PENGUIN

RAFFLES: THE AMATEUR CRACKSMAN

ERNEST WILLIAM HORNUNG was born 7 June 1866 at Marton, near Middlesbrough, the son of a German ironmaster and an English mother. He was educated at Uppingham School in Rutland where he first gave evidence of his literary talents in the School Magazine. He left before reaching the Upper Sixth because of ill-health and spent the next two years in Australia. His experiences abroad, his love of cricket, and incidents from his own life provided the inspiration for his fiction. Under the tutelage of the Irish novelist Richard Dowling his stories began to appear in the late 1880s, and he first made his name with *A Bride from the Bush* (1890). In September 1893 he married Constance Doyle, the sister of Arthur Conan Doyle, and in 1898 created his most famous character, Raffles, who is considered by some to be the equal of Sherlock Holmes. *The Amateur Cracksman* (1899) was followed by *The Black Mask* (1901), *A Thief in the Night* (1905), and a novel, *Mr Justice Raffles* (1909). His other major work, *Stingaree*, containing stories about a gentleman-bushranger, was published in 1905. In 1915, after his son was killed in action, he joined the Anti-Aircraft Corps and two years later accepted a post as secretary and librarian of the YMCA at Arras. He was a member of the MCC and a friend, among others, of Jerome K. Jerome, J. M. Barrie, George Gissing, Rudyard Kipling and Hilaire Belloc. He died at St-Jean-de-Luz on 22 March 1921 and is buried in the cemetary above the town.

RICHARD LANCELYN GREEN was born in the Wirral and is the son of Roger Lancelyn Green. He read English at University College, Oxford, and is an authority on the life and work of Sir Arthur Conan Doyle. With J. M. Gibson, he compiled the *Bibliography of A. Conan Doyle* and edited several volumes of Conan Doyle's previously uncollected work. He is the editor of two volumes in the Oxford Sherlock Holmes (World's Classics) series, and of *The Uncollected Sherlock Holmes* and *The Further Adventures of Sherlock Holmes*, which are published by Penguin.

E. W. HORNUNG

Raffles

THE AMATEUR CRACKSMAN

Edited with an Introduction and Notes by
RICHARD LANCELYN GREEN

PENGUIN BOOKS

Published by the Penguin Group
Penguin Books Ltd, 80 Strand, London WC2R ORL, England
Penguin Group (USA) Inc., 375 Hudson Street, New York, New York 10014, USA
Penguin Group (Canada), 90 Eglinton Avenue East, Suite 700, Toronto, Ontario, Canada M4P 2Y3
(a division of Pearson Penguin Canada Inc.)
Penguin Ireland, 25 St Stephen's Green, Dublin 2, Ireland (a division of Penguin Books Ltd)
Penguin Group (Australia), 250 Camberwell Road, Camberwell, Victoria 3124, Australia
(a division of Pearson Australia Group Pty Ltd)
Penguin Books India Pvt Ltd, 11 Community Centre, Panchsheel Park, New Delhi – 110 017, India
Penguin Group (NZ), 67 Apollo Drive, Rosedale, North Shore 0632, New Zealand
(a division of Pearson New Zealand Ltd)
Penguin Books (South Africa) (Pty) Ltd, 24 Sturdee Avenue,
Rosebank, Johannesburg 2196, South Africa

Penguin Books Ltd, Registered Offices: 80 Strand, London WC2R ORL, England

www.penguin.com

First published 1899
This edition published in Penguin Classics 2003

1

This edition produced for The Book People Ltd,
Hall Wood Avenue, Haydock, St Helens, WA11 9UL

Introduction and editorial notes copyright © Richard Lancelyn Green, 2003
All rights reserved

The moral right of the editor has been asserted

Set in 10.25/12.25 pt PostScript Adobe Sabon
Typeset by Rowland Phototypesetting Ltd, Bury St Edmunds, Suffolk
Printed in England by Clays Ltd, St Ives plc

ISBN 978–1–856–13282–4

www.greenpenguin.co.uk

Contents

The Amateur Cracksman

Acknowledgements

My thanks are due to the Librarians at Princeton University Library and at the Lilly Library, Bloomington, Indiana, for permission to examine and quote from original manuscript material in their possession; to all the authors whose works are quoted within the introduction and notes; and to all those who have assisted me in this pleasant task over many years, in particular E. W. Hornung's nephew, the late Brigadier John Doyle; his great-nephew, the late Stephen Hornung; and his niece (by marriage), the late Barbara Foley and her son, Robert; also to Pierre Coustillas, the authority on the life and work of George Gissing; the late Bryan Matthews, the Uppingham archivist and historian; and in particular to Otto Penzler of New York, who on many occasions has generously allowed me access to his extensive collection of books and manuscripts by E. W. Hornung.

Chronology

1866 Ernest William ('Willie') Hornung born on 7 June at Erdely Villa, Marton, near Middlesbrough, fourth son and eighth child of an ironmaster, Johan Petrus Hornung (1821–86), and Harriet, née Armstrong (1824–96).

1878 Attends local Dame's School.

1879–80 At St Ninian's preparatory school, Moffat, Dumfriesshire, one of nine boys under the tutelage of A. J. C. Dowding and W. H. Churchill.

1880–83 At Uppingham School, Rutland (A. J. Tuck's house); first literary contributions published in the Uppingham School Magazine (1882); leaves December 1883 on account of poor health, having reached the Remove.

1884–6 In Australia, as tutor to the family of Cecil Joseph Parsons, at Mossgiel Station in the Riverina, New South Wales; pays several visits to Melbourne; visits Queensland and travels in New South Wales (September 1884); 'A Visit to the Blue Mountains, New South Wales' published in the Uppingham School Magazine (February 1885).

1885 Hornung's father declared bankrupt after the loss of two cargo boats; his partner absconds to South America.

1886 Returns to England (February); the family moves to 49 Waldegrave Park, Teddington; death of Johan Petrus Hornung (11 November); Hornung meets Richard Dowling (1846–98), who acts as his literary mentor.

1887 A short story, 'The Stroke of Five', published in the *Belgravia Magazine* (November).

1888 Further stories published in the *Belgravia Magazine*

(March) and *Every Boy's Annual* (September/November);
first contributions to the *Pictorial World*.

1889 Further stories published (in the summer and Christmas
numbers of the *Pictorial World* and elsewhere); works on first
novel, *At Large* (serialized in the *Pictorial World*, May–
September 1891); James Payn accepts *A Bride from the Bush*
for the *Cornhill Magazine*.

1890 *A Bride from the Bush* serialized in the *Cornhill Magazine*
(July–November); and published in book form (October).

1891 Further stories published in the *Strand Magazine* (April/
May), and elsewhere. Moves to 17 Abingdon Mansions,
Abingdon Road, Kensington.

1892 'Kenyon's Innings' published in *Longman's Magazine*
(April); *Under Two Skies* (short stories) published; Hornung
meets his future wife, Constance ('Connie') Aimée Monica
Doyle (1869–1924), and her brother, Arthur Conan Doyle
(1859–1930); plays in the Idler's cricket match (6 September); visits the Black Museum at Scotland Yard with Doyle
and Jerome K. Jerome (10 December).

1893 *Tiny Luttrell* published (April); marriage to Constance
Doyle at St Edward's Roman Catholic church, London
(27 September), with the novelist Gilbert Parker as witness;
honeymoon in Paris; *The Boss of Taroomba* serialized in the
Detroit Free Press (Christmas number); Hornung and his
wife move to 14 Rossetti Garden Mansions, Flood Street,
Chelsea.

1894 *The Unbidden Guest* ('A Bad Lot') serialized in *Longman's
Magazine* (May–October); published in book form (August).

1895 Birth of only child, Arthur Oscar Hornung (25 March);
Hornung completes *My Lord Duke* (5 April; serialized in
Chambers's Journal, January–May 1897, and in America by
the McClure Syndicate; published in book form, May 1897);
completes *The New Owner or Irralie's Bushranger*, featuring
Stingaree (6 October; published as *Irralie's Bushranger* in a
special supplement to the 1895 Christmas number of *Cassell's
Magazine*, and in book form as part of the New Vagabond
Library, December 1896); *The Rogue's March* serialized in

Tit-Bits (December 1895–June 1896; and published in book form, October 1896).

1896 'After the Fact', the story which inspired Raffles, published in *Chambers's Journal* (4–25 January; collected in *Some Persons Unknown*, 1897); death of Hornung's mother (6 June).

1897 Writes *Young Blood* (syndicated by Tillotson's, February–March 1898; published in book form, June 1898); spends October with his mother-in-law, Mary Doyle, at Masongill, Kirkby Lonsdale; writes *The Sole Survivor* (published as *Dead Men Tell No Tales*, the first volume of Methuen's 'Novelist Series', May 1899); stays with Conan Doyle at Undershaw, Hindhead, meets Grant Allen (November 1897); sails to Italy on board the Norddeutscher-Lloyd, SS *Königin Luise* (22 November 1897); arrives in Genoa (30 November 1897); visits his sister-in-law Ida Foley on the island of Gaiola, at Posilippo, Naples (December 1897).

1898 Visits Pompeii (January); spends five months at 38 Via Gregoriana, Rome, in the rooms where children's author and translator Mary Howitt died (January–May); writes first of the Raffles stories (January); meets George Gissing and H. G. Wells (March); dinner with Gissing, the Wellses, and Conan Doyle at the Trattoria Colonna (8 April); the first six Raffles stories appear in *Cassell's Magazine* under the heading 'In the Chains of Crime' (June–November 1898); and in *Collier's Magazine*, New York, as 'Adventures of A. J. Raffles' (September–October); death of Richard Dowling (28 July); returns to Gaiola and takes the 'villa in the vineyard' for six months (July 1898–January 1899); *Some Persons Unknown* (short stories) published (November).

1899 Publication of *The Amateur Cracksman* (March); 'A Villa in a Vineyard' published in the *Cornhill Magazine* (May); moves to 9 Pitt Street, Kensington (July); plays in the Artists v. Authors team (June) and in Conan Doyle's Undershaw XI (August).

1900 Plans a further series of Raffles stories for *Scribner's Magazine* (January); 'In Memoriam' (poem) published in the *Spectator* (3 February); William Gillette declines the role of

Raffles when offered the part by Charles Frohman in an as yet unwritten adaptation of the stories (February); first three stories of the new Raffles series written in London (June–August); *The Belle of Toorak* published (July; after serialization in *Lippincott's Magazine*); Hornung reprimands A. Conan Doyle for his marital infidelity (August); revises *Peccavi* (August to October, with publication in October); returns to Gaiola (October–December) where he writes the remaining five Raffles stories ('More Adventures of the Amateur Cracksman'), serialized in *Scribner's Magazine*, January–September 1901, published in England, with prefatory note, as *The Black Mask* (Grant Richards), and in America as *Raffles, Further Adventures of the Amateur Cracksman* (without the note, Scribner's, 1901).

1901 Plays cricket in J. M. Barrie's Allahakbarries cricket team (May), for the Authors v. Artists, and on the Incogniti Schools Tour (June); the second Stingaree story ('The Taking of Stingaree') published in the *Graphic* (July) and *Frank Leslie's Magazine* (August); Hornung and his family spend the summer at Zermatt (August–October), writes *No Hero*; *The Shadow of the Law* serialized in *Munsey's Magazine* (October 1901–November 1902; published in book form as *The Shadow of the Rope*, April 1902).

1902 Hornung's early novel, *At Large*, published in America (February); plays in Conan Doyle's Undershaw XI (August); the Liebler Company plans dramatization of Raffles (November).

1903 *No Hero* serialized in the *Pall Mall Magazine* (January–May); published in book form (April); plays cricket for the Authors v. Artists (May); *Denis Dent* serialized in America (March–December; published in book form, November); Hornung plans new series of Stingaree stories (May); 'Letters to a Young Writer' appears anonymously in the *Cornhill Magazine* (July); he takes a country house at East Ruston, Norfolk (September–December); *Raffles, The Amateur Cracksman*, a play in four acts by E. W. Hornung and Eugene Wiley Presbrey, starring Kyrle Bellew, previewed at Young's Pier Theatre, Atlantic City (19 September), then in Philadelphia, Baltimore,

Washington (12 October); opens at the Princess Theatre, New York (27 October).

1904 Travels up the Nile; visits Gaiola (March); plays cricket for the Authors' team (May, June); 'Stingaree Stories' published in the British and American editions of the *Strand Magazine* (September 1904 – April 1905; published in book form, April 1905); undertakes to write a series of twelve stories for the *Pall Mall Magazine* and *Ainslee's Magazine* about a smart money-lender or 'honest Raffles'; but instead revives Raffles (serialized in the *Pall Mall Magazine* and *Collier's Weekly*); buys new house at 7 Hornton Street, Kensington (December); acquires first motor-car.

1905 Plays for the Authors' team (May); first unauthorized film, *Raffles, The Amateur Cracksman* released in America by the Vitagraph Company (August); *A Thief in the Night* published (October) by Chatto & Windus.

1906 Speaks at the Old Uppinghamian dinner (10 January); works on a dramatization of *Stingaree* (January–February); *Raffles, The Amateur Cracksman*, with Gerald du Maurier, receives first performance in London (Comedy Theatre, 12 May; 353 performances, ending 2 April 1907; first French production at the Théatre Réjane, Paris, 14 June 1907); *Raffles, the Amateur Cracksman* (*The Amateur Cracksman* and *The Black Mask*) issued by Eveleigh Nash (June 1906); plays for the Authors' (May, July); motor tour in south of France (August); writes obituary of his close friend Lionel Martineau (Uppingham School Magazine, November).

1907 Elected to the MCC; plays in six matches (June–August); plays for the Authors' at Lords (August).

1908 *Stingaree, the Bushranger*, a play in four acts, starring Henry Ainley, opens at the Queen's Theatre, London, 1 February 1908; runs for 26 performances, and closes 22 February 1908; Oscar Hornung's first term at Eton College in Hugh de Havilland's House (September); Hornung plays again for the MCC; summer spent at Winchelsea (July); starts *Mr Justice Raffles* (November–December; serialized in the *Grand Magazine*, January–July 1909, and *Gunter's Maga-*

zine, New York, September–November 1909; published in book form, September 1909).

1909 Starts work on *The Camera Fiend* (March; serialized in the *Royal Magazine*, December 1910–February 1911; published in book form, March 1911); summer at Nesbit Cottage, Winchelsea (July–September).

1911 Speaks at the Old Uppinghamian dinner (12 January); completes *Fathers of Men* (August) based on his experiences at Uppingham; writes the 'Witching Hill' stories (September; serialized in *Scribner's Magazine*, February–September 1912; published in book form, February 1913); works on *The Thousandth Woman* (December; serialized in *Harper's Bazaar*, September 1913–March 1914; published in book form, October 1913).

1912 Winters in Engelberg, Switzerland, with Rudyard Kipling; friendship between Oscar Hornung and John Kipling; *Fathers of Men* published (January); moves to Rome (April); starts work on *The Crime Doctor* (May; serialized in *Everybody's Magazine*, New York, and the *Red Magazine* during 1913; published in book form, July 1914).

1913 Returns to Italy (March), staying at the Hotel Elysée, Rome; lectures at the Keats/Shelley Memorial House (22 April); dines with Louis N. Parker; moves north to Roncegno (May–June); returns to England in the summer; the 'Uppingham Song' published in the Jubilee number of the Uppingham School Magazine (April); starts work on a novel, *A European Reputation* – later set aside because of the war.

1914 Oscar Hornung leaves Eton (April); Hornung's letter in defence of 'Laura Grey' published in *The Times* (14 June); war declared (4 August); Oscar receives his commission for the 3rd Essex Regiment (15 August); *Raffles, the Amateur Cracksman* (play) revived in London with Gerald du Maurier (Wyndham's Theatre, 23 December; 180 performances, closing 26 May 1915).

1915 Oscar leaves for France (April); killed in action (6 July); Hornung joins the Anti-Aircraft Corps, RNVR Temple Company, based at the Cannon Street Hotel (July); starts work on a memoir of his son containing his letters from the Front (*'Trusty and Well Beloved'*, privately printed, 1915); 'Last Post (To A[rthur] O[scar] H[ornung]) published in the *Spectator* (20 November); Kalem Film Company release twelve *Adventures of Stingaree* (November 1915 – February 1916), starring Tom Boardman.

1916 Connie in nursing home in London (July); the Hornungs leave Hornton Street and move to South Lodge, on the West Grinstead Park estate of Hornung's brother John Peter ('Pitt') Hornung; Hornung signs contract for a further series of *Stingaree* films (September).

1917 Mary Doyle, Hornung's mother-in-law, moves from Masongill to Bowshott Cottage on the West Grinstead Park estate to be near Connie (April); *The Further Adventures of Stingaree* (Kalem Film Company) released (June–September); Hornung's poems, 'Wooden Crosses' and 'Bond and Free' published in *The Times* (20 July, 25 September); accepts a job as secretary to the YMCA at the Hotel de Ville, Arras, where he remains until the summer of 1918; *Raffles, the Amateur Cracksman*, a film starring John Barrymore, released in America by L. Lawrence Weber (December); 'The Ballad of Ensign Joy' (poem) published in *Land and Water* (December); writes five new Raffles stories for Joseph Menchen for use in the cinema.

1918 The Hornungs move to Midway Cottage, Partridge Green, near West Grinstead Park (July); completes *Notes of a Camp-Follower on the Western Front* (October), based on his letters sent from France.

1919 Paramount Pictures Corporation releases *Out of the Shadow*, based on *The Shadow of the Rope* (January); death of Hornung's brother-in-law Innes Doyle (February); Hornung visits Germany (May–June) with the YMCA, Army of the Rhine, to entertain the troops in Cologne; 'Shell Shock in Arras' (poem) published in the *Cologne Post* (3 May); *Notes of a Camp-Follower on the Western Front* published (August); visits Ypres and the surrounding battle-fields (September); writes introduction for a new edition of *Fathers of Men* (John Murray); *The Young Guard* (poems) published (December); 'About the Battlefields' published in the *Cologne Post* souvenir number (December 1919).

1920 Vitagraph Company releases *Dead Men Tell No Tales* (November); Hornung works on essay on Charles Reade for the *London Mercury* (published posthumously, June 1921); serves as a member of the Uppingham War Shrine Committee and selects the eight watchwords to run round the octagonal chapel (dedicated 16 October 1921); Hornung's health in decline at end of the year.

1921 Travels to the south of France; dies of aggravated influenza, 22 March, at St-Jean-de-Luz; funeral attended by Arthur Conan Doyle; buried near the grave of George Gissing in the cemetery above the town.

1923 *Old Offenders and a Few Old Scores* (short stories), with an introduction by Hornung's brother-in-law A. Conan Doyle, published (May).

1924 Death of Hornung's wife, Connie (9 July).

Introduction

One of the great merits of *The Amateur Cracksman* is that it can be read for enjoyment without the need for an introduction or for any of the scholarly apparatus which its classic status deserves. Raffles will already be familiar to the vast majority of readers, for he has entered the dictionary and every gentleman-burglar has been given his name. Yet there is a place for an introduction, because of a natural curiosity about the ingredients which went into the making of the book.

The author is far less well known than his famous character. To many of his contemporaries he appeared to be a typical Englishman, with a great love of cricket and a clever wit, yet, as the name suggests, E. W. Hornung had a German father: Johan Petrus Hornung, who came from Mediasch, in Transylvania. He was educated in Vienna and was an ironmaster by profession. He moved to Middlesbrough in the 1840s, where he met and married Harriet Armstrong. They had eight children of whom Ernest William Hornung, or 'Willie', was the youngest. He was born on 7 June 1866 and educated at a local Dame's school, a preparatory school in Scotland, and then at Uppingham, in Rutland, where he went in 1880. It is one of the great public schools and was an ideal choice as it was famous for cricket, a game to which Hornung was already devoted and about which he had an encyclopaedic knowledge.

The Old School, Cricket, and Bushrangers

A. J. Raffles and his accomplice, Bunny, are also a product of Uppingham. Raffles was given the same initials as Hornung's housemaster, A. J. Tuck, and his cricketing skills were based to a large extent on those of J. A. Turner, who was captain of cricket in 1882. Other elements came from H. H. Stephenson, the school's professional cricket coach, and from Lionel Martineau, Hornung's closest friend, who followed Turner as captain in 1885. Bunny was to a large extent a self-portrait of the author, and though Hornung's own nickname had been 'Dodo' on account of his failing health, 'Bunny' would have suited him equally well.

Hornung left the school in December 1883, before he had reached the upper sixth, and spent the next two years in Australia serving as a tutor to the children of Cecil Joseph Parsons, at the Mossgiel Station in the Riverina, New South Wales. The opportunity to visit the 'back blocks' in the interior and see the outback and the bush, and to hear tales of bushrangers, provided him with the inspiration for much of his subsequent fiction, and his experiences there represented the first step in his career in the same way that India had done for Rudyard Kipling.

The First Step

When he returned to England in February 1886, Hornung found that his father had been declared bankrupt and the family had moved to 49 Waldegrave Road between Twickenham and Teddington (on the outskirts of London). His father died on 11 November 1886. By then Hornung, who shared the house with his mother and other members of the family, had found work as a clerk in the City, but his ambition was to be a writer. With the help and advice of Irish novelist Richard Dowling, the author of *The Mystery of Killard*, he published his first stories, one of which a direct bearing on the later Raffles stories as it deals with the attraction of evil. In 'The Stroke of Five' (in the *Belgravia Magazine*, November 1887), the narrator describes how he had become 'absorbed' in the evil of Mephistopheles while watching *Faust* at the Lyceum Theatre:

My heart turned to this scarlet prince of darkness! His plausibility played upon my fancy in the beginning, his ingenuity fanned my fancy into admiration, his unfathomable cunning turned admiration to unholy reverence! The supreme badness of the fiend won me over to the wrong side in spite of myself. The influence of the fiend intoxicated me. Each poisoned arrow of subtle sarcasm struck acute enjoyment into my soul. All through the play, when the fiend was on the stage, my eyes saw no other form, my ears heard no other voice. But on the Brocken, I absolutely revelled in the majesty of the fiend!

On the way home the narrator is accosted by a person whom he believes to be the Devil, and is persuaded to effect his own death by lying on the railway tracks, but as the train thunders towards him, at 'the stroke of five' he struggles free and the spell is broken.

The Author's Encounter with a Burglar

It was also while he was at Teddington that Hornung had his only experience with a real burglar, and this he later described in an interview with *Tit-Bits* (2 January 1909), when asked about the origin of Raffles:

I only met a burglar once, and he was one of the sorriest specimens of humanity I ever saw in my life. I was living at Teddington at the time, and while out for a walk one day passed a large house, at the door of which a woman stood with a baby in her arms. She beckoned, and then asked if I would go into the house and help her husband to catch a burglar. It appeared they were living in the house as caretakers.

Now, I never was a very athletic sort of person, but I was carrying a good heavy blackthorn, and I went in and met the husband in the corridor in a great state of excitement. 'You go on the lawn,' he said, 'and I'll drive him through.' He was such a long time, however, that I went into the house again to reconnoitre on my own account, and ultimately we discovered that the burglar had taken refuge underneath the kitchen floor, having gained access to his hiding-place through a small grating.

There was space to the depth of two or three feet below the kitchen floor, but we could not induce the burglar to come out. Ultimately, it was decided to pull the flooring up, and just when the caretaker and a jobbing gardener had commenced to do so, a policeman, who looked quite imposing in his long winter overcoat, came in. He got into the hole already made, and peered underneath the floor with his lantern, at which the burglar began throwing bits of builders' chips. Suddenly the policeman beamed upon us all. 'He hit me on the leg!' he cried. 'I'll charge him with that!'

They had to pull up the whole floor before they unearthed a wizened half-starved creature, who whiningly exclaimed, 'I ain't been doin' nothing. I only came in to 'ave a smoke!'

The poor little performer got two months, but I never heard how much of it was for assaulting the six-foot constable with a missile perhaps the size of a pea!

Hornung worked on his first novel, *At Large*, in 1889, but this was not serialized until after he had made his name with another novel, *A Bride from the Bush*, which appeared in the *Cornhill Magazine* in 1890. He also quickly established himself as a very able writer of short stories, which were sought after by many of the leading periodicals of the day. Some dealt with social manners, many with the rise of the 'new woman', but it is in his stories with Australian themes that the precursors of Raffles are to be found, in particular those which involve gentlemen-bushrangers. In 'The Romance of a Township' (*Pictorial World*, October 1889), George Constantine Drake, the *aide de camp* of the Governor, masquerades as a bushranger and is mistaken for the notorious Captain Coffin; and in *Irralie's Bushranger* (*Cassell's Magazine*, December 1895), Stingaree, a monocled bushranger with a passion for music, made his first appearance. He had the dash and panache later found in Raffles and was the hero of a series of stories published in 1905.

Raffles and 'Bunny' in Embryo

Raffles and Bunny first appeared in embryo in 'After the Fact', which was published in *Chambers's Journal* in January 1896. The story was inspired by the incident with the burglar at Teddington, although it is set in Australia. The narrator comes upon a burglar hiding in an empty house and recognizes him: '"We were at school together," I explained. "I was your fag when you were captain of footer." "The Beetle!" cried Deedes, not unkindly; a moment later he was shaking my hand and smiling on my confusion . . . We were twenty-eight and twenty-four now, instead of eighteen and fourteen; yet, as we walked, only one of us was a man, and I was once more his fag. I felt quite proud when he accepted a cigarette from my case, prouder yet when he took my arm.' The Beetle becomes an accessory 'after the fact' because he is unwilling to betray his friend. Deedes attempts to escape, but is shot and killed by the police as he swims out to sea.

Hornung explained in an interview with *Tit-Bits* in 1909 how this led to Raffles: 'I'll tell you exactly how Raffles started':

A good many years ago I wrote a story about a public-school villain; he committed a terrible crime in Australia, and was met by his old fag, who shielded him. Unfortunately, I killed the villain at the end of the story.

One day my brother-in-law, Sir Arthur Conan Doyle, to whom I owe a very great deal, said to me, 'What a pity you killed that fellow! A public-school villain would be a new figure for a series. Why not revive him?'

'I don't believe I could write such a series to save my life,' I replied. However, I was advised to think the suggestion over. I did so, and the eventual result was a variation of the type in the shape of Raffles.

A. Conan Doyle

Hornung moved to lodgings at 17 Abingdon Mansions, off Kensington High Street, in 1891, and remained there until his marriage to Arthur Conan Doyle's sister Connie (Constance) in September 1893. He first met her in Portugal when she was working as a governess and he was on a visit to his brother Pitt (who had a Portuguese wife). On her return to England in 1892 Connie moved in with Conan Doyle at 12 Tennison Road, South Norwood, and Hornung called to see her and soon fell in love. He and Conan Doyle were often together (it is not known if Hornung had met Doyle before he called on Connie). They played in the same cricket teams, wrote for the same magazines, and shared the same interests – indeed, their signatures appear together, alongside that of Jerome K. Jerome, in the visitors' book for the Black Museum at Scotland Yard on 10 December 1892. Jerome, recalling the visit he paid to Norway with Conan Doyle and his sister, described her as 'a handsome girl' who 'might have posed as Brunhilda' (*My Life and Times*, Hodder and Stoughton, 1926). For Hornung she was the ideal of the new woman, and proved a loving and loyal wife. His marriage and the birth of a son compensated in large measure for the loss of his mother, who died in June 1896.

Hornung and Connie moved to 14 Rossetti Garden Mansions, in Flood Street, Chelsea, after their marriage, and it was here that their only child, Arthur Oscar Hornung, was born on 25 March 1895. His first name (which was later given to Raffles) was in honour of Conan Doyle, who was both his uncle and godfather.

The suggestion about the public school villain could have been made at any time after January 1896 when Conan Doyle and Hornung spent time together, perhaps at a New Vagabonds Club dinner, or at the Café Monico on 13 February 1897, when Doyle lectured on Irish literature, or at the Reform Club on 28 July 1897 when Hamilton Mabie was a guest, but the most likely date would be the third week of November 1897 when Hornung and his wife stayed at Conan Doyle's new house in Hindhead.

Grant Allen and the Literature of Roguery

The visit was important for another reason, as Hornung met Conan Doyle's neighbour Grant Allen, who had just published *An African Millionaire* (1897). This featured the scheming Colonel Clay, who constantly outwits the millionaire of the title and deprives him of his money, and who has often been described as a precursor of Raffles.

Hornung had said he had doubted whether he could write a series of stories about a villain, but nevertheless he was very well-equipped to do so. In his convict novel *The Rogue's March* (1896) he had used original sources, such as the *Newgate Calen-*

dar and Charles White's study of *Convict Life in New South Wales and Van Diemens Land*. He also had a wide-ranging knowledge of crime and criminal behaviour, gleaned from his visit to the Black Museum, from friends in the legal profession, such as Edward Shortt (to whom he dedicated *The Shadow of the Rope* in 1902), and from books, newspapers and magazines.

Hornung was also familiar with the 'literature of roguery', which had emerged as a distinctive genre with the Spanish picaresque novels of the sixteenth century, but in England runs in an unbroken line from Chaucer, through the Tudor 'cony-catchers' and the picaresque novels of Robert Greene and Thomas Nash, the art of Hogarth, the plays of Gay, and stories by Defoe, Fielding and Smollett, to the romantic novels of the early nineteenth century, which glamorized the lives of outlaws and highwaymen such as Robin Hood, Dick Turpin and Jack Sheppard.

The Gentleman-Burglar in Fact and Fiction

The gentleman-burglar was already a familiar figure in fact and fiction. There was the 'Spider' in the play *The Silver King* (1882) by Henry Arthur Jones and Henry Herman; and there were numerous more recent examples, such as *Lady Turpin*, by Henry Herman (published as *Beeton's Christmas Annual* for 1895), or the humorous Christmas story by William Waldorf Astor, 'Jack Sheppard up to Date' (*Pall Mall Magazine*, December 1895), which featured a sophisticated modern-day burglar, who was 'chief of all the scientific cracksmen in London'. In real life there were men such as Adam Worth, who stole the Gainsborough portrait of the Duchess of Devonshire from Agnew's in Bond Street in 1876, or Robert Graham, Esq., a cracksman, who had all the attributes of the gentleman-burglar. According to the *Weekly Dispatch* (in an article in April 1899) Graham was 'most aesthetic in his taste, buying the very best articles, whilst in order to avoid injuring his hands, which are remarkably white and well-shapen, he always worked in old kid gloves which he preserved for the purpose'. He had an assistant to whom he paid a weekly wage, a 'fence', and when committing his crimes he wore a black mask, 'a simple piece of black Italian cloth lining', taken from the suit in which he had been married.

George Cecil Ives, of the Albany:
The Model for Raffles

Raffles, however, is more than a reworking of an existing type, because he had a model in real life, in the same way that Joseph Bell had served as the model for Sherlock Holmes. The model for Raffles was to be George Cecil Ives (1867–1950), a cricketer and a criminologist, who lived at the Albany. He had been adopted and brought up by his grandmother, the daughter of the 3rd Viscount Maynard, and was educated at home and at Magdalene College, Cambridge. After leaving university he came to London where he joined the MCC and moved in literary circles. Ives first became known to Hornung as a promising young cricketer, so promising that J. M. Barrie included him in his 1893 Allahakbarries team (in which Conan Doyle and Jerome K. Jerome were also members). He moved to the Albany – Number E4 – in 1895 and remained there until 1897. The surviving correspondence between Hornung and Ives deals exclusively with cricket and shows no great intimacy, but Hornung certainly visited Ives's rooms in the Albany and based those occupied by Raffles upon them.

It was also in those Albany rooms that Oscar Wilde met the Oxford undergraduate Jack Bloxam, whose story 'The Priest and the Acolyte' caused outrage when it was published in the *Chameleon* in December 1894. As a consequence of that visit Wilde gave Ernest Worthing rooms at B4, the Albany, and used the name 'Bloxam' in *The Importance of Being Earnest*.

Ives had been introduced to Wilde for the first time at the Authors' Club in June 1892 and he met Lord Alfred Douglas the following year. He was openly sympathetic to their views, and had published an article in the *Fortnightly Review* in October 1894 attacking Grant Allen, who had condemned homosexuality. Ives also founded a secret society, called the 'Order of Chaeronea', for those who shared his sexual orientation. His first collection of poems was the *Book of Chains*, which was published anonymously in 1897. The 'chains' of the title referred to the real chains of prison and the metaphorical chains that bind the human soul. His purpose, according to the preface, was 'to fight the cause of our unhappy prisoners' and 'other victims of the crimes of the State'. The poems dealt with free love, suicide, death by drowning, imprisonment and the 'ghosts of the captive dead'.

A second volume of poems, *Eros's Throne*, followed in 1900, but his main interest was criminology and the study of the prison and penal systems of England and Europe. In 1914 he published *A History of Penal Methods, Criminals, Witches, Lunatics*, based on the premise that crime could be combated only if the true causes were understood and if taboos were openly addressed and swept away. He wrote several further books on the penal system and essays on the psychology of sex, but he is now best remembered for the forty-eight scrapbooks which he kept throughout his life and which he filled with curious tit-bits of the 'man bites man' variety (that being the title of a selection from the scrapbooks chosen by Paul Sieveking and published by Jay Landesman in 1980).

Ives was not Raffles, any more than Joseph Bell had been Sherlock Holmes, but he did have similar Jekyll-and-Hyde qualities. He had independent means and could afford rooms in the Albany; he moved in the best literary circles and was a keen and active member of the MCC, with a love of swimming and the outdoors. Yet he was also burdened by his sexual nature; criminology allowed him to give expression to his feelings and to side with the criminal against the state. Hornung found Ives an intriguing character. He was a good cricketer, but also a minor poet; he was a gentleman, but had an almost unhealthy interest in crime; he conformed to the social norms, but had a philosophy of 'rational anarchy', which turned morality on its head. Hornung was not fully aware of the hidden side of Ives's life, but he did sense that something was being concealed. When they met on later occasions or played cricket in the same team (as they did, for example, when both played for the Authors against the Artists on 22 May 1903) it is unlikely that either of them would have mentioned Raffles, but he would not have

existed in the same form, nor would he have had his rooms in
the Albany had Ives not existed.

Hornung in Italy

Hornung and his wife had planned a visit to Italy in order
to stay with Connie's sister Ida, who had married a distant
cousin, Nelson Foley, and moved to the island of Gaiola at
Posilippo, near Naples. They sailed on 22 November 1897 on
the Norddeutscher-Lloyd SS *Königin Luise* (the inspiration for
the *Uhlan* in 'The Gift of the Emperor') and reached Genoa on
30 November. They then sailed past Elba (where Raffles was to
disappear) to Naples, where they were met by the Foleys, who
took them by boat across the bay to Gaiola.

The island is divided from the mainland by a narrow strip of
water and the villa stood on Roman foundations which had
formed part of the imperial villas of Pausilypon. The ruins
stretched across the neighbouring hillside, which also had the
tunnels that had carried water to the Emperors' artificial lakes.
Dotted among the vineyards were a number of modern villas,
including the Villa Bechi, which was owned by the author
Norman Douglas, who had been a contemporary of Hornung's
at Uppingham. Slightly further away in the Via Posilippo was
the Villa Guidice, which, by another curious quirk of fate, was
occupied by Oscar Wilde. He had been released from Pentonville
prison in May 1897 and had arrived in Naples in September.
He was then joined by Lord Alfred Douglas and they moved
into the villa at the end of the month. Douglas left in December,
but Wilde remained until the beginning of January 1898.
Hornung also remained until early January, when he left for
Rome. Although he may have been aware of Wilde's presence,
there is no evidence that they met. It is, however, a remarkable
coincidence given the connection between Wilde and Ives.

Hornung recalled in an interview with the *Roman Herald* on
12 April 1913 that it was at Posilippo 'in the midst of this
wonderful panorama, Naples, Vesuvius, Nisida, Procida, Ischia
and Capri that "Raffles" was born'. However, the writing was
done in Rome where he took rooms at 38 Via Gregoriana (a

road running from the top of the Spanish Steps), having moved there from Naples with his wife in January 1898. The city provided a stimulating atmosphere, and Hornung found himself in good company. A 'Roman Correspondent' in the journal *Academy* wrote on 19 February 1898: 'the Eternal City has now quite a little circle of English and American literary people. Mr Gissing, Mr Hall Caine, and Mr Hornung represent fiction; Lord Rosebery and Mr Haweis, criticism; and Mr Astor, patronage. The principal poet is Mrs Julia Ward Howe, the author of the magnificent *Battle Hymn of the Republic*, who is staying with her daughter, Mrs Elliott. Mrs Howe, the other day, read a paper on "Pessimism and Optimism", which was listened to, among others, by Bjornsterne Bjornson.'

George Gissing

George Gissing had arrived in Rome in February 1898 and was joined by H. G. Wells on 9 March. Three days later Hornung sent his card. 'It was the novelist (of whom I have read nothing),' Gissing noted in his diary: 'A man of 30, suffering much from asthma; married to a sister of Conan Doyle. Invited us all to call tomorrow.' The invitation was accepted and the three novelists met next day. Gissing visited the Hornungs twice during the following week, and they called on him on 22 March 1898.

Hornung described his meetings in a letter to Frederic Whyte, a close friend who worked for Cassell's in London and had been with Hornung at the time that Connie gave birth to her son (the reference in the course of the letter to 'Oscar' is to the son, not Oscar Wilde). He said: 'We have seen quite a lot of Gissing and Wells during the last fortnight. Wells has joined Gissing here for two or three weeks. We like them both quite immensely. Wells is a very good little chap when you know him, humorous, modest, unaffected. As for Gissing, he is really a sweet fellow – Connie says so and it is the only word . . . He has charm and sympathy, humour too and a louder laugh than Oscar's. That man is not wilfully a pessimist. But he is lonely – there has been some great sorrow and ill-health. I took him the *Academy* this forenoon . . . and found him writing a short story in his insect's hand – 1,000 words on each (quarto) page. I spoilt his morning's work but left him merry. I could have stopped there jawing all day.' The copy of the *Academy* which he took was the one in which their names were mentioned, and the reference to Gissing's pessimism suggests that Hornung may have attended Mrs Howe's lecture and also raises the possibility that he was the 'Roman Correspondent'.

Gissing attended a musical evening at the Via Gregoriana on 26 March, and on 8 April 1898 he and Wells joined the Hornungs and Conan Doyle (who was on a brief visit) for dinner at the Trattoria Colonna. They saw the Colosseum by moonlight and ended the evening in Hornung's rooms. The friendship between Gissing and Hornung outlasted their stay in Italy. They corresponded and met again in London. After Gissing's death in 1903 Hornung wrote his obituary for the *Author* (1 February 1904), in which he spoke of him as a friend, recalling 'his fine face, his noble head, his winning ways' and his charm, sensitivity and humour: 'There was an appreciative sympathy, a cordial humanity, which it would be difficult to deduce from his writings.' By a strange quirk of fate, both men died in St-Jean-de-Luz and are buried in the same cemetery within a few yards of each other. It is remarkable that their friendship should have begun at exactly the time the Raffles stories were being written.

The Stuff of Fiction: Adam Worth and Barney Barnato

Hornung felt that Gissing could have been a great classical scholar, and being in Rome brought to mind the classics and the work of the Romantic poets, in particular the work of Keats, who had lived close to where he was staying. Yet, although the Romantics coloured his narrative, the plots were taken from events and personalities in England. The burglary in 'The Ides of March', for example, was inspired by the theft of jewels from the Diamond Merchants Alliance at 68 Piccadilly (on the corner of Dover Street) on the night of 30–31 October 1897. The premises had seemed secure, with the windows protected by revolving steel shutters and the doors with shutters fastened to the doorsteps by steel bolts, yet the thieves entered through the side door in Dover Street by cutting the steel bolts and raising the shutter. They tried and failed to crack the main safe, which contained £100,000 worth of jewellery, and then turned their attention to the showcases in the window, from which they took a pair of diamond and ruby earrings, diamond and pearl pins, gem watches, diamond and sapphire links, pearl necklaces, pendants, diamond combs, a diamond necklace, and a diamond tiara, worth in all about £15,000. *The Times* described it as the work of 'experienced cracksmen' ('Diamond Robbery in Piccadilly', 2 November 1897) and it was only later revealed to have been the work of Adam Worth, who was living close by in Piccadilly.

The central figure in the second story, 'A Costume Piece', was based on Barney Barnato (who had also provided the inspiration for Grant Allen in *The African Millionaire* and for George Griffith in a series of stories for *Pearson's Magazine* about Illicit Diamond Buyers, published in book form as *Knaves of Diamonds*). Barnato, whose real name was Isaacs, was born in Whitechapel in 1852, and started his career in the rag trade and the music hall. In 1873 he sailed steerage to South Africa, where he joined his brother in the diamond fields at Kimberley. They traded as diamond dealers and by 1876 were producing profits of £90,000 a year, although there were rumours that they had engaged in illicit diamond-buying. In 1880 Barney established the firm of Barnato Brothers, and in 1888 he became a millionaire several times over when it was amalgamated with the De Beers company.

His antics caused raised eyebrows whenever he was in London. During an extended visit from March 1894 to June 1895 he became a familiar figure at the National Sporting Club and the Empire Music Hall, and he flaunted his wealth by acquiring the freehold on 25 Park Lane as the site for a mansion. The high water mark was in May 1895 when several dinners were given in his honour, including one at the Criterion Restaurant in the presence of the Lord Mayor of London and two hundred and fifty guests. In his speech he bragged of his wealth and spoke of his humble beginnings.

Financial problems began to mount after the Jameson Raid

at the end of 1895, and by 1896 he was drinking heavily and was given to aggressive outbursts. The final chapter of his life was the most dramatic. He set out from South Africa for London on board the *Scot* at the beginning of June 1897 in order to attend Queen Victoria's Diamond Jubilee celebrations. On 14 June he was seen walking on deck, then a cry went up that he had jumped (or been thrown) overboard. He was spotted in the water, but was dead when the lifeboat reached him.

Although Barnato does not match the physical description of Reuben Rosenthall in 'A Costume Piece', they are otherwise alike – the boasting and bragging, the drunken outbursts, the retinue of prize-fighters, and so on – but the influence extends beyond the character. The disappearance of Raffles resembles that of Barnato. The places associated with him (such as Willesden, Whitechapel and Shoreditch) recur in the stories. The brash Queensland legislator in 'Nine Points of the Law' is in the same *nouveau riche* category; and there are innumerable touches and allusions which suggest that Hornung had read the *Memoir* of Barnato, which was published at the end of November 1897.

'Gentlemen and Players'

The third story is the one which best defines the book because it uses the metaphor of the Gentlemen and Players match to express the rivalry between the amateur and the professional cracksmen and to illustrate the analogy between cricket and crime. The theft of jewels from a country house may recall *The Moonstone* by Wilkie Collins (1868) and to a lesser extent Anthony Trollope's novel *The Eustace Diamonds* (1872), but it was probably suggested by one of the many similar cases in real life. Lady Melrose was not alone. The Duchess of Cleveland had had her jewels stolen from Battle Abbey in November 1877; the Countess of Aberdeen was robbed at Halstead Place in 1878. Lady Miles lost her jewels at Leigh Court, Bristol, in 1892; Baroness Schroeder was robbed at Worleston in March 1893; the Countess Wilton was robbed at the Hatch, near Maidenhead, in August 1893; and there were many others who lost necklaces and jewel cases.

Work in Progress

The manuscripts were sent as they were written to Cassell's in London, who had acquired the serial rights for *Cassell's Magazine*. Copies were then forwarded to S.S. McClure in New York, who had acquired the American rights. He bought them in January 1898 at a rate of £10 per story, and announced them as 'Burglar Stories' in his February 1898 list. 'The Ides of March' was sent on 23 March 1898; 'Gentlemen and Players' followed in April, and 'A Costume Piece' (or 'The Costume Piece' as it was first known) at the beginning of May. McClure also received a synopsis of the remaining stories from his son Robert (who worked in his London office). The fourth, it was said, would be a love story in which 'Raffles all but elopes with a young lady of title and wealth'; in the fifth he would 'commit, or think he had committed a murder'; and the sixth would be 'the most exciting of all. Nothing shall be said of it here, save that it uncovers an unscrupulous statesman, a celebrated aeronaut, a steeplechase in balloons, the final disappearance of Raffles, and the escape of "Bunny".'

This was not the way they turned out. When it came, the fourth of the stories received by McClure (which would be the fifth in the book) had no love interest. It was 'The Murder of Angus Baird' (later called 'Wilful Murder') in which Raffles witnessed the killing of his 'fence'. It had a precedent in the 'wilful murder' of the popular actor William Terriss, who had been stabbed to death at the stage door of the Adelphi Theatre on 16 December 1897, and contained echoes of Thomas de Quincey's essay on 'Murder Considered as One of the Fine Arts'. It caused alarm in New York, however, where McClure was hoping to sell the stories as a series to a magazine, instead of syndicating them in newspapers. He feared that the editors, who were already mystified by many of the references to cricket, might be further deterred by the gruesome nature of the story. He asked his son to find out if Hornung would be willing to provide another in its place, and if he would consider amending the earlier ones. Robert McClure put this to Hornung, and wrote back to his father on 19 June 1898: 'The 4th story entitled

"The Murder of Angus Baird" will be withdrawn and one less gruesome substituted for it. With regard to recasting these tales, Hornung does not seem very ready to undertake the work, but he says you are at liberty to make any changes you like – in fact you have a free hand. I am aware that you would rather he did the cutting and altering but this is all that I have been able to arrange at present.'

'Nine Points of the Law' (which recalls 'The Episode of the Old Master' in Grant Allen's *African Millionaire*) was sent from Rome on 1 July 1898. Hornung then returned to Posilippo, where he spent the next six months in 'a villa in a vineyard' on the slopes overlooking the island of Gaiola (which he described in an article for the *Cornhill Magazine* in May 1899, and used as the setting for a later Raffles story, 'The Fate of Faustina'). The last two stories which make up *The Amateur Cracksman* were written there, in a small 'villino' that served as his study. 'The Return Match' (suggested by the escape from Dartmoor of William Morgan on 2 January 1898) and 'The Gift of the Emperor' (drawing on his recent memories of the ship which had brought him to Italy) were with McClure at the end of August 1898.

'In the Chains of Crime'

The stories were announced by *Cassell's Magazine* in May 1898: 'Mr Hornung's work is familiar to most of us. He is an exceedingly picturesque and pleasant writer of short stories; but this time we find him in a new role. It is scarcely an exaggeration to say that these stories are, in their way, worthy to be compared with the famous "Sherlock Holmes". They are tales of the darker side of London life, and their interest is quite extraordinary.' The first story appeared in June 1898 and the last in November, under the series title 'In the Chains of Crime. Being the Confessions of a late Prisoner of the Crown, and sometime accomplice of the more notorious A. J. Raffles, Cricketer and Criminal, whose fate is unknown.' The phrase 'in the chains of crime' had been used by the Baptist preacher Charles Haddon Spurgeon, but also recalls *In Vinculis* (1889), the poems by Wilfrid Scawen

Blunt, written after his release from prison, and the *Book of Chains* (1897) by George Ives. John Henry Bacon (1866–1914), who illustrated the stories, provided a heading showing Bunny chained to a skeletal figure in a hooded cape.

The Amateur Cracksman

The English book rights went to Methuen (who had taken Hornung's previous book, *Dead Men Tell No Tales*) and the American rights were offered to Charles Scribner. Hornung wrote to Scribner on 17 August 1898: 'I am almost ashamed to speak of yet another book; my name is so often in your list; but I should be still more ashamed to take a book elsewhere without showing it first to your firm. The book in question is a *series* of stories now appearing in *Cassell's Magazine* and the McClure papers; but it will be more like one story when I put it together in book-form. Title – *The Amateur Cracksman*. Subject – light-hearted Crime! It is not very shocking, and seems a popular serial in London. But I do not pretend that it is my best work – though on the mere execution I have spared no pains. By this post I am sending half the book, in magazine proofs, on approval. It should be published in February next. 60,000 words will be the length.'

Scribner did not reply at once as he wanted to gauge the public reaction in America before he committed himself. Moreover, although Hornung was under the impression that the stories were appearing in newspapers, McClure had instead sold them to *Collier's Weekly*, and none had yet been printed. The first was published on 17 September 1898, and they ran at weekly intervals until 22 October, under the heading 'The Adventures of A. J. Raffles', with illustrations by E. V. Nadherny. As they were well received, Scribner's sent a contract.

Unaware of this Hornung wrote again on 12 October: 'I am afraid (as I think I wrote to Mr Scribner) that for various reasons you may not care to handle this particular book of mine. Of course I shall be only too delighted if I am wrong – in which case the delay in hearing from you will not matter. If, however, I am to make other arrangements, I have not time to lose.' No sooner had the letter been sent than he heard that the contract had arrived.

Hornung returned the contract on 20 November 1898, explaining that the delay was caused by the English publisher, Methuen, who had been unable to decide on the publication date for *The Amateur Cracksman* (which was provisionally set for February 1899), and who were pressing him to change the title to *The Adventures of A. J. Raffles*.

Methuen felt that the word 'amateur' might be misconstrued, but Hornung was able to persuade them otherwise. The word (from the French) is used in the sporting sense where an amateur is as proficient as a professional, but plays the game for its own sake rather than for money. It was first used of a person who loved 'the polite arts of painting, sculpture, or architecture, without any regard to any pecuniary advantage', and then spread to embrace any person of means who engaged in an activity for artistic or aesthetic reasons. Robert Louis Stevenson described himself as 'The Amateur Emigrant' in his account of life on board an emigrant ship, and Conan Doyle referred in one of the early Sherlock Holmes stories to the 'Amateur Mendicant Society'. With Raffles it goes further. He is not 'an amateur cracksman', but '*The* Amateur Cracksman'. It becomes a title, rather than a description.

'Cracksman' was also an ideal choice, and far better than 'burglar' or 'thief', as it suggests proficiency in the art of crime. It was originally thieves' slang for a housebreaker or burglar who 'cracked a crib', and came into the mainstream language in the early nineteenth century. The added glamour of the false association with the word for 'expert' (as in 'crack shot') made it popular with writers of all types. It had been used by the Revd Frederick Langbridge in the title of a humorous novel, *The Clerical Cracksman, A Tale for the Burgling Season*, which was published in 1889 under his pen name 'Alfred Fitzmaurice King' (the cracksman is a clergyman who is deemed to be over-worthy by a bishop's daughter; he therefore dons a black mask and breaks into her father's house in order to win her hand).

Hornung worked on the proofs at Gaiola, where he remained until the early part of 1899. On his return to London he and his wife took a house at 36 Edwardes Square before moving a few months later to 9 Pitt Street. By then the final revisions had been made to the text, and with 'Le Premier Pas' and 'Wilful Murder' added, *The Amateur Cracksman* was ready for publication in March 1899 (a month later than originally planned). In America it carried the following blurb: 'Raffles, the hero of Mr Hornung's new story, is one of the most fascinating rascals of modern fiction. Born and bred a gentleman, he enters upon an astonishing career of crime, bringing to every enterprise high spirits, an iron nerve, a buoyant wit, and a perfect ease and self-possession. The combination of precision, of head work and of handiwork, stamps him a veritable artist in crime, well worthy to rank with his counterpart, Sherlock Holmes. His adventures are described with infinite zest and with delicious humor.'

'This Form of Flattery'

It was inevitable that the publicity should mention Sherlock Holmes, and Hornung appeared to acknowledge a connection by dedicating the book to Conan Doyle: 'To / A.C.D. / This Form of Flattery'. The *Scotsman* (13 March 1899) interpreted it 'as acknowledging the stories to be imitated after the works of Mr Conan Doyle' and said that Raffles was a 'converse gentleman to the renowned Sherlock Holmes'. The *Academy* (19 March 1899) was even more emphatic: 'The initials stand for A. Conan Doyle and the form of flattery is imitation . . . Mr Hornung is imitating Mr Conan Doyle.' Even Conan Doyle himself apparently believed this to be the case. In his autobiography, *Memories and Adventures* (1924), he said of his brother-in-law: 'I think I may claim that his famous character Raffles was a kind of inversion of Sherlock Holmes, Bunny playing Watson. He admits as much in his kindly dedication.'

In fact, Hornung did not 'admit as much'. The dedication was intended to acknowledge his debt to Doyle for having suggested the series of stories. It might also have been an acknowledgement for the name of the protagonist, 'Raffles', which Conan Doyle had used in his novel *The Doings of Raffles Haw* (1892) – though it could as easily have come from Sir

Stamford Raffles, the founder of Singapore. Hornung did not 'imitate' Sherlock Holmes. Had he done so, Raffles would have been a 'Napoleon of crime' similar to Professor Moriarty and he would have matched wits with a great detective. He would have been similar to Arsene Lupin, the criminal hero created by Maurice Leblanc, who was a foil for a great detective. The dedication has had a lasting influence on the way the book has been viewed, and it might have been very different if, for example, it had instead been dedicated 'To My Old Friend/ George Cecil Ives', or 'In Memory of My Friends at Uppingham School and of the adventures I shared with them'.

The dedication may have been misinterpreted, but the critics were unanimous in their praise of the book. The *Outlook* (11 March 1899) found it 'unconventional and stirring'; the *Athenaeum* (15 April 1899) called it 'highly pleasing', and the *New York Times* (1 April 1899) said that seldom had a book of stories taken 'a more artistic form than that which characterizes those which go to make up the book entitled *The Amateur Cracksman*. Mr Hornung has risen to a very high plane in his creation and treatment of the tales, and into them all he has contrived to put heart and soul that gives to them a strong human interest.'

Critical Acclaim

The book was hailed as a welcome departure from the detective story and its offshoots by critics in England and America. The *Spectator* (18 March 1899) said: 'It has been reserved to Mr Hornung to show us the other side of the medal in *The Amateur Cracksman*, which stern moralists will hardly fail to reprobate as a new, ingenious, artistic, but most reprehensible application of the crude principles involved in the old-fashioned hero-worship of Jack Sheppard and Dick Turpin.' The *World* (29 March 1899) praised the 'remarkable freshness and originality' of the book:

It is difficult to imagine anything better in their way than the eight stories of crime here delineated. Short and to the point, each is suggested with admirable art, and each is finished to perfection. From the moment we make the acquaintance of Raffles the resourceful, we are fascinated by his individuality, his daring, his wonderful coolness, and his delightful *savoir faire*, and follow him breathlessly in his career of crime until the inevitable moment arrives when Nemesis overtakes him. His method of cracking cribs would have earned the commendations of the late Mr Peace. The frankly egotistic nature of the man is truly refreshing, his coolness and daring unsurpassed. Ingeniously strung together, the tales may be read separately, but it is unlikely that any one commencing the book will lay it down until it has been read from cover to cover, for the writer has placed the burglar Raffles upon a pinnacle of fame from which he is not likely to be dislodged for a long time.

The critics did not express undue concern about the moral ramifications of the book as they felt that the narrator retained his sense of right and wrong and that the last story redeemed it from what the *Bookman* (April 1899) called 'the reproach of its being the greatest incentive ever penned to spirited youth to make a brilliant living by the burglar's art'.

The Later Raffles Stories

Several newspapers, such as the *Daily Mail*, ended their reviews by saying that they suspected that more would be heard of Raffles – and they did not have long to wait. At the end of 1899 Hornung received a generous offer from Collier's for a new series of stories, but out of loyalty to Scribner gave him first refusal on their serial publication, which to his surprise Scribner accepted. The first three stories were written in London between June and August 1900, and the remainder at Gaiola, where Hornung spent the last three months of the year. They were serialized in *Scribner's Magazine* and published in book form in England as *The Black Mask* (Grant Richards, 1901) and by Scribner in America as *Raffles, Further Adventures of the Amateur Cracksman*. The stories dealt with the period after Raffles had returned from Italy as an outcast from society, and ended with his death in the Boer War.

This was followed by a third series of stories, *A Thief in the*

Night (Chatto & Windus, 1905), and by a novel, *Mr Justice
Raffles* (Smith, Elder, 1909). *A Thief in the Night* consisted of
additional stories from his heyday at the Albany and the later
period. They were serialized very successfully in England in the
Pall Mall Magazine, but in America, where they were taken
by *Collier's Weekly* to follow *The Return of Sherlock Holmes*,
they encountered problems because of a campaign by the New
York weekly magazine *Town Topics*. It was directed against
the publisher, who was accused of undermining the youth of
America, in particular a young cracksman called Christopher
Smith, who said he had been drawn to crime after seeing the
play of Raffles. The vituperation reached such a pitch that
Collier curtailed the serialization, while pointing out that no
such claim had been made when the earlier stories had been
serialized. When the book was published it enjoyed even greater
sales than might otherwise have been the case.

Raffles on Stage and Screen

The play to which Christopher Smith referred was *Raffles, The
Amateur Cracksman*, written by Eugene W. Presbrey (who
shared the credit with E. W. Hornung). It starred Kyrle Bellew
and opened in Atlantic City on 19 September 1903, before
moving to the Princess Theatre, New York. It was first performed in London at the Comedy Theatre on 12 May 1906 with
Gerald du Maurier in the title role. It subsequently inspired
numerous films. The first came out in 1905, but the most famous
are those which starred John Barrymore (Weber, 1917), House
Peters (Universal, 1925), Ronald Colman (Samuel Goldwyn/
United Artists, 1930), and David Niven (Samuel Goldwyn,
1939). The play was performed in many European capitals and
was revived in London in 1914. Raffles was also the subject of
numerous travesties and curtain-raisers such as *Waffles, or The
Amateur Cracker* by Edgar Smith (1903) as well the hero of a
play by Graham Greene, *The Return of A. J. Raffles*, which was
produced by the Royal Shakespeare Company in December
1976. Raffles also made his mark on radio and television, including a series made in 1977 by Yorkshire Television with Anthony

Valentine and Christopher Strauli, and more recently in *Gentleman Thief* by Matthew Green (shown on the BBC in June 2001), which starred Nigel Havers as Raffles, but did away with Bunny, who was replaced by a 'thieving ruffian' called Ellis Bride.

The Creator of Raffles

The Raffles stories are Hornung's greatest achievement, but many of his other works also merit attention. The Australian novels and stories are closely observed, fresh in their style, and true in their sentiment. His semi-autobiographical works, such as *Young Blood*, based on his father's bankruptcy, and *Fathers of Men*, about his days at Uppingham, have the innocence of youth, while a greater sophistication is found in the stories of love and intrigue, such as *The Shadow of the Rope* and *No Hero*. *The Camera Fiend*, about a man who attempts to photograph the soul as it leaves the body, *Witching Hill*, a series of stories about a modern housing estate in which the spirit of the past persists, and *The Crime Doctor*, which treats crime as a psychological disorder, are all notable for the originality of their plots.

Hornung suffered all his life from asthma, which was at times debilitating, but this did not prevent him from leading a full and active life. As well as being devoted to cricket, he was fond of skating and swimming. He was a member of the Reform, the National Liberal Club, the RAC, and of many literary societies. He rowed on the river, walked, bicycled, and was one of the first to own his own motor-car. He enjoyed good company, good food and wine, and the luxuries of life, such as Turkish baths.

His house in Pitt Street (which he immortalized in one of the later Raffles stories, and which also features in Conan Doyle's Sherlock Holmes story 'The Six Napoleons') and the larger house in Hornton Street (where he moved in 1904) were often the venue for musical evenings, parties and family meetings (including those of his brother-in-law's ill-fated 'Automatic Sculpture Syndicate').

He was devoted to the schools at which he had been a pupil and often returned to them. He gave sermons, attended Old Boys' days, and offered encouragement and advice to both teachers and boys.

The greatest tragedy of his life was the loss of his son, Oscar, who was killed in action in July 1915. His grief was all the greater because the body was never found. He shared his suffering with others who mourned the loss of their children, such as Rudyard Kipling, whose son John, who had been a friend of Oscar's, was also killed. The awful suspense which Hornung had endured while his son was in the trenches, and the emptiness he felt when he learnt of his death, was encapsulated in a poignant privately printed collection of his son's letters called 'Trusty and Well Beloved'.

At the end of 1915 Hornung worked as an air-raid warden for the Anti-Aircraft Corps, and in 1917 he accepted a position with the YMCA as the secretary and honorary librarian at Arras. He remained there until the summer of 1918 and his letters home formed the basis of his book Notes of a Camp-Follower on the Western Front. He returned to Germany in May 1919, and again in September when he visited the battle-fields. He also arranged for a plaque (with lines by Kipling) to be placed in the house at Eton where his son had been a pupil, and served as a member of the committee which planned the War Memorial Shrine at Uppingham.

Hornung left London and moved to a house on his brother's estate in West Grinstead in 1917, and the following year bought Midway Cottage at Partridge Green (where Hilaire Belloc was a neighbour). He spent his last few years working on scenarios for films (including new stories of Raffles and Stingaree) and wrote a detailed study of the writings of Charles Reade. His health began to deteriorate early in 1921 and in search of a cure he travelled to St-Jean-de-Luz, where he died on 22 March 1921.

E. W. Hornung and A. Conan Doyle: a Retrospect

Conan Doyle (who died in 1930) was in Paris at the time of his brother-in-law's death, having just returned from Australia, and was able to attend the funeral. Their relationship had not always been easy. They fell out over Conan Doyle's affair with Jean Leckie, when Hornung reprimanded him in 1900 for walking arm in arm with her at Lord's, and they disagreed about spiritualism, which Doyle promoted and Hornung abhorred (making it clear that he did not wish to be given any messages purporting to be from his son, who had been killed in action during the Great War). However, they agreed to disagree and continued to play cricket in the same teams and were members of the same clubs (including the 'Crimes Club').

Conan Doyle seemed at times to be jealous of his brother-in-law's success and never acknowledged his own debt or paid him the compliment of a dedication. Raffles had made a comeback before Sherlock Holmes and the means by which he did so was an inspiration for Conan Doyle, who was also indebted to Hornung for several of his plots, such as that used in 'Charles Augustus Milverton' (which was suggested by 'Wilful Murder'). He could be generous in his praise, but was generally churlish in his attitude to Hornung. In *The Wanderings of a Spiritualist* (1921), which described how he had heard of his brother-in-law's illness and only arrived in time for the funeral, he called him 'one of the wits of our time', but chose to remember that he had been witty about his own 'physical disabilities'. In the introduction to *Old Offenders* (1923), a posthumous collection of stories, Conan Doyle said that Hornung had always brought to his work 'a fine artistic sense, and a remarkable power of vivid narrative', and that the Raffles stories were an example of this: 'one could not find any better example of clever plot and terse admirable narrative'. However, he then went on to suggest that they 'harmed' him because 'they got between the public and his better work', and that this 'better' work 'fell little short of achieving the high mark at which it was aimed'. In his autobiography, *Memories and Adventures* (1924), Conan Doyle devoted just one paragraph to his brother-in-law. After claiming that Raffles was an inversion of Sherlock Holmes, he went on to say that he considered the Raffles stories were 'rather dangerous in their suggestion. I told him so before he put pen to paper, and the result has, I fear, borne me out. You must not make the criminal a hero.'

The Enduring Popularity of Raffles

Conan Doyle's words perhaps say more about himself than about Hornung. By the early 1930s, when Barry Perowne (a pseudonym of Philip Atkey, the nephew of the writer Bertram Atkey) began his long-running series of sequels to Raffles, the work was already being hailed as a 'classic'. 'Old Fag' in *John O' London's Weekly* (30 April 1937) said the stories deserved this status because of their consummate artistry and topsy-turvy morality; he answered Conan Doyle's criticism by saying: 'You return to the real world afterwards none the worse for your adventures with Raffles and Bunny. They rob you of neither your honour nor your honesty.'

The same high opinion was shared by Malcolm Elwin in *Old Gods Falling* (1939). He took issue with Anthony Hope (the author of *The Prisoner of Zenda*), who had called Raffles a 'low scoundrel'. He may have been a scoundrel, Elwin said: 'But Raffles was not low; he never invites contempt, like Casanova or Cellini, or Mr Meyerstein's Terence Duke, but remains ever the most winning of rascals, such as have wrought havoc with the hearts of women since the beginning of time, though Raffles has nothing of the bounder about him like most men successful with women, but, on the contrary, possesses the graces of a prince of good fellows, ever welcomed with a glad hand in club or tavern.' Even as an outcast from society he retained 'the irresistible charm of genius', and he appealed to readers because they shared Bunny's feelings towards him: 'It was Raffles I loved. It was not the dark life we led together, still less its base rewards; it was the man himself, his gaiety, his humour, his dazzling audacity, his incomparable courage and resource.'

The most influential critic was George Orwell in his essay 'Raffles and Miss Blandish', which was first published in *Hori-*

zon in October 1944. He compared *Raffles* to James Hadley Chase's gangster novel, *No Orchids for Miss Blandish*, on the pretext that both were glamorized versions of crime, but, having expressed his dismay at the raw power-lust and sadism of Hadley Chase, he devoted most of the article to Raffles, who he felt had achieved greatness through being 'a gentleman – and specifically a public school man – who had gone astray. *Raffles*, not less than *Great Expectations* or *Le Rouge et Le Noir*, is a story of snobbery, and it gains a great deal from the precariousness of Raffles's social position. A cruder writer would have made the "gentleman burglar" a member of the peerage, or at least a baronet. Raffles, however, is of upper-middle-class origin and is only accepted by the aristocracy because of his personal charm. "We were in Society but not of it," he says to Bunny towards the end of the book; "and I was asked about for my cricket."'

Anthony Powell made the same point about the stories in the introduction to the Century Library edition of 1950, although he used the word 'respectability' rather than 'snobbery': 'Their spirit at once revolts against respectability, and chants a paean in respectability's praise. Perhaps this closeness to their period's inconsistencies has caused their survival; because after the passing of fifty years, they have lost none of their flavour. If anything, they have gained by becoming, as it were, a costume piece.' The stories, in his opinion, combined 'a touch of the philosophies of both Kipling and Wilde' and embodied '*fin-de-siecle* sentiment in more than one of its protean forms'.

A Classic Status

M. R. Ridley, in the introduction to the Collins Clear Type Classics edition of 1955, said he was in no doubt that the stories deserved classic status: 'The inclusion of them in this series is anything but a rescue from oblivion. Their stamina, their continuing vitality and appeal, are proved by the hard numerical test of the multitude of readers who have wanted to read them and want to read them today.' Those who lived in the post-war world had the advantage over earlier readers because they could see beyond the glamour and could appreciate Raffles as a fully rounded and very human figure: 'We are not in the least blind to his dislikeable qualities; but he has great qualities too, steely courage and lightning presence of mind among them. He is, in fact, a lesser and somewhat shop-soiled Satan. But above all – and here, I fancy, is what catches the attention of the present generation of readers – he is a quite interesting psychological study . . . I am not at all clear that Hornung fully knew what he was doing, but even if he was working only half-consciously the result is admirably true to life. And Bunny is not only a skilfully devised foil, but interesting in his own right, not least because his self-perception is a great deal keener than his leader's.'

For Oliver Edwards (writing in *The Times* in 1956), the defining quality was the 'Jekyll and Hyde' contrast between the two sides of Raffles – one respectable and conventional, the other unpredictable and incalculable:

The point is that while the respectable Raffles is as firmly rooted in the mind's eye, as certain in every detail, as the most conventional of our friends, the other Raffles forever remains a completely uncertain quantity. It was so with every hero we had at school. Part of our education is to find out exactly where each man's feet of clay begin. Hornung understood that queer mixture called schoolboy honour as few writers have done. The longer we read of Raffles the greater are the number of episodes from our own boyhood tragedies and comedies that come back to us. There comes back, too, the London of Atlas buses, of the hansom cab, of the sulphurous fogs, of the lazy country-house life, of the long, lovely decade of the Edwardian age. (Chronologically, of course, Raffles was Victorian, but in spirit he was Edwardian.) No one, I think, has given us in fewer words so true a feeling of all that we lost when that life vanished. They were, moreover, words of one syllable. For not the least attractive part of the Raffles books is the simple, plain, unaffected language in which each one of them is written.

The only dissenting voices were those who tried to pigeon-hole Hornung alongside writers such as 'Sapper', Dornford Yates, and others who were guilty of the great sin of 'snobbery'. Colin Watson in *Snobbery with Violence* (1971) argued that

Raffles confirmed the prejudices and pattern of thought of a privileged elite, and claimed that a modern reader would be repelled by the sentimentality and 'sadistic overtones'. This was denied by William Vivian Butler, in *The Durable Desperadoes* (1973), but he agreed that the stories had satisfied the vague yearnings of the denizens of the *fin-de-siècle* no man's land, who were fascinated by anything that was uninhibited and bravura – especially 'lawlessness'. Hornung had allowed them to indulge their fantasies, while Bunny worried on their behalf about the ethics of such exploits with a self-disgust that was 'almost Poe-like in its intensity'. Butler believed that Bunny was as great a creation as Raffles. 'To show a whole generation a living embodiment of their frustrated romantic urges (illicit romantic urges, if you insist) is itself a considerable thing to do; but to show, at one and the same time, the flaws in that embodiment – to split oneself in two, to be Raffles and Bunny functioning throughout as both your reader's temptation and his conscience, his demon and his guardian angel – that is something that must, in popular crime fiction at any rate, be very nearly unique.'

C. P. Snow, in a review in the *Financial Times* (3 April 1975), defended Bunny's 'outpouring of emotion', which, in his opinion, was not a fault, but was the reason why Raffles was 'one of the most remarkable triumphs of the late 19th century romantic imagination': 'The feeling is juvenile. It is also inno-cent, which isn't the same thing. It is not erotic, but it has homosexual undertones about which Hornung was not in the slightest inhibited. He just reveals that here was a kind of love.' The nineteenth-century writers, Snow believed, had a greater emotional range than their modern counterparts: 'These writers were much more open emotionally than we are. We have become increasingly tight-lipped, except about sex and perhaps an unen-dearing form of social anger. It is likely that, if in a hundred years anyone is interested in us, our literature will seem, not emancipated, but embarrassingly unfree.'

Peter Haining, in his introduction to the Souvenir Press edi-tion in 1984 (later reissued by Penguin Books), pointed out that the name had entered the language and that Raffles reigned supreme as the greatest of all cracksmen. He commended the work 'with the observation that perhaps only one of W. G. Grace's classic innings or a Sherlock Holmes adventure might bear comparison'. Jeremy Lewis, in J. M. Dent's Classic Thrillers edition a year later (subsequently issued as one of the Everyman Classics), noted that Raffles was 'endearingly fallible' and 'a good deal more interesting and less predictable' than commonly supposed. Clive Bloom, in an introduction for the Oxford Popular Classics (1995), rose to greater critical heights, pointing out that when Hornung faced the 'literary and moral conundrum' of how he might create 'a criminal who was neither immoral nor ungentlemanly and whose character was neither perverse nor prone to degeneracy', he achieved something remarkable: 'Compared to Holmes, Raffles has a positively *healthy* disposition unfettered by the morbidity of Holmes's own obsessions and bizarrerie.' He praised the work as 'supremely entertaining, witty, and fun', noting the 'Wildean wit' and the occasional 'striking classicism which brings to the tales a touch of Homeric grandeur'. In the stories, he said, there is neither modern introspection nor any psychological questioning: 'As such the tales are perverse comedies of social manners; their generic partners are Jane Austen and P. G. Wodehouse rather than the more obvious romances of Stevenson, Rider Haggard, or Conan Doyle.'

Peter Rowland devoted a book to Hornung (*Raffles and His Creator*, 1991) and placed the stories in the wider context of the author's works, while Kurt Kausler, in his introduction to *The A. J. Raffles Omnibus* (2000), provided a fund of detail about the stage and film career of Raffles, and praised the lucidity of the work. Hornung's 'word pictures', he said, were 'as precise and memorable as a photograph'.

Ellery Queen listed *The Amateur Cracksman* as one of the hundred and six 'Most Important Books of Detective-Crime-Mystery Short Stories' in the *Queen's Quorum* (1951), and the book is often bracketed with the best detective fiction. Yet it is not a detective story. It has a detective, the dour Inspector Mackenzie, who is one of the most realistic in fiction, but he does very little detecting. It is not a mystery story, even though Raffles does not always make his plans clear in advance to

Bunny. It is not even a crime story in the usual sense, though it is a story about crime.

The Amateur Cracksman could be considered as an extension of the school story, where the prank becomes a crime, and the master a police detective. It could be said to be a novel based on cricket, where Raffles and Bunny play in the same team (one as a high scorer, the other as a 'lower order' batsman) against assorted teams, such as the country house, the diamond millionaires, or the *nouveaux riches*; where Raffles represents the gentlemen against the players, or the amateurs against the professionals, under the eye of the umpire, who is the law. It could be called a satire on the eccentricities of its age, on the muscular aestheticism of men such as George Ives, who mixed elements of Kipling and Wilde. But it is more than any of these. It is not written to any formula. It is an original work, which draws its strength from the great themes of literature and has the inevitability of a Greek tragedy (with Bunny as the Chorus). It is clear in style, accessible and entertaining. It is not pretentious or morbid, even though it is a lament for the false aspirations of youth. It cannot be faulted, because it is aware of its faults. It is the triumph of virtuosity over virtue, and it demonstrates in its own particular way the truth of the saying that there is honour among thieves.

Further Reading

Raffles Stories

The Amateur Cracksman (Methuen, 1899); *The Black Mask* (Grant Richards, 1901)/USA: *Raffles, Further Adventures of the Amateur Cracksman* (Scribner's, 1901); *A Thief in the Night* (Chatto & Windus, 1905); *Mr Justice Raffles* (Smith, Elder, 1909); *Raffles, A Play in Four Acts* (Samuel French, 1914).

The introductions to the *Raffles* stories by Anthony Powell (Century Library, Eyre and Spottiswoode, 1950, 1956), by M. R. Ridley (Collins New Classics, Collins, 1955), by Anthony Curtis (Landmark Library, Chatto & Windus, 1972), and by the publisher of the Bison Books edition (University of Nebraska Press, 1976) deserve attention, as does Otto Penzler's introduction to the American edition of Barry Perowne's *Raffles Revisited* (New York, Harper & Row, 1974). There are also introductions to collected editions by Peter Haining (Souvenir Press, 1984; Penguin Books, 1985), Jeremy Lewis (J. M. Dent, 1985, 1992), and Kurt Kausler (in *The A. J. Raffles Omnibus*, Shelburne, Battered Silicon Dispatch Box, 2000). The last includes the text of the play by Eugene W. Presbrey.

Other Works by E. W. Hornung

A Bride from the Bush (Smith, Elder, 1890); *Under Two Skies* (A. & C. Black, 1892); *Tiny Luttrell* (Cassell, 1893); *The Boss of Taroomba* (Bliss, Sands & Foster, 1894); *The Unbidden Guest* (Longmans, Green, 1894); *The Rogue's March* (Cassell, 1896); *The Cricket on the Green* (Jordison, 1895); *Irralie's Bushranger* (Neville Beeman, 1896); *My Lord Duke* (Cassell,

1897); *Young Blood* (Cassell, 1898); *Some Persons Unknown* (Cassell, 1898); *Dead Men Tell No Tales* (Methuen, 1899); *The Belle of Toorak* (Grant Richards, 1900)/USA: *The Shadow of a Man* (Scribner's, 1900); *Peccavi* (Grant Richards, 1900); *At Large* (USA only, Scribner's, 1902); *The Shadow of the Rope* (Chatto & Windus, 1902); *No Hero* (Smith, Elder, 1903); *Denis Dent* (Isbister, 1903); *Stingaree* (Chatto & Windus, 1905); *The Camera Fiend* (T. Fisher Unwin, 1911); *Witching Hill* (Hodder & Stoughton, 1912); *Fathers of Men* (Smith, Elder, 1912; with introduction, John Murray, 1919); *The Thousandth Woman* (Eveleigh Nash, 1913); *The Crime Doctor* (Eveleigh Nash, 1914); *'Trusty and Well Beloved'* (privately printed, 1915); *Notes of a Camp-Follower on the Western Front* (Constable, 1919); *The Young Guard* (Constable, 1919), including two poems which had been issued separately, *Wooden Cross* (Nisbet, 1918) and *The Ballad of Ensign Joy* (USA, E. P. Dutton, 1919); *Old Offenders and a Few Old Scores* (John Murray, 1923); *E. W. Hornung and His Young Guard, 1914*, edited by Shane R. Chichester (Wellington College Press, 1941).

Plays

Raffles, The Amateur Cracksman by E. W. Hornung and Eugene Wiley Presbrey, starring Kyrle Bellew (Raffles), Young's Pier Theatre, Atlantic City (19 September 1903); Princess Theatre, New York (27 October 1903), transferred to the Savoy Theatre; on tour, 1904–12, starring S. Miller Kent, William Ingersoll and others; first English production, starring Gerald du Maurier (with mid-run performances by Henry Ainley), Comedy Theatre (12 May 1906); Wyndham's Theatre, with Gerald Du Maurier (23 December 1914); touring productions, 1907–12, starring Leonard Boyne, Reginald Dance, Claud Allister, and others; Théatre Réjane, Paris, starring André Brulé (14 June 1907); Teatro de la Comedia, Madrid, with Sr. Calle (11 February 1908). *The Burglar and the Lady* by Langdon McCormick, with James J. Corbett as Raffles, Opera Glass, Wilke-Barre, Pennsylvania (6 September 1906), and on tour (1906–8); *The*

Further Adventures of the Amateur Cracksman by Eugene Presbrey (n.d.); *A Visit from Raffles*, by E. W. Hornung and Charles
Sansom, starring H. A. Saintsbury, Empress Theatre, Brixton
(1 November 1909); *The Return of A. J. Raffles*, by Graham
Greene, starring Denholm Elliott, RSC, Aldwych Theatre
(4 December 1975); also Royal Shakespeare Theatre, Stratford-
upon-Avon (13–17 January 1976); revived, with Jeremy Child,
Oxford Playhouse (22 October 1979).

Travesties and Burlesques

Waffles by Edgar Smith, New York (December 1903); *The Girl
Raffles* by Charles E. Blaney, New York (1906); *An Amateur
Raffles* by Herbert Clayton, London (2 March 1908); *Holmes
y Raffles* by Gonzalo Jover and Emilio Gonzales, Madrid (15
June 1908); *La Captura de Raffles*, by Luis Millá & G. X.
Roura, Madrid (29 November 1908); *Nadie más fuerte que
Sherlock-Holmes*, by Luis Millá and Guillermo X. Roura, Bar-
celona (27 February 1909); *The Raffle-ing of Sherlock Holmes*,
by N. Thorpe-Mayne, London (17 March 1913); *El Robo del
Milon*, by Miguel Sierra Montayo (published 1916).

Films and Television

Raffles, The Amateur Cracksman starring John Barney Sherry,
Vitagraph, 1905; *The Dog Raffles*, Edison, 1905; *Sherlock
Holmes I Livisfare (Sherlock Holmes in Danger of His Life)*
and *Sherlock Holmes II (Raffles' Escape from Prison)*, with
Forrest Holger-Madsen as Raffles, Nordisk Films, 1908; *Raffles,
Gentleman-Cambrioleur*, Ambrosio, 1911; *Raffles Caught*,
Pathé, 1911; *Raffles, Gentleman-Burglar*, Keystone, 1914; *The
Lady Raffles* and *Lady Raffles' Return*, Gold Seal, 1915–16,
two series; *Raffles, The Amateur Cracksman*, starring John
Barrymore, Weber, 1917; UK, 1918; *Mr Justice Raffles*, starring
Gerald Ames, Hepworth, 1921; *Raffles*, starring House Peters,
Universal, 1925; *Raffles*, starring Ronald Colman, Samuel
Goldwyn/United Artists, 1930; *The Return of Raffles*, starring
George Barraud, Mansfield Markham, 1932; *Raffles*, with

David Niven, Samuel Goldwyn, 1939; *Raffles*, with Anthony
Valentine, Yorkshire Television, February–May 1977, thirteen
episodes; *Gentleman Thief*, with Nigel Havers, BBC Television,
24 June 2001.

Sequels and Related Works

John Kendrick Bangs: *Mrs Raffles, being the Adventures of An
Amateur Crackswoman* (Harper & Brothers, 1905); *R. Holmes
& Co., Being the Remarkable Adventures of Raffles Holmes,
Esq., Detective and Amateur Cracksman by Birth* (Harper &
Brothers, 1906).

Barry Perowne [Philip Atkey]: *Raffles After Dark* (Cassell,
1930)/USA: *The Return of Raffles* (John Day, 1933); *Raffles
in Pursuit* (Cassell, 1934); *Raffles Under Sentence* (Cassell,
1936); *She Married Raffles* (Cassell, 1936); *Raffles Versus
Sexton Blake* (Sexton Blake Library, Amalgamated Press, 1937);
Raffles' Crime in Gibraltar (Sexton Blake Library, Amalgamated Press, 1937)/USA: *They Hang Them in Gibraltar* (Hill-
man-Curl, 1939); *Scuttler's Cache* (*Sexton Blake Annual*,
1939)/USA: *Raffles and the Key Man* (J. B. Lippincott, 1940);
The A.R.P. Mystery (Sexton Blake Library, Amalgamated Press,
1939); *Raffles Revisited* (Harper & Row, New York, 1974/
Hamish Hamilton, 1975); *Raffles of the Albany* (St Martin's
Press, New York/Hamish Hamilton, 1976); *Raffles of the
M.C.C.* (St Martin's Press, New York/Macmillan, 1979).

Graham Greene: *The Return of A. J. Raffles*, a play (The
Bodley Head, 1975).

David Fletcher [Dulan Barber]: *Raffles*, based on the Yorkshire Television series (Macmillan, 1977).

Peter Tremayne, *The Return of Raffles* (Magnum Books,
1981).

Biographical Sources

Several of E. W. Hornung's works are semi-autobiographical.
Young Blood (Cassell, 1898) recalls his youth; *Fathers of Men*
(Smith, Elder, 1912) is based on his experiences at Uppingham

School. 'A Visit to the Blue Mountains, New South Wales' (Uppingham School Magazine, 23, February 1885) and 'A Christmastide in the Bush; and how I spent it three years ago' (*Every Boy's Annual*, 1888) describe his experiences in Australia (1884–6); 'Letters to a Young Writer' (*Cornhill Magazine*, 87, July 1903) has extracts from the letters of Richard Dowling, the Irish novelist, commenting upon his work; 'A Villa in a Vineyard' (*Cornhill Magazine*, 79, May 1899) describes his stay at Posilippo in 1898; *Notes of a Camp-Follower on the Western Front* (Constable, 1919) relates his experiences with the YMCA at Arras in 1918, and a posthumously published essay on Charles Reade (*London Mercury*, 4, June 1921) is evidence of his skills as a literary critic. *E. W. Hornung and His Young Guard* (Wellington College Press, 1941), edited by Shane R. Chichester, reprints four sermons given at the Old Stone House (the successor of his first school) and has a memoir of the author (and in later issues an obituary of his son, Oscar Hornung, from the *Eton College Chronicle*). Bertha M. Collin's biography of Hornung's elder brother, *J. P. Hornung, A Family Portrait* (privately printed, Orpington Press, 1970), provides background information on the family.

The important interview 'Raffles and the "Rabbit"' appeared in *Tit-Bits* (55, 2 January 1909) and was reused in a shorter form in 'Popular Characters in Modern Fiction' (*Tit-Bits*, 67, 28 November 1914). Other articles of interest can be found in the *Detroit Free Press* (13 May 1893); the *Book-Buyer*, New York (22, March 1901), and *Harper's Weekly*, New York (50, 27 January 1906). The *Roman Herald* for 12 April 1913 contains 'A Chat with E. W. Hornung'; anecdotes are given by Herbert Greenhough Smith, the editor of the *Strand Magazine*, in 'Authors I Have Known' (*John O' London's Weekly*, 1, 3 May 1919; *Odd Moments*, George Newnes, 1925), and by Percy Cross Standing in 'Author-Cricketers' (*World of Cricket*, 1914; *Some Cover Shots*, Jonathan Cape, 1924).

The obituaries of E. W. Hornung which appeared on 24 March 1921 (*The Times, Daily Mail, Daily News, Evening Standard*) and on later dates (*Daily Chronicle*, 26 March 1921; *New York Times*, 8 April 1921) provide only a rough outline of his life; one by J. P. Graham in the Uppingham School Magazine (463, June 1921) describes his involvement with the planning of the memorial chapel at Uppingham School. Sir Arthur Conan Doyle was interviewed by *L'Intransigeant*, Paris (24 March 1921) on the eve of his departure for St-Jean-de-Luz; he wrote of his brother-in-law's death in *The Wanderings of a Spiritualist* (Hodder & Stoughton, 1921), contributed a preface to a post-humous volume of short stories, *Old Offenders and a Few Old Scores* (John Murray, 1923), and gave some personal recollections in his autobiography, *Memories and Adventures* (John Murray, 1924). *The Life of Arthur Conan Doyle* (John Murray, 1949) by John Dickson Carr and *Conan Doyle* (Didier, Paris, 1964; John Murray, 1966) by Pierre Nordon offer additional details. Trumbull White in 'An Editorial Adventure Story' (*Bookman*, New York, 5, July 1922) describes the attempt to persuade Hornung and Doyle to collaborate on a play with Raffles and Sherlock Holmes; Hugh Castier's review of *Old Offenders*, 'The Friend of Raffles' (*Outlook*, 51, May 1923), assesses the author's achievement. *A Bachelor's London* (Grant Richards, 1931) by Frederic Whyte, an editor at Cassell's, and *Crowded Company* (Allan Wingate, 1949) by Philip Gibbs include personal memories; George Gissing's diary (*London and the Life of Literature in Late Victorian England*, edited by Pierre Coustillas, Harvester Press, 1978) includes Gissing's descriptions of his meetings with Hornung in Rome in 1898; Hornung's obituary of George Gissing appeared in the *Author* (14, 1 February 1904). 'Raffles in Vienna' by Joseph Gollomb (*Strand Magazine*, 63, 1922) and *Raffles in Real Life, The Confessions of George Smithson, alias 'Gentlemen George'* (Hutchinson, 1930) are of interest (particularly for their choice of title).

The entry on Hornung in *Who's Who* (*Who Was Who, 1916–1928*, A. & C. Black, 1929) is based on information provided by him; Kunitz and Haycraft's *Twentieth Century Authors* (H. W. Wilson, New York, 1942) and Steinbrunner and Penzler's *Ency-*

clopaedia of Crime and Mystery Writers (Routledge & Kegan Paul, 1976) have entries on Hornung, while Reilly's *Twentieth Century Crime and Mystery Writers* (St Martin's Press, New York, 1980) includes a note by H. R. F. Keating. A well-researched article on Hornung, written by Stephen Knight, appears in the *Australian Dictionary of Biography, 1891–1939* (Melbourne University Press, 1983), and is more informative than the less reliable entry written by G. H. L. Le May for the *Dictionary of National Biography, Missing Persons* (Oxford University Press, 1993).

Critical Articles

Contemporary reviews of *The Amateur Cracksman* include those found in the following newspapers and magazines: *Outlook* (3, 11 March 1899); *New York Tribune* (58, Illustrated Supplement, 12 March 1899); *Scotsman* (13 March 1899); *Academy* (56, 18 March 1899); *Spectator* (18 March 1899); *Daily Mail* (21 March 1899); *Daily Telegraph* (24 March 1899); *World* (29 March 1899); *Bookman* (16, April 1899; reprinted, *Bookman*, New York, 9, June 1899); *Literary Gazette* (1, April 1899); *New York Times* (Saturday Review, 1 April 1899); *Publishers' Circular* (70, 1 April 1899); *Daily Chronicle* (5 April 1899); *Pall Mall Gazette* (5 April 1899); *Athenaeum* (15 April 1899); *Punch* (116, 19 April 1899); *Critic* (New York, 34, June 1899).

Frank Wadleigh Chandler's two-volume study, *The Literature of Roguery* (Houghton, Mifflin, Boston, 1907), remains the best work on the subject. 'Does "Raffles" Exist? or, The Myth of the Gentleman-Burglar' by Alphonse Bertillon (*Strand Magazine*, 46, October 1913) is of significance because of the standing of its author; *Sherlock Holmes, Raffles, und Ihre Vorbilder* by Friedrich Depken (Carl Winter's Universitätsbuchhandlung, Heidelberg, 1914), loosely translated and edited by Jay Finley Christ as *Sherlock Holmes, Raffles, and their Prototypes* (The Fanlight Press, Chicago, 1949), is less useful than the title suggests. Malcolm Elwin's *Old Gods Falling* (Macmillan, 1939) is of interest, as are studies on the genre by Colin Wilson (*Snobbery with Violence*, Eyre & Spottiswoode, 1971; revised edition, Eyre Methuen, 1979), by William Vivian Butler (*The Durable Desperadoes*, Macmillan, 1973) and by Hugh David (*Heroes, Mavericks and Bounders*, Michael Joseph, 1991).

Raffles is the subject of one of the 'Letters to John Doe' (*John O' London's Weekly*, 37, 30 April 1937) and of an important essay by George Orwell, 'Raffles and Miss Blandish', which compares the work of Hornung to that of James Hadley Chase (*Horizon*, 10, October 1944; *Critical Essays*, Secker & Warburg/USA: *Dickens, Dali, and Others*, Harcourt Brace, 1946). A 'middle' section in the *Times Literary Supplement* is devoted to the subject ('The Amateur Cracksman', 11 August 1950), as are two articles in *The Times* by Oliver Edwards [William Haley] ('A. J. Raffles', 22 March 1956, collected in *Talking of Books*, Heinemann, 1957; 'The Rest of Willie', 2 June 1966); C. P. Snow wrote about Raffles in a review for the *Financial Times* ('Raffles Rides Again', 3 April 1975). Conan Doyle's plagiarism of Raffles in *The Return of Sherlock Holmes* (1905) is mentioned by Christopher Morley (*Baker Street Journal*, old series, 2, January 1947) and dealt with more fully by Roger Lancelyn Green in '*Holmes, this is amazing*' (privately printed, London, 1975) – and the volume also includes a chronology of Raffles. The relationship between Raffles and Sherlock Holmes is also considered by Evan M. Wilson ('Sherlock Holmes and A. J. Raffles', *Baker Street Journal*, 34, September 1984) and an issue of the *Baker Street Miscellanea* (37, spring 1984) is devoted to Raffles with articles by Michael Harrison, Donald F. Pollock, and Philip Atkey ['Barry Perowne']. The essay by Nick Rance on 'The Immorally Rich and the Richly Immoral. Raffles and the Plutocracy' (in *Twentieth Century Suspense*, Macmillan, 1990) deserves attention, as does an article by Steven T. Doyle, 'In the Chains of Crime: A. J. Raffles, Amateur Cracksman and Sherlock Holmes, Amateur Detective' (*Sherlock Holmes Review*, 14, February, 1993). Werner P. Friederich discusses Hornung's Australian fiction in his book *Australia in Western Imaginative Prose Writings 1600–1960* (University of North

Carolina Press, Chapel Hill, 1967). There is one full-length study of E. W. Hornung and his work by Peter Rowland (*Raffles and His Creator*, Nekta Publications, 1999).

A Note on the Text

This edition of *The Amateur Cracksman* uses the text of the first edition, published by Methuen & Co. in 1899. Major alterations and additions made after the serialization (of six of the eight stories) in *Cassell's Magazine*, London ('In the Chains of Crime', June–November 1898), and *Collier's Weekly*, New York ('Adventures of A. J. Raffles', 17 September–22 October 1898), are cited in the notes at the end of the book.

The Amateur Cracksman

TO
A.C.D.
THIS FORM OF FLATTERY

THE IDES OF MARCH

I

It was about half-past twelve when I returned to the Albany[1] as a last desperate resort. The scene of my disaster was much as I had left it. The baccarat-counters[2] still strewed the table, with the empty glasses and the loaded ash-trays. A window had been opened to let the smoke out, and was letting in the fog instead. Raffles himself had merely discarded his dining jacket for one of his innumerable blazers. Yet he arched his eyebrows as though I had dragged him from his bed.

'Forgotten something?' said he, when he saw me on his mat.

'No,' said I, pushing past him without ceremony. And I led the way into his room with an impudence amazing to myself.

'Not come back for your revenge, have you? Because I'm afraid I can't give it you single-handed. I was sorry myself that the others –'

We were face to face by his fireside, and I cut him short.

'Raffles,' said I, 'you may well be surprised at my coming back in this way and at this hour. I hardly know you. I was never in your rooms before to-night. But I fagged for you at school,[3] and you said you remembered me. Of course that's no excuse; but will you listen to me – for two minutes?'

In my emotion I had at first to struggle for every word; but his face reassured me as I went on, and I was not mistaken in its expression.

'Certainly, my dear man,' said he; 'as many minutes as you like. Have a Sullivan[4] and sit down.' And he handed me his silver cigarette-case.

'No,' said I, finding a full voice as I shook my head; 'no, I won't smoke, and I won't sit down, thank you. Nor will you ask me to do either when you've heard what I have to say.'

'Really?' said he, lighting his own cigarette with one clear blue eye upon me. 'How do you know?'

'Because you'll probably show me the door,' I cried bitterly; 'and you'll be justified in doing it! But it's no good beating about the bush. You know I dropped over two hundred just now?'

He nodded.

'I hadn't the money in my pocket.'

'I remember.'

'But I had my cheque-book, and I wrote each of you a cheque at that desk.'

'Well?'

'Not one of them was worth the paper it was written on, Raffles. I am overdrawn already at my bank!'

'Surely only for the moment?'

'No. I have spent everything.'

'But somebody told me you were so well off. I heard you had come in for money?'

'So I did. Three years ago. It has been my curse; now it's all gone – every penny! Yes, I've been a fool; there never was nor will be such a fool as I've been . . . Isn't this enough for you? Why don't you turn me out?' He was walking up and down with a very long face instead.

'Couldn't your people do anything?' he asked at length.

'Thank God,' I cried, 'I have no people! I was an only child. I came in for everything there was. My one comfort is that they're gone, and will never know.'

I cast myself into a chair and hid my face. Raffles continued to pace the rich carpet that was of a piece with everything else in his rooms. There was no variation in his soft and even footfalls.

'You used to be a literary little cuss,'[5] he said at length; 'didn't you edit the mag.[6] before you left? Anyway I recollect fagging you to do my verses; and literature of sorts is the very thing nowadays; any fool can make a living at it.'

I shook my head. 'Any fool couldn't write off my debts,' said I.

'Then you have a flat somewhere?' he went on.

'Yes, in Mount Street.'[7]

'Well, what about the furniture?'

I laughed aloud in my misery. 'There's been a bill of sale[8] on every stick for months!'

And at that Raffles stood still, with raised eyebrows and stern eyes that I could meet the better now that he knew the worst; then, with a shrug, he resumed his walk, and for some minutes neither of us spoke. But in his handsome unmoved face I read my fate and death-warrant; and with every breath I cursed my folly and my cowardice in coming to him at all. Because he had been kind to me at school, when he was captain of the eleven,[9] and I his fag, I had dared to look for kindness from him now; because I was ruined, and he rich enough to play cricket all the summer, and do nothing for the rest of the year, I had fatuously counted on his mercy, his sympathy, his help! Yes, I had relied on him in my heart, for all my outward diffidence and humility; and I was rightly served. There was as little of mercy as of sympathy in that curling nostril, that rigid jaw, that cold blue eye which never glanced my way. I caught up my hat. I blundered to my feet. I would have gone without a word; but Raffles stood between me and the door.

'Where are you going?' said he.

'That's my business,' I replied. 'I won't trouble *you* any more.'

'Then how am I to help you?'

'I didn't ask your help.'

'Then why come to me?'

'Why, indeed!' I echoed. 'Will you let me pass?'

'Not until you tell me where you are going and what you mean to do.'

'Can't you guess?' I cried. And for many seconds we stood staring in each other's eyes.

'Have you got the pluck?'[10] said he, breaking the spell in a tone so cynical that it brought my last drop of blood to the boil.

'You shall see,' said I, as I stepped back and whipped the pistol from my overcoat pocket. 'Now, will you let me pass or shall I do it here?'

The barrel touched my temple, and my thumb the trigger. Mad with excitement as I was, ruined, dishonoured, and now

finally determined to make an end of my misspent life, my only
surprise to this day is that I did not do so then and there. The
despicable satisfaction of involving another in one's destruction
added its miserable appeal to my baser egoism; and had fear or
horror flown to my companion's face, I shudder to think I might
have died diabolically happy with that look for my last impious
consolation. It was the look that came instead which held my
hand. Neither fear nor horror were in it; only wonder, admiration, and such a measure of pleased expectancy as caused me
after all to pocket my revolver with an oath.

'You devil!' I said. 'I believe you wanted me to do it!'

'Not quite,' was the reply, made with a little start, and a
change of colour that came too late. 'To tell you the truth,
though, I half thought you meant it, and I was never more
fascinated in my life. I never dreamt you had such stuff in you,
Bunny![11] No, I'm hanged if I let you go now. And you'd better
not try that game again, for you won't catch me stand and look
on a second time. We must think of some way out of the mess.
I had no idea you were a chap of that sort! There, let me have
the gun.'

One of his hands fell kindly on my shoulder, while the other
slipped into my overcoat pocket, and I suffered him to deprive
me of my weapon without a murmur. Nor was this simply
because Raffles had the subtle power of making himself irresistible at will. He was beyond comparison the most masterful man
whom I have ever known; yet my acquiescence was due to more
than the mere subjection of the weaker nature to the stronger.
The forlorn hope which had brought me to the Albany was
turned as by magic into an almost staggering sense of safety.
Raffles would help me after all! A.J. Raffles[12] would be my
friend! It was as though all the world had come round suddenly
to my side; so far therefore from resisting his action, I caught
and clasped his hand with a fervour as uncontrollable as the
frenzy which had preceded it.

'God bless you!' I cried. 'Forgive me for everything. I will tell
you the truth. I *did* think you might help me in my extremity,
though I well knew that I had no claim upon you. Still – for the
old school's sake – the sake of old times – I thought you might

give me another chance. If you wouldn't I meant to blow out my brains – and will still if you change your mind!'

In truth I feared that it was changing, with his expression, even as I spoke, and in spite of his kindly tone and kindlier use of my old school nickname. His next words showed me my mistake.

'What a boy it is for jumping to conclusions! I have my vices, Bunny, but backing and filling[13] is not one of them. Sit down, my good fellow, and have a cigarette to soothe your nerves. I insist. Whisky? The worst thing for you; here's some coffee that I was brewing when you came in. Now listen to me. You speak of "another chance". What do you mean? Another chance at baccarat? Not if I know it! You think the luck must turn; suppose it didn't? We should only have made bad worse. No, my dear chap, you've plunged enough. Do you put yourself in my hands or do you not? Very well, then you plunge no more, and I undertake not to present my cheque. Unfortunately there are the other men; and still more unfortunately, Bunny, I'm as hard up at this moment as you are yourself!'

It was my turn to stare at Raffles. 'You?' I vociferated. 'You hard up? How am I to sit here and believe that?'

'Did I refuse to believe it of you?' he returned, smiling. 'And, with your own experience, do you think that because a fellow has rooms in this place, and belongs to a club or two, and plays a little cricket, he must necessarily have a balance at the bank? I tell you, my dear man, that at this moment I'm as hard up as you ever were. I have nothing but my wits to live on – absolutely nothing else. It was as necessary for me to win some money this evening as it was for you. We're in the same boat, Bunny; we'd better pull together.'

'Together!' I jumped at it. 'I'll do anything in this world for you, Raffles,' I said, 'if you really mean that you won't give me away. Think of anything you like, and I'll do it! I was a desperate man when I came here, and I'm just as desperate now. I don't mind what I do if only I can get out of this without a scandal.'

Again I see him, leaning back in one of the luxurious chairs with which his room was furnished. I see his indolent, athletic figure; his pale, sharp, clean-shaven features; his curly black

hair; his strong, unscrupulous mouth. And again I feel the clear
beam of his wonderful eye, cold and luminous as a star, shining
into my brain – sifting the very secrets of my heart.[14]

'I wonder if you mean all that!' he said at length. 'You do in
your present mood; but who can back his mood to last? Still,
there's hope when a chap takes that tone. Now I think of it, too,
you were a plucky little devil at school; you once did me rather
a good turn, I recollect. Remember it, Bunny? Well, wait a bit,
and perhaps I'll be able to do you a better one. Give me time to
think.'

He got up, lit a fresh cigarette, and fell to pacing the room
once more, but with a slower and more thoughtful step, and for
a much longer period than before. Twice he stopped at my chair
as though on the point of speaking, but each time he checked
himself and resumed his stride in silence. Once he threw up the
window, which he had shut some time since, and stood for
some moments leaning out into the fog which filled the Albany
courtyard. Meanwhile a clock on the chimney-piece struck one,
and one again for the half-hour, without a word between us.

Yet I not only kept my chair with patience, but I acquired
an incongruous equanimity in that half-hour. Insensibly I had
shifted my burden to the broad shoulders of this splendid friend,
and my thoughts wandered with my eyes as the minutes passed.
The room was the good-sized, square one, with the folding
doors, the marble mantel-piece, and the gloomy, old-fashioned
distinction peculiar to the Albany. It was charmingly furnished
and arranged, with the right amount of negligence and the
right amount of taste. What struck me most, however, was the
absence of the usual insignia of a cricketer's den. Instead of
the conventional rack of war-worn bats, a carved oak book-case,
with every shelf in a litter, filled the better part of one wall; and
where I looked for cricketing groups, I found reproductions of
such works as *Love and Death* and *The Blessed Damozel*,[15] in
dusty frames and different parallels. The man might have been
a minor poet instead of an athlete of the first water.[16] But there
had always been a fine streak of æstheticism in his complex
composition; some of these very pictures I had myself dusted in
his study at school; and they set me thinking of yet another of

his many sides – and of the little incident to which he had just referred.

Everybody knows how largely the tone of a public school depends on that of the eleven, and on the character of the captain of cricket in particular; and I have never heard it denied that in A.J. Raffles's time our tone was good, or that such influence as he troubled to exert was on the side of the angels.[17] Yet it was whispered in the school that he was in the habit of parading the town at night in loud checks and a false beard. It was whispered, and disbelieved. I alone knew it for a fact; for night after night had I pulled the rope up after him[18] when the rest of the dormitory were asleep, and kept awake by the hour to let it down again on a given signal. Well, one night he was over-bold, and within an ace of ignominious expulsion in the hey-day of his fame. Consummate daring and extraordinary nerve on his part, aided, doubtless, by some little presence of mind on mine, averted that untoward result; and no more need be said of a discreditable incident. But I cannot pretend to have forgotten it in throwing myself on this man's mercy in my desperation. And I was wondering how much of his leniency was owing to the fact that Raffles had not forgotten it either, when he stopped and stood over my chair once more.

'I've been thinking of that night we had the narrow squeak,' he began. 'Why do you start?'

'I was thinking of it too.'

He smiled, as though he had read my thoughts.

'Well, you were the right sort of little beggar then, Bunny; you didn't talk and you didn't flinch. You asked no questions and you told no tales. I wonder if you're like that now?'

'I don't know,' said I, slightly puzzled by his tone. 'I've made such a mess of my own affairs that I trust myself about as little as I'm likely to be trusted by anybody else. Yet I never in my life went back on a friend. I will say that; otherwise perhaps I mightn't be in such a hole to-night.'

'Exactly,' said Raffles, nodding to himself, as though in assent to some hidden train of thought; 'exactly what I remember of you, and I'll bet it's as true now as it was ten years ago. We don't alter, Bunny. We only develop. I suppose neither you nor

I are really altered since you used to let down that rope and I used to come up it hand over hand. You would stick at nothing for a pal – what?'

'At nothing in this world,' I was pleased to cry.

'Not even at a crime?' said Raffles, smiling.

I stopped to think, for his tone had changed, and I felt sure he was chaffing me. Yet his eye seemed as much in earnest as ever, and for my part I was in no mood for reservations.

'No, not even at that,' I declared; 'name your crime, and I'm your man.'

He looked at me one moment in wonder, and another moment in doubt; then turned the matter off with a shake of his head, and the little cynical laugh that was all his own.

'You're a nice chap, Bunny! A real desperate character – what? Suicide one moment, and any crime I like the next! What you want is a drag,[19] my boy, and you did well to come to a decent law-abiding citizen with a reputation to lose. None the less we must have that money to-night – by hook or crook.'[20]

'To-night, Raffles?'

'The sooner the better. Every hour after ten o'clock to-morrow morning is an hour of risk. Let one of those cheques get round to your own bank, and you and it are dishonoured together. No, we must raise the wind[21] to-night and reopen your account first thing to-morrow. And I rather think I know where the wind can be raised.'

'At two o'clock in the morning?'

'Yes.'

'But how – but where – at such an hour?'

'From a friend of mine here in Bond Street.'[22]

'He must be a very intimate friend!'

'Intimate's not the word. I have the run of his place and a latch-key all to myself.'

'You would knock him up at this hour of the night?'

'If he's in bed.'

'And it's essential that I should go in with you?'

'Absolutely.'

'Then I must; but I'm bound to say I don't like the idea, Raffles.'

'Do you prefer the alternative?' asked my companion, with a sneer. 'No, hang it, that's unfair!' he cried apologetically in the same breath. 'I quite understand. It's a beastly ordeal. But it would never do for you to stay outside. I tell you what, you shall have a peg before we start – just one. There's the whisky, here's a syphon, and I'll be putting on an overcoat while you help yourself.'

Well, I daresay I did so with some freedom, for this plan of his was not the less distasteful to me from its apparent inevitability. I must own, however, that it possessed fewer terrors before my glass was empty. Meanwhile Raffles rejoined me, with a covert coat[23] over his blazer, and a soft felt hat set carelessly on the curly head he shook with a smile as I passed him the decanter.

'When we come back,' said he. 'Work first, play afterwards. Do you see what day it is?' he added, tearing a leaflet from a Shakesperian calendar,[24] as I drained my glass. 'March 15th. "The Ides of March, the Ides of March, remember."[25] Eh, Bunny, my boy? You won't forget them, will you?'

And, with a laugh, he threw some coals on the fire before turning down the gas like a careful householder. So we went out together as the clock on the chimney-piece was striking two.

II

Piccadilly was a trench of raw white fog, rimmed with blurred street-lamps, and lined with a thin coating of adhesive mud. We met no other wayfarers on the deserted flagstones, and were ourselves favoured with a very hard stare from the constable of the beat, who, however, touched his helmet on recognizing my companion.

'You see, I'm known to the police,' laughed Raffles as we passed on. 'Poor devils, they've got to keep their weather eye open[26] on a night like this! A fog may be a bore to you and me, Bunny, but it's a perfect godsend to the criminal classes, especially so late in their season. Here we are, though – and I'm hanged if the beggar isn't in bed and asleep after all!'

We had turned into Bond Street, and had halted on the kerb

a few yards down on the right. Raffles was gazing up at some windows across the road,[27] windows barely discernible through the mist, and without the glimmer of a light to throw them out. They were over a jeweller's shop, as I could see by the peep-hole in the shop door, and the bright light burning within. But the entire 'upper part', with the private street-door next the shop, was black and blank as the sky itself.

'Better give it up for to-night,' I urged. 'Surely the morning will be time enough!'

'Not a bit of it,' said Raffles. 'I have his key. We'll surprise him. Come along.'

And seizing my right arm, he hurried me across the road, opened the door with his latch-key, and in another moment had shut it swiftly but softly behind us. We stood together in the dark. Outside, a measured step was approaching; we had heard it through the fog as we crossed the street; now, as it drew nearer, my companion's fingers tightened on my arm.

'It may be the chap himself,' he whispered. 'He's the devil of a night-bird.[28] Not a sound, Bunny! We'll startle the life out of him. Ah!'

The measured step had passed without a pause. Raffles drew a deep breath, and his singular grip of me slowly relaxed.

'But still, not a sound,' he continued in the same whisper; 'we'll take a rise out of him,[29] wherever he is! Slip off your shoes and follow me.'

Well, you may wonder at my doing so; but you can never have met A. J. Raffles. Half his power lay in a conciliating trick of sinking the commander in the leader.[30] And it was impossible not to follow one who led with such a zest. You might question, but you followed first. So now, when I heard him kick off his own shoes, I did the same, and was on the stairs at his heels before I realized what an extraordinary way was this of approaching a stranger for money in the dead of night. But obviously Raffles and he were on exceptional terms of intimacy, and I could not but infer that they were in the habit of playing practical jokes upon each other.

We groped our way so slowly upstairs that I had time to make more than one note before we reached the top. The stair was uncarpeted. The spread fingers of my right hand encountered nothing on the damp wall; those of my left trailed through a dust that could be felt on the banisters. An eerie sensation had been upon me since we entered the house. It increased with every step we climbed. What hermit were we going to startle in his cell?

We came to a landing. The banisters led us to the left, and to the left again. Four steps more, and we were on another and a longer landing, and suddenly a match blazed from the black. I never heard it struck. Its flash was blinding. When my eyes became accustomed to the light, there was Raffles holding up the match with one hand, and shading it with the other, between bare boards, stripped walls, and the open doors of empty rooms.

'Where have you brought me?' I cried. 'The house is unoccupied!'

'Hush! Wait!' he whispered, and he led the way into one of the empty rooms. His match went out as we crossed the threshold, and he struck another without the slightest noise. Then he stood with his back to me, fumbling with something that I could not see. But, when he threw the second match away, there was some other light in its stead, and a slight smell of oil. I stepped forward to look over his shoulder, but before I could do so he had turned and flashed a tiny lantern in my face.

'What's this?' I gasped. 'What rotten trick are you going to play?'

'It's played,' he answered, with his quiet laugh.

'On me?'

'I'm afraid so, Bunny.'

'Is there no one in the house, then?'

'No one but ourselves.'

'So it was mere chaff[31] about your friend in Bond Street, who could let us have that money?'

'Not altogether. It's quite true that Danby[32] is a friend of mine.'

'Danby?'

'The jeweller underneath.'

'What do you mean?' I whispered, trembling like a leaf as his meaning dawned upon me. 'Are we to get the money from the jeweller?'

'Well, not exactly.'

'What then?'

'The equivalent – from his shop.'

There was no need for another question. I understood every-thing but my own density. He had given me a dozen hints, and I had taken none. And there I stood staring at him, in that empty room; and there he stood with his dark lantern,[33] laughing at me.

'A burglar!' I gasped. 'You – you!'

'I told you I lived by my wits.'

'Why couldn't you tell me what you were going to do? Why couldn't you trust me? Why must you lie?' I demanded, piqued to the quick for all my horror.

'I wanted to tell you,' said he. 'I was on the point of telling you more than once. You may remember how I sounded you about crime, though you have probably forgotten what you said your-self. I didn't think you meant it at the time, but I thought I'd put you to the test. Now I see you didn't, and I don't blame you. I only am to blame. Get out of it, my dear boy, as quick as you can; leave it to me. You won't give me away, whatever else you do!'

Oh, his cleverness! His fiendish cleverness! Had he fallen back on threats, coercion, sneers, all might have been different even yet. But he set me free to leave him in the lurch. He would not blame me. He did not even bind me to secrecy; he trusted me. He knew my weakness and my strength, and was playing on both with his master's touch.

'Not so fast,' said I. 'Did I put this into your head, or were you going to do it in any case?'

'Not in any case,' said Raffles. 'It's true I've had the key for days, but when I won to-night I thought of chucking it; for, as a matter of fact, it's not a one-man job.'

'That settles it. I'm your man.'

'You mean it?'

'Yes – for to-night.'

'Good old Bunny,' he murmured, holding the lantern for one moment to my face; the next he was explaining his plans, and I was nodding, as though we had been fellow-cracksmen all our days.

'I know the shop,' he whispered, 'because I've got a few things there. I know this upper part too; it's been to let for a month, and I got an order to view, and took a cast of the key before using it. The one thing I don't know is how to make a connection between the two; at present there's none. We may make it up here, though I rather fancy the basement myself. If you wait a minute I'll tell you.'

He set his lantern on the floor, crept to a back window, and opened it with scarcely a sound: only to return, shaking his head, after shutting the window with the same care.

'That was our one chance,' said he: 'a back window above a back window; but it's too dark to see anything, and we daren't show an outside light. Come down after me to the basement; and remember, though there's not a soul on the premises, you can't make too little noise. There – there – listen to that!'

It was the measured tread that we had heard before on the flag-stones outside. Raffles darkened his lantern, and again we stood motionless till it had passed.

'Either a policeman,' he muttered, 'or a watchman that all these jewellers run between them. The watchman's the man for us to watch; he's simply paid to spot this kind of thing.'

We crept very gingerly down the stairs, which creaked a bit in spite of us, and we picked up our shoes in the passage; then down some narrow stone steps, at the foot of which Raffles showed his light, and put on his shoes once more, bidding me do the same in a rather louder tone than he had permitted himself to employ overhead. We were now considerably below the level of the street, in a small space with as many doors as it had sides. Three were ajar, and we saw through them into empty cellars; but in the fourth a key was turned and a bolt drawn; and this one presently let us out into the bottom of a deep, square well of fog. A similar door faced it across this area, and Raffles had the lantern close against it, and was hiding the light with his body, when a short and sudden crash made my heart stand still. Next moment I saw the door wide open, and Raffles standing within and beckoning me with a jemmy.

'Door number one,' he whispered. 'Deuce knows how many more there'll be, but I know of two at least. We won't have to make much noise over them, either; down here there's less risk.'

We were now at the bottom of the exact fellow to the narrow stone stair which we had just descended: the yard, or well, being the one part common to both the private and the business premises. But this flight led to no open passage; instead, a singularly solid mahogany door confronted us at the top.

'I thought so,' muttered Raffles, handing me the lantern, and pocketing a bunch of skeleton keys, after tampering for a few minutes with the lock. 'It'll be an hour's work to get through that!'

'Can't you pick it?'

'No. I know these locks. It's no use trying. We must cut it out, and it'll take us an hour.'

It took us forty-seven minutes by my watch; or, rather, it took Raffles; and never in my life have I seen anything more deliberately done. My part was simply to stand by with the dark lantern in one hand, and a small bottle of rock-oil[34] in the other. Raffles had produced a pretty embroidered case, intended obviously for his razors,[35] but filled instead with the tools of his secret trade, including the rock-oil. From this case he selected a 'bit', capable of drilling a hole an inch in diameter, and fitted it to a small but very strong steel 'brace'. Then he took off his covert-coat and his blazer, spread them neatly on the top step – knelt on them – turned up his shirt-cuffs – and went to work with brace-and-bit near the key-hole. But first he oiled the bit to minimize the noise, and this he did invariably before beginning a fresh hole, and often in the middle of one. It took thirty-two separate borings to cut round that lock.

I noticed that through the first circular orifice Raffles thrust a forefinger; then, as the circle became an ever-lengthening oval, he got his hand through up to the thumb; and I heard him swear softly to himself.

'I was afraid so!'

'What is it?'

'An iron gate on the other side!'

'How on earth are we to get through that?' I asked in dismay.

'Pick the lock. But there may be two. In that case they'll be top and bottom, and we shall have two fresh holes to make, as the door opens inwards. It won't open two inches as it is.'

I confess I did not feel sanguine about the lock-picking, seeing that one lock had baffled us already; and my disappointment and impatience must have been a revelation to me had I stopped to think. The truth is that I was entering into our nefarious undertaking with an involuntary zeal of which I was myself quite unconscious at the time. The romance and the peril of the whole proceeding held me spellbound and entranced. My moral sense and my sense of fear were stricken by a common paralysis. And there I stood, shining my light and holding my phial with a keener interest than I had ever brought to any honest avocation. And there knelt A. J. Raffles, with his black hair tumbled, and the same watchful, quiet, determined half-smile with which I have seen him send down over after over in a county match!

At last the chain of holes was complete, the lock wrenched out bodily, and a splendid bare arm plunged up to the shoulder through the aperture, and through the bars of the iron gate beyond.

'Now,' whispered Raffles, 'if there's only one lock it'll be in the middle. Joy! Here it is! Only let me pick it, and we're through at last.'

He withdrew his arm, a skeleton key was selected from the bunch,[36] and then back went his arm to the shoulder. It was a breathless moment. I heard the heart throbbing in my body, the very watch ticking in my pocket, and ever and anon the tinkle-tinkle of the skeleton key. Then – at last – there came a single unmistakable click. In another minute the mahogany door and the iron gate yawned behind us; and Raffles was sitting on an office table, wiping his face, with the lantern throwing a steady beam by his side.

We were now in a bare and roomy lobby behind the shop, but separated therefrom by an iron curtain, the very sight of which filled me with despair. Raffles, however, did not appear in the least depressed, but hung up his coat and hat on some pegs in the lobby before examining this curtain with his lantern.

'That's nothing,' said he, after a minute's inspection; 'we'll be through that in no time, but there's a door on the other side which may give us trouble.'

'Another door!' I groaned. 'And how do you mean to tackle this thing?'

'Prise it up with the jointed jemmy.[37] The weak point of these iron curtains is the leverage you can get from below. But it makes a noise, and this is where you're coming in, Bunny; this is where I couldn't do without you. I must have you overhead to knock through when the street's clear. I'll come with you and show a light.'

Well, you may imagine how little I liked the prospect of this lonely vigil; and yet there was something very stimulating in the vital responsibility which it involved. Hitherto I had been a mere spectator. Now I was to take part in the game. And the fresh excitement made me more than ever insensible to those consider-ations of conscience and of safety which were already as dead nerves in my breast.

So I took my post without a murmur in the front room above the shop. The fixtures had been left for the refusal of the incoming tenant, and fortunately for us they included Venetian blinds which were already down. It was the simplest matter in the world to stand peeping through the laths into the street, to beat twice with my foot when anybody was approaching, and once when all was clear again. The noises that even I could hear below, with the exception of one metallic crash at the beginning, were indeed incredibly slight; but they ceased altogether at each double rap from my toe; and a policeman passed quite half a dozen times beneath my eyes, and the man whom I took to be the jeweller's watchman oftener still, during the better part of an hour that I spent at the window. Once, indeed, my heart was in my mouth, but only once. It was when the watchman stopped and peered through the peep-hole into the lighted shop. I waited for his whistle – I waited for the gallows or the gaol! But my signals had been studiously obeyed, and the man passed on in undisturbed serenity. In the end I had a signal in my turn, and retraced my steps with lighted matches, down the broad stairs, down the narrow ones, across the area, and up into the lobby where Raffles awaited me with an outstretched hand.

'Well done, my boy!' said he. 'You're the same good man in a pinch, and you shall have your reward. I've got a thousand pounds' worth if I've got a penn'orth. It's all in my pockets. And here's something else I found in this locker; very decent port and some cigars, meant for poor dear Danby's business friends. Take a pull, and you shall light up presently. I've found a lavatory, too, and we must have a wash-and-brush-up before we go, for I'm as black as your boot.'

The iron curtain was down, but he insisted on raising it until I could peep through the glass door on the other side and see his handiwork in the shop beyond. Here two electric lights were left burning all night long, and in their cold white rays I could at first see nothing amiss. I looked along an orderly lane, an empty glass counter on my left, glass cupboards of untouched silver on my right, and facing me the filmy black eye of the peep-hole that shone like a stage moon on the street. The counter had not been emptied by Raffles; its contents were in the Chubb's safe,[38] which he had given up at a glance; nor had he looked at the silver, except to choose a cigarette-case for me. He had confined himself entirely to the shop window. This was in three compartments, each secured for the night by removable panels with separate locks. Raffles had removed them a few hours before their time, and the electric light shone on a corrugated shutter bare as the ribs of an empty carcase. Every article of value was gone from the one place which was invisible from the little window in the door; elsewhere all was as it had been left overnight. And but for a train of mangled doors behind the iron curtain, a bottle of wine and a cigar-box with which liberties had been taken, a rather black towel in the lavatory, a burnt match here and there, and our finger-marks on the dusty banisters,[39] not a trace of our visit did we leave.

'Had it in my head for long?' said Raffles, as we strolled through the streets towards dawn, for all the world as though we were returning from a dance. 'No, Bunny, I never thought of it till I saw that upper part empty about a month ago, and bought a few things in the shop to get the lie of the land. That reminds me that I never paid for them; but, by Jove, I will to-morrow, and if that isn't poetic justice, what is? One visit showed me the possibilities of the place, but a second convinced me of its impossibilities without a pal. So I had practically given up the idea, when you came along on the very night and in the very plight for it! But here we are at the Albany, and I hope there's some fire left; for I don't know how you feel, Bunny, but for my part I'm as cold as Keats's owl.'[40]

He could think of Keats on his way from a felony! He could hanker for his fireside like another! Floodgates were loosed within me, and the plain English of our adventure rushed over me as cold as ice. Raffles was a burglar. I had helped him to commit one burglary, therefore I was a burglar too. Yet I could stand and warm myself by his fire, and watch him empty his pockets, as though we had done nothing wonderful or wicked!

My blood froze. My heart sickened. My brain whirled. How I had liked this villain! How I had admired him! Now my liking and admiration must turn to loathing and disgust. I waited for the change. I longed to feel it in my heart. But – I longed and I waited in vain!

I saw that he was emptying his pockets; the table sparkled with their hoard. Rings by the dozen, diamonds by the score; bracelets, pendants, aigrettes,[41] necklaces; pearls, rubies, amethysts, sapphires; and diamonds always, diamonds in everything, flashing bayonets of light, dazzling me – blinding me – making me disbelieve because I could no longer forget. Last of all came no gem, indeed, but my own revolver from an inner pocket. And that struck a chord. I suppose I said something – my hand flew out. I can see Raffles now, as he looked at me once more with a high arch over each clear eye. I can see him pick out the cartridges with his quiet, cynical smile, before he would give me my pistol back again.

'You mayn't believe it, Bunny,' said he, 'but I never carried a loaded one before. On the whole I think it gives one confidence. Yet it would be very awkward if anything went wrong; one might use it, and that's not the game at all, though I have often thought that the murderer who has just done the trick must have great sensations before things get too hot for him. Don't look so distressed, my dear chap. I've never had those sensations, and I don't suppose I ever shall.'

'But this much you have done before?' said I hoarsely.

'Before? My dear Bunny, you offend me! Did it look like a first attempt? Of course I have done it before.'

'Often?'

'Well – no! Not often enough to destroy the charm, at all events; never, as a matter of fact, unless I'm cursedly hard up. Did you hear about the Thimbleby diamonds?[42] Well, that was the last time – and a poor lot of paste[43] they were. Then there was the little business of the Dormer house-boat at Henley[44] last year. That was mine also – such as it was. I've never brought off a really big coup yet; when I do I shall chuck it up.'

Yes, I remembered both cases very well. To think that he was their author! It was incredible, outrageous, inconceivable. Then my eyes would fall upon the table, twinkling and glittering in a hundred places, and incredulity was at an end.

'How came you to begin?' I asked, as curiosity overcame mere wonder, and a fascination for his career gradually wove itself into my fascination for the man.

'Ah! that's a long story,' said Raffles. 'It was in the Colonies,[45] when I was out there playing cricket. It's too long a story to tell you now, but I was in much the same fix that you were in to-night, and it was my only way out. I never meant it for anything more; but I'd tasted blood, and it was all over with me. Why should I work when I could steal? Why settle down to some humdrum uncongenial billet, when excitement, romance, danger and a decent living were all going begging together? Of course it's very wrong, but we can't all be moralists, and the distribution of wealth is very wrong to begin with. Besides, you're not at it all the time. I'm sick of quoting Gilbert's lines[46] to myself, but they're profoundly true. I only wonder if you'll like the life as much as I do!'

'Like it?' I cried out. 'Not I! It's no life for me. Once is enough!'

'You wouldn't give me a hand another time?'

'Don't ask me, Raffles. Don't ask me, for God's sake!'

'Yet you said you would do anything for me! You asked me to name my crime! But I knew at the time you didn't mean it; you didn't go back on me to-night, and that ought to satisfy me, goodness knows! I suppose I'm ungrateful, and unreasonable, and all that. I ought to let it end at this. But you're the very man for me, Bunny, the – very – man! Just think how we got through to-night. Not a scratch – not a hitch! There's nothing very terrible in it, you see; there never would be, while we worked together.'

He was standing in front of me with a hand on either shoulder; he was smiling as he knew so well how to smile. I turned on my heel, planted my elbows on the chimneypiece, and my burning head between my hands. Next instant a still heartier hand had fallen on my back.

'All right, my boy! You are quite right and I'm worse than wrong. I'll never ask it again. Go, if you want to, and come again about mid-day for the cash. There was no bargain; but, of course, I'll get you out of your scrape – especially after the way you've stood by me to-night.'

I was round again with my blood on fire.

'I'll do it again,' I said, through my teeth.

He shook his head. 'Not you,' he said, smiling quite good-humouredly on my insane enthusiasm.

'I will,' I cried with an oath. 'I'll lend you a hand as often as you like! What does it matter now? I've been in it once. I'll be in it again. I've gone to the devil anyhow. I can't go back, and wouldn't if I could. Nothing matters another rap![47] When you want me I'm your man.'

And that is how Raffles and I joined felonious forces on the Ides of March.

A COSTUME PIECE

London was just then talking of one whose name is already a name and nothing more. Reuben Rosenthall[1] had made his millions on the diamond fields of South Africa, and had come home to enjoy them according to his lights; how he went to work will scarcely be forgotten by any reader of the halfpenny evening papers,[2] which revelled in endless anecdotes of his original indigence and present prodigality, varied with interesting particulars of the extraordinary establishment which the millionaire set up in St John's Wood.[3] Here he kept a retinue of Kaffirs,[4] who were literally his slaves; and hence he would sally, with enormous diamonds in his shirt and on his finger, in the convoy of a prize-fighter[5] of heinous repute, who was not, however, by any means the worst element in the Rosenthall *ménage*. So said common gossip; but the fact was sufficiently established by the interference of the police on at least one occasion, followed by certain magisterial proceedings[6] which were reported with justifiable gusto and huge headlines in the newspapers aforesaid. And this was all one knew of Reuben Rosenthall up to the time when the Old Bohemian Club,[7] having fallen on evil days, found it worth its while to organize a great dinner in honour of so wealthy an exponent of the club's principles. I was not at the banquet myself, but a member took Raffles, who told me all about it that very night.

'Most extraordinary show I ever went to in my life,' said he. 'As for the man himself – well, I was prepared for something grotesque, but the fellow fairly took my breath away. To begin with, he's the most astounding brute to look at, well over six feet, with a chest like a barrel, and a great hook-nose, and the reddest hair and whiskers you ever saw. Drank like a fire-engine, but only got drunk enough to make us a speech that I wouldn't have missed for ten pounds. I'm only sorry you weren't there too, Bunny, old chap.'

I began to be sorry myself, for Raffles was anything but an excitable person, and never had I seen him so excited before. Had he been following Rosenthall's example? His coming to my rooms at midnight, merely to tell me about his dinner, was in itself enough to excuse a suspicion which was certainly at variance with my knowledge of A. J. Raffles.

'What did he say?' I inquired mechanically, divining some subtler explanation of this visit, and wondering what on earth it could be.

'Say?' cried Raffles. 'What did he not say! He boasted of his rise, he bragged of his riches, and he blackguarded society for taking him up for his money and dropping him out of sheer pique and jealousy because he had so much. He mentioned names, too, with the most charming freedom, and swore he was as good a man as the Old Country[8] had to show – *pace* the Old Bohemians. To prove it he pointed to a great diamond in the middle of his shirt-front with a little finger loaded with another just like it: which of our bloated princes[9] could show a pair like that? As a matter of fact they seemed quite wonderful stones, with a curious purple gleam to them that must mean a pot of money. But old Rosenthall swore he wouldn't take fifty thousand pounds for the two, and wanted to know where the other man was who went about with twenty-five thousand in his shirt-front, and another twenty-five on his little finger. He didn't exist. If he did, he wouldn't have the pluck to wear them. But *he* had – he'd tell us why. And before you could say Jack Robinson[10] he had whipped out a whacking great revolver!'

'Not at the table?'

'At the table! In the middle of his speech! But it was nothing to what he wanted to do. He actually wanted us to let him write his name in bullets on the opposite wall[11] to show us why he wasn't afraid to go about in all his diamonds! That brute Purvis, the prize-fighter, who is his paid bully, had to bully his master before he could be persuaded out of it. There was quite a panic for the moment; one fellow was saying his prayers under the table, and the waiters bolted to a man.'

'What a grotesque scene!'

'Grotesque enough, but I rather wish they had let him go the whole hog and blaze away. He was as keen as knives to show us how he could take care of his purple diamonds; and, do you know, Bunny, *I* was as keen as knives to see.'

And Raffles leant towards me with a sly, slow smile that made the hidden meaning of his visit only too plain to me at last.

'So you think of having a try for his diamonds yourself?'

He shrugged his shoulders.

'It is horridly obvious, I admit. But – yes, I have set my heart upon them! To be quite frank, I have had them on my conscience for some time; one couldn't hear so much of the man, and his prize-fighter, and his diamonds, without feeling it a kind of duty to have a go for them; but when it comes to brandishing a revolver and practically challenging the world, the thing becomes inevitable. It is simply thrust upon one. I was fated to hear that challenge, Bunny, and I, for one, must take it up. I was only sorry I couldn't get on my hind legs and say so then and there.'

'Well,' I said, 'I don't see the necessity as things are with us; but, of course, I'm your man.'

My tone may have been half-hearted. I did my best to make it otherwise. But it was barely a month since our Bond Street exploit, and we certainly could have afforded to behave ourselves for some time to come. We had been getting along so nicely: by his advice I had scribbled a thing or two; inspired by Raffles, I had even done an article on our own jewel robbery; and for the moment I was quite satisfied with this sort of adventure. I thought we ought to know when we were well off, and could see no point in our running fresh risks before we were obliged. On the other hand, I was anxious not to show the least disposition to break the pledge that I had given a month ago. But it was not on my manifest disinclination that Raffles fastened.

'Necessity, my dear Bunny? Does the writer only write when the wolf is at the door? Does the painter paint for bread alone?[12] Must you and I be *driven* to crime like Tom of Bow and Dick

of Whitechapel?[13] You pain me, my dear chap; you needn't
laugh, because you do. Art for art's sake[14] is a vile catchword,
but I confess it appeals to me. In this case my motives are
absolutely pure, for I doubt if we shall ever be able to dispose
of such peculiar stones. But if I don't have a try for them – after
to-night – I shall never be able to hold up my head again.'

His eye twinkled, but it glittered too.

'We shall have our work cut out,' was all I said.

'And do you suppose I should be keen on it if we hadn't?'
cried Raffles. 'My dear fellow, I would rob St Paul's Cathedral[15]
if I could, but I could no more scoop a till when the shop-walker
wasn't looking than I could bag the apples out of an old woman's
basket. Even that little business last month was a sordid affair,
but it was necessary, and I think its strategy redeemed it to some
extent. Now there's some credit, and more sport, in going where
they boast they're on their guard against you. The Bank of
England,[16] for example, is the ideal crib; but that would need
half a dozen of us with years to give to the job; and meanwhile
Reuben Rosenthall is high enough game for you and me. We
know he's armed. We know how Billy Purvis[17] can fight. It'll be
no soft thing, I grant you. But what of that, my good Bunny –
what of that? A man's reach must exceed his grasp, dear boy,
or what the dickens is a heaven for?'[18]

'I would rather we didn't exceed ours just yet,' I answered
laughing, for his spirit was irresistible, and the plan was growing
upon me, despite my qualms.

'Trust me for that,' was his reply; 'I'll see you through. After
all I expect to find that the difficulties are nearly all on the
surface. These fellows both drink like the devil, and that should
simplify matters considerably. But we shall see, and we must
take our time. There will probably turn out to be a dozen
different ways in which the thing might be done, and we shall
have to choose between them. It will mean watching the house
for at least a week in any case; it may mean lots of other things
that will take much longer; but give me a week, and I will tell
you more. That's to say if you're really on?'

'Of course I am,' I replied indignantly. 'But why should I give
you a week? Why shouldn't we watch the house together?'

'Because two eyes are as good as four and take up less room. Never hunt in couples unless you're obliged. But don't you look offended, Bunny; there'll be plenty for you to do when the time comes, that I promise you. You shall have your share of the fun, never fear, and a purple diamond all to yourself – if we're lucky.'

On the whole, however, this conversation left me less than lukewarm, and I still remember the depression which came upon me when Raffles was gone. I saw the folly of the enterprise to which I had committed myself – the sheer, gratuitous, unnecessary folly of it. And the paradoxes in which Raffles revelled, and the frivolous casuistry which was nevertheless half sincere, and which his mere personality rendered wholly plausible at the moment of utterance, appealed very little to me when recalled in cold blood. I admired the spirit of pure mischief in which he seemed prepared to risk his liberty and his life, but I did not find it an infectious spirit on calm reflection. Yet the thought of withdrawal was not to be entertained for a moment. On the contrary, I was impatient of the delay ordained by Raffles; and, perhaps, no small part of my secret disaffection came of his galling determination to do without me until the last moment.

It made it no better that this was characteristic of the man and of his attitude towards me. For a month we had been, I suppose, the thickest thieves in all London,[19] and yet our intimacy was curiously incomplete. With all his charming frankness, there was in Raffles a vein of capricious reserve which was perceptible enough to be very irritating. He had the instinctive secretiveness of the inveterate criminal. He would make mysteries of matters of common concern; for example, I never knew how or where he disposed of the Bond Street jewels, on the proceeds of which we were both still leading the outward lives of hundreds of other young fellows about town. He was consistently mysterious about that and other details, of which it seemed to me that I had already earned the right to know everything. I could not but remember how he had led me into my first felony, by means of a trick, while yet uncertain whether he could trust me or not. That I could no longer afford to resent, but I did resent his want of confidence in me now. I said nothing about it, but it rankled every day, and never more than in the week that succeeded the Rosenthall dinner. When I met Raffles at the club he would tell me nothing; when I went to his rooms he was out, or pretended to be. One day he told me he was getting on well, but slowly; it was a more ticklish game than he had thought; but when I began to ask questions he would say no more. Then and there, in my annoyance, I took my own decision. Since he would tell me nothing of the result of his vigils, I determined to keep one on my own account, and that very evening found my way to the millionaire's front gates.

The house he was occupying is, I believe, quite the largest in the St John's Wood district. It stands in the angle formed by two broad thoroughfares,[20] neither of which, as it happens, is a 'bus route, and I doubt if many quieter spots exist within the four-mile radius.[21] Quiet also was the great square house, in its garden of grass-plots and shrubs; the lights were low, the millionaire and his friends obviously spending their evening elsewhere. The garden walls were only a few feet high. In one there was a side door opening into a glass passage; in the other two five-barred, grained-and-varnished gates, one at either end of the little semi-circular drive, and both wide open. So still was the place that I had a great mind to walk boldly in and learn something of the premises; in fact, I was on the point of doing so, when I heard a quick, shuffling step on the pavement behind me. I turned round and faced the dark scowl and the dirty clenched fists of a dilapidated tramp.

'You fool!' said he. 'You utter idiot!'

'Raffles!'

'That's it,' he whispered savagely; 'tell all the neighbourhood – give me away at the top of your voice!'

With that he turned his back upon me, and shambled down the road, shrugging his shoulders and muttering to himself as though I had refused him alms. A few moments I stood astounded, indignant, at a loss; then I followed him. His feet trailed, his knees gave, his back was bowed, his head kept nodding; it was the gait of a man eighty years of age. Presently he waited for me midway between two lamp-posts. As I came up he was lighting rank tobacco, in a cutty pipe,[22] with an evil-smelling match, and the flame showed me the suspicion of a smile.

'You must forgive my heat, Bunny, but it really was very foolish of you. Here am I trying every dodge – begging at the door one night – hiding in the shrubs the next – doing every mortal thing but stand and stare at the house as you went and did. It's a costume piece, and in you rush in your ordinary clothes. I tell you they're on the look-out for us night and day. It's the toughest nut I ever tackled!'

'Well,' said I, 'if you had told me so before I shouldn't have come. You told me nothing.'

He looked hard at me from under the broken brim of a battered billycock.[23]

'You're right,' he said at length. 'I've been too close. It's become second nature with me when I've anything on. But here's an end of it, Bunny, so far as you're concerned. I'm going home now, and I want you to follow me; but for heaven's sake keep your distance, and don't speak to me again till I speak to you. There – give me a start.' And he was off again, a decrepit vagabond, with his hands in his pockets, his elbows squared, and frayed coat-tails swinging raggedly from side to side.

I followed him to the Finchley Road.[24] There he took an Atlas omnibus,[25] and I sat some rows behind him on the top, but not far enough to escape the pest of his vile tobacco. That he could carry his character-sketch to such a pitch – he who would only smoke one brand of cigarettes! It was the last, least touch of the insatiable artist, and it charmed away what mortification there still remained in me. Once more I felt the fascination of a comrade who was for ever dazzling one with a fresh and unsuspected facet of his character.

As we neared Piccadilly I wondered what he would do. Surely he was not going into the Albany like that? No, he took another omnibus to Sloane Street,[26] I sitting behind him as before. At Sloane Street we changed again, and were presently in the long lean artery of the King's Road.[27] I was now all agog to know our destination, nor was I kept many more minutes in doubt. Raffles got down. I followed. He crossed the road and disappeared up a dark turning. I pressed after him, and was in time to see his coat-tails as he plunged into a still darker flagged alley to the right. He was holding himself up and stepping out like a

young man once more; also, in some subtle way, he already
looked less disreputable. But I alone was there to see him, the
alley was absolutely deserted, and desperately dark. At the
further end he opened a door with a latch-key, and it was darker
yet within.

Instinctively I drew back and heard him chuckle. We could
no longer see each other.

'All right, Bunny! There's no hanky-panky this time. These
are studios, my friend, and I'm one of the lawful tenants.'

Indeed, in another minute we were in a lofty room with
skylight, easels, dressing-cupboard, platform, and every other
adjunct save the signs of actual labour. The first thing I saw, as
Raffles lit the gas, was its reflection in his silk hat[28] on the pegs
beside the rest of his normal garments.

'Looking for the works of art?' continued Raffles, lighting a
cigarette and beginning to divest himself of his rags. 'I'm afraid
you won't find any, but there's the canvas I'm always going to
make a start upon. I tell them I'm looking high and low for my
ideal model. I have the stove lit on principle twice a week, and
look in and leave a newspaper and a smell of Sullivans – how
good they are after shag![29] Meanwhile I pay my rent and am a
good tenant in every way; and it's a very useful little *pied-à-
terre*[30] – there's no saying how useful it might be at a pinch. As
it is, the billycock comes in and the topper goes out, and nobody
takes the slightest notice of either; at this time of night the
chances are that there's not a soul in the building except ourselves.'

'You never told me you went in for disguises,' said I, watching
him as he cleansed the grime from his face and hands.

'No, Bunny, I've treated you very shabbily all round. There
was really no reason why I shouldn't have shown you this place
a month ago, and yet there was no point in my doing so, and
circumstances are just conceivable in which it would have suited
us both for you to be in genuine ignorance of my whereabouts.
I have something to sleep on, as you perceive, in case of need,
and, of course, my name is not Raffles in the King's Road. So
you will see that one might bolt further and fare worse.'

'Meanwhile you use the place as a dressing-room?'

'It's my private pavilion,'[31] said Raffles. 'Disguises? In some cases they're half the battle, and it's always pleasant to feel that, if the worst comes to the worst, you needn't necessarily be convicted under your own name. Then they're indispensable in dealing with the fences. I drive all my bargains in the tongue and raiment of Shoreditch.[32] If I didn't there'd be the very devil to pay in blackmail. Now, this cupboard's full of all sorts of toggery.[33] I tell the woman who cleans the room that it's for my models when I find 'em. By the way, I only hope I've got something that'll fit you, for you'll want a rig[34] for to-morrow night.'

'To-morrow night!' I exclaimed. 'Why, what do you mean to do?'

'The trick,' said Raffles. 'I intended writing to you as soon as I got back to my rooms, to ask you to look me up to-morrow afternoon; then I was going to unfold my plan of campaign, and take you straight into action then and there. There's nothing like putting the nervous players in first; it's the sitting with their pads on that upsets their applecart;[35] that was another of my reasons for being so confoundedly close. You must try to forgive me. I couldn't help remembering how well you played up last trip, without any time to weaken on it before-hand. All I want is for you to be as cool and smart to-morrow night as you were then; though, by Jove, there's no comparison between the two cases!'

'I thought you would find it so.'

'You were right. I have. Mind you, I don't say this will be the tougher job all round; we shall probably get in without any difficulty at all; it's the getting out again that may flummox us. That's the worst of an irregular household!' cried Raffles, with quite a burst of virtuous indignation. 'I assure you, Bunny, I spent the whole of Monday night in the shrubbery of the garden next door, looking over the wall, and, if you'll believe me, somebody was about all night long! I don't mean the Kaffirs. I don't believe they ever get to bed at all – poor devils! No, I mean Rosenthall himself, and that pasty-faced beast Purvis. They were up and drinking from midnight, when they came in, to broad daylight, when I cleared out. Even then I left them sober enough to slang each other. By the way, they very nearly came to blows in the garden, within a few yards of me, and I heard something that might come in useful and make Rosenthall shoot crooked at a critical moment. You know what an I. D. B. is?'

'Illicit Diamond Buyer?'[36]

'Exactly. Well, it seems that Rosenthall was one. He must have let it out to Purvis in his cups. Anyhow, I heard Purvis taunting him with it, and threatening him with the breakwater at Capetown;[37] and I begin to think our friends are friend and foe. But about to-morrow night: there's nothing subtle in my plan. It's simply to get in while these fellows are out on the loose, and to lie low till they come back, and longer. If possible we must doctor the whisky. That would simplify the whole thing, though it's not a very sporting game to play; still, we must remember Rosenthall's revolver; we don't want him to sign his name on *us*. With all those Kaffirs about, however, it's ten to one on the whisky, and a hundred to one against us if we go looking for it. A brush with the heathen[38] would spoil everything, if it did no more. Besides, there are the ladies —'

'The deuce there are!'

'Ladies with an *i*,[39] and the very voices for raising Cain.[40] I fear, I fear the clamour! It would be fatal to us. *Au contraire*, if we can manage to stow ourselves away unbeknownst, half the battle will be won. If Rosenthall turns in drunk, it's a purple diamond a-piece. If he sits up sober, it may be a bullet instead. We will hope not, Bunny; and all the firing wouldn't be on one side; but it's on the knees of the gods.'[41]

And so we left it when we shook hands in Piccadilly – not by any means as much later as I could have wished. Raffles would not ask me to his rooms that night. He said he made it a rule to have a long night before playing cricket and – other games. His final word to me was framed on the same principle.

'Mind, only one drink to-night, Bunny. Two at the outside – as you value your life – and mine!'

I remember my abject obedience; and the endless, sleepless night it gave me; and the roofs of the houses opposite standing out at last against the blue-grey London dawn. I wondered whether I should ever see another, and was very hard on myself for that little expedition which I had made on my own wilful account.

It was between eight and nine o'clock in the evening when we took up our position in the garden adjoining that of Reuben Rosenthall; the house itself was shut up, thanks to the outrageous libertine next door, who, by driving away the neighbours, had gone far towards delivering himself into our hands. Practically secure from surprise on that side, we could watch our house under cover of a wall just high enough to see over, while a fair margin of shrubs in either garden afforded us additional protection. Thus entrenched, we had stood an hour, watching a pair of lighted bow-windows with vague shadows flitting continually across the blinds, and listening to the drawing of corks, the clink of glasses, and a gradual crescendo of coarse voices within. Our luck seemed to have deserted us: the owner of the purple diamonds was dining at home and dining at undue length. I thought it was a dinner-party. Raffles differed; in the end he proved right. Wheels grated in the drive, a carriage and pair stood at the steps; there was a stampede from the dining-room, and the loud voices died away, to burst forth presently from the porch.

Let me make our position perfectly clear. We were over the wall, at the side of the house, but a few feet from the dining-room windows. On our right, one angle of the building cut the back lawn in two diagonally; on our left, another angle just permitted us to see the jutting steps and the waiting carriage. We saw Rosenthall come out – saw the glimmer of his diamonds before anything. Then came the pugilist; then a lady with a head of hair like a bath sponge;[42] then another, and the party was complete.

Raffles ducked and pulled me down in great excitement.

'The ladies are going with them,' he whispered. 'This is great!'

'That's better still.'

'The Gardenia!'[43] the millionaire had bawled.

'And that's best of all,' said Raffles, standing upright as hoofs and wheels crunched through the gates and rattled off at a fine speed.

'Now what?' I whispered, trembling with excitement.

'They'll be clearing away. Yes, here come their shadows. The drawing-room windows open on the lawn. Bunny, it's the psychological moment.[44] Where's that mask?'

I produced it with a hand whose trembling I tried in vain to still, and could have died for Raffles when he made no comment on what he could not fail to notice. His own hands were firm and cool as he adjusted my mask for me, and then his own.

'By Jove, old boy,' he whispered cheerily, 'you look about the greatest ruffian I ever saw! These masks alone will down a nigger, if we meet one. But I'm glad I remembered to tell you not to shave. You'll pass for Whitechapel if the worst comes to the worst and you don't forget to talk the lingo. Better sulk like a mule if you're not sure of it, and leave the dialogue to me; but, please our stars, there will be no need. Now, are you ready?'

'Quite.'

'Got your gag?'

'Yes.'

'Shooter?'

'Yes.'

'Then follow me.'

In an instant we were over the wall, in another on the lawn behind the house. There was no moon. The very stars in their courses had veiled themselves for our benefit. I crept at my leader's heels to some French windows opening upon a shallow verandah. He pushed. They yielded.

'Luck again,' he whispered; 'nothing *but* luck! Now for a light.'

And the light came!

A good score of electric burners glowed red for the fraction of a second, then rained merciless white beams into our blinded eyes. When we found our sight four revolvers covered us, and between two of them the colossal frame of Reuben Rosenthall shook with a wheezy laughter from head to foot.

'Good evening, boys,' he hiccoughed. 'Glad to see ye at last! Shift foot or finger, you on the left, though, and you're a dead boy. I mean you, you greaser!' he roared out at Raffles. 'I know you. I've been waitin' for you. I've been *watchin'* you all this week! Plucky smart you thought yerself, didn't you? One day beggin', next time shammin' tight, and next one o' them old pals from Kimberley[45] what never come when I'm in. But you left the same tracks every day, you buggins,[46] an' the same tracks every night, all round the blessed premises.'

'All right, guv'nor,' drawled Raffles; 'don't excite. It's a fair cop. We don't sweat to know 'ow you brung it orf. On'y don't you go for to shoot, 'cos we 'int awmed, s'help me Gord!'

'Ah, you're a knowin' one,' said Rosenthall, fingering his triggers. 'But you've struck a knowin'er.'

'Ho, yuss, we know all abaht thet! Set a thief to ketch a thief[47] – ho, yuss.'

My eyes had torn themselves from the round black muzzles, from the accursed diamonds that had been our snare, the pasty pig-face of the over-fed pugilist, and the flaming cheeks and hook nose of Rosenthall himself. I was looking beyond them at the doorway filled with quivering silk and plush, black faces, white eye-balls, woolly pates. But a sudden silence recalled my attention to the millionaire. And only his nose retained its colour.

'What d'ye mean?' he whispered with a hoarse oath. 'Spit it out, or, by Christmas, I'll drill you!'[48]

'Whort price thet brikewater?'[49] drawled Raffles coolly.

'Eh?'

Rosenthall's revolvers were describing widening orbits.

'Whort price thet brikewater – old *I.D.B.*?'

'Where in hell did you get hold o' that?' asked Rosenthall, with a rattle in his thick neck[50] meant for mirth.

'You may well arst,' says Raffles. 'It's all over the plice w'ere *I* come from.'

'Who can have spread such rot?'

'I dunno,' says Raffles; 'arst the gen'leman on yer left; p'r'aps '*e* knows.'

The gentleman on his left had turned livid with emotion. Guilty conscience never declared itself in plainer terms. For a moment his small eyes bulged like currants in the suet of his face; the next, he had pocketed his pistols on a professional instinct, and was upon us with his fists.

'Out o' the light – out o' the light!' yelled Rosenthall in a frenzy.

He was too late. No sooner had the burly pugilist obstructed his fire than Raffles was through the window at a bound; while I, for standing still and saying nothing, was scientifically felled to the floor.

I cannot have been many moments without my senses. When I recovered them there was a great to-do in the garden, but I had the drawing-room to myself. I sat up. Rosenthall and Purvis were rushing about outside, cursing the Kaffirs and nagging at each other.

'Over *that* wall, I tell yer!'

'I tell you it was this one. Can't you whistle for the police?'

'Police be damned! I've had enough of the blessed police.'

'Then we'd better get back and make sure of the other rotter.'

'Oh, make sure o' yer skin. That's what you'd better do. Jala,[51] you black hog, if I catch *you* skulkin' . . .'

I never heard the threat. I was creeping from the drawing-room on my hands and knees, my own revolver swinging by its steel ring from my teeth.

For an instant I thought that the hall also was deserted. I was wrong, and I crept upon a Kaffir on all fours. Poor devil, I could not bring myself to deal him a base blow, but I threatened him most hideously with my revolver, and left the white teeth chattering in his black head as I took the stairs three at a time. Why I went upstairs in that decisive fashion, as though it were my only course, I cannot explain. But garden and ground floor seemed alive with men, and I might have done worse.

I turned into the first room I came to. It was a bedroom – empty, though lit up; and never shall I forget how I started as I entered, on encountering the awful villain that was myself at full length in a pier-glass![52] Masked, armed, and ragged, I was indeed fit carrion for a bullet or the hangman, and to one or the other I made up my mind. Nevertheless, I hid myself in the wardrobe behind the mirror; and there I stood shivering and cursing my fate, my folly, and Raffles most of all – Raffles first and last – for I daresay half an hour. Then the wardrobe door was flung suddenly open; they had stolen into the room without a sound; and I was hauled downstairs, an ignominious captive.

Gross scenes followed in the hall; the ladies were now upon

the stage, and at sight of the desperate criminal they screamed
with one accord. In truth I must have given them fair cause,
though my mask was now torn away and hid nothing but my
left ear. Rosenthall answered their shrieks with a roar for silence;
the woman with the bath-sponge hair swore at him shrilly in
return; the place became a Babel[53] impossible to describe. I
remember wondering how long it would be before the police
appeared. Purvis and the ladies were for calling them in and
giving me in charge without delay. Rosenthall would not hear
of it. He swore that he would shoot man or woman who left his
sight. He had had enough of the police. He was not going to
have them coming there to spoil sport; he was going to deal with
me in his own way. With that he dragged me from all other
hands, flung me against a door, and sent a bullet crashing
through the wood within an inch of my ear.

'You drunken fool! It'll be murder!' shouted Purvis, getting
in the way a second time.

'Wha' do I care? He's armed, isn't he? I shot him in self-
defence. It'll be a warning to others. Will you stand aside, or
d'ye want it yourself?'

'You're drunk,' said Purvis, still between us. 'I saw you take
a neat tumblerful since you come in, and it's made you drunk
as a fool. Pull yourself together, old man. You ain't a-going to
do what you'll be sorry for.'

'Then I won't shoot at him, I'll only shoot roun' an' roun'
the beggar. You're quite right, ole feller. Wouldn't hurt him.
Great mishtake. Roun' an' roun'. There – like that!'

His freckled paw shot up over Purvis's shoulder, mauve
lightning came from his ring, a red flash from his revolver, and
shrieks from the women as the reverberations died away. Some
splinters lodged in my hair.

Next instant the prize-fighter disarmed him; and I was safe
from the devil, but finally doomed to the deep sea. A policeman
was in our midst. He had entered through the drawing-room
window; he was an officer of few words and creditable prompti-
tude. In a twinkling he had the handcuffs on my wrists, while
the pugilist explained the situation, and his patron reviled the
force and its representative with impotent malignity. A fine

watch they kept; a lot of good they did; coming in when all was over and the whole household might have been murdered in their sleep. The officer only deigned to notice him as he marched me off.

'We know all about *you*, sir,' said he contemptuously, and he refused the sovereign Purvis proffered. 'You will be seeing me again, sir, at Marylebone.'[54]

'Shall I come now?'

'As you please, sir. I rather think the other gentleman requires you more, and I don't fancy this young man means to give much trouble.'

'Oh, I'm coming quietly,' I said.

And I went.

In silence we traversed perhaps a hundred yards. It must have been midnight. We did not meet a soul. At last I whispered:

'How on earth did you manage it?'

'Purely by luck,' said Raffles. 'I had the luck to get clear away through knowing every brick of those back-garden walls, and the double luck to have these togs with the rest over at Chelsea. The helmet is one of a collection I made up at Oxford;[55] here it goes over this wall, and we'd better carry the coat and belt before we meet a real officer. I got them once for a fancy ball – ostensibly – and thereby hangs a yarn. I always thought they might come in useful a second time. My chief crux to-night was getting rid of the hansom[56] that brought me back. I sent him off to Scotland Yard with ten bob[57] and a special message to good old Mackenzie. The whole detective department will be at Rosenthall's in about half an hour. Of course, I speculated on our gentleman's hatred of the police – another huge slice of luck. If you'd got away, well and good; if not, I felt he was the man to play with his mouse as long as possible. Yes, Bunny, it's been more of a costume piece than I intended, and we've come out of it with a good deal less credit. But, by Jove, we're jolly lucky to have come out of it at all!'

GENTLEMEN AND PLAYERS

Old Raffles may or may not have been an exceptional criminal, but as a cricketer I dare swear he was unique. Himself a dangerous bat, a brilliant field, and perhaps the very finest slow bowler of his decade, he took incredibly little interest in the game at large. He never went up to Lord's[1] without his cricket-bag, or showed the slightest interest in the result of a match in which he was not himself engaged. Nor was this mere hateful egotism on his part. He professed to have lost all enthusiasm for the game, and to keep it up only from the very lowest motives.

'Cricket,' said Raffles, 'like everything else, is good enough sport until you discover a better. As a source of excitement it isn't in it with other things you wot of, Bunny, and the involuntary comparison becomes a bore. What's the satisfaction of taking a man's wicket when you want his spoons? Still, if you can bowl a bit your low cunning won't get rusty, and always looking for the weak spot's just the kind of mental exercise one wants. Yes, perhaps there's some affinity between the two things after all. But I'd chuck up cricket to-morrow, Bunny, if it wasn't for the glorious protection it affords a person of my proclivities.'

'How so?' said I. 'It brings you before the public, I should have thought, far more than is either safe or wise.'

'My dear Bunny, that's exactly where you make a mistake. To follow Crime with reasonable impunity you simply *must* have a parallel, ostensible career – the more public the better. The principle is obvious. Mr Peace, of pious memory, disarmed suspicion by acquiring a local reputation for playing the fiddle and taming animals,[2] and it's my profound conviction that Jack the Ripper was a really eminent public man,[3] whose speeches

were very likely reported alongside his atrocities. Fill the bill in
some prominent part, and you'll never be suspected of doubling
it with another of equal prominence. That's why I want you to
cultivate journalism, my boy, and sign all you can. And it's the
one and only reason why I don't burn my bats for firewood.'

Nevertheless, when he did play there was no keener performer
on the field, nor one more anxious to do well for his side. I
remember how he went to the nets, before the first match of the
season, with his pocket full of sovereigns, which he put on the
stumps instead of bails.[4] It was a sight to see the professionals
bowling like demons for the hard cash, for whenever a stump
was hit a pound was tossed to the bowler and another balanced
in its stead, while one man took £3 with a ball that spread-eagled
the wicket. Raffles's practice cost him either eight or nine
sovereigns; but he had absolutely first-class bowling all the time;
and he made fifty-seven runs next day.

It became my pleasure to accompany him to all his matches,
to watch every ball he bowled, or played, or fielded, and to sit
chatting with him in the pavilion when he was doing none of
these three things. You might have seen us there, side by side,
during the greater part of the Gentlemen's first innings against
the Players (who had lost the toss) on the second Monday in
July.[5] We were to be seen, but not heard, for Raffles had failed
to score, and was uncommonly cross for a player who cared so
little for the game. Merely taciturn with me, he was positively
rude to more than one member who wanted to know how it
had happened, or who ventured to commiserate him on his luck;
there he sat, with a straw hat tilted over his nose and a cigarette
stuck between lips that curled disagreeably at every advance. I
was therefore much surprised when a young fellow of the exquisite type[6] came and squeezed himself in between us, and met with
a perfectly civil reception despite the liberty. I did not know the
boy by sight, nor did Raffles introduce us; but their conversation
proclaimed at once a slightness of acquaintanceship and a
licence on the lad's part which combined to puzzle me. Mys-
tification reached its height when Raffles was informed that
the other's father was anxious to meet him, and he instantly
consented to gratify that whim.

'He's in the Ladies' Enclosure.[7] Will you come round now?'

'With pleasure,' says Raffles. 'Keep a place for me, Bunny.'

And they were gone.

'Young Crowley,' said some voice further back. 'Last year's Harrow Eleven.'[8]

'I remember him. Worst man in the team.'

'Keen cricketer, however. Stopped till he was twenty to get his colours. Governor made him. Keen breed. Oh, pretty, sir! Very pretty!'

The game was boring me. I only came to see old Raffles perform. Soon I was looking wistfully for his return, and at length I saw him beckoning me from the palings to the right.

'Want to introduce you to old Amersteth,'[9] he whispered, when I joined him. 'They've a cricket week[10] next month, when this boy Crowley comes of age, and we've both got to go down and play.'

'Both!' I echoed. 'But I'm no cricketer!'

'Shut up,' says Raffles. 'Leave that to me. I've been lying for all I'm worth,' he added sepulchrally as we reached the bottom of the steps. 'I trust to you not to give the show away.'

There was the gleam in his eye that I knew well enough elsewhere, but was unprepared for in those healthy, sane sur-roundings; and it was with very definite misgivings and surmises that I followed the Zingari blazer[11] through the vast flower-bed of hats and bonnets that bloomed beneath the ladies' awning.

Lord Amersteth was a fine-looking man with a short mous-tache and a double chin. He received me with much dry courtesy, through which, however, it was not difficult to read a less flattering tale. I was accepted as the inevitable appendage of the invaluable Raffles, with whom I felt deeply incensed as I made my bow.

'I have been bold enough,' said Lord Amersteth, 'to ask one of the Gentlemen of England to come down and play some rustic cricket for us next month. He is kind enough to say that he would have liked nothing better, but for this little fishing expedition of yours, Mr —, Mr —,' and Lord Amersteth succeeded in remembering my name.

It was, of course, the first I had ever heard of that fishing expedition, but I made haste to say that it could easily, and should certainly, be put off. Raffles gleamed approval through his eyelashes. Lord Amersteth bowed and shrugged.

'You're very good, I'm sure,' said he. 'But I understand you're a cricketer yourself?'

'He was one at school,' said Raffles, with infamous readiness.

'Not a real cricketer,' I was stammering meanwhile.

'In the eleven?' said Lord Amersteth.

'I'm afraid not,' said I.

'But only just out of it,' declared Raffles, to my horror.

'Well, well, we can't all play for the Gentlemen,' said Lord Amersteth slyly. 'My son Crowley only just scraped into the eleven at Harrow, and *he's* going to play. I may even come in myself at a pinch; so you won't be the only duffer, if you are one, and I shall be very glad if you will come down and help us too. You shall flog a stream[12] before breakfast and after dinner, if you like.'

'I should be very proud,' I was beginning, as the mere prelude to resolute excuses; but the eye of Raffles opened wide upon me; and I hesitated weakly, to be duly lost.

'Then that's settled,' said Lord Amersteth, with the slightest suspicion of grimness. 'It's to be a little week, you know, when my son comes of age. We play the Free Foresters,[13] the Dorsetshire Gentlemen, and probably some local lot as well. But Mr Raffles will tell you all about it, and Crowley shall write. Another wicket! By Jove, they're all out! Then I rely on you both.' And, with a little nod, Lord Amersteth rose and sidled to the gangway.

Raffles rose also, but I caught the sleeve of his blazer.

'What are you thinking of?' I whispered savagely. 'I was nowhere near the eleven. I'm no sort of cricketer. I shall have to get out of this!'

'Not you,' he whispered back. 'You needn't play, but come you must. If you wait for me after half-past six I'll tell you why.'

But I could guess the reason; and I am ashamed to say that it revolted me much less than did the notion of making a public fool of myself on a cricket-field. My gorge rose at this as it no longer rose at crime, and it was in no tranquil humour that I

strolled about the ground while Raffles disappeared in the pavilion. Nor was my annoyance lessened by a little meeting I
witnessed between young Crowley and his father, who shrugged
as he stopped and stooped to convey some information which
made the young man look a little blank. It may have been pure
self-consciousness on my part, but I could have sworn that the
trouble was their inability to secure the great Raffles without
his insignificant friend.

Then the bell rang,[14] and I climbed to the top of the pavilion
to watch Raffles bowl. No subtleties are lost up there; and if
ever a bowler was full of them, it was A. J. Raffles on his day,
as, indeed, all the cricket world remembers. One had not to be
a cricketer oneself to appreciate his perfect command of pitch
and break,[15] his beautifully easy action, which never varied with
the varying pace, his great ball on the leg-stump[16] – his dropping
head-ball[17] – in a word, the infinite ingenuity of that versatile
attack. It was no mere exhibition of athletic prowess, it was an
intellectual treat, and one with a special significance in my
eyes. I saw the 'affinity between the two things', saw it in that
afternoon's tireless warfare against the flower of professional
cricket. It was not that Raffles took many wickets for few runs;
he was too fine a bowler to mind being hit; and time was short,
and the wicket good. What I admired, and what I remember,
was the combination of resource and cunning, of patience and
precision, of head-work and handiwork, which made every over
an artistic whole. It was all so characteristic of that other Raffles
whom I alone knew!

'I felt like bowling this afternoon,' he told me later in the
hansom. 'With a pitch to help me, I'd have done something big;
as it is, three for forty-one, out of the four that fell,[18] isn't so
bad for a slow bowler on a plumb wicket against those fellows.
But I felt venomous! Nothing riles me more than being asked
about for my cricket as though I were a pro. myself.'

'Then why on earth go?'

'To punish them, and – because we shall be jolly hard up,
Bunny, before the season's over!'

'Ah!' said I. 'I thought it was that.'

'Of course, it was! It seems they're going to have the very devil of a week of it – balls – dinner-parties – swagger house-party[19] – general junketings – and obviously a houseful of diamonds as well. Diamonds galore! As a general rule nothing would induce me to abuse my position as a guest. I've never done it, Bunny. But in this case we're engaged like the waiters and the band, and by heaven we'll take our toll! Let's have a quiet dinner somewhere and talk it over.'

'It seems rather a vulgar sort of theft,' I could not help saying; and to this, my single protest, Raffles instantly assented.

'It *is* a vulgar sort,' said he; 'but I can't help that. We're getting vulgarly hard up again, and there's an end on 't. Besides, these people deserve it, and can afford it. And don't you run away with the idea that all will be plain sailing; nothing will be easier than getting some stuff, and nothing harder than avoiding all suspicion, as, of course, we must. We may come away with no more than a good working plan of the premises. Who knows? In any case there's weeks of thinking in it for you and me.'

But with those weeks I will not weary you further than by remarking that the 'thinking' was done entirely by Raffles, who did not always trouble to communicate his thoughts to me. His reticence, however, was no longer an irritant. I began to accept it as a necessary convention of these little enterprises. And, after our last adventure of the kind, more especially after its *dénouement*, my trust in Raffles was much too solid to be shaken by a want of trust in me, which I still believe to have been more the instinct of the criminal than the judgment of the man.

It was on Monday, the tenth of August,[20] that we were due at Milchester Abbey, Dorset;[21] and the beginning of the month found us cruising about that very county, with fly-rods actually in our hands. The idea was that we should acquire at once a local reputation as decent fishermen, and some knowledge of the countryside, with a view to further and more deliberate operations in the event of an unprofitable week. There was another idea which Raffles kept to himself until he had got me down there. Then one day he produced a cricket-ball in a meadow we were crossing, and threw me catches for an hour together. More hours he spent in bowling to me on the nearest green; and, if I was never a cricketer, at least I came nearer to being one, by the end of that week, than ever before or since.

Incident began early on the Monday. We had sallied forth from a desolate little junction within quite a few miles of Milchester, had been caught in a shower, had run for shelter to a wayside inn. A florid, overdressed man was drinking in the parlour, and I could have sworn it was at the sight of him that Raffles recoiled on the threshold, and afterwards insisted on returning to the station through the rain. He assured me, however, that the odour of stale ale had almost knocked him down. And I had to make what I could of his speculative, downcast eyes and knitted brows.

Milchester Abbey is a grey, quadrangular pile, deep-set in rich woody country, and twinkling with triple rows of quaint windows, every one of which seemed alight as we drove up just in time to dress for dinner. The carriage had whirled us under I know not how many triumphal arches in process of construction, and past the tents and flag-poles of a juicy-looking cricket-field, on which Raffles undertook to bowl up to his reputation. But the chief signs of festival were within, where we found an enormous house-party assembled, including more persons of pomp, majesty, and dominion than I had ever encountered in one room before. I confess I felt overpowered. Our errand and my own pretences combined to rob me of an address upon which I have sometimes plumed myself; and I have a grim recollection of my nervous relief when dinner was at last announced. I little knew what an ordeal it was to prove.

I had taken in a much less formidable young lady than might have fallen to my lot. Indeed I began by blessing my good fortune in this respect. Miss Melhuish was merely the rector's daughter, and she had only been asked to make an even number. She informed me of both facts before the soup reached us, and her subsequent conversation was characterized by the same engaging candour. It exposed what was little short of a mania for imparting information. I had simply to listen, to nod, and to be thankful. When I confessed to knowing very few of those present, even by sight, my entertaining companion proceeded to tell me who everybody was, beginning on my left and working conscientiously round to her right. This lasted quite a long time, and really interested me; but a great deal that followed did not; and, obviously to recapture my unworthy attention, Miss Melhuish suddenly asked me, in a sensational whisper, whether I could keep a secret.

I said I thought I might, whereupon another question followed, in still lower and more thrilling accents:

'Are you afraid of burglars?'

Burglars! I was roused at last. The word stabbed me. I repeated it in horrified query.

'So I've found something to interest you at last!' said Miss Melhuish, in naïve triumph. 'Yes – burglars! But don't speak so loud. It's supposed to be kept a great secret. I really oughtn't to tell you at all!'

'But what is there to tell?' I whispered with satisfactory impatience.

'You promise not to speak of it?'

'Of course!'

'Well, then, there are burglars in the neighbourhood.'

'Have they committed any robberies?'

'Not yet.'

'Then how do you know?'

'They've been seen. In the district. Two well-known London thieves!'

Two! I looked at Raffles. I had done so often during the evening, envying him his high spirits, his iron nerve, his buoyant wit, his perfect ease and self-possession. But now I pitied him; through all my own terror and consternation, I pitied him as he sat eating and drinking, and laughing and talking, without a cloud of fear or of embarrassment on his handsome, taking, daredevil face. I caught up my champagne and emptied the glass.

'Who has seen them?' I then asked calmly.

'A detective. They were traced down from town a few days ago. They are believed to have designs on the Abbey!'

'But why aren't they run in?'

'Exactly what I asked papa on the way here this evening; he says there is no warrant out against the men at present, and all that can be done is to watch their movements.'

'Oh! so they are being watched?'

'Yes, by a detective who is down here on purpose. And I heard Lord Amersteth tell papa that they had been seen this afternoon at Warbeck Junction!'[22]

The very place where Raffles and I had been caught in the rain! Our stampede from the inn was now explained; on the other hand, I was no longer to be taken by surprise by anything that my companion might have to tell me; and I succeeded in looking her in the face with a smile.

'This is really quite exciting, Miss Melhuish,' said I. 'May I ask how you come to know so much about it?'

'It's papa,' was the confidential reply. 'Lord Amersteth consulted him, and he consulted me. But for goodness' sake don't let it get about! I can't think *what* tempted me to tell you!'

'You may trust me, Miss Melhuish. But – aren't you frightened?'

Miss Melhuish giggled.

'Not a bit! They won't come to the rectory. There's nothing for them there. But look round the table: look at the diamonds: look at old Lady Melrose's necklace alone!'

The Dowager Marchioness of Melrose[23] was one of the few persons whom it had been unnecessary to point out to me. She sat on Lord Amersteth's right, flourishing her ear-trumpet, and drinking champagne with her usual notorious freedom, as dissipated and kindly a dame as the world has ever seen. It was a necklace of diamonds and sapphires that rose and fell about her ample neck.

'They say it's worth five thousand pounds at least,' continued my companion. 'Lady Margaret told me so this morning (that's Lady Margaret next your Mr Raffles, you know); and the old dear *will* wear them every night. Think what a haul they would be! No; we don't feel in immediate danger at the rectory.'

When the ladies rose, Miss Melhuish bound me to fresh vows of secrecy; and left me, I should think, with some remorse for her indiscretion, but more satisfaction at the importance which it had undoubtedly given her in my eyes. The opinion may smack of vanity, though, in reality, the very springs of conversation reside in that same human, universal itch to thrill the auditor. The peculiarity of Miss Melhuish was that she must be thrilling at all costs. And thrilling she had surely been.

I spare you my feelings of the next two hours. I tried hard to get a word with Raffles, but again and again I failed. In the dining-room he and Crowley lit their cigarettes with the same match, and had their heads together all the time. In the drawing-room I had the mortification of hearing him talk interminable nonsense into the ear-trumpet of Lady Melrose, whom he knew in town. Lastly, in the billiard-room, they had a great and lengthy pool,[24] while I sat aloof and chafed more than ever in the company of a very serious Scotchman, who had arrived since dinner, and who would talk of nothing but the recent improvements in instantaneous photography.[25] He had not come to play in the matches (he told me), but to obtain for Lord Amersteth such a series of cricket photographs as had never been taken before; whether as an amateur or a professional photographer I was unable to determine. I remember, however, seeking distraction in little bursts of resolute attention to the conversation of this bore. And so at last the long ordeal ended; glasses were emptied, men said good-night, and I followed Raffles to his room.

'It's all up!' I gasped, as he turned up the gas and I shut the door. 'We're being watched. We've been followed down from town. There's a detective here on the spot!'

'How do *you* know?' asked Raffles, turning upon me quite sharply, but without the least dismay. And I told him how I knew.

'Of course,' I added, 'it was the fellow we saw in the inn this afternoon.'

'The detective?' said Raffles. 'Do you mean to say you don't know a detective when you see one, Bunny?'

'If that wasn't the fellow, which is?'

Raffles shook his head.

'To think that you've been talking to him for the last hour in the billiard-room, and couldn't spot what he was!'

'The Scotch photographer –'

I paused aghast.

'Scotch he is,' said Raffles, 'and photographer he may be. He

is also Inspector Mackenzie of Scotland Yard[26] – the very man
I sent the message to that night last April. And you couldn't spot
who he was in a whole hour! O Bunny, Bunny, you were never
built for crime!'

'But,' said I, 'if that was Mackenzie, who was the fellow you
bolted from at Warbeck?'

'The man he's watching.'

'But he's watching us!'

Raffles looked at me with a pitying eye, and shook his head
again before handing me his open cigarette-case.

'I don't know whether smoking's forbidden in one's bedroom, but you'd better take one of these and stand tight, Bunny,
because I'm going to say something offensive.'

I helped myself with a laugh.

'Say what you like, my dear fellow, if it really isn't you and I
that Mackenzie's after.'

'Well, then, it isn't, and it couldn't be, and nobody but a
born Bunny would suppose for a moment that it was! Do you
seriously think he would sit there and knowingly watch his man
playing pool under his nose? Well, he might; he's a cool hand,
Mackenzie; but I'm not cool enough to win a pool under such
conditions. At least I don't think I am; it would be interesting
to see. The situation wasn't free from strain as it was, though I
knew he wasn't thinking of us. Crowley told me all about it
after dinner, you see, and then I'd seen one of the men for myself
this afternoon. You thought it was a detective who made me
turn tail at that inn. I really don't know why I didn't tell you at
the time, but it was just the opposite. That loud, red-faced brute
is one of the cleverest thieves in London, and I once had a drink
with him and our mutual fence.[27] I was an East-ender from
tongue to toe at the moment, but you will understand that I
don't run unnecessary risks of recognition by a brute like that.'

'He's not alone, I hear.'

'By no means; there's at least one other man with him; and
it's suggested that there may be an accomplice here in the house.'

'Did Lord Crowley tell you so?'

'Crowley and the champagne between them. In confidence,
of course, just as your girl told you; but even in confidence he

never let on about Mackenzie. He told me there was a detective in the background, but that was all. Putting him up as a guest is evidently their big secret, to be kept from the other guests because it might offend them, but more particularly from the servants whom he's here to watch. That's my reading of the situation, Bunny, and you will agree with me that it's infinitely more interesting than we could have imagined it would prove.'

'But infinitely more difficult for us,' said I, with a sigh of pusillanimous relief. 'Our hands are tied for this week, at all events.'

'Not necessarily, my dear Bunny, though I admit that the chances are against us. Yet I'm not so sure of that either. There are all sorts of possibilities in these three-cornered combinations. Set A to watch B, and he won't have an eye left for C. That's the obvious theory, but then Mackenzie's a very big A. I should be sorry to have any boodle[28] about me with that man in the house. Yet it would be great to nip in between A and B and score off them both at once! It would be worth a risk, Bunny, to do that; it would be worth risking something merely to take on old hands like B and his men at their own old game! Eh, Bunny? That would be something like a match. Gentlemen and Players at single wicket,[29] by Jove!'

His eyes were brighter than I had known them for many a day. They shone with the perverted enthusiasm which was roused in him only by the contemplation of some new audacity. He kicked off his shoes and began pacing his room with noiseless rapidity; not since the night of the Old Bohemian dinner to Reuben Rosenthall had Raffles exhibited such excitement in my presence; and I was not sorry at the moment to be reminded of the fiasco to which that banquet had been the prelude.

'My dear A. J.,' said I in his very own tone, 'you're far too fond of the uphill game; you will eventually fall a victim to the sporting spirit and nothing else. Take a lesson from our last escape, and fly lower as you value our skins. Study the house as much as you like, but do – not – go and shove your head into Mackenzie's mouth!'

My wealth of metaphor brought him to a standstill, with his cigarette between his fingers and a grin beneath his shining eyes.

'You're quite right, Bunny. I won't. I really won't. Yet – you saw old Lady Melrose's necklace? I've been wanting it for years! But I'm not going to play the fool; honour bright, I'm not; yet – by Jove! – to get to windward of the professors[30] and Mackenzie too! It would be a great game, Bunny, it would be a great game!'

'Well, you mustn't play it this week.'

'No, no, I won't. But I wonder how the professors think of going to work? That's what one wants to know. I wonder if they've really got an accomplice in the house? How I wish I knew their game! But it's all right, Bunny; don't you be jealous; it shall be as you wish.'

And with that assurance I went off to my own room, and so to bed with an incredibly light heart. I had still enough of the honest man in me to welcome the postponement of our actual felonies, to dread their performance, to deplore their necessity: which is merely another way of stating the too patent fact that I was an incomparably weaker man than Raffles, while every whit as wicked. I had, however, one rather strong point. I possessed the gift of dismissing unpleasant considerations, not intimately connected with the passing moment, entirely from my mind. Through the exercise of this faculty I had lately been living my frivolous life in town with as much ignoble enjoyment as I had derived from it the year before; and similarly, here at Milchester, in the long-dreaded cricket week, I had after all a quite excellent time.

It is true that there were other factors in this pleasing disappointment. In the first place, *mirabile dictu*,[31] there were one or two even greater duffers than I on the Abbey cricket-field. Indeed, quite early in the week, when it was of most value to me, I gained considerable kudos for a lucky catch; a ball, of which I had merely heard the hum, stuck fast in my hand, which Lord Amersteth himself grasped in public congratulation. This happy accident was not to be undone even by me, and, as nothing succeeds like success, and the constant encouragement of the one great cricketer on the field was in itself an immense stimulus, I actually made a run or two in my very next innings. Miss Melhuish said pretty things to me that night at the great ball in honour of Viscount Crowley's majority;[32] she also told me that was the night on which the robbers would assuredly make their raid, and was full of arch tremors when we sat out in the garden, though the entire premises were illuminated all night long. Meanwhile, the quiet Scotchman took countless photographs by day, which he developed by night in a dark room admirably situated in the servants' part of the house; and it is my firm belief that only two of his fellow-guests knew Mr Clephane of Dundee for Inspector Mackenzie of Scotland Yard.

The week was to end with a trumpery match[33] on the Saturday, which two or three of us intended abandoning early in order to return to town that night. The match, however, was never played. In the small hours of the Saturday morning a tragedy took place at Milchester Abbey.

Let me tell of the thing as I saw and heard it. My room opened upon the central gallery, and was not even on the same floor as that on which Raffles – and I think all the other men – were quartered. I had been put, in fact, into the dressing-room of one of the grand suites, and my two near neighbours were old Lady Melrose and my host and hostess. Now, by the Friday evening the actual festivities were at an end, and, for the first time that week, I must have been sound asleep since midnight, when all at once I found myself sitting up breathless. A heavy thud had come against my door, and now I heard hard breathing and the dull stamp of muffled feet.

'I've got ye,' muttered a voice. 'It's no use struggling.'

It was the Scotch detective, and a new fear turned me cold. There was no reply, but the hard breathing grew harder still, and the muffled feet beat the floor to a quicker measure. In sudden panic I sprang out of bed and flung open my door. A light burnt low on the landing, and by it I could see Mackenzie swaying and staggering in a silent tussle with some powerful adversary.

'Hold this man!' he cried, as I appeared. 'Hold the rascal!'

But I stood like a fool until the pair of them backed into me, when, with a deep breath I flung myself on the fellow, whose face I had seen at last. He was one of the footmen who waited at table; and no sooner had I pinned him than the detective loosed his hold.

'Hang on to him,' he cried. 'There's more of 'em below.'

And he went leaping down the stairs, as other doors opened and Lord Amersteth and his son appeared simultaneously in their pyjamas. At that my man ceased struggling; but I was still holding him when Crowley turned up the gas.

'What the devil's all this?' asked Lord Amersteth, blinking. 'Who was that ran downstairs?'

'Mac – Clephane!' said I hastily.

'Aha!' said he, turning to the footman. 'So you're the scoundrel, are you? Well done! Well done! Where was he caught?'

I had no idea.

'Here's Lady Melrose's door open,' said Crowley. 'Lady Melrose! Lady Melrose!'

'You forget she's deaf,' said Lord Amersteth. 'Ah! that'll be her maid.'

An inner door had opened; next instant there was a little shriek, and a white figure gesticulated on the threshold.

'Où donc est l'écrin[34] de Madame la Marquise? La fenêtre est ouverte. Il a disparu!'

'Window open and jewel-case gone, by Jove!' exclaimed Lord Amersteth. 'Mais comment est Madame la Marquise? Est-elle bien?'[35]

'Oui, milor. Elle dort.'

'Sleeps through it all,' said my lord. 'She's the only one, then!'

'What made Mackenzie – Clephane – bolt?' young Crowley asked me.

'Said there were more of them below.'

'Why the devil couldn't you tell us so before?' he cried, and went leaping downstairs in his turn.

He was followed by nearly all the cricketers, who now burst upon the scene in a body, only to desert it for the chase. Raffles was one of them, and I would gladly have been another, had not the footman chosen this moment to hurl me from him, and to make a dash in the direction from which they had come. Lord Amersteth had him in an instant; but the fellow fought desperately, and it took the two of us to drag him downstairs, amid a terrified chorus from half-open doors. Eventually we handed him over to two other footmen who appeared with their nightshirts tucked into their trousers, and my host was good enough to compliment me as he led the way outside.

'I thought I heard a shot,' he added. 'Didn't you?'

'I thought I heard three.'

And out we dashed into the darkness.

I remember how the gravel pricked my feet, how the wet grass numbed them as we made for the sound of voices on an outlying lawn. So dark was the night that we were in the cricketers' midst before we saw the shimmer of their pyjamas; and then Lord Amersteth almost trod on Mackenzie as he lay prostrate in the dew.

'Who's this?' he cried. 'What on earth's happened?'

'It's Clephane,' said a man who knelt over him. 'He's got a bullet in him somewhere.'

'Is he alive?'

'Barely.'

'Good God! Where's Crowley?'

'Here I am,' called a breathless voice. 'It's no good, you fellows. There's nothing to show which way they've gone. Here's Raffles; he's chucked it, too.' And they ran up panting.

'Well, we've got one of them, at all events,' muttered Lord Amersteth. 'The next thing is to get this poor fellow indoors. Take his shoulders, somebody. Now his middle. Join hands under him. Altogether, now; that's the way. Poor fellow! Poor fellow! His name isn't Clephane at all. He's a Scotland Yard detective, down here for these very villains!'

Raffles was the first to express surprise; but he had also been the first to raise the wounded man. Nor had any of them a stronger or more tender hand in the slow procession to the house. In a little we had the senseless man stretched on a sofa in the library. And there, with ice on his wound and brandy in his throat, his eyes opened and his lips moved.

Lord Amersteth bent down to catch the words.

'Yes, yes,' said he; 'we've got one of them safe and sound. The brute you collared upstairs.' Lord Amersteth bent lower. 'By Jove! Lowered the jewel-case out of the window, did he? And they've got clean away with it! Well, well! I only hope we'll be able to pull this good fellow through. He's off again.'

An hour passed: the sun was rising.

It found a dozen young fellows on the settees in the billiard-room, drinking whisky and soda-water in their overcoats and pyjamas, and still talking excitedly in one breath. A time-table was being passed from hand to hand: the doctor was still in the library. At last the door opened, and Lord Amersteth put in his head.

'It isn't hopeless,' said he, 'but it's bad enough. There'll be no cricket to-day.'

Another hour, and most of us were on our way to catch the early train; between us we filled a compartment almost to suffocation. And still we talked all together of the night's event; and still I was a little hero in my way, for having kept my hold of the one ruffian who had been taken; and my gratification was subtle and intense. Raffles watched me under lowered lids. Not a word had we had together; not a word did we have until we had left the others at Paddington,[36] and were skimming through the streets in a hansom with noiseless tyres[37] and a tinkling bell.

'Well, Bunny,' said Raffles, 'so the professors have it, eh?'

'Yes,' said I. 'And I'm jolly glad!'

'That poor Mackenzie has a ball in his chest?'

'That you and I have been on the decent side for once.'

He shrugged his shoulders.

'You're hopeless, Bunny, quite hopeless! I take it you wouldn't have refused your share if the boodle had fallen to us? Yet you positively enjoy coming off second best – for the second time running! I confess, however, that the professors' methods were full of interest to me. I, for one, have probably gained as much in experience as I have lost in other things. That lowering the jewel-case out of the window was a very simple and effective expedient; two of them had been waiting below for it for hours.'

'How do you know?' I asked.

'I saw them from my own window, which was just above the dear old lady's. I was fretting for that necklace in particular, when I went up to turn in for our last night – and I happened to look out of my window. In point of fact, I wanted to see whether the one below was open, and whether there was the slightest chance of working the oracle with my sheet[38] for a rope. Of course I took the precaution of turning my light off first, and it was a lucky thing I did. I saw the pros. right down below, and they never saw me. I saw a little tiny luminous disc just for an instant, and then again for an instant a few minutes later. Of course I knew what it was, for I have my own watch-dial daubed with luminous paint; it makes a lantern of sorts when you can get no better. But these fellows were not using theirs as a lantern. They were under the old lady's window. They were watching the time. The whole thing was arranged with their accomplice inside. Set a thief to catch a thief: in a minute I had guessed what the whole thing proved to be.'

'And you did nothing!' I exclaimed.

'On the contrary, I went downstairs and straight into Lady Melrose's room –'

'You did?'

'Without a moment's hesitation. To save her jewels. And I was prepared to yell as much into her ear-trumpet for all the house to hear. But the dear lady is too deaf and too fond of her dinner to wake easily.'

'Well?'

'She didn't stir.'

'And yet you allowed the professors, as you call them, to take her jewels, case and all!'

'All but this,' said Raffles, thrusting his fist into my lap. 'I would have shown it you before, but really, old fellow, your face all day has been worth a fortune to the firm!'

And he opened his fist, to shut it next instant on the bunch of diamonds and of sapphires that I had last seen encircling the neck of Lady Melrose.

LE PREMIER PAS

That night[1] he told me the story of his earliest crime. Not since the fateful morning of the Ides of March, when he had just mentioned it as an unreported incident of a certain cricket tour, had I succeeded in getting a word out of Raffles on the subject. It was not for want of trying; he would shake his head, and watch his cigarette smoke thoughtfully; a subtle look in his eyes, half cynical, half wistful, as though the decent honest days that were no more[2] had had their merits after all. Raffles would plan a fresh enormity, or glory in the last, with the unmitigated enthusiasm of the artist. It was impossible to imagine one throb or twitter of compunction beneath those frankly egoistic and infectious transports. And yet the ghost of a dead remorse seemed still to visit him with the memory of his first felony, so that I had given the story up long before the night of our return from Milchester. Cricket, however, was in the air, and Raffles's cricket-bag back where he sometimes kept it, in the fender, with the remains of an Orient label[3] still adhering to the leather. My eyes had been on this label for some time, and I suppose his eyes had been on mine, for all at once he asked me if I still burned to hear that yarn.

'It's no use,' I replied. 'You won't spin it. I must imagine it for myself.'

'How can you?'

'Oh, I begin to know your methods.'

'You take it I went in with my eyes open, as I do now, eh?'

'I can't imagine your doing otherwise.'

'My dear Bunny, it was the most unpremeditated thing I ever did in my life!'

His chair wheeled back into the books as he sprang up with sudden energy. There was quite an indignant glitter in his eyes.

'I can't believe that,' said I craftily. 'I can't pay you such a poor compliment!'

'Then you must be a fool –'

He broke off, stared hard at me, and in a trice stood smiling in his own despite.

'Or a better knave than I thought you, Bunny, and by Jove it's the knave! Well – I suppose I'm fairly drawn; I give you best, as they say out there. As a matter of fact I've been thinking of the thing myself; last night's racket reminds me of it in one or two respects. I tell you what, though, this is an occasion in any case, and I'm going to celebrate it by breaking the one good rule of my life. I'm going to have a second drink!'

The whisky tinkled, the syphon fizzed, the ice plopped home; and seated there in his pyjamas, with the inevitable cigarette, Raffles told me the story that I had given up hoping to hear. The windows were wide open; the sounds of Piccadilly floated in at first. Long before he finished, the last wheels had rattled, the last brawler was removed, we alone broke the quiet of the summer night.

'. . . No, they do you very well indeed. You pay for nothing but drinks, so to speak, but I'm afraid mine were of a comprehensive character. I had started in a hole, I ought really to have refused the invitation; then we all went to the Melbourne Cup,[4] and I had the certain winner that didn't win, and that's not the only way you can play the fool in Melbourne. I wasn't the steady old stager I am now, Bunny; my analysis was a confession in itself. But the others didn't know how hard up I was, and I swore they shouldn't. I tried the Jews, but they're extra fly[5] out there. Then I thought of a kinsman of sorts, a second cousin of my father's[6] whom none of us knew anything about, except that he was supposed to be in one or other of the Colonies. If he was a rich man, well and good, I would work him; if not there would be no harm done. I tried to get on his tracks, and, as luck would have it, I succeeded (or thought I had) at the very moment when I happened to have a few days to myself. I was cut over on the hand,[7] just before the big Christmas match, and couldn't have bowled a ball if they had played me.

'The surgeon who fixed me up happened to ask me if I was any relation of Raffles of the National Bank,[8] and the pure luck of it almost took my breath away. A relation who was a high official in one of the banks, who would finance me on my mere name – could anything be better? I made up my mind that this Raffles was the man I wanted, and was awfully sold to find next moment that he wasn't a high official at all. Nor had the doctor so much as met him, but had merely read of him in connection with a small sensation at the suburban branch which my name-sake managed; an armed robber had been rather pluckily beaten off, with a bullet in him, by this Raffles; and the sort of thing was so common out there that this was the first I had heard of it! A suburban branch – my financier had faded into some excellent fellow with a billet to lose if he called his soul his own. Still a manager was a manager, and I said I would soon see whether this was the relative I was looking for, if he would be good enough to give me the name of that branch.

' "I'll do more," says the doctor. "I'll get you the name of the branch he's been promoted to, for I think I heard they'd moved him up one already." And the next day he brought me the name of the township of Yea,[9] some fifty miles north of Melbourne; but, with the vagueness which characterized all his information, he was unable to say whether I should find my relative there or not.

' "He's a single man, and his initials are W.F.,"[10] said the doctor, who was certain enough of the immaterial points. "He left his old post several days ago, but it appears he's not due at the new one till the New Year. No doubt he'll go before then to take things over and settle in. You might find him up there and you might not. If I were you I should write."

' "That'll lose two days," said I, "and more if he isn't there," for I'd grown quite keen on this up-country manager, and I felt that if I could get at him while the holidays were still on, a little conviviality might help matters considerably.

' "Then," said the doctor, "I should get a quiet horse and ride. You needn't use that hand."

' "Can't I go by train?"[11]

' "You can and you can't. You would still have to ride. I suppose you're a horseman?"

' "Yes."

' "Then I should certainly ride all the way. It's a delightful road, through Whittlesea and over the Plenty Ranges.[12] It'll give you some idea of the bush, Mr Raffles, and you'll see the sources of the water supply of this city, sir. You'll see where every drop of it comes from, the pure Yan Yean![13] I wish I had time to ride with you."

' "But where can I get a horse?"

'The doctor thought a moment.

' "I've a mare of my own that's as fat as butter for want of work," said he. "It would be a charity to me to sit on her back for a hundred miles or so, and then I should know you'd have no temptation to use that hand."

' "You're far too good!" I protested.

' "You're A. J. Raffles," he said.

'And if ever there was a prettier compliment, or a finer instance of even Colonial hospitality, I can only say, Bunny, that I never heard of either.'

He sipped his whisky, threw away the stump of his cigarette, and lit another before continuing.

'Well, I managed to write a line to W. F. with my own hand, which, as you will gather, was not very badly wounded; it was simply this third finger that was split and in splints; and next morning the doctor packed me off on a bovine beast[14] that would have done for an ambulance. Half the team came up to see me start; the rest were rather sick with me for not stopping to see the match out, as if I could help them to win by watching them. They little knew the game I'd got on myself, but still less did I know the game I was going to play.

'It was an interesting ride enough, especially after passing the place called Whittlesea, a real wild township on the lower slope of the ranges, where I recollect having a deadly meal of hot mutton and tea, with the thermometer at three figures in the shade. The first thirty miles or so was a good metal road, too good to go half round the world to ride on, but after Whittlesea it was a mere track over the ranges, a track I often couldn't see and left entirely to the mare. Now it dipped into a gully and ran through a creek,[15] and all the time the local colour was inches thick: gum-trees galore and parrots all colours of the rainbow. In one place a whole forest of gums had been ring-barked,[16] and were just as though they had been painted white, without a leaf or a living thing for miles. And the first living thing I did meet was the sort to give you the creeps; it was a riderless horse coming full tilt through the bush, with the saddle twisted round and the stirrup-irons ringing. Without thinking, I had a shot at heading him with the doctor's mare, and blocked him just enough to allow a man who came galloping after to do the rest.

' "Thank ye, mister," growled the man, a huge chap in a red checked shirt, with a beard like W. G. Grace,[17] but the very devil of an expression.

' "Been an accident?" said I, reining up.

' "Yes," said he, scowling as though he defied me to ask any more.

' "And a nasty one," I said, "if that's blood on the saddle!"

'Well, Bunny, I may be a blackguard myself, but I don't think I ever looked at a fellow as that chap looked at me. But I stared him out, and forced him to admit that it was blood on the twisted saddle, and after that he became quite tame. He told me exactly what had happened. A mate of his had been dragged under a branch, and had his nose smashed, but that was all; had sat tight after it till he dropped from loss of blood; another mate was with him back in the bush.

'As I've said already, Bunny, I wasn't the old stager that I am now – in any respect – and we parted good enough friends. He asked me which way I was going, and, when I told him, he said I should save seven miles, and get a good hour earlier to Yea, by striking off the track and making for a peak that we could see through the trees, and following a creek that I should see from the peak. Don't smile, Bunny! I began by saying I was a child in those days. Of course, the short cut was the long way round; and it was nearly dark when that unlucky mare and I saw the single street of Yea.

'I was looking for the bank when a fellow in a white suit ran down from a verandah.

' "Mr Raffles?" said he.

' "Mr Raffles!" said I, laughing as I shook his hand.

' "You're late."

' "I was misdirected."

' "That all? I'm relieved," he said. "Do you know what they are saying? There are some brand-new bushrangers on the road between Whittlesea and this – a second Kelly gang![18] They'd have caught a Tartar in you,[19] eh?"

' "They would in you," I retorted, and my *tu quoque*[20] shut him up and seemed to puzzle him. Yet there was much more sense in it than in his compliment to me, which was absolutely pointless.

' "I'm afraid you'll find things pretty rough," he resumed, when he had unstrapped my valise, and handed my reins to his man. "It's lucky you're a bachelor like myself."

'I could not quite see the point of this remark either, since, had I been married, I should hardly have sprung my wife upon him in this free-and-easy fashion. I muttered the conventional sort of thing, and then he said I should find it all right when I settled, as though I had come to graze upon him for weeks! "Well," thought I, "these Colonials do take the cake[21] for hospitality!" And, still marvelling, I let him lead me into the private part of the bank.

' "Dinner will be ready in a quarter of an hour," said he as we entered. "I thought you might like a tub first, and you'll find all ready in the room at the end of the passage. Sing out if there's anything you want. Your luggage hasn't turned up yet, by the way, but here's a letter that came this morning."

' "Not for me?"

' "Yes; didn't you expect one?"

' "I certainly did not!"

' "Well, here it is."

'And, as he lit me to my room, I read my own superscription of the previous day – to W. F. Raffles!

*

'Bunny, you've had your wind bagged at footer,[22] I daresay; you know what that's like? All I can say is that my moral wind was bagged by that letter as I hope, old chap, I have never yet bagged yours. I couldn't speak. I could only stand with my own letter in my hands until he had the good taste to leave me by myself.

'W. F. Raffles! We had mistaken *each other* for W. F. Raffles – for the new manager who had not yet arrived! Small wonder we had conversed at cross-purposes; the only wonder was that we had not discovered our mutual mistake. How the other man would have laughed! But I – I could not laugh. By Jove, no, it was no laughing matter for me! I saw the whole thing in a flash, without a tremor, but with the direst depression from my own single point of view. Call it callous if you like, Bunny, but remember that I was in much the same hole as you've since been in yourself, and that I had counted on this W. F. Raffles even as you counted on A. J. I thought of the man with the W. G. beard – the riderless horse with the bloody saddle – the deliberate misdirection that had put me off the track and out of the way – and now the missing manager and the report of bushrangers at this end. But I simply don't pretend to have felt any personal pity for a man whom I had never seen; that kind of pity's usually cant; and besides, all mine was needed for myself.

'I was in as big a hole as ever. What the devil was I to do? I doubt if I have sufficiently impressed upon you the absolute necessity of my returning to Melbourne in funds. As a matter of fact it was less the necessity than my own determination which I can truthfully describe as absolute.

'Money I would have – but how – but how? Would this stranger be open to persuasion – if I told him the truth? No; that would set us all scouring the country for the rest of the night. Why should I tell him? Suppose I left him to find out his mistake . . . would anything be gained? Bunny, I give you my word that I went in to dinner without a definite intention in my head, or one premeditated lie upon my lips. I might do the decent natural thing, and explain matters without loss of time; on the other hand, there was no hurry. I had not opened the letter, and could always pretend I had not noticed the initials;

meanwhile something might turn up. I could wait a little and see. Tempted I already was, but as yet the temptation was vague, and its very vagueness made me tremble.

' "Bad news, I'm afraid?" said the manager, when at last I sat down at his table.

' "A mere annoyance," I answered – I do assure you – on the spur of the moment and nothing else. But my lie was told; my position was taken; from that moment onward there was no retreat. By implication, without realizing what I was doing, I had already declared myself W. F. Raffles. Therefore, W. F. Raffles I would be, in that bank, for that night. And the devil teach me how to use my lie!'

Again he raised his glass to his lips – I had forgotten mine. His cigarette-case caught the gaslight as he handed it to me. I shook my head without taking my eyes from his.

'The devil played up,' continued Raffles, with a laugh. 'Before I tasted my soup I had decided what to do. I had determined to rob that bank instead of going to bed, and to be back in Melbourne for breakfast if the doctor's mare could do it. I would tell the old fellow that I had missed my way and been bushed for hours, as I easily might have been, and had never got to Yea at all. At Yea, on the other hand, the personation and robbery would ever after be attributed to a member of the gang that had waylaid and murdered the new manager with that very object. You are acquiring some experience in such matters, Bunny. I ask you, was there ever a better get-out? Last night's was something like it, only never such a certainty. And I saw it from the beginning – saw to the end before I had finished my soup!

'To increase my chances, the cashier, who also lived in the bank, was away over the holidays, had actually gone down to Melbourne to see us play; and the man who had taken my horse also waited at table; for he and his wife were the only servants, and they slept in a separate building. You may depend I ascertained this before we had finished dinner. Indeed I was by way of asking too many questions (the most oblique and delicate was that which elicited my host's name, Ewbank),[23] nor was I careful enough to conceal their drift.

'"Do you know," said this fellow Ewbank, who was one of the downright sort, "if it wasn't you, I should say you were in a funk of robbers?[24] Have you lost your nerve?"

'"I hope not," said I, turning jolly hot, I can tell you; "but – well, it's not a pleasant thing to have to put a bullet through a fellow!"

'"No?" said he, coolly. "I should enjoy nothing better, myself; besides, yours didn't go through."

'"I wish it had!" I was smart enough to cry.

'"Amen!" said he.

'And I emptied my glass; actually I did not know whether my wounded bank-robber was in prison, dead, or at large!

'But, now that I had had more than enough of it, Ewbank would come back to the subject. He admitted that the staff was small; but as for himself, he had a loaded revolver under his pillow all night, under the counter all day, and he was only waiting for his chance.

'"Under the counter, eh?" I was ass enough to say.

'"Yes; so had you!"

'He was looking at me in surprise, and something told me that to say "of course – I had forgotten!" would have been quite fatal, considering what I was supposed to have done. So I looked down my nose and shook my head.

'"But the papers said you had!" he cried.

'"Not under the counter," said I.

'"But it's the regulation!"

'For the moment, Bunny, I felt stumped, though I trust I only looked more superior than before, and I think I justified my look.

'"The regulation!" I said at length, in the most offensive tone at my command. "Yes, the regulation would have us all dead men! My dear sir, do you expect your bank-robber to let you reach for your gun in the place where he knows it's kept? I had mine in my pocket, and I got my chance by retreating from the counter with all visible reluctance."

'Ewbank stared at me with open eyes and a five-barred forehead,[25] then down came his fist on the table.

'"By God that was smart! Still," he added, like a man who

would not be in the wrong, "the papers said the other thing, you know!"

' "Of course," I rejoined, "because they said what I told them. You wouldn't have had me advertise the fact that I improved upon the bank's regulations, would you?"

'So that cloud rolled over, and by Jove it was a cloud with a golden lining! Not silver – real good Australian gold! For old Ewbank hadn't quite appreciated me till then; he was a hard nut, a much older man than myself, and I felt pretty sure he thought me young for the place, and my supposed feat a fluke. But I never saw a man change his mind more openly. He got out his best brandy, he made me throw away the cigar I was smoking, and opened a fresh box. He was a convivial-looking party, with a red moustache, and a very humorous face (not unlike Tom Emmett's),[26] and from that moment I laid myself out to attack him on his convivial flank. But he wasn't a Rosenthall, Bunny; he had a treble-seamed, hand-sewn head,[27] and could have drunk me under the table ten times over.

' "All right," I thought, "you may go to bed sober, but you'll sleep like a timber-yard!"[28] And I threw half he gave me through the open window, when he wasn't looking.

'But he was a good chap, Ewbank, and don't you imagine he was at all intemperate. Convivial I called him, and I only wish he had been something more. He did, however, become more and more genial as the evening advanced, and I had not much difficulty in getting him to show me round the bank at what was really an unearthly hour for such a proceeding. It was when he went to fetch the revolver before turning in. I kept him out of his bed another twenty minutes, and I knew every inch of the business premises before I shook hands with Ewbank in my room.

'You won't guess what I did with myself for the next hour. I undressed and went to bed. The incessant strain involved in even the most deliberate impersonation is the most wearing thing I know; then how much more so when the impersonation is impromptu! There's no getting your eye in; the next word may bowl you out; it's batting in a bad light all through. I haven't told you of half the tight places I was in during a

conversation that ran into hours and became dangerously intimate towards the end. You can imagine them for yourself, and
then picture me spread out on my bed, getting my second wind
for the big deed of the night.

'Once more I was in luck, for I had not been lying there long
before I heard my dear Ewbank snoring like a harmonium, and
the music never ceased for a moment; it was as loud as ever
when I crept out and closed my door behind me, as regular as
ever when I stopped to listen at his. And I have still to hear the
concert that I shall enjoy much more. The good fellow snored
me out of the bank, and was still snoring when I again stood
and listened under his open window.

'Why did I leave the bank first? To catch and saddle the mare
and tether her in a clump of trees close by: to have the means of
escape nice and handy before I went to work. I have often
wondered at the instinctive wisdom of the precaution; unconsci-
ously I was acting on what has been one of my guiding principles
ever since. Pains and patience were required: I had to get my
saddle without waking the man, and I was not used to catching
horses in a horse-paddock. Then I distrusted the poor mare, and
I went back to the stables for a hatful of oats, which I left with
her in the clump, hat and all. There was a dog, too, to reckon
with (our very worst enemy, Bunny); but I had been 'cute enough
to make immense friends with him during the evening; and he
wagged his tail, not only when I came downstairs, but when I
reappeared at the back-door.

'As the *soi-disant* new manager, I had been able, in the most
ordinary course, to pump poor Ewbank about anything and
everything connected with the working of the bank, especially
in those twenty last invaluable minutes before turning in. And I
had made a very natural point of asking him where he kept, and
would recommend me to keep, the keys at night. Of course I
thought he would take them with him to his room; but no such
thing; he had a dodge worth two of that. What it was doesn't
much matter, but no outsider would have found those keys in a
month of Sundays.

'I, of course, had them in a few seconds, and in a few more I
was in the strong-room itself. I forgot to say that the moon had

risen and was letting quite a lot of light into the bank. I had, however, brought a bit of candle with me from my room; and in the strong-room, which was down some narrow stairs behind the counter in the banking chamber, I had no hesitation in lighting it. There was no window down there, and, though I could no longer hear old Ewbank snoring, I had not the slightest reason to anticipate disturbance from that quarter. I did think of locking myself in while I was at work, but, thank goodness, the iron door had no key-hole on the inside.

'Well, there was heaps of gold in the safe, but I only took what I needed and could comfortably carry, not much more than a couple of hundred altogether. Not a note would I touch, and my native caution came out also in the way I divided the sovereigns between all my pockets, and packed them up so that I shouldn't be like the old woman of Banbury Cross.[29] Well, you think me too cautious still, but I was insanely cautious then. And so it was that, just as I was ready to go, whereas I might have been gone ten minutes, there came a violent knocking at the outer door.

'Bunny, it was the outer door of the banking chamber! My candle must have been seen! And there I stood, with the grease running hot over my fingers, in that brick grave of a strong-room!

'There was only one thing to be done. I must trust to the sound sleeping of Ewbank upstairs, open the door myself, knock the visitor down, or shoot him with the revolver I had been new chum[30] enough to buy before leaving Melbourne, and make a dash for that clump of trees and the doctor's mare. My mind was made up in an instant, and I was at the top of the strong-room stairs, the knocking still continuing, when a second sound drove me back. It was the sound of bare feet coming along a corridor.

'My narrow stair was stone, I tumbled down it with little noise, and had only to push open the iron door, for I had left the keys in the safe. As I did so I heard a handle turn overhead, and thanked my gods that I had shut every single door behind me. You see, old chap, one's caution doesn't always let one in!

' "Who's that knocking?" said Ewbank up above.

'I could not make out the answer, but it sounded to me like the irrelevant supplication of a spent man. What I did hear, plainly, was the cocking of the bank revolver before the bolts were shot back. Then, a tottering step, a hard, short, shallow breathing, and Ewbank's voice in horror –

' "Good Lord! What's happened to you? You're bleeding like a pig!"

' "Not now," came with a grateful sort of sigh.

' "But you have been! What's done it?"

' "Bushrangers."

' "Down the road?"

' "This and Whittlesea – tied to tree – cock shots[31] – left me – bleed to death . . ."

'The weak voice failed, and the bare feet bolted. Now was my time – if the poor devil had fainted. But I could not be sure, and there I crouched down below in the dark, at the half-shut iron door, not less spellbound than imprisoned. It was just as well, for Ewbank wasn't gone a minute.

' "Drink this," I heard him say, and, when the other spoke again, his voice was stronger.

' "Now I begin to feel alive . . ."

' "Don't talk!"

' "It does me good. You don't know what it was, all those miles alone, one an hour at the outside! I never thought I should come through. You must let me tell you – in case I don't!"

' "Well, have another sip."

' "Thank you . . . I said bushrangers; of course, there are no such things nowadays."[32]

' "What were they, then?"

' "Bank-thieves; the one that had the pot shots was the very brute I drove out of the bank at Coburg,[33] with a bullet in him!" '

'I knew it!'

'Of course you did, Bunny; so did I, down in that strong-room; but old Ewbank didn't, and I thought he was never going to speak again.

' "You're delirious," he says at last. "Who in blazes do you think you are?"

' "The new manager."

' "The new manager's in bed and asleep upstairs!"

' "When did he arrive?"

' "This evening."

' "Call himself Raffles?"

' "Yes."

' "Well, I'm damned!" whispered the real man. "I thought it was just revenge, but now I see what it was. My dear sir, the man upstairs is an impostor – if he's upstairs still! He must be one of the gang. He's going to rob the bank – if he hasn't done so already!"

' "If he hasn't done so already," muttered Ewbank after him; "if he's upstairs still! By God, if he is I'm sorry for him!"

'His tone was quiet enough, but about the nastiest I ever heard. I tell you, Bunny, I was glad I'd brought that revolver. It looked as though it must be mine against his, muzzle to muzzle.

' "Better have a look down here, first," said the new manager.

' "While he gets through his window? No no, he's not down here."

' "It's easy to have a look."

'Bunny, if you ask me what was the most thrilling moment of my infamous career, I say it was that moment. There I stood at the bottom of those narrow stone stairs, inside the strong-room, with the door a good foot open, and I didn't know whether it would creak or not. The light was coming nearer – and I didn't know! I had to chance it. And it didn't creak a bit; it was far too solid and well-hung; and I couldn't have banged it if I'd tried, it was too heavy; and it fitted so close that I felt and heard the air squeeze out in my face. Every shred of light went out, except the streak underneath, and it brightened. How I blessed that door!

' "No, he's not down *there*," I heard as though through cotton-wool; then the streak went out too, and in a few seconds I ventured to open once more, and was in time to hear them creeping to my room.

'Well, now there was not a fifth of a second to be lost; but I'm proud to say I came up those stairs on my toes and fingers, and out of that bank (they'd gone and left the door open) just as gingerly as though my time had been my own. I didn't even

forget to put on the hat that the doctor's mare was eating her
oats out of, as well as she could with a bit, or it alone would
have landed me. I didn't even gallop away, but just jogged off
quietly in the thick dust at the side of the road (though I own
my heart was galloping), and thanked my stars the bank was at
that end of the township, in which I really hadn't set foot. The
very last thing I heard was the two managers raising Cain and
the coachman. And now, Bunny –'

He stood up and stretched himself, with a smile that ended in
a yawn. The black windows had faded through every shade of
indigo; they now framed their opposite neighbours, stark and
livid in the dawn; and the gas seemed turned to nothing in the
globes.

'But that's not all?' I cried.

'I'm sorry to say it is,' said Raffles apologetically. 'The thing
should have ended with an exciting chase, I know, but somehow
it didn't. I suppose they thought I had got no end of a start; then
they had made up their minds that I belonged to the gang, which
was not so many miles away; and one of them had got as much
as he could carry from that gang as it was. But I wasn't to know
all that, and I'm bound to say that there was plenty of excitement
left for me. Lord, how I made that poor brute travel when I got
among the trees! Though we must have made it well over fifty
miles from Melbourne, we had done it at a snail's pace; and those
stolen oats had brisked the old girl up to such a pitch that she
fairly bolted when she felt her nose turned south. By Jove it was
no joke, in and out among those trees, and under branches with
your face in the mane! I told you about the forest of dead gums?
It looked perfectly ghostly in the moonlight. And I found it as still
as I had left it – so still that I pulled up there, my first halt, and lay
with my ear to the ground for two or three minutes. But I heard
nothing – not a thing but the mare's bellows and my own heart.
I'm sorry, Bunny; but if ever you write my memoirs, you won't
have any difficulty in working up that chase. Play those dead
gum-trees for all they're worth, and let the bullets fly like hail. I'll
turn round in my saddle to see Ewbank coming up hell-to-leather
in his white suit, and I'll duly paint it red. Do it in the third person,
and they won't know how it's going to end.'

'But I don't know myself,' I complained. 'Did the mare carry you all the way back to Melbourne?'

'Every rod, pole or perch![34] I had her well seen to at our hotel, and returned her to the doctor in the evening. He was tremendously tickled to hear I had been bushed;[35] next morning he brought me the paper to show me what I had escaped at Yea!'

'Without suspecting anything?'

'Ah!' said Raffles, as he put out the gas; 'that's a point on which I've never made up my mind. The mare and her colour was a coincidence – luckily she was only a bay – and I fancy the condition of the beast must have told a tale. The doctor's manner was certainly different. I'm inclined to think he suspected something, though not the right thing. I wasn't expecting him, and I fear my appearance may have increased his suspicions.'

I asked him why.

'I used to have rather a heavy moustache,' said Raffles, 'but I lost it the day after I lost my innocence.'

WILFUL MURDER

Of the various robberies in which we were both concerned, it is but the few, I find, that will bear telling at any length. Not that the others contained details which even I would hesitate to recount; it is, rather, the very absence of untoward incident which renders them useless for my present purpose. In point of fact our plans were so craftily laid (by Raffles) that the chances of a hitch were invariably reduced to a minimum before we went to work. We might be disappointed in the market value of our haul; but it was quite the exception for us to find ourselves confronted by unforeseen impediments, or involved in a really dramatic dilemma. There was a sameness even in our spoil; for, of course, only the most precious stones are worth the trouble we took and the risks we ran. In short, our most successful escapades would prove the greatest weariness of all in narrative form; and none more so than the dull affair of the Ardagh emeralds,[1] some eight or nine weeks after the Milchester cricket week. The former, however, had a sequel that I would rather forget than all our burglaries put together.

It was the evening after our return from Ireland, and I was waiting at my rooms for Raffles, who had gone off as usual to dispose of the plunder. Raffles had his own method of conducting this very vital branch of our business, which I was well content to leave entirely in his hands. He drove the bargains, I believe, in a thin but subtle disguise of the flashy-seedy order, and always in the Cockney dialect of which he had made himself a master. Moreover, he invariably employed the same 'fence', who was ostensibly a money-lender in a small (but yet notorious) way, and in reality a rascal as remarkable as Raffles himself.

Only lately I also had been to the man, but in my proper person. We had needed capital for the getting of these very emeralds, and I had raised a hundred pounds, on the terms you would expect, from a soft-spoken greybeard with an ingratiating smile, an incessant bow, and the shiftiest old eyes that ever flew from rim to rim of a pair of spectacles. So the original sinews and the final spoils of war[2] came in this case from the self-same source – a circumstance which appealed to us both.

But these same final spoils I was still to see, and I waited and waited with an impatience that grew upon me with the growing dusk. At my open window I had played Sister Ann[3] until the faces in the street below were no longer distinguishable. And now I was tearing to and fro in the grip of horrible hypotheses – a grip that tightened when at last the lift-gates opened with a clatter outside – that held me breathless until a well-known tattoo[4] followed on my door.

'In the dark!' said Raffles as I dragged him in. 'Why, Bunny, what's wrong?'

'Nothing – now you've come,' said I, shutting the door behind him in a fever of relief and anxiety. 'Well? Well? What did they fetch?'

'Five hundred.'

'Down?'

'Got it in my pocket.'

'Good man!' I cried. 'You don't know what a stew I've been in. I'll switch on the light. I've been thinking of you and nothing else for the last hour. I – I was ass enough to think something had gone wrong!'

Raffles was smiling when the white light filled the room, but for the moment I did not perceive the peculiarity of his smile. I was fatuously full of my own late tremors and present relief; and my first idiotic act was to spill some whisky and squirt the soda-water all over in my anxiety to do instant justice to the occasion.

'So you thought something had happened?' said Raffles, leaning back in my chair as he lit a cigarette, and looking much amused. 'What should you say if something had? Sit tight, my dear chap! It was nothing of the slightest consequence, and it's all over now. A stern chase and a long one,[5] Bunny, but I think I'm well to windward this time.'

And suddenly I saw that his collar was limp, his hair matted, his boots thick with dust.

'The police?' I whispered aghast.

'Oh dear, no; only old Baird.'[6]

'Baird! But wasn't it Baird who took the emeralds?'

'It was.'

'Then how came he to chase you?'

'My dear fellow, I'll tell you if you give me a chance; it's really nothing to get in the least excited about. Old Baird has at last spotted that I'm not quite the common cracksman I would have him think me. So he's been doing his best to run me to my burrow.'

'And you call that nothing!'

'It would be something if he had succeeded; but he has still to do that. I admit, however, that he made me sit up for the time being. It all comes of going on the job so far from home. There was the old brute with the whole thing in his morning paper. He *knew* it must have been done by some fellow who could pass himself off for a gentleman, and I saw his eyebrows go up the moment I told him I was the man, with the same old twang that you could cut with a paper-knife.[7] I did my best to get out of it – swore I had a pal who was a real swell – but I saw very plainly that I had given myself away. He gave up haggling. He paid my price as though he enjoyed doing it. But I *felt* him following me when I made tracks; though, of course, I didn't turn round to see.'

'Why not?'

'My dear Bunny, it's the very worst thing you can do. As long as you look unsuspecting they'll keep their distance, and so long as they keep their distance you stand a chance. Once show that you know you're being followed, and it's flight or fight for all you're worth. I never even looked round; and mind you never do in the same hole. I just hurried up to Blackfriars and booked for High Street, Kensington, at the top of my voice; and as the train was leaving Sloane Square[8] out I hopped, and up all those stairs like a lamplighter,[9] and round to the studio by the back streets. Well, to be on the safe side, I lay low there all the afternoon, hearing nothing in the least suspicious, and only wishing I had a window to look through instead of that beastly skylight. However, the coast seemed clear enough, and thus far it was my mere idea that he would follow me; there was nothing to show he had. So at last I marched out in my proper rig – almost straight into old Baird's arms!'

'What on earth did you do?'

'Walked past him as though I had never set eyes on him in my life, and didn't then; took a hansom in the King's Road, and drove like the deuce to Clapham Junction; rushed on to the nearest platform, without a ticket, jumped into the first train I saw, got out at Twickenham, walked full tilt back to Richmond, took the District to Charing Cross,[10] and here I am! Ready for tub and a change, and the best dinner the club can give us. I came to you first, because I thought you might be getting anxious. Come round with me, and I won't keep you long.'

'You're certain you've given him the slip?' I said, as we put on our hats.

'Certain enough; but we can make assurance doubly sure,'[11] said Raffles, and went to my window, where he stood for a minute or two looking down into the street.

'All right?' I asked him.

'All right,' said he; and we went downstairs forthwith, and so to the Albany arm-in-arm.

But we were both rather silent on the way. I, for my part, was wondering what Raffles would do about the studio in Chelsea, whither, at all events, he had been successfully dogged. To me the point seemed one of immediate importance, but when I mentioned it he said there was time enough to think about that. His one other remark was made after we had nodded (in Bond Street) to a young blood[12] of our acquaintance who happened to be getting himself a bad name.

'Poor Jack Rutter!'[13] said Raffles, with a sigh. 'Nothing's sadder than to see a fellow going to the bad like that. He's about mad with drink and debt, poor devil; did you see his eye? Odd that we should have met him to-night, by the way; it's old Baird who's said to have skinned[14] him. I've a jolly good mind to skin old Baird!'

And his tone took a sudden low fury, made the more notice-able by another long silence, which lasted, indeed, throughout an admirable dinner at the club, and for some time after we had settled down in a quiet corner of the smoking-room with our coffee and cigars. Then at last I saw Raffles looking at me with his lazy smile, and I knew that the morose fit was at an end.

'I daresay you wonder what I've been thinking about all this time?' said he. 'I've been thinking what rot it is to go doing things by halves!'

'Well,' said I, returning his smile, 'that's not a charge that you can bring against yourself, is it?'

'I'm not so sure,' said Raffles, blowing a meditative puff; 'as a matter of fact, I was thinking less of myself than of that poor devil of a Jack Rutter. There's a fellow who does things by halves; he's only half gone to the bad; and look at the difference between him and us! He's under the thumb of a villainous money-lender; we are solvent citizens. He's taken to drink; we're as sober as we are solvent. His pals are beginning to cut him; our difficulty is to keep the pal from the door. *Enfin*, he begs or borrows, which is stealing by halves; and we steal outright and are done with it. Obviously ours is the more honest course. Yet I'm not sure, Bunny, but we're doing the thing by halves ourselves!'

'Why? What more could we do?' I exclaimed in soft derision, looking round, however, to make sure that we were not overheard.

'What more?' said Raffles. 'Well, murder – for one thing.'

'Rot!'

'A matter of opinion, my dear Bunny; I don't mean it for rot. I've told you before that the biggest man alive is the man who's committed a murder, and not yet been found out; at least he ought to be, but he so very seldom has the soul to appreciate himself. Just think of it! Think of coming in here and talking to the men, very likely about the murder itself; and knowing you've done it; and wondering how they'd look if *they* knew! Oh, it would be great, simply great! But, besides all that, when you were caught there'd be a merciful and dramatic end of you. You'd fill the bill[15] for a few weeks, and then snuff out with a flourish of extra-specials;[16] you wouldn't rust with a vile repose[17] for seven or fourteen years.'

'Good old Raffles!' I chuckled. 'I begin to forgive you for being in bad form at dinner.'

'But I was never more earnest in my life.'

'Go on!'

'I mean it.'

'You know very well that you wouldn't commit a murder, whatever else you might do.'

'I know very well I'm going to commit one to-night!'

He had been leaning back in the saddle-bag chair,[18] watching me with keen eyes sheathed by languid lids; now he started forward, and his eyes leapt to mine like cold steel from the scabbard. They struck home to my slow wits; their meaning was no longer in doubt. I, who knew the man, read murder in his clenched hands, and murder in his locked lips, but a hundred murders in those hard blue eyes.

'Baird?' I faltered, moistening my lips with my tongue.

'Of course.'

'But you said it didn't matter about the room in Chelsea?'

'I told a lie.'

'Anyway you gave him the slip afterwards!'

'That was another. I didn't. I thought I had when I came up to you this evening; but when I looked out of your window – you remember? to make assurance doubly sure – there he was on the opposite pavement down below.'

'And you never said a word about it!'

'I wasn't going to spoil your dinner, Bunny, and I wasn't going to let you spoil mine. But there he was as large as life, and, of course, he followed us to the Albany. A fine game for him to play, a game after his mean old heart: blackmail from me, bribes from the police, the one bidding against the other; but he shan't play it with me, he shan't live to, and the world will have an extortioner the less. Waiter! Two Scotch whiskies and sodas. I'm off at eleven, Bunny; it's the only thing to be done.'

'You know where he lives, then?'

'Yes, out Willesden[19] way, and alone; the fellow's a miser among other things. I long ago found out all about him.'

Again I looked round the room; it was a young man's club, and young men were laughing, chatting, smoking, drinking, on every hand. One nodded to me through the smoke. Like a machine I nodded to him, and turned back to Raffles with a groan.

'Surely you will give him a chance!' I urged. 'The very sight of your pistol should bring him to terms.'

'It wouldn't make him keep them.'

'But you might try the effect?'

'I probably shall. Here's a drink for you, Bunny. Wish me luck.'

'I'm coming too.'[20]

'I don't want you.'

'But I must come!'

An ugly gleam shot from the steel-blue eyes.

'To interfere?' said Raffles.

'Not I.'

'You give me your word?'

'I do.'

'Bunny, if you break it –'

'You may shoot me too!'

'I most certainly should,' said Raffles, solemnly. 'So you come at your own peril, my dear man; but, if you are coming – well, the sooner the better, for I must stop at my rooms on the way.'

Five minutes later I was waiting for him at the Piccadilly entrance to the Albany. I had a reason for remaining outside. It was the feeling – half hope, half fear – that Angus Baird might still be on our trail – that some more immediate and less cold-blooded way of dealing with him might result from a sudden encounter between the money-lender and myself. I would not warn him of his danger; but I would avert tragedy at all costs. And when no such encounter had taken place, and Raffles and I were fairly on our way to Willesden, that, I think, was still my honest resolve. I would not break my word if I could help it, but it was a comfort to feel that I could break it if I liked, on an understood penalty. Alas! I fear my good intentions were tainted with a devouring curiosity, and overlaid by the fascination which goes hand in hand with horror.

I have a poignant recollection of the hour it took us to reach the house. We walked across St James's Park (I can see the lights now, bright on the bridge[21] and blurred in the water), and we had some minutes to wait for the last train to Willesden. It left at 11.21, I remember, and Raffles was put out to find it did not go on to Kensal Rise. We had to get out at Willesden Junction[22] and walk on through the streets into fairly open country that happened to be quite new to me. I could never find the house again. I remember, however, that we were on a dark footpath between woods and fields when the clocks began striking twelve.

'Surely,' said I, 'we shall find him in bed and asleep?'

'I hope we do,' said Raffles grimly.

'Then you mean to break in?'

'What else did you think?'

I had not thought about it at all; the ultimate crime had monopolized my mind. Beside it burglary was a bagatelle, but one to deprecate none the less. I saw obvious objections: the man was *au fait* with cracksmen and their ways; he would certainly have firearms, and might be the first to use them.

'I could wish nothing better,' said Raffles. 'Then it will be man to man, and devil take the worst shot. You don't suppose I prefer foul play to fair, do you? But die he must, by one or the other, or it's a long stretch for you and me.'

'Better that than this!'

'Then stay where you are, my good fellow. I told you I didn't want you; and this is the house. So good-night.'

I could see no house at all, only the angle of a high wall rising solitary in the night, with the starlight glittering on battlements of broken glass; and in the wall a tall green gate, bristling with spikes, and showing a front for battering-rams in the feeble rays an outlying lamp-post cast across the new-made road. It seemed to me a road of building sites, with but this one house built, all by itself, at one end; but the night was too dark for more than a mere impression.

Raffles, however, had seen the place by daylight, and had come prepared for the special obstacles; already he was reaching up and putting champagne corks on the spikes,[23] and in another moment he had his folded covert-coat across the corks. I stepped back as he raised himself, and saw a little pyramid of slates[24] snip the sky above the gate; as he squirmed over I ran forward, and had my own weight on the spikes and corks and covert-coat when he gave the latter a tug.

'Coming after all?'

'Rather!'

'Take care, then; the place is all bell-wires and springs.[25] It's no soft thing, this! There – stand still while I take off the corks.'

The garden was very small and new, with a grass-plot still in separate sods, but a quantity of full-grown laurels stuck into the raw clay beds. 'Bells in themselves,' as Raffles whispered; 'there's nothing else rustles so – cunning old beast!' And we gave them a wide berth as we crept across the grass.

'He's gone to bed!'

'I don't think so, Bunny. I believe he's seen us.'

'Why?'

'I saw a light.'

'Where?'

'Downstairs, for an instant, when I –'

His whisper died away; he had seen the light again; and so had I.

It lay like a golden rod under the front-door – and vanished. It reappeared like a gold thread under the lintel – and vanished for good. We heard the stairs creak, creak, and cease, also for good. We neither saw nor heard any more, though we stood waiting on the grass till our feet were soaked with the dew.

'I'm going in,' said Raffles at last. 'I don't believe he saw us at all. I wish he had. This way.'

We trod gingerly on the path, but the gravel stuck to our wet soles, and grated horribly in a little tiled verandah with a glass door leading within. It was through this glass that Raffles had first seen the light; and he now proceeded to take out a pane, with the diamond, the pot of treacle, and the sheet of brown paper[26] which were seldom omitted from his impedimenta. Nor did he dispense with my own assistance, though he may have accepted it as instinctively as it was proffered. In any case it was these fingers that helped to spread the treacle on the brown paper, and pressed the latter to the glass until the diamond had completed its circuit and the pane fell gently back into our hands.

Raffles now inserted his hand, turned the key in the lock, and, by making a long arm, succeeded in drawing the bolt at the bottom of the door; it proved to be the only one, and the door opened, though not very wide.

'What's that?' said Raffles, as something crunched beneath his feet on the very threshold.

'A pair of spectacles,' I whispered, picking them up. I was still fingering the broken lenses and the bent rims when Raffles tripped and almost fell, with a gasping cry that he made no effort to restrain.

'Hush, man, hush!' I entreated under my breath. 'He'll hear you!'

For answer his teeth chattered – even his – and I heard him fumbling with his matches . . .

'No, Bunny; he won't hear us,' whispered Raffles, presently; and he rose from his knees and lit a gas as the match burnt down.

Angus Baird was lying on his own floor, dead, with his grey hairs glued together by his blood; near him a poker with the black end glistening; in a corner his desk, ransacked, littered. A clock ticked noisily on the chimney-piece; for perhaps a hundred seconds there was no other sound.

Raffles stood very still, staring down at the dead, as a man might stare into an abyss after striding blindly to its brink. His breath came audibly through wide nostrils; he made no other sign, and his lips seemed sealed.

'That light!' said I, hoarsely; 'the light we saw under the door!'

With a start he turned to me.

'It's true! I had forgotten it. It was in here I saw it first!'

'He must be upstairs still!'

'If he is we'll soon rout him out. Come on!'

Instead I laid a hand upon his arm, imploring him to reflect – that his enemy was dead now – that we should certainly be involved – that now or never was our own time to escape. He shook me off in a sudden fury of impatience, a reckless contempt in his eyes, and, bidding me save my own skin if I liked, he once more turned his back upon me, and this time left me half resolved to take him at his word. Had he forgotten on what errand he himself was here? Was he determined that this night should end in black disaster? As I asked myself these questions his match flared in the hall; in another moment the stairs were creaking under his feet, even as they had creaked under those of the murderer; and the humane instinct that inspired him in defiance of his risk was borne in also upon my slower sensibilities. Could we let the murderer go? My answer was to bound up the creaking stairs and to overhaul Raffles on the landing.

But three doors presented themselves; the first opened into a bedroom with the bed turned down but undisturbed; the second room was empty in every sense; the third door was locked.

Raffles lit the landing gas.

'He's in there,' said he, cocking his revolver. 'Do you remember how we used to break into the studies at school?[27] Here goes!'

His flat foot crashed over the keyhole, the lock gave, the door flew open, and in the sudden draught the landing gas heeled over like a cobble in a squall;[28] as the flame righted itself I saw a fixed bath, two bath-towels knotted together – an open window – a cowering figure – and Raffles struck aghast on the threshold.

'*Jack – Rutter?*'

The words came thick and slow with horror, and in horror I heard myself repeating them, while the cowering figure by the bathroom window rose gradually erect.

'It's you!' he whispered, in amazement no less than our own; 'it's you two! What's it mean, Raffles? I saw you get over the gate; a bell rang, the place is full of them. Then you broke in. What's it all mean?'

'We may tell you that, when you tell us what in God's name you've done, Rutter!'

'Done? What have I done?' The unhappy wretch came out into the light with bloodshot, blinking eyes, and a bloody shirt-front. 'You know – you've seen – but I'll tell you if you like. I've killed a robber; that's all. I've killed a robber, a usurer, a jackal, a blackmailer, the cleverest and the cruellest villain unhung. I'm ready to hang for him. I'd kill him again!'

And he looked us fiercely in the face, a fine defiance in his dissipated eyes; his breast heaving, his jaw like a rock.

'Shall I tell you how it happened?' he went passionately on. 'He's made my life a hell these weeks and months past. You may know that. A perfect hell! Well, to-night I met him in Bond Street. Do you remember when I met you fellows? He wasn't twenty yards behind you; he was on your tracks, Raffles; he saw me nod to you, and stopped me and asked me who you were. He seemed as keen as knives to know, I couldn't think why, and didn't care either, for I saw my chance. I said I'd tell him all about you if he'd give me a private interview. He said he wouldn't. I said he should, and held him by the coat; by the time I let him go you were out of sight, and I waited where I was till he came back in despair. I had the whip-hand of him then. I could dictate where the interview should be, and I made him take me home with him, still swearing to tell him all about you when we'd had our talk. Well, when we got here I made him give me something to eat, putting him off and off; and about ten o'clock I heard the gate shut. I waited a bit, and then asked him if he lived alone.

'"Not at all," says he; "did you not see the servant?"

'I said I'd seen her, but I thought I'd heard her go; if I was mistaken no doubt she would come when she was called; and I yelled three times at the top of my voice. Of course there was no servant to come. I knew that, because I came to see him one night last week, and he interviewed me himself through the gate, but wouldn't open it. Well, when I had done yelling, and not a soul had come near us he was as white as that ceiling. Then I told him we could have our chat at last; and I picked the poker out of the fender, and told him how he'd robbed me, but by God he shouldn't rob me any more. I gave him three minutes to write and sign a settlement of all his iniquitous claims against me, or have his brains beaten out over his own carpet. He thought a minute, and then went to his desk for pen and paper. In two seconds he was round like lightning with a revolver, and I went for him bald-headed.[29] He fired two or three times and missed; you can find the holes if you like; but I hit him every time – my God! I was like a savage till the thing was done. And then I didn't care. I went through his desk looking for my own bills, and was coming away when you turned up. I said I didn't care, nor do I; but I was going to give myself up to-night, and shall still; so you see I shan't give you fellows much trouble!'

He was done; and there we stood on the landing of the lonely house, the low, thick, eager voice still racing and ringing through our ears; the dead man below, and in front of us his impenitent slayer. I knew to whom the impenitence would appeal when he had heard the story, and I was not mistaken.

'That's all rot,' said Raffles, speaking after a pause; 'we shan't let you give yourself up.'

'You shan't stop me! What would be the good? The woman saw me; it would only be a question of time; and I can't face waiting to be taken. Think of it: waiting for them to touch you on the shoulder! No, no, no; I'll give myself up and get it over.'

His speech was changed; he faltered, floundered. It was as though a clearer perception of his position had come with the bare idea of escape from it.

'But listen to me,' urged Raffles; 'we're here at our peril ourselves. We broke in like thieves to enforce redress for a grievance very like your own. But don't you see? We took out a pane – did the thing like regular burglars. We shall get the credit of all the rest!'

'You mean that I shan't be suspected?'

'I do.'

'But I don't want to get off scot-free,' cried Rutter hysterically. 'I've killed him. I know that. But it was in self-defence; it wasn't murder. I must own up and take the consequences. I shall go mad if I don't!'

His hands twitched; his lips quivered; the tears were in his eyes. Raffles took him roughly by the shoulder.

'Look here, you fool! If the three of us were caught here now, do you know what those consequences would be? We should swing in a row at Newgate[30] in six weeks' time! You talk as though we were sitting in a club; don't you know it's one o'clock in the morning, and the lights on, and a dead man down below? For God's sake pull yourself together, and do what I tell you, or you're a dead man yourself.'

'I wish I was one!' Rutter sobbed. 'I wish I had his revolver,

I'd blow my own brains out. It's somewhere under him! O my God, my God!'

His knees knocked together: the frenzy of reaction was at its height. We had to take him downstairs between us, and so through the front door out into the open air.

All was still outside – all but the smothered weeping of the unstrung wretch upon our hands. Raffles returned for a moment to the house; then all was dark as well. The gate opened from within; we closed it carefully behind us; and so left the starlight shining on broken glass and polished spikes, one and all as we had found them.

We escaped; no need to dwell on our escape. Our murderer seemed set upon the scaffold: drunk with his deed, he was more trouble than six men drunk with wine.[31] Again and again we threatened to leave him to his fate, to wash our hands of him. But incredible and unmerited luck was with the three of us. Not a soul did we meet between that and Willesden; and of those who saw us later, did one think of the two young men with crooked white ties, supporting a third in a seemingly unmistakable condition, when the evening papers apprised the town of a terrible tragedy at Kensal Rise?

We walked to Maida Vale,[32] and thence drove openly to my rooms. But I alone went upstairs; the other two proceeded to the Albany, and I saw no more of Raffles for forty-eight hours. He was not at his rooms when I called in the morning; he had left no word. When he reappeared the papers were full of the murder; and the man who had committed it was on the wide Atlantic, a steerage passenger from Liverpool to New York.[33]

'There was no arguing with him,' so Raffles told me; 'either he must make a clean breast of it or flee the country. So I rigged him up at the studio, and we took the first train to Liverpool. Nothing would induce him to sit tight and enjoy the situation as I should have endeavoured to do in his place; and it's just as well! I went to his diggings[34] to destroy some papers, and what do you think I found? The police in possession; there's a warrant out against him already! The idiots think that window wasn't genuine, and the warrant's out. It won't be my fault if it's ever served!'

Nor, after all these years, can I think it will be mine.

NINE POINTS OF THE LAW

'Well,' said Raffles, 'what do you make of it?'

I read the advertisement once more before replying. It was in the last column of the *Daily Telegraph*,[1] and it ran:–

TWO THOUSAND POUNDS REWARD. – The above sum may be earned by any one qualified to undertake delicate mission and prepared to run certain risk. – Apply by telegram, Security, London.

'I think,' said I, 'it's the most extraordinary advertisement that ever got into print!'

Raffles smiled.

'Not quite all that, Bunny; still, extraordinary enough, I grant you.'

'Look at the figure!'

'It is certainly large.'

'And the mission – and the risk!'

'Yes; the combination is frank, to say the least of it. But the really original point is requiring applications by telegram to a telegraphic address![2] There's something in the fellow who thought of that, and something in his game; with one word he chokes off the million who answer an advertisement every day – when they can raise the stamp. My answer cost me five bob;[3] but then I prepaid another.'

'You don't mean to say that you've applied?'

'Rather,' said Raffles. 'I want two thousand pounds as much as any man.'

'Put your own name?'

'Well – no, Bunny, I didn't. In point of fact, I smell something interesting and illegal, and you know what a cautious chap I am. I signed myself Glasspool,[4] care of Hickey, 38, Conduit Street; that's my tailor,[5] and after sending the wire I went round and told him what to expect. He promised to send the reply along the moment it came. I shouldn't be surprised if that's it!'

And he was gone before a double-knock on the outer door had done ringing through the rooms, to return next minute with an open telegram and a face full of news.

'What do you think?' said he. 'Security's that fellow Addenbrooke,[6] the police-court lawyer, and he wants to see me *instanter*!'[7]

'Do you know him, then?'

'Merely by repute. I only hope he doesn't know me. He's the chap who got six weeks for sailing too close to the wind in the Sutton-Wilmer case; everybody wondered why he wasn't struck off the rolls.[8] Instead of that he's got a first-rate practice on the seamy side, and every blackguard with half a case takes it straight to Bennett Addenbrooke. He's probably the one man who would have the cheek to put in an advertisement like that, and the one man who could do it without exciting suspicion. It's simply in his line; but you may be sure there's something shady at the bottom of it. The odd thing is that I have long made up my mind to go to Addenbrooke myself if accidents should happen.'

'And you're going to him now?'

'This minute,' said Raffles, brushing his hat; 'and so are you.'

'But I came in to drag you out to lunch.'

'You shall lunch with me when we've seen this fellow. Come on, Bunny, and we'll choose your name on the way. Mine's Glasspool, and don't you forget it.'

Mr Bennett Addenbrooke occupied substantial offices in Wellington Street, Strand, and was out when we arrived; but he had only just gone 'over the way to the court';[9] and five minutes sufficed to produce a brisk, fresh-coloured, resolute-looking man, with a very confident, rather festive air, and black eyes that opened wide at the sight of Raffles.

'Mr – Glasspool?' exclaimed the lawyer.

'My name,' said Raffles, with dry effrontery.

'Not up at Lord's, however!' said the other, slyly. 'My dear sir, I have seen you take far too many wickets to make any mistake!'

For a single moment Raffles looked venomous; then he shrugged and smiled, and the smile grew into a little cynical chuckle.

'So you have bowled me out in my turn?' said he. 'Well, I don't think there's anything to explain. I am harder up than I wished to admit under my own name, that's all, and I want that thousand pounds reward.'

'Two thousand,' said the solicitor. 'And the man who is not above an alias happens to be just the sort of man I want; so don't let that worry you, my dear sir. The matter, however, is of a strictly private and confidential character.' And he looked very hard at me.

'Quite so,' said Raffles. 'But there was something about a risk?'

'A certain risk is involved.'

'Then surely three heads will be better than two. I said I wanted that thousand pounds; my friend here wants the other. We are both cursedly hard up, and we go into this thing together or not at all. Must you have his name too? I should give him my real one, Bunny.'

Mr Addenbrooke raised his eyebrows over the card I found for him; then he drummed upon it with his finger-nail, and his embarrassment expressed itself in a puzzled smile.

'The fact is, I find myself in a difficulty,' he confessed at last. 'Yours is the first reply I have received; people who can afford to send long telegrams don't rush to the advertisements in the *Daily Telegraph*; but, on the other hand, I was not quite prepared to hear from men like yourselves. Candidly, and on consideration, I am not sure that you *are* the stamp of men for me – men who belong to good clubs! I rather intended to appeal to the – er – adventurous classes.'

'We are adventurers,' said Raffles gravely.

'But you respect the law?'

The black eyes gleamed shrewdly.

'We are not professional rogues, if that's what you mean,'

said Raffles, smiling. 'But on our beam-ends[10] we are; we would do a good deal for a thousand pounds apiece, eh, Bunny?'

'Anything,' I murmured.

The solicitor rapped his desk.

'I'll tell you what I want you to do. You can but refuse. It's illegal, but it's illegality in a good cause; that's the risk, and my client is prepared to pay for it. He will pay for the attempt, in case of failure; the money is as good as yours once you consent to run the risk. My client is Sir Bernard Debenham, of Broom Hall, Esher.'[11]

'I know his son,' I remarked.

Raffles knew him too, but said nothing, and his eye drooped disapproval in my direction. Bennett Addenbrooke turned to me.

'Then,' said he, 'you have the privilege of knowing one of the most complete young blackguards about town, and the *fons et origo*[12] of the whole trouble. As you know the son, you may know the father too, at all events by reputation; and in that case I needn't tell you that he is a very peculiar man. He lives alone in a storehouse of treasures which no eyes but his ever behold. He is said to have the finest collection of pictures in the south of England, though nobody ever sees them to judge; pictures, fiddles and furniture are his hobby, and he is undoubtedly very eccentric. Nor can one deny that there has been considerable eccentricity in his treatment of his son. For years Sir Bernard paid his debts, and the other day, without the slightest warning, not only refused to do so any more, but absolutely stopped the lad's allowance. Well, I'll tell you what has happened; but first of all you must know, or you may remember, that I appeared for young Debenham in a little scrape he got into a year or two ago. I got him off all right, and Sir Bernard paid me handsomely on the nail. And no more did I hear or see of either of them until one day last week.'

The lawyer drew his chair nearer ours, and leant forward with a hand on either knee.

'On Tuesday of last week I had a telegram from Sir Bernard; I was to go to him at once. I found him waiting for me in the drive; without a word he led me to the picture-gallery, which was locked and darkened, drew up a blind, and stood simply pointing to an empty picture-frame. It was a long time before I could get a word out of him. Then at last he told me that that frame had contained one of the rarest and most valuable pictures in England – in the world – an original Velasquez.[13] I have checked this,' said the lawyer, 'and it seems literally true; the picture was a portrait of the Infanta Maria Teresa,[14] said to be one of the artist's greatest works, second only to another portrait of one of the Popes in Rome[15] – so they told me at the National Gallery,[16] where they had its history by heart. They say there that the picture is practically priceless. And young Debenham has sold it for five thousand pounds!'

'The deuce he has,' said Raffles.

I inquired who had bought it.

'A Queensland legislator of the name of Craggs – the Hon. John Montagu Craggs, M.L.C.,[17] to give him his full title. Not that we knew anything about him on Tuesday last; we didn't even know for certain that young Debenham had stolen the picture. But he had gone down for money on the Monday evening, had been refused, and it was plain enough that he had helped himself in this way; he had threatened revenge, and this was it. Indeed, when I hunted him up in town on the Tuesday night, he confessed as much in the most brazen manner imaginable. But he wouldn't tell me who was the purchaser, and finding out took the rest of the week; but I did find out, and a nice time I've had of it ever since! Backwards and forwards between Esher and the Métropole,[18] where the Queenslander is staying, sometimes twice a day; threats, offers, prayers, entreaties, not one of them a bit of good!'

'But,' said Raffles, 'surely it's a clear case? The sale was illegal; you can pay him back his money and force him to give the picture up.'

'Exactly; but not without an action and a public scandal, and that my client declines to face. He would rather lose even his picture than have the whole thing get into the papers; he has disowned his son, but he will not disgrace him; yet his picture he must have by hook or crook, and there's the rub![19] I am to get it back by fair means or foul. He gives me *carte blanche* in the matter, and, I verily believe, would throw in a blank cheque if asked. He offered one to the Queenslander, but Craggs simply tore it in two; the one old boy is as much a character as the other, and between the two of them I'm at my wits' end.'

'So you put that advertisement in the paper?' said Raffles, in the dry tones he had adopted throughout the interview.

'As a last resort. I did.'

'And you wish us to *steal* this picture?'

It was magnificently said; the lawyer flushed from his hair to his collar.

'I knew you were not the men!' he groaned. 'I never thought of men of your stamp! But it's *not* stealing,' he exclaimed heatedly; 'it's recovering stolen property. Besides, Sir Bernard will pay him his five thousand as soon as he has the picture; and, you'll see, old Craggs will be just as loth to let it come out as Sir Bernard himself. No, no – it's an enterprise, an adventure, if you like – but not stealing.'

'You yourself mentioned the law,' murmured Raffles.

'And the risk,' I added.

'We pay for that,' he said once more.

'But not enough,' said Raffles, shaking his head. 'My good sir, consider what it means to us. You spoke of those clubs; we should not only get kicked out of them, but put in prison like common burglars! It's true we're hard up, but it simply isn't worth it at the price. Double your stakes, and I for one am your man.'

Addenbrooke wavered.

'Do you think you could bring it off?'

'We could try.'

'But you have no –'

'Experience? Well, hardly!'

'And you would really run the risk for four thousand pounds?'

Raffles looked at me. I nodded.

'We would,' said he, 'and blow the odds!'

'It's more than I can ask my client to pay,' said Addenbrooke, growing firm.

'Then it's more than you can expect us to risk.'

'You are in earnest?'

'God wot!'[20]

'Say three thousand if you succeed!'

'Four is our figure, Mr Addenbrooke.'

'Then I think it should be nothing if you fail.'

'Doubles or quits?' cried Raffles. 'Well, that's sporting. Done!'

Addenbrooke opened his lips, half rose, then sat back in his chair, and looked long and shrewdly at Raffles – never once at me.

'I know your bowling,' said he reflectively. 'I go up to Lord's whenever I want an hour's real rest, and I've seen you bowl again and again – yes, and take the best wickets in England on a plumb pitch. I don't forget the last Gentlemen and Players; I was there. You're up to every trick – every one . . . I'm inclined to think that if anybody could bowl out this old Australian . . . Damme, I believe you're my very man!' . . .

The bargain was clinched at the Café Royal,[21] where Bennett Addenbrooke insisted on playing host at an extravagant luncheon. I remember that he took his whack of champagne with the nervous freedom of a man at high pressure, and have no doubt I kept him in countenance by an equal indulgence; but Raffles, ever an exemplar in such matters, was more abstemious even than his wont, and very poor company to boot. I can see him now, his eyes in his plate – thinking – thinking. I can see the solicitor glancing from him to me in an apprehension of which I did my best to disabuse him by reassuring looks. At the close Raffles apologized for his preoccupation, called for an A.B.C. time-table,[22] and announced his intention of catching the 3.2 to Esher.

'You must excuse me, Mr Addenbrooke,' said he, 'but I have my own idea, and for the moment I should much prefer to keep it to myself. It may end in fizzle,[23] so I would rather not speak about it to either of you just yet. But speak to Sir Bernard I must, so will you write me one line to him on your card? Of course, if you wish, you must come down with me and hear what I say; but I really don't see much point in it.'

And as usual Raffles had his way, though Bennett Addenbrooke showed some temper when he was gone, and I myself shared his annoyance to no small extent. I could only tell him that it was in the nature of Raffles to be self-willed and secretive, but that no man of my acquaintance had half his audacity and determination; that I for my part would trust him through and through, and let him gang his own gait[24] every time. More I dared not say, even to remove those chill misgivings with which I knew that the lawyer went his way.

That day I saw no more of Raffles, but a telegram reached me when I was dressing for dinner:–

Be in your rooms to-morrow from noon and keep rest of day clear
Raffles.

It had been sent off from Waterloo at 6.42.

So Raffles was back in town; at an earlier stage of our relations I should have hunted him up then and there, but now I knew better. His telegram meant that he had no desire for my society that night or the following forenoon; that when he wanted me I should see him soon enough.

And see him I did, towards one o'clock next day. I was watching for him from my window in Mount Street, when he drove up furiously in a hansom, and jumped out without a word to the man. I met him next minute at the lift gates, and he fairly pushed me back into my rooms.

'Five minutes, Bunny!' he cried. 'Not a moment more.'

And he tore off his coat before flinging himself into the nearest chair.

'I'm fairly on the rush,' he panted; 'having the very devil of a time! Not a word till I tell you all I've done. I settled my plan of campaign yesterday at lunch. The first thing was to get in with this man Craggs; you can't break into a place like the Métropole, it's got to be done from the inside. Problem one, how to get at the fellow. Only one sort of pretext would do – it must be something to do with this blessed picture, so that I might see where he'd got it and all that. Well, I couldn't go and ask to see it out of curiosity, and I couldn't go as a second representative of the other old chap, and it was thinking how I could go that made me such a bear at lunch.[25] But I saw my way before we got up. If I could only lay hold of a copy of the picture I might ask leave to go and compare it with the original. So down I went to Esher to find out if there was a copy in existence, and was at Broom Hall for one hour and a half yesterday afternoon. There was no copy there, but they must exist, for Sir Bernard himself (there's 'copy' *there*!)[26] has allowed a couple to be made since the picture has been in his possession. He hunted up the painters' addresses, and the rest of the evening I spent in hunting up the painters themselves; but their work had been done on commission; one copy had gone out of the country, and I'm still on the track of the other.'

'Then you haven't seen Craggs yet?'

'Seen him and made friends with him, and if possible he's the funnier old cuss of the two; but you should study 'em both. I took the bull by the horns this morning, went in and lied like Ananias,[27] and it was just as well I did – the old ruffian sails for Australia by to-morrow's boat. I told him a man wanted to sell me a copy of the celebrated Infanta Maria Teresa of Velasquez, that I'd been down to the supposed owner of the picture, only to find that he had just sold it to him. You should have seen his face when I told him that! He grinned all round his wicked old head. 'Did *old* Debenham admit the sale?' says he; and when I said he had he chuckled to himself for about five minutes. He was so pleased that he did just what I hoped he would do; he showed me the great picture – luckily it isn't by any means a large one – also the case he's got it in. It's an iron map-case in which he brought over the plans of his land in Brisbane; he wants to know who would suspect it of containing an Old Master, too? But he's had it fitted with a new Chubb's lock, and I managed to take an interest in the key while he was gloating over the canvas. I had the wax in the palm of my hand,[28] and I shall make my duplicate this afternoon.'

Raffles looked at his watch and jumped up saying he had given me a minute too much.

'By the way,' he added, 'you've got to dine with him at the Métropole to-night!'

'I?'

'Yes; don't look so scared. Both of us are invited – I swore

you were dining with me. I accepted for us both; but I shan't be
there.'

His clear eye was upon me, bright with meaning and with
mischief. I implored him to tell me what his meaning was.

'You will dine in his private sitting-room,' said Raffles; 'it
adjoins his bedroom. You must keep him sitting as long as
possible, Bunny, and talking all the time!'

In a flash I saw his plan.

'You're going for the picture while we're at dinner?'

'I am.'

'If he hears you!'

'He shan't.'

'But if he does!'

And I fairly trembled at the thought.

'If he does,' said Raffles, 'there will be a collision, that's all.
Revolvers would be out of place in the Métropole,[29] but I shall
certainly take a life-preserver.'[30]

'But it's ghastly!' I cried. 'To sit and talk to an utter stranger
and to know that you're at work in the next room!'

'Two thousand apiece,' said Raffles, quietly.

'Upon my soul I believe I shall give it away!'

'Not you, Bunny. I know you better than you know yourself.'

He put on his coat and his hat.

'What time have I to be there?' I asked him, with a groan.

'Quarter to eight. There will be a telegram from me saying I
can't turn up. He's a terror to talk, you'll have no difficulty in
keeping the ball rolling; but head him off his picture for all
you're worth. If he offers to show it you, say you must go. He
locked up the case elaborately this afternoon, and there's no
earthly reason why he should unlock it again in this hemisphere.'

'Where shall I find you when I get away?'

'I shall be down at Esher. I hope to catch the 9.55.'

'But surely I can see you again this afternoon?' I cried in a
ferment, for his hand was on the door. 'I'm not half coached up
yet! I know I shall make a mess of it!'

'Not you,' he said again, 'but I shall if I waste any more time.
I've got a deuce of a lot of rushing about to do yet. You won't
find me at my rooms. Why not come down to Esher yourself by

the last train? That's it – down you come with the latest news!
I'll tell old Debenham to expect you: he shall give us both a bed.
By Jove! he won't be able to do us too well if he's got his picture.'

'If!' I groaned as he nodded his adieu; and he left me limp with
apprehension, sick with fear, in a perfectly pitiable condition of
pure stage-fright.

For, after all, I had only to act my part; unless Raffles failed
where he never did fail, unless Raffles the neat and noiseless was
for once clumsy and inept, all I had to do was indeed to 'smile and
smile and be a villain'.[31] I practised that smile half the afternoon.
I rehearsed putative parts in hypothetical conversations. I got up
stories. I dipped in a book on Queensland at the club. And at last
it was 7.45, and I was making my bow to a somewhat elderly man
with a small bald head and a retreating brow.

'So you're Mr Raffles's friend?' said he, overhauling me rather
rudely with his light small eyes. 'Seen anything of him? Expected
him early to show me something, but he's never come.'

No more, evidently, had his telegram, and my troubles were
beginning early. I said I had not seen Raffles since one o'clock,
telling the truth with unction while I could; even as we spoke
there came a knock at the door; it was the telegram at last, and,
after reading it himself, the Queenslander handed it to me.

'Called out of town!' he grumbled. 'Sudden illness of near
relative! What near relatives has he got?'

I knew of none,[32] and for an instant I quailed before the perils
of invention; then I replied that I had never met any of his
people, and again felt fortified by my veracity.

'Thought you were bosom pals?' said he, with (as I imagined)
a gleam of suspicion in his crafty little eyes.

'Only in town,' said I. 'I've never been to his place.'

'Well,' he growled, 'I suppose it can't be helped. Don't know
why he couldn't come and have his dinner first. Like to see the
death-bed *I'd* go to without *my* dinner; it's a full-skin billet,[33] if
you ask me. Well, must just dine without him, and he'll have to
buy his pig in a poke after all. Mind touching that bell? Suppose
you know what he came to see me about? Sorry I shan't see
him again, for his own sake. I liked Raffles – took to him
amazingly. He's a cynic. Like cynics. One myself. Rank bad

form of his mother or his aunt, and I hope she will kick the bucket.'[34]

I connect these specimens of his conversation, though they were doubtless detached at the time, and interspersed with remarks of mine here and there. They filled the interval until dinner was served, and they gave me an impression of the man which his every subsequent utterance confirmed. It was an impression which did away with all remorse for my treacherous presence at his table. He was that terrible type, the Silly Cynic,[35] his aim a caustic commentary on all things and all men, his achievement mere vulgar irreverence and unintelligent scorn. Ill-bred and ill-informed, he had (on his own showing) fluked into fortune on a rise in land; yet cunning he possessed, as well as malice, and he chuckled till he choked over the misfortunes of less astute speculators in the same boom. Even now I cannot feel much compunction for my behaviour by the Hon. J.M. Craggs, M.L.C.

But never shall I forget the private agonies of the situation, the listening to my host with one ear and for Raffles with the other! Once I heard him – though the rooms were not divided by the old-fashioned folding-doors, and though the door that did divide them was not only shut but richly curtained, I could have sworn I heard him once. I spilt my wine and laughed at the top of my voice at some coarse sally of my host's. And I heard nothing more, though my ears were on the strain. But later, to my horror, when the waiter had finally withdrawn, Craggs himself sprang up and rushed to his bedroom without a word. I sat like stone till he returned.

'Thought I heard a door go,' he said. 'Must have been mistaken . . . imagination . . . gave me quite a turn. Raffles tell you priceless treasure I got in there?'

It was the picture at last; up to this point I had kept him to Queensland and the making of his pile. I tried to get him back there now, but in vain. He was reminded of his great ill-gotten possession. I said that Raffles had just mentioned it, and that set him off. With the confidential garrulity of a man who has dined too well, he plunged into his darling topic, and I looked past him at the clock. It was only a quarter to ten.

In common decency I could not go yet. So there I sat (we

were still at port) and learnt what had originally fired my host's ambition to possess what he was pleased to call a 'real, genuine, twin-screw, double-funnelled, copper-bottomed Old Master';[36] it was to 'go one better' than some rival legislator of pictorial proclivities. But even an epitome of his monologue would be so much weariness; suffice it that it ended inevitably in the invitation I had dreaded all the evening.

'But you must see it. Next room. This way.'

'Isn't it packed up?' I inquired hastily.

'Lock and key. That's all.'

'Pray don't trouble,' I urged.

'Trouble be hanged!' said he. 'Come along.'

And all at once I saw that to resist him further would be to heap suspicion upon myself against the moment of impending discovery. I therefore followed him into his bedroom without further protest, and suffered him first to show me the iron map-case which stood in one corner; he took a crafty pride in this receptacle, and I thought he would never cease descanting on its innocent appearance and its Chubb's lock. It seemed an interminable age before the key was in the latter. Then the ward clicked, and my pulse stood still.

'By Jove!' I cried next instant.

The canvas was in its place among the maps!

'Thought it would knock you,' said Craggs, drawing it out and unrolling it for my benefit. 'Grand thing, ain't it? Wouldn't think it had been painted two hundred and thirty years?[37] It has, though, *my* word! Old Johnson's face will be a treat when he sees it; won't go bragging about *his* pictures much more. Why, this one's worth all the pictures in Colony o' Queensland put together. Worth fifty thousand pounds,[38] my boy – and I got it for five!'

He dug me in the ribs, and seemed in the mood for further confidences. My appearance checked him, and he rubbed his hands.

'If you take it like that,' he chuckled, 'how will old Johnson take it? Go out and hang himself to his own picture-rods, I hope!'

Heaven knows what I contrived to say at last. Struck speechless first by my relief, I continued silent from a very different cause. A new tangle of emotions tied my tongue. Raffles had failed – Raffles had failed! Could I not succeed? Was it too late? Was there no way?

'So long,' he said, taking a last look at the canvas before he rolled it up – 'so long till we get to Brisbane.'

The flutter I was in as he closed the case!

'For the last time,' he went on, as his keys jingled back into his pocket. 'It goes straight into the strong-room on board.'

For the last time! If I could but send him out to Australia with only its legitimate contents in his precious map-case! If I could but succeed where Raffles had failed!

We returned to the other room. I have no notion how long he talked, or what about. Whisky and soda-water became the order of the hour. I scarcely touched it, but he drank copiously, and before eleven I left him incoherent. And the last train for Esher was the 11.50 out of Waterloo.

I took a hansom to my rooms. I was back at the hotel in thirteen minutes. I walked upstairs. The corridor was empty; I stood an instant on the sitting-room threshold, heard a snore within, and admitted myself softly with my gentleman's own key,[39] which it had been a very simple matter to take away with me.

Craggs never moved; he was stretched on the sofa fast asleep. But not fast enough for me. I saturated my handkerchief with the chloroform[40] I had brought, and I laid it gently over his mouth. Two or three stertorous breaths,[41] and the man was a log.

I removed the handkerchief; I extracted the keys from his pocket. In less than five minutes I put them back, after winding the picture about my body beneath my Inverness cape.[42] I took some whisky and soda-water before I went.

The train was easily caught – so easily that I trembled for ten minutes in my first-class smoking carriage, in terror of every footstep on the platform – in unreasonable terror till the end. Then at last I sat back and lit a cigarette, and the lights of Waterloo reeled out behind.

Some men were returning from the theatre. I can recall their conversation even now. They were disappointed with the piece they had seen. It was one of the later Savoy operas, and they spoke wistfully of the days of *Pinafore* and *Patience*. One of them hummed a stave, and there was an argument as to whether the air was out of *Patience* or the *Mikado*.[43] They all got out at Surbiton,[44] and I was alone with my triumph for a few intoxicating minutes. To think that I had succeeded where Raffles had failed! Of all our adventures this was the first in which I had played a commanding part; and, of them all, this was infinitely the least discreditable. It left me without a conscientious qualm; I had but robbed a robber, when all was said. And I had done it myself, single-handed – *ipse egomet*![45]

I pictured Raffles, his surprise, his delight. He would think a little more of me in future. And that future, it should be different. We had two thousand pounds apiece – surely enough to start afresh as honest men – and all through me!

In a glow I sprang out at Esher, and took the one belated cab that was waiting under the bridge. In a perfect fever I beheld Broom Hall, with the lower storey still lit up, and saw the front door open as I climbed the steps.

'Thought it was you,' said Raffles cheerily. 'It's all right. There's a bed for you. Sir Bernard's sitting up to shake your hand.'

His good spirits disappointed me. But I knew the man: he was one of those who wear their brightest smile in the blackest hour. I knew him too well by this time to be deceived.

'I've got it!' I cried in his ear. 'I've got it!'

'Got what?' he asked me, stepping back.

'The picture!'

'*What?*'

'The picture. He showed it me. You had to go without it; I saw that. So I determined to have it. And here it is.'

'Let's see,' said Raffles grimly.

I threw off my cape and unwound the canvas from about my body. While I was doing so an untidy old gentleman made his appearance in the hall, and stood looking on with raised eyebrows.

'Looks pretty fresh for an Old Master, doesn't she?' said Raffles.

His tone was strange. I could only suppose that he was jealous of my success.

'So Craggs said. I hardly looked at it myself.'

'Well, look now – look closely. By Jove, I must have faked her better than I thought!'

'It's a copy!' I cried.

'It's *the* copy,' he answered. 'It's the copy I've been tearing all over the country to procure. It's the copy I faked back and front, so that, on your own showing, it imposed upon Craggs, and might have made him happy for life. And you go and rob him of that!'

I could not speak.

'How did you manage it?' inquired Sir Bernard Debenham.

'Have you killed him?' asked Raffles sardonically.

I did not look at him; I turned to Sir Bernard Debenham, and to him I told my story, hoarsely, excitedly, for it was all that I could do to keep from breaking down. But as I spoke I became calmer, and I finished in mere bitterness, with the remark that another time Raffles might tell me what he meant to do.

'Another time!' he cried instantly. 'My dear Bunny, you speak as though we were going to turn burglars for a living!'

'I trust you won't,' said Sir Bernard, smiling, 'for you are certainly two very daring young men. Let us hope our friend from Queensland will do as he said, and not open his map-case till he gets back there. He will find my cheque awaiting him, and I shall be very much surprised if he troubles any of us again.'

Raffles and I did not speak till I was in the room which had been prepared for me. Nor was I anxious to do so then. But he followed me and took my hand.

'Bunny,' said he, 'don't you be hard on a fellow! I was in the deuce of a hurry, and didn't know that I should ever get what I wanted in time, and that's a fact. But it serves me right that you should have gone and undone one of the best things I ever did. As for *your* handiwork, old chap, you won't mind my saying that I didn't think you had it in you. In future –'

'Don't talk to me about the future!' I cried. 'I hate the whole thing! I'm going to chuck it up!'

'So am I,' said Raffles, 'when I've made my pile.'

THE RETURN MATCH

I had turned into Piccadilly, one thick evening in the following November, when my guilty heart stood still at the sudden grip of a hand upon my arm. I thought – I was always thinking – that my inevitable hour was come at last. It was only Raffles, however, who stood smiling at me through the fog.

'Well met!' said he. 'I've been looking for you at the club.'

'I was just on my way there,' I returned, with an attempt to hide my tremors. It was an ineffectual attempt, as I saw from his broader smile, and by the indulgent shake of his head.

'Come up to my place instead,' said he. 'I've something amusing to tell you.'

I made excuses, for his tone foretold the kind of amusement, and it was a kind against which I had successfully set my face for months. I have stated before, however, and I can but reiterate, that to me, at all events, there was never anybody in the world so irresistible as Raffles when his mind was made up. That we had both been independent of crime since our little service to Sir Bernard Debenham – that there had been no occasion for that masterful mind to be made up in any such direction for many a day – was the undeniable basis of a longer spell of honesty than I had hitherto enjoyed during the term of our mutual intimacy. Be sure I would deny it if I could; the very thing I am to tell you would discredit such a boast. I made my excuses, as I have said. But his arm slid through mine, with his little laugh of light-hearted mastery. And even while I argued we were on his staircase in the Albany.

His fire had fallen low. He poked and replenished it after

lighting the gas. As for me, I stood by sullenly in my overcoat until he dragged it off my back.

'What a chap you are!' said Raffles playfully. 'One would really think I had proposed to crack another crib[1] this blessed night! Well, it isn't that, Bunny; so get into that chair, and take one of these Sullivans and sit tight.'

He held the match to my cigarette; he brought me a whisky and soda. Then he went out into the lobby, and just as I was beginning to feel happy, I heard a bolt shot home. It cost me an effort to remain in that chair; next moment he was straddling another and gloating over my discomfiture across his folded arms.

'You remember Milchester, Bunny, old boy?'

His tone was as bland as mine was grim when I answered that I did.

'We had a little match there that wasn't down on the card.[2] Gentlemen and Players, if you recollect?'

'I don't forget it.'

'Seeing that you never got an innings, so to speak, I thought you might. Well, the Gentlemen scored pretty freely, but the Players were all caught –'

'Poor devils!'

'Don't be too sure. You remember the fellow we saw in the inn? The florid, overdressed chap who I told you was one of the cleverest thieves in town?'

'I remember him. Crawshay[3] his name turned out to be.'

'Well, it was certainly the name he was convicted under, so Crawshay let it be. You needn't waste any pity on *him*, old chap; he escaped from Dartmoor[4] yesterday afternoon.'

'Well done!'

Raffles smiled, but his eyebrows had gone up and his shoulders followed suit.

'You are perfectly right; it was very well done indeed. I wonder you didn't see it in the paper. In a dense fog on the moor yesterday good old Crawshay made a bolt for it, and got away without a scratch under heavy fire. All honour to him, I agree; a fellow with that much grit deserves his liberty. But Crawshay has a good deal more. They hunted him all night long; couldn't find him for nuts; and that was all you missed in the morning papers.'

He unfolded a *Pall Mall*,[5] which he had brought in with him.

'But listen to this; here's an account of the escape, with just the addition which puts the thing on a higher level. "The fugitive has been traced to Totnes, where he appears to have committed a peculiarly daring outrage in the early hours of this morning. He is reported to have entered the lodgings of the Rev. A. H. Ellingworth, curate of the parish, who missed his clothes on rising at the usual hour; later in the morning those of the convict were discovered neatly folded at the bottom of a drawer. Meanwhile Crawshay had made good his second escape, though it is believed that so distinctive a guise will lead to his recapture during the day." What do you think of that, Bunny?'

'He is certainly a sportsman,' said I, reaching for the paper.

'He's more,' said Raffles; 'he's an artist, and I envy him. The curate, of all men! Beautiful – beautiful! But that's not all. I saw just now on the board at the club that there's been an outrage on the line near Dawlish. Parson found insensible in the six-foot way.[6] Our friend again! The telegram doesn't say so, but it's obvious; he's simply knocked some other fellow out, changed clothes again, and come on gaily to town. Isn't it great? I do believe it's the best thing of the kind that's ever been done!'

'But why should he come to town?'

In an instant the enthusiasm faded from Raffles's face; clearly I had reminded him of some prime anxiety, forgotten in his impersonal joy over the exploit of a fellow-criminal. He looked over his shoulder towards the lobby before replying.

'I believe,' said he, 'that the beggar's on *my* tracks!'

And as he spoke he was himself again – quietly amused – cynically unperturbed – characteristically enjoying the situation and my surprise.

'But look here, what do you mean?' said I. 'What does Crawshay know about you?'

'Not much; but he suspects.'

'Why should he?'

'Because, in his way, he's very nearly as good a man as I am; because, my dear Bunny, with eyes in his head and brains behind them, he couldn't help suspecting. He saw me once in town with old Baird. He must have seen me that day in the pub, on the way to Milchester, as well as afterwards on the cricket-field. As a matter of fact, I know he did, for he wrote and told me so before his trial.'

'He wrote to you! And you never told me!'

The old shrug answered the old grievance.

'What was the good, my dear fellow? It would only have worried you.'

'Well, what did he say?'

'That he was sorry he had been run in before getting back to town, as he had proposed doing himself the honour of paying me a call; however, he trusted it was only a pleasure deferred, and he begged me not to go and get lagged[7] myself before he came out. Of course he knew the Melrose necklace was gone, though he hadn't got it; and he said that the man who could take that and leave the rest was a man after his own heart. And so on, with certain little proposals for the far future, which I fear may be the very near future indeed! I'm only surprised he hasn't turned up yet.'

He looked again towards the lobby, which he had left in darkness, with the inner door shut as carefully as the outer one. I asked him what he meant to do.

'Let him knock – if he gets so far. The porter is to say I'm out of town; it will be true, too, in another hour or so.'

'You're going off to-night?'

'By the 7.15 from Liverpool Street.[8] I don't say much about my people, Bunny, but I have the best of sisters married to a country parson in the eastern counties.[9] They always make me welcome, and let me read the lessons for the sake of getting me to church. I'm sorry you won't be there to hear me on Sunday, Bunny. I've figured out some of my best schemes in that parish, and I know of no better port in a storm. But I must pack. I thought I'd just let you know where I was going, and why, in case you cared to follow my example.'

He flung the stump of his cigarette into the fire, stretched himself as he rose, and remained so long in the inelegant attitude that my eyes mounted from his body to his face; a second later they had followed his eyes across the room, and I also was on my legs. On the threshold of the folding doors that divided bedroom and sitting-room, a well-built man stood in ill-fitting broadcloth,[10] and bowed to us until his bullet head presented an unbroken disc of short red hair.

Brief as was my survey of this astounding apparition, the interval was long enough for Raffles to recover his composure; his hands were in his pockets, and a smile upon his face, when my eyes flew back to him.

'Let me introduce you, Bunny,' said he, 'to our distinguished colleague, Mr Reginald Crawshay.'

The bullet head bobbed up, and there was a wrinkled brow above the coarse, shaven face, crimson also, I remember, from the grip of a collar several sizes too small. But I noted nothing consciously at the time. I had jumped to my own conclusion, and I turned on Raffles with an oath.

'It's a trick!' I cried. 'It's another of your cursed tricks! You got him here, and then you got me. You want me to join you, I suppose? I'll see you damned!'

So cold was the stare which met this outburst that I became ashamed of my words while they were yet upon my lips.

'Really, Bunny!' said Raffles, and turned his shoulder with a shrug.

'Lord love yer,' cried Crawshay, ' '*e* knew nothin'. '*E* didn't expect me; '*e's* all right. And you're the cool canary,[11] *you* are,' he went on to Raffles. 'I knoo you were, but do me proud, you're one after my own kidney!'[12] And he thrust out a shaggy hand.

'After that,' said Raffles, taking it, 'what am I to say? But you must have heard my opinion of you. I am proud to make your acquaintance. How the deuce did you get in?'

'Never you mind,' said Crawshay, loosening his collar; 'let's talk about how I'm to get out. Lord love yer, but that's better!' There was a livid ring round his bull-neck, that he fingered tenderly. 'Didn't know how much longer I might have to play the gent,' he explained; 'didn't know who you'd bring in.'

'Drink whisky and soda?' inquired Raffles, when the convict was in the chair from which I had leapt.

'No, I drink it neat,' replied Crawshay, 'but I talk business first. You don't get over me[13] like that, Lor' love yer!'

'Well, then, what can I do for you?'

'You know without me tellin' you.'

'Give it a name.'

'Clean heels,[14] then; that's what I want to show, and I leaves the way to you. We're brothers in arms, though I ain't armed this time. It ain't necessary. You've too much sense. But brothers we are, and you'll see a brother through. Let's put it at that. You'll see me through in yer own way. I leaves it all to you.'

His tone was rich with conciliation and concession; he bent over and tore a pair of button boots from his bare feet, which he stretched towards the fire, painfully uncurling his toes.

'I hope you take a larger size than them,' said he. 'I'd have had a see if you'd given me time. I wasn't in long afore you.'

'And you won't tell me how you got in?'

'Wot's the use? I can't teach *you* nothin'. Besides, I want out. I want out of London, an' England, an' bloomin' Europe too. That's all I want of you, mister. I don't arst how *you* go on the job. You know w'ere I come from, 'cos I 'eard you say; you know w'ere I want to 'ead for, 'cos I've just told yer; the details I leaves entirely to you.'

'Well,' said Raffles, 'we must see what can be done.'

'We must,' said Mr Crawshay, and leaned back comfortably, and began twirling his stubby thumbs.

Raffles turned to me with a twinkle in his eye; but his forehead was scored with thought, and resolve mingled with resignation in the lines of his mouth. And he spoke exactly as though he and I were alone in the room.

'You seize the situation, Bunny? If our friend here is "copped",[15] to speak his language, he means to "blow the gaff" on you and me. He is considerate enough not to say so in so many words, but it's plain enough, and natural enough for that matter. I would do the same in his place. We had the bulge[16] before; he has it now; it's perfectly fair. We must take on this job; we aren't in a position to refuse it; even if we were, I should take it on! Our friend is a great sportsman; he has got clear away from Dartmoor; it would be a thousand pities to let him go back. Nor shall he; not if I can think of a way of getting him abroad.'

'Any way you like,' murmured Crawshay, with his eyes shut. 'I leaves the 'ole thing to you.'

'But you'll have to wake up and tell us things.'

'All right, mister; but I'm fair on the rocks for a sleep!'[17]

And he stood up, blinking.

'Think you were traced to town?'

'Must have been.'

'And here?'

'Not in this fog – not with any luck.'

Raffles went into the bedroom, lit the gas there, and returned next minute.

'So you got in by the window?'

'That's about it.'

'It was devilish smart of you to know which one; it beats me how you brought it off in daylight, fog or no fog! But let that pass. You don't think you were seen?'

'I don't think it, sir.'

'Well, let's hope you are right. I shall reconnoitre and soon find out. And you'd better come too, Bunny, and have something to eat and talk it over.'

As Raffles looked at me, I looked at Crawshay, anticipating trouble; and trouble brewed in his blank, fierce face, in the glitter of his startled eyes, in the sudden closing of his fists.

'And what's to become o' me?' he cried out with an oath.

'You wait here.'

'No, you don't,' he roared, and at a bound had his back to the door. 'You don't get round me like that, you cuckoos!'[18]

Raffles turned to me with a twitch of the shoulders.

'That's the worst of these professors,' said he: 'they never will use their heads. They see the pegs, and they mean to hit 'em;[19] but that's all they do see and mean, and they think we're the same. No wonder we licked them last time!'

'Don't talk through yer neck,' snarled the convict. 'Talk out straight, curse you!'

'Right,' said Raffles. 'I'll talk as straight as you like. You say you put yourself in my hands – you leave it all to me – yet you don't trust me an inch! I know what's to happen if I fail. I accept the risk. I take this thing on. Yet you think I'm going straight out to give you away and make you give me away in my turn. You're a fool, Mr Crawshay, though you have broken Dartmoor; you've got to listen to a better man, and obey him. I see you through in my own way, or not at all. I come and go as I like, and with whom I like, without your interference; you stay here and lie just as low as you know how, be as wise as your word, and leave the whole thing to me. If you won't – if you're fool enough not to trust me – there's the door. Go out and say what you like, and be damned to you!'

Crawshay slapped his thigh.

'That's talking!' said he. 'Lord love yer, I know where I am when you talk like that. I'll trust yer. I know a man when he gets his tongue between his teeth;[20] you're all right. I don't say so much about this other gent, though I saw him along with you on the job that time in the provinces; but if he's a pal of yours, Mr Raffles, he'll be all right too. I only hope you gents ain't too stony –'

And he touched his pockets with a rueful face.

'I only went for their togs,' said he. 'You never struck two such stony-broke cusses in yer life!'

'That's all right,' said Raffles. 'We'll see you through properly. Leave it to us, and you sit tight.'

'Rightum!'[21] said Crawshay. 'And I'll have a sleep time you're gone. But no sperrits – no, thank'ee – not yet! Once let me loose on the lush, and, Lord love yer, I'm a gone coon!'[22]

Raffles got his overcoat, a long, light driving-coat,[23] I remember, and even as he put it on our fugitive was dozing in the chair; we left him murmuring incoherently, with the gas out, and his bare feet toasting.

'Not such a bad chap, that professor,' said Raffles on the stairs; 'a real genius in his way, too, though his methods are a little elementary for my taste. But technique isn't everything; to get out of Dartmoor and into the Albany in the same twenty-four hours is a whole that justifies its parts. Good Lord!'

We had passed a man in the foggy courtyard, and Raffles had nipped my arm.

'Who was it?'

'The last man we want to see! I hope to heaven he didn't hear me!'

'But who is he, Raffles?'

'Our old friend Mackenzie, from the Yard!'

I stood still with horror.

'Do you think he's on Crawshay's track?'

'I don't know. I'll find out.'

And before I could remonstrate he had wheeled me round; when I found my voice he merely laughed, and whispered that the bold course was the safe one every time.

'But it's madness –'

'Not it. Shut up! Is that *you*, Mr Mackenzie?'

The detective turned about and scrutinized us keenly; and through the gaslit mist I noticed that his hair was grizzled at the temples, and his face still cadaverous, from the wound that had nearly been his death.

'Ye have the advantage o' me, sirs,' said he.

'I hope you're fit again,' said my companion. 'My name is Raffles, and we met at Milchester last year.'

'Is that a fact?' cried the Scotchman, with quite a start. 'Yes, now I remember your face, and yours too, sir. Ay, yon was a bad business, but it ended vera well, an' that's the main thing.'

His native caution had returned to him. Raffles pinched my arm.

'Yes, it ended splendidly, but for you,' said he. 'But what about this escape of the leader of the gang, that fellow Crawshay? What do you think of that, eh?'

'I havena the parteeculars,' replied the Scot.

'Good!' cried Raffles. 'I was only afraid you might be on his tracks once more!'

Mackenzie shook his head with a dry smile, and wished us good evening as an invisible window was thrown up, and a whistle blown softly through the fog.

'We must see this out,' whispered Raffles. 'Nothing more natural than a little curiosity on our part. After him, quick!'

And we followed the detective into another entrance on the same side as that from which we had emerged, the left-hand side on one's way to Piccadilly;[24] quite openly we followed him, and at the foot of the stairs met one of the porters of the place. Raffles asked him what was wrong.

'Nothing, sir,' said the fellow glibly.

'Rot!' said Raffles. 'That was Mackenzie, the detective. I've just been speaking to him. What's he here for? Come on, my good fellow; we won't give you away, if you've instructions not to tell.'

The man looked quaintly wistful, the temptation of an audience hot upon him; a door shut upstairs, and he fell.

'It's like this,' he whispered. 'This arfternoon a gen'leman comes arfter rooms, and I sent him to the orfice; one of the clurks, 'e goes round with 'im an' shows 'im the empties,[25] an' the gen'leman's partic'ly struck on the set the coppers is up in now. So he sends the clurk to fetch the manager, as there was one or two things he wished to speak about; an' when they come back, blowed if the gent isn't gone! Beg yer pardon, sir, but he's clean disappeared off the face o' the premises!' And the porter looked at us with shining eyes.

'Well?' said Raffles.

'Well, sir, they looked about, an' looked about, an' at larst they give him up for a bad job; thought he'd changed his mind an' didn't want to tip the clurk; so they shut up the place an' come away. An' that's all till about 'alf an hour ago, when I takes the manager his extry-speshul *Star*;[26] in about ten minutes he comes running out with a note, an' sends me with it to Scotland Yard in a hansom. An' that's all I know, sir – straight. The coppers is up there now, and the tec,[27] and the manager, and they think their gent is about the place somewhere still. Least, I reckon that's their idea; but who he is, or what they want him for, I dunno.'

'Jolly interesting!' said Raffles. 'I'm going up to inquire. Come on, Bunny; there should be some fun.'

'Beg yer pardon, Mr Raffles, but you won't say nothing about me?'

'Not I; you're a good fellow. I won't forget it if this leads to sport. Sport!' he whispered as we reached the landing. 'It looks like precious poor sport for you and me, Bunny!'

'What are you going to do?'

'I don't know. There's no time to think. This, to start with.'

And he thundered on the shut door; a policeman opened it. Raffles strode past him with the air of a chief commissioner,[28] and I followed before the man had recovered from his astonishment. The bare boards rang under us; in the bedroom we found a knot of officers stooping over the window-ledge with a constable's lantern. Mackenzie was the first to stand upright, and he greeted us with a glare.

'May I ask what you gentlemen want?' said he.

'We want to lend a hand,' said Raffles briskly. 'We lent one once before, and it was my friend here who took over from you the fellow who split on all the rest, and held him tight. Surely that entitles him, at all events, to see any fun that's going? As for myself, well, it's true I only helped to carry you to the house; but for old acquaintance I do hope, my dear Mr Mackenzie, that you will permit us to share such sport as there may be. I myself can only stop a few minutes, in any case.'

'Then ye'll not see much,' growled the detective, 'for he's not up here. Constable, go you and stand at the foot o' the stairs, and let no other body come up on any conseederation; these gentlemen may be able to help us after all.'

'That's kind of you, Mackenzie!' cried Raffles warmly. 'But what is it all? I questioned a porter I met coming down, but could get nothing out of him, except that somebody had been to see these rooms and not since been seen himself.'

'He's a man we want,' said Mackenzie. 'He's concealed himself somewhere about these premises, or I'm vera much mistaken. D'ye reside in the Albany, Mr Raffles?'

'I do.'

'Will your rooms be near these?'

'On the next staircase but one.'

'Ye'll just have left them?'

'Just.'

'Been in all the afternoon, likely?'

'Not all.'

'Then I may have to search your rooms, sir. I am prepared to search every room in the Albany! Our man seems to have gone for the leads;[29] but unless he's left more marks outside than in, or we find him up there, I shall have the entire building to ransack.'

'I will leave you my key,' said Raffles at once. 'I am dining out, but I'll leave it with the officer down below.'

I caught my breath in mute amazement. What was the meaning of this insane promise? It was wilful, gratuitous, suicidal; it made me catch at his sleeve in open horror and disgust; but, with a word of thanks, Mackenzie had returned to his window-sill, and we sauntered unwatched through the folding-doors into the adjoining room. Here the window looked down into the courtyard; it was still open; and as we gazed out in apparent idleness, Raffles reassured me.

'It's all right, Bunny; you do what I tell you and leave the rest to me. It's a tight corner, but I don't despair. What you've got to do is to stick to these chaps, especially if they search my rooms; they musn't poke about more than necessary, and they won't if you're there.'

'But where will you be? You're never going to leave me to be landed alone?'

'If I do, it will be to turn up trumps at the right moment. Besides, there are such things as windows, and Crawshay's the man to take his risks. You must trust me, Bunny; you've known me long enough.'

'And you're going now?'

'There's no time to lose. Stick to them, old chap; don't let them suspect *you*, whatever else you do.' His hand lay an instant on my shoulder; then he left me at the window, and recrossed the room.

'I've got to go now,' I heard him say; 'but my friend will stay and see this through, and I'll leave the gas on in my rooms, and my key with the constable downstairs. Good luck, Mackenzie; only wish I could stay.'

'Goodbye, sir,' came in a preoccupied voice, 'and many thanks.'

Mackenzie was still busy at his window, and I remained at mine, a prey to mingled fear and wrath, for all my knowledge of Raffles and of his infinite resource. By this time I felt that I knew

more or less what he would do in any given emergency; at least
I could conjecture a characteristic course of equal cunning and
audacity. He would return to his rooms, put Crawshay on his
guard, and – stow him away? No – there were such things as
windows. Then why was Raffles going to desert us all? I thought
of many things – lastly of a cab. These bedroom windows looked
into a narrow side-street;[30] they were not very high; from them
a man might drop on to the roof of a cab – even as it passed –
and be driven away – even under the noses of the police! I
pictured Raffles driving that cab, unrecognizable in the foggy
night; the vision came to me as he passed under the window,
tucking up the collar of his great driving-coat on the way to his
rooms; it was still with me when he passed again on his way
back, and stopped to hand the constable his key.

'We're on his track,' said a voice behind me. 'He's got up on
the leads, sure enough, though how he managed it from yon
window is a myst'ry to me. We're going to lock up here and try
what like it is from the attics. So you'd better come with us if
you've a mind.'

The top floor at the Albany, as elsewhere, is devoted to the
servants – a congeries of little kitchens and cubicles,[31] used by
many as lumber-rooms – by Raffles among the many. The
annexe in this case was, of course, empty as the rooms below;
and that was lucky, for we filled it, what with the manager, who
now joined us, and another tenant whom he brought with him
to Mackenzie's undisguised annoyance.

'Better let in all Piccadilly at a crown a head,'[32] said he. 'Here,
my man, out you go on the roof to make one less, and have your
truncheon handy.'

We crowded to the little window, which Mackenzie took
care to fill; and a minute yielded no sound but the crunch and
slither of constabulary boots upon sooty slates. Then came a
shout.

'What now?' cried Mackenzie.

'A rope,' we heard, 'hanging from the spout by a hook!'

'Sirs,' purred Mackenzie, 'yon's how he got up from below!
He would do it with one o' they telescope sticks,[33] an' I never
thocht o't! How long a rope, my lad?'

'Quite short. I've got it.'

'Did it hang over a window? Ask him that!' cried the manager. 'He can see by leaning over the parapet.'

The question was repeated by Mackenzie; a pause, then 'Yes, it did.'

'Ask him how many windows along!' shouted the manager in high excitement.

'Six, he says,' said Mackenzie next minute; and he drew in his head and shoulders. 'I should just like to see those rooms, six windows along.'

'Mr Raffles's,' announced the manager after a mental calculation.

'Is that a fact?' cried Mackenzie. 'Then we shall have no difficulty at all. He's left me his key down below.'

The words had a dry, speculative intonation, which even then I found time to dislike; it was as though the coincidence had already struck the Scotchman as something more.

'Where is Mr Raffles?' asked the manager, as we all filed downstairs.

'He's gone out to his dinner,' said Mackenzie.

'Are you sure?'

'I saw him go,' said I. My heart was beating horribly. I would not trust myself to speak again. But I wormed my way to a front place in the little procession, and was, in fact, the second man to cross the threshold that had been the Rubicon of my life.[34] As I did so I uttered a cry of pain, for Mackenzie had trod back heavily on my toes; in another second I saw the reason, and saw it with another and a louder cry.

A man was lying at full length before the fire, on his back, with a little wound in the white forehead, and the blood draining into his eyes. And the man was Raffles himself!

'Suicide,' said Mackenzie calmly. 'No – here's the poker – looks more like murder.' He went on his knees and shook his head quite cheerfully. 'An' it's not even murder,' said he, with a shade of disgust in his matter-of-fact voice; 'yon's no more than a flesh-wound, and I have my doubts whether it felled him; but, sirs, he just stinks o' chloryform!'

He got up and fixed his keen grey eyes upon me; my own were full of tears, but they faced him unashamed.

'I understood ye to say ye saw him go out?' said he sternly.

'I saw that long driving-coat; of course I thought he was inside it.'

'And I could ha' sworn it was the same gent when he give me the key!'

It was the disconsolate voice of the constable in the background; on him turned Mackenzie, white to the lips.

'You'd think anything, some of you damned policemen,' said he. 'What's your number, you rotter? P 34?[35] You'll be hearing more of this, Mr P 34! If that gentleman was dead – instead of coming to himself while I'm talking – do you know what you'd be? Guilty of his manslaughter, you stuck pig in buttons![36] Do you know who you've let slip, butter-fingers? Crawshay – no less – him that broke Dartmoor yesterday. By the God that made ye, P 34, if I lose him I'll hound ye from the forrce!'

Working face – shaking fist – a calm man on fire. It was a new side of Mackenzie, and one to mark and to digest. Next moment he had flounced from our midst.

'Difficult thing to break your own head,' said Raffles later; 'infinitely easier to cut your own throat. Chloroform's another matter; when you've used it on others, you know the dose to a nicety. So you thought I was really gone? Poor old Bunny! But I hope Mackenzie saw your face?'

'He did,' said I. I would not tell him all Mackenzie must have seen, however.

'That's all right. I wouldn't have had him miss it for worlds; and you mustn't think me a brute, old boy, for I fear that man; and, you know, we sink or swim together.'

'And now we sink or swim with Crawshay too,' said I dolefully.

'Not we!' cried Raffles with conviction. 'Old Crawshay's a true sportsman, and he'll do by us as we've done by him;[37] besides, this makes us quits; and I don't think, Bunny, that we'll take on the professors again!'

THE GIFT OF THE EMPEROR

I

When the King of the Cannibal Islands[1] made faces at Queen Victoria,[2] and a European monarch[3] set the cables tingling with his compliments[4] on the exploit, the indignation in England was not less than the surprise, for the thing was not so common as it has since become. But when it transpired that a gift of peculiar significance was to follow the congratulations, to give them weight, the inference prevailed that the white potentate and the black had taken simultaneous leave of their fourteen senses. For the gift was a pearl of price unparalleled,[5] picked aforetime by British cutlasses from a Polynesian setting,[6] and presented by British royalty to the sovereign who seized this opportunity of restoring it to its original possessor.

The incident would have been a godsend to the Press a few weeks later.[7] Even in June there were leaders, letters, large headlines, leaded type; the *Daily Chronicle* devoting half its literary page[8] to a charming drawing of the island capital which the new *Pall Mall*,[9] in a leading article headed by a pun, advised the Government to blow to flinders.[10] I was myself driving a poor but not dishonest quill at the time, and the topic of the hour goaded me into satiric verse which obtained a better place than anything I had yet turned out. I had let my flat in town, and taken inexpensive quarters at Thames Ditton,[11] on the plea of a disinterested passion for the river.

'First-rate, old boy!' said Raffles (who must needs come and see me there), lying back in the boat while I sculled and steered. 'I suppose they pay you pretty well for these, eh?'

'Not a penny.'

'Nonsense, Bunny! I thought they paid so well? Give them time, and you'll get your cheque.'

'Oh, no, I shan't,' said I gloomily. 'I've got to be content with the honour of getting in; the editor wrote to say so, in so many words,' I added. But I gave the gentleman his distinguished name.

'You don't mean to say you've written for payment already?'

No; it was the last thing I had intended to admit. But I had done it. The murder was out; there was no sense in further concealment. I had written for my money because I really needed it; if he must know, I was cursedly hard up. Raffles nodded as though he knew already. I warmed to my woes. It was no easy matter to keep your end up as a raw free lance of letters; for my part, I was afraid I wrote neither well enough nor ill enough for success. I suffered from a persistent ineffectual feeling after style. Verse I could manage; but it did not pay. To personal paragraphs and the baser journalism I could not and I would not stoop.[12]

Raffles nodded again, this time with a smile that stayed in his eyes as he leant back watching me. I knew that he was thinking of other things I had stooped to, and I thought I knew what he was going to say. He had said it before so often; he was sure to say it again. I had my answer ready, but evidently he was tired of asking the same question. His lids fell, he took up the paper he had dropped, and I sculled the length of the old red wall of Hampton Court[13] before he spoke again.

'And they gave you nothing for these! My dear Bunny, they're capital, not only *qua* verses[14] but for crystallizing your subject and putting it in a nutshell. Certainly you've taught *me* more about it than I knew before. But is it really worth fifty thousand pounds[15] – a single pearl?'

'A hundred, I believe; but that wouldn't scan.'

'A hundred thousand pounds!' said Raffles, with his eyes shut. And again I made certain what was coming, but again I was mistaken. 'If it's worth all that,' he cried at last, 'there would be no getting rid of it at all; it's not like a diamond that you can subdivide. But I beg your pardon, Bunny. I was forgetting!'

And we said no more about the emperor's gift; for pride

thrives on an empty pocket, and no privation would have drawn from me the proposal which I had expected Raffles to make. My expectation had been half a hope, though I only knew it now. But neither did we touch again on what Raffles professed to have forgotten – my 'apostasy',[16] my 'lapse into virtue', as he had been pleased to call it. We were both a little silent, a little constrained, each preoccupied with his own thoughts. It was months since we had met, and, as I saw him off towards eleven o'clock that Sunday night, I fancied it was for more months that we were saying goodbye.

But as we waited for the train I saw those clear eyes peering at me under the station lamps, and when I met their glance Raffles shook his head.

'You don't look well on it, Bunny,' said he. 'I never did believe in this Thames Valley. You want a change of air.'

I wished I might get it.

'What you really want is a sea voyage.'

'And a winter at St Moritz, or do you recommend Cannes or Cairo?[17] It's all very well, A. J., but you forget what I told you about my funds.'

'I forget nothing. I merely don't want to hurt your feelings. But, look here, a sea voyage you shall have. I want a change myself, and you shall come with me as my guest. We'll spend July in the Mediterranean.'

'But you're playing cricket –'

'Hang the cricket!'

'Well, if I thought you meant it –'

'Of course I mean it. Will you come?'

'Like a shot – if you go.'

And I shook his hand, and waved mine in farewell, with the perfectly good-humoured conviction that I should hear no more of the matter. It was a passing thought, no more, no less. I soon wished it were more; that week found me wishing myself out of England for good and all. I was making nothing. I could but subsist on the difference between the rent I paid for my flat and the rent at which I had sublet it, furnished, for the season. And the season was near its end, and creditors awaited me in town. Was it possible to be entirely honest? I had run no bills when I had money in my pocket, and the more downright dishonesty seemed to me the less ignoble.

But from Raffles, of course, I heard nothing more; a week went by, and half another week; then, late on the second Wednesday night, I found a telegram from him at my lodgings, after seeking him vainly in town, and dining with desperation at the solitary club to which I still belonged.

'Arrange to leave Waterloo by North German Lloyd special,'[18] he wired, '9.25 a.m. Monday next will meet you Southampton aboard *Uhlan*[19] with tickets am writing.'

And write he did, a light-hearted letter enough, but full of serious solicitude for me and for my health and prospects; a letter almost touching in the light of our past relations, in the twilight of their complete rupture. He said that he had booked two berths to Naples, that we were bound for Capri,[20] which was clearly the Island of the Lotos-eaters,[21] that we would bask there together, 'and for a while forget'.[22] It was a charming letter. I had never seen Italy; the privilege of initiation should be his. No mistake was greater than to deem it an impossible country for the summer. The Bay of Naples was never so divine, and he wrote of 'faëry lands forlorn',[23] as though the poetry sprang unbidden to his pen. To come back to earth and prose, I might think it unpatriotic of him to choose a German boat, but on no other line did you receive such attention and accommodation for your money. There was a hint of better reasons. Raffles wrote, as he had telegraphed, from Bremen;[24] and I gathered that the personal use of some little influence with the authorities there had resulted in a material reduction in our fares.

Imagine my excitement and delight! I managed to pay what I owed at Thames Ditton, to squeeze a small editor for a very small cheque, and my tailors for one more flannel suit. I remember that I broke my last sovereign to get a box of Sullivan's cigarettes for Raffles to smoke on the voyage. But my heart was as light as my purse on the Monday morning, the fairest morning of an unfair summer, when the special whirled me through the sunshine to the sea.

A tender awaited us at Southampton. Raffles was not on board, nor did I really look for him till we reached the liner's

side. And then I looked in vain. His face was not among the
many that fringed the rail; his hand was not of the few that
waved to friends. I climbed aboard in a sudden heaviness. I had
no ticket, nor the money to pay for one. I did not even know
the number of my room. My heart was in my mouth as I waylaid
a steward and asked if a Mr Raffles was on board. Thank heaven
– he was! But where? The man did not know, was plainly on
some other errand, and a-hunting I must go.[25] But there was no
sign of him on the promenade deck, and none below in the
saloon; the smoking-room was empty but for a little German
with a red moustache twisted into his eyes; nor was Raffles in
his own cabin, whither I inquired my way in desperation, but
where the sight of his own name on the baggage was certainly a
further reassurance. Why he himself kept in the background,
however, I could not conceive, and only sinister reasons would
suggest themselves in explanation.

'So there you are! I've been looking for you all over the ship!'

Despite the graven prohibition, I had tried the bridge as a last
resort; and there, indeed, was A. J. Raffles, seated on a skylight,
and leaning over one of the officers' long chairs,[26] in which
reclined a girl in a white drill coat[27] and skirt – a slip of a girl
with a pale skin, dark hair, and rather remarkable eyes. So much
I noted as he rose and quickly turned; thereupon I could think
of nothing but the swift grimace which preceded a start of
well-feigned astonishment.

'Why – *Bunny*?' cried Raffles. 'Where have *you* sprung from?'

I stammered something as he pinched my hand.

'And are you coming in this ship? And to Naples, too? Well,
upon my word! Miss Werner, may I introduce him?'

And he did so without a blush, describing me as an old
schoolfellow whom he had not seen for months, with wilful
circumstance and gratuitous detail that filled me at once with
confusion, suspicion, and revolt. I felt myself blushing for us
both, and I did not care. My address utterly deserted me, and I
made no effort to recover it, to carry the thing off. All I would
do was to mumble such words as Raffles actually put into my
mouth, and that I doubt not with a thoroughly evil grace.

'So you saw my name in the list of passengers, and came in

search of me? Good old Bunny! I say, though, I wish you'd share my cabin? I've got a beauty on the promenade deck, but they wouldn't promise to keep me by myself. We ought to see about it before they shove in some alien. In any case we shall have to get out of this.'

For a quartermaster had entered the wheel-house, and even while we had been speaking the pilot had taken possession of the bridge; as we descended, the tender left us with flying handkerchiefs and shrill goodbyes; and as we bowed to Miss Werner on the promenade deck, there came a deep, slow throbbing under-foot, and our voyage had begun.

It did not begin pleasantly between Raffles and me. On deck he had overborne my stubborn perplexity by dint of a forced though forceful joviality; in his cabin the gloves were off.

'You idiot,' he snarled, 'you've given me away again!'

'How have I given you away?'

I ignored the separate insult in his last word.

'How? I should have thought any clod could see that I meant us to meet by chance!'

'After taking both tickets yourself?'

'They know nothing about that on board; besides, I hadn't decided when I took the tickets.'

'Then you should have let me know when you did decide. You lay your plans, and never say a word, and expect me to tumble to them by light of nature.[28] How was I to know you had anything on?'

I had turned the tables with some effect. Raffles almost hung his head.

'The fact is, Bunny, I didn't mean you to know. You – you've grown such a pious rabbit in your old age!'

My nickname and his tone went far to mollify me, other things went farther, but I had much to forgive him still.

'If you were afraid of writing,' I pursued, 'it was your business to give me the tip the moment I set foot on board. I would have taken it all right. I am not so virtuous as all that.'

Was it my imagination, or did Raffles look slightly ashamed? If so, it was for the first and last time in all the years I knew him; nor can I swear to it even now.

'That,' said he, 'was the very thing I meant to do – to lie in wait in my room and get you as you passed. But –'

'You were better engaged?'

'Say otherwise.'

'The charming Miss Werner?'

'She is quite charming.'

'Most Australian girls are,' said I.

'How did you know she was one?' he cried.

'I heard her speak.'

'Brute!' said Raffles, laughing; 'she has no more twang than you have. Her people are German, she has been to school in Dresden, and is on her way out alone.'

'Money?' I inquired.

'Confound you!' he said, and, though he was laughing, I thought it was a point at which the subject might be changed.

'Well,' I said, 'it wasn't for Miss Werner you wanted us to play strangers, was it? You have some deeper game than that, eh?'

'I suppose I have.'

'Then hadn't you better tell me what it is?'

Raffles treated me to the old cautious scrutiny that I knew so well; the very familiarity of it, after all these months, set me smiling in a way that might have reassured him; for dimly already I divined his enterprise.

'It won't send you off in the pilot's boat, Bunny?'

'Not quite.'

'Then – you remember the pearl you wrote the –'

I did not wait for him to finish his sentence.

'You've got it!' I cried, my face on fire, for I caught sight of it that moment in the stateroom mirror.

Raffles seemed taken aback.

'Not yet,' said he; 'but I mean to have it before we get to Naples.'

'Is it on board?'

'Yes.'

'But how – where – who's got it?'

'A little German officer, a whipper-snapper with perpendicular moustaches.'[29]

'I saw him in the smoke-room.'

'That's the chap; he's always there. Herr Capitain Wilhelm von Heumann,[30] if you look in the list. Well, he's the special envoy of the emperor, and he's taking the pearl out with him!'

'You found this out in Bremen?'

'No, in Berlin, from a newspaper man I know there. I'm ashamed to tell you, Bunny, that I went there on purpose!'

I burst out laughing.

'You needn't be ashamed. You are doing the very thing I was rather hoping you were going to propose the other day on the river.'

'You were *hoping* it?' said Raffles, with his eyes wide open. Indeed, it was his turn to show surprise, and mine to be much more ashamed than I felt.

'Yes,' I answered, 'I was quite keen on the idea, but I wasn't going to propose it.'

'Yet you would have listened to me the other day?'

Certainly I would, and I told him so without reserve; not brazenly, you understand; not even now with the gusto of a man who savours such an adventure for its own sake, but doggedly, defiantly, through my teeth, as one who had tried to live honestly and failed. And, while I was about it, I told him much more. Eloquently enough I daresay, I gave him chapter and verse of my hopeless struggle, my inevitable defeat; for hopeless and inevitable they were to a man with my record, even though that record was written only in one's own soul. It was the old story of the thief trying to turn honest man; the thing was against nature,[31] and there was an end of it.

Raffles entirely disagreed with me. He shook his head over my conventional view. Human nature was a board of chequers;[32] why not reconcile oneself to alternate black and white? Why desire to be all one thing or all the other, like our forefathers on the stage or in the old-fashioned fiction? For his part, he enjoyed himself on all squares of the board, and liked the light the better for the shade. My conclusion he considered absurd.

'But you err in good company, Bunny, for all the cheap moralists who preach the same twaddle: old Virgil[33] was the first and worst offender of you all. I back myself to climb out of

Avernus[34] any day I like, and sooner or later I shall climb out for good. I suppose I can't very well turn myself into a Limited Liability Company. But I could retire and settle down and live blamelessly ever after. I'm not sure that it couldn't be done on this pearl alone!'

'Then you don't still think it too remarkable to sell?'

'We might take a fishery and haul it up with smaller fry. It would come after months of ill luck, just as we were going to sell the schooner; by Jove, it would be the talk of the Pacific!'

'Well, we've got to get it first. Is this von What's-his-name a formidable cuss?'

'More so than he looks; and he has the cheek of the devil!'

As he spoke a white drill skirt fluttered past the open state-room door, and I caught a glimpse of an upturned moustache beyond.

'But is he the chap we have to deal with? Won't the pearl be in the purser's keeping?'

Raffles stood at the door, frowning out upon the Solent,[35] but for an instant he turned to me with a sniff.

'My good fellow, do you suppose the whole ship's company knows there's a gem like that aboard? You said that it was worth a hundred thousand pounds; in Berlin they say it's priceless. I doubt if the skipper himself knows that von Heumann has it on him.'

'And he has?'

'Must have.'

'Then we have only him to deal with?'

He answered me without a word. Something white was fluttering past once more, and Raffles, stepping forth, made the promenaders three.

II

I do not ask to set foot aboard a finer steamship than the *Uhlan* of the Norddeutscher Lloyd, to meet a kindlier gentleman than her then commander, or better fellows than his officers. This much at least let me have the grace to admit. I hated the voyage.

It was no fault of anybody connected with the ship; it was no fault of the weather, which was monotonously ideal. Not even in my own heart did the reason reside; conscience and I were divorced at last, and the decree made absolute. With my scruples had fled all fear, and I was ready to revel between bright skies and sparkling sea with the lighthearted detachment of Raffles himself. It was Raffles himself who prevented me, but not Raffles alone. It was Raffles and that Colonial minx on her way home from school.

What he could see in her – but that begs the question. Of course he saw no more than I did, but to annoy me, or perhaps to punish me for my long defection, he must turn his back on me and devote himself to this chit[36] from Southampton to the Mediterranean. They were always together. It was too absurd. After breakfast they would begin, and go on until eleven or twelve at night; there was no intervening hour at which you might not hear her nasal laugh, or his quiet voice talking soft nonsense into her ear. Of course it was nonsense! Is it conceivable that a man like Raffles, with his knowledge of the world, and his experience of women[37] (a side of his character upon which I have purposely never touched, for it deserves another volume); is it credible, I ask, that such a man could find anything but nonsense to talk by the day together to a giddy young schoolgirl? I would not be unfair for the world. I think I have admitted that the young person had points. Her eyes, I suppose, were really fine, and certainly the shape of the little brown face was charming, so far as mere contour can charm. I admit also more audacity than I cared about, with enviable health, mettle, and vitality. I may not have occasion to report any of this young lady's speeches (they would scarcely bear it), and am therefore the more anxious to describe her without injustice. I confess to some little prejudice against her. I resented her success with Raffles, of whom, in consequence, I saw less and less each day. It is a mean thing to have to confess, but there must have been something not unlike jealousy rankling within me.

Jealousy there was in another quarter – crude, rampant, undignified jealousy. Captain von Heumann would twirl his moustaches into twin spires, shoot his white cuffs over his rings,

and stare at me insolently through his rimless eye-glasses; we
ought to have consoled each other, but we never exchanged a
syllable. The captain had a murderous scar across one of his
cheeks, a present from Heidelberg,[38] and I used to think how he
must long to have Raffles there to serve the same. It was not as
though von Heumann never had his innings. Raffles let him go
in several times a day, for the malicious pleasure of bowling him
out as he was 'getting set';[39] those were his words when I taxed
him disingenuously with obnoxious conduct towards a German
on a German boat.

'You'll make yourself disliked on board!'

'By von Heumann merely.'

'But is that wise when he's the man we've got to diddle?'[40]

'The wisest thing I ever did. To have chummed up with him
would have been fatal – the common dodge.'

I was consoled, encouraged, almost content. I had feared
Raffles was neglecting things, and I told him so in a burst. Here
we were near Gibraltar, and not a word since the Solent. He
shook his head with a smile.

'Plenty of time, Bunny, plenty of time. We can do nothing
before we get to Genoa, and that won't be till Sunday night.
The voyage is still young, and so are we; let's make the most of
things while we can.'

It was after dinner on the promenade deck, and as Raffles
spoke he glanced sharply fore and aft, leaving me next moment
with a step full of purpose. I retired to the smoking-room, to
smoke and read in a corner, and to watch von Heumann, who
very soon came to drink beer and to sulk in another.

Few travellers tempt the Red Sea[41] at mid-summer; the *Uhlan*
was very empty indeed. She had, however, but a limited supply
of cabins on the promenade deck, and there was just that excuse
for my sharing Raffles's room. I could have had one to myself
downstairs, but I must be up above. Raffles had insisted that I
should insist on the point. So we were together, I think, without
suspicion, though also without any object that I could see.

On the Sunday afternoon I was asleep in my berth, the lower
one, when the curtains were shaken by Raffles, who was in his
shirt-sleeves on the settee.

'Achilles sulking in his bunk!'[42]

'What else is there to do?' I asked him as I stretched and yawned. I noted, however, the good-humour of his tone, and did my best to catch it.

'I have found something else, Bunny.'

'I daresay!'

'You misunderstand me. The whippersnapper's making his century this afternoon. I've had other fish to fry.'

I swung my legs over the side of my berth and sat forward, as he was sitting, all attention. The inner door, a grating, was shut and bolted, and curtained like the open porthole.

'We shall be at Genoa before sunset,' continued Raffles. 'It's the place where the deed's got to be done.'

'So you still mean to do it!'

'Did I ever say I didn't?'

'You have said so little either way.'

'Advisedly so, my dear Bunny; why spoil a pleasure trip by talking unnecessary shop? But now the time has come. It must be done at Genoa or not at all.'

'On land?'

'No, on board, to-morrow night. To-night would do, but to-morrow is better, in case of mishap. If we were forced to use violence we could get away by the earliest train, and nothing be known till the ship was sailing and von Heumann found dead or drugged –'

'Not dead!' I exclaimed.

'Of course not,' assented Raffles, 'or there would be no need for us to bolt; but if we should have to bolt, Tuesday morning is our time, when this ship has got to sail, whatever happens. But I don't anticipate any violence. Violence is a confession of terrible incompetence. In all these years how many blows have you known me strike? Not one, I believe; but I have been quite ready to kill my man every time, if the worst came to the worst.'

I asked him how he proposed to enter von Heumann's state-room unobserved, and even through the curtained gloom of ours his face lighted up.

'Climb into my bunk, Bunny, and you shall see.'

I did so, but could see nothing. Raffles reached across me and tapped the ventilator, a sort of trap-door in the wall above his bed, some eighteen inches long and half that height. It opened outwards into the ventilating shaft.

'That,' said he, 'is our door to fortune. Open it if you like; you won't see much, because it doesn't open far; but loosening a couple of screws will set that all right. The shaft, as you may see, is more or less bottomless; you pass under it whenever you go to your bath, and the top is a skylight on the bridge. That's why this thing has to be done while we're at Genoa, because they keep no watch on the bridge in port. The ventilator opposite ours is von Heumann's. It again will only mean a couple of screws, and there's a beam to stand on while you work.'

'But if anybody should look up from below?'

'It's extremely unlikely that anybody will be astir below, so unlikely that we can afford to chance it. No, I can't have you there to make sure. The great point is that neither of us should be seen from the time we turn in. A couple of ship's boys do sentry-go[43] on these decks, and they shall be our witnesses; by Jove, it'll be the biggest mystery that ever was made!'

'If von Heumann doesn't resist.'

'Resist! He won't get the chance. He drinks too much beer to sleep light, and nothing is so easy as to chloroform a heavy sleeper; you've even done it yourself on an occasion of which it's perhaps unfair to remind you. Von Heumann will be past sensation almost as soon as I get my hand through his ventilator. I shall crawl in over his body, Bunny, my boy!'

'And I?'

'You will hand me what I want, and hold the fort in case of accidents, and generally lend me the moral support you've made me require. It's a luxury, Bunny, but I found it devilish difficult to do without it after you turned pi!'[44]

He said that von Heumann was certain to sleep with a bolted door, which he, of course, would leave unbolted, and spoke of other ways of laying a false scent while rifling the cabin. Not that Raffles anticipated a tiresome search. The pearl would be about von Heumann's person; in fact, Raffles knew exactly where and in what he kept it. Naturally I asked how he could have come by such knowledge, and his answer led up to a momentary unpleasantness.

'It's a very old story, Bunny. I really forget in what Book it comes; I'm only sure of the Testament. But Samson was the unlucky hero, and one Delilah the heroine.'[45]

And he looked so knowing that I could not be in a moment's doubt as to his meaning.

'So the fair Australian has been playing Delilah?' said I.

'In a very harmless, innocent sort of way.'

'She got his mission out of him?'

'Yes, I've forced him to score all the points he could, and that was his great stroke, as I hoped it would be. He has even shown Amy the pearl.'

'Amy, eh! and she promptly told you?'

'Nothing of the kind. What makes you think so? I had the greatest trouble in getting it out of her.'

His tone should have been a sufficient warning to me. I had not the tact to take it as such. At last I knew the meaning of his furious flirtation, and stood wagging my head and shaking my finger, blinded to his frowns by my own enlightenment.

'Wily worm!' said I. 'Now I see through it all; how dense I've been!'

'Sure you're not still?'

'No; now I understand what has beaten me all the week. I simply couldn't fathom what you saw in that little girl. I never dreamt it was part of the game.'

'So you think it was that and nothing more?'

'You deep old dog – of course I do!'

'You didn't know she was the daughter of a wealthy squatter?'[46]

'There are wealthy women by the dozen who would marry you to-morrow.'

'It doesn't occur to you that I might like to draw stumps,[47] start clean, and live happily ever after – in the bush?'

'With that voice? It certainly does not!'

'Bunny!' he cried, so fiercely that I braced myself for a blow. But no more followed.

'Do you think you would live happily?' I made bold to ask him.

'God knows!' he answered. And with that he left me, to marvel at his look and tone, and, more than ever, at the insufficiently exciting cause.

III

Of all the mere feats of cracksmanship which I have seen Raffles perform, at once the most delicate and most difficult was that which he accomplished between one and two o'clock on the Tuesday morning, aboard the North German steamer *Uhlan*, lying at anchor in Genoa harbour.

Not a hitch occurred. Everything had been foreseen; everything happened as I had been assured everything must. Nobody was about below, only the ship's boys on deck, and nobody on the bridge. It was twenty-five minutes past one when Raffles, without a stitch of clothing on his body, but with a glass phial, corked with cotton-wool, between his teeth, and a tiny screwdriver behind his ear, squirmed feet first through the ventilator over his berth; and it was nineteen minutes to two when he returned, head first, with the phial still between his teeth, and the cotton-wool rammed home to still the rattling of that which lay like a great grey bean within. He had taken screws out and put them in again; he had unfastened von Heumann's ventilator and had left it fast as he had found it – fast as he instantly proceeded to make his own. As for von Heumann, it had been enough to place the drenched wad first on his moustache, and then to hold it between his gaping lips; thereafter the intruder had climbed both ways across his shins without eliciting a groan.

And here was the prize – this pearl as large as a filbert[48] – with a pale pink tinge like a lady's finger-nail – this spoil of a filibustering age[49] – this gift from a European emperor to a South Sea chief. We gloated over it when all was snug. We toasted it in whisky and soda-water laid in overnight in view of the great moment. But the moment was greater, more triumphant, than our most sanguine dreams. All we had now to do was to secrete the gem (which Raffles had prised from its setting, replacing the latter), so that we could stand the strictest search and yet take it ashore with us at Naples; and this Raffles was doing when I turned in. I myself would have landed incontinently, that night, at Genoa, and bolted with the spoil; he would not hear of it, for a dozen good reasons which will be obvious.

On the whole I do not think that anything was discovered or suspected before we weighed anchor; but I cannot be sure. It is difficult to believe that a man could be chloroformed in his sleep and feel no tell-tale effects, sniff no suspicious odour, in the morning. Nevertheless, von Heumann reappeared as though nothing had happened to him, his German cap[50] over his eyes and his moustaches brushing the peak. And by ten o'clock we were quit of Genoa; the last lean, blue-chinned official had left our decks; the last fruitseller had been beaten off with bucketsful of water and left cursing us from his boat; the last passenger had come aboard at the last moment – a fussy greybeard who kept the big ship waiting while he haggled with his boatman over half a lira. But at length we were off, the tug was shed, the lighthouse[51] passed, and Raffles and I leaned together over the rail, watching our shadows on the pale green, liquid, veined marble that again washed the vessel's side.

Von Heumann was having his innings once more; it was part of the design that he should remain in all day, and so postpone the inevitable hour; and, though the lady looked bored, and was for ever glancing in our direction, he seemed only too willing to avail himself of his opportunities. But Raffles was moody and ill-at-ease. He had not the air of a successful man. I could but opine that the impending parting at Naples sat heavily on his spirit.

He would neither talk to me, nor would he let me go.

'Stop where you are, Bunny. I've things to tell you. Can you swim?'

'A bit.'

'Ten miles?'

'Ten?' I burst out laughing. 'Not one! Why do you ask?'

'We shall be within a ten miles' swim of the shore most of the day.'

'What on earth are you driving at, Raffles?'

'Nothing; only I shall swim for it if the worst comes to the worst. I suppose you can't swim under water at all?'

I did not answer his question. I scarcely heard it: cold beads were bursting through my skin.

'Why should the worst come to the worst?' I whispered. 'We aren't found out, are we?'

'No.'

'Then why speak as though we were?'

'We may be; an old enemy of ours is on board.'

'An old enemy?'

'Mackenzie.'

'Never!'

'The man with the beard who came aboard last.'

'Are you sure?'

'Sure! I was only sorry to see you didn't recognize him too.'

I took my handkerchief to my face; now that I thought of it, there had been something familiar in the old man's gait, as well as something rather youthful for his apparent years; his very beard seemed unconvincing, now that I recalled it in the light of this horrible revelation. I looked up and down the deck, but the old man was nowhere to be seen.

'That's the worst of it,' said Raffles. 'I saw him go into the captain's cabin twenty minutes ago.'

'But what can have brought him?' I cried miserably. 'Can it be a coincidence – is it somebody else he's after?'

Raffles shook his head.

'Hardly this time.'

'Then you think he's after you?'

'I've been afraid of it for some weeks.'

'Yet there you stand!'

'What am I to do? I don't want to swim for it before I must. I begin to wish I'd taken your advice, Bunny, and left the ship at Genoa. But I've not the smallest doubt that Mac was watching both ship and station till the last moment. That's why he ran it so fine.'

He took a cigarette and handed me the case, but I shook my head impatiently.

'I still don't understand,' said I. 'Why should he be after you? He couldn't come all this way about a jewel which was perfectly safe for all he knew. What's your own theory?'

'Simply that he's been on my track for some time, probably ever since friend Crawshay slipped clean through his fingers last November. There have been other indications. I am really not unprepared for this. But it can only be pure suspicion. I'll defy him to bring anything home, and I'll defy him to find the pearl! Theory, my dear Bunny? I know how he's got here as well as though I'd been inside that Scotchman's skin, and I know what he'll do next. He found out I'd gone abroad, and looked for a motive; he found out about von Heumann and his mission, and there was his motive cut-and-dried. Great chance – to nab me on a new job altogether. But he won't do it, Bunny; mark my words, he'll search the ship and search us all, when the loss is known; but he'll search in vain. And there's the skipper beckoning the whipper-snapper to his cabin: the fat will be in the fire in five minutes!'

Yet there was no conflagration, no fuss, no searching of the passengers, no whisper of what had happened in the air; instead of a stir there was portentous peace; and it was clear to me that Raffles was not a little disturbed at the falsification of all his predictions. There was something sinister in silence under such a loss, and the silence was sustained for hours during which Mackenzie never reappeared. But he was abroad during the luncheon-hour – he was in our cabin! I had left my book in Raffles's berth, and in taking it after lunch I touched the quilt. It was warm from the recent pressure of flesh and blood, and on an instinct I sprang to the ventilator; as I opened it the ventilator opposite was closed with a snap.

I waylaid Raffles. 'All right! Let him find the pearl.'

'Have you dumped it overboard?'

'That's a question I shan't condescend to answer.'

He turned on his heel, and at subsequent intervals I saw him making the most of his last afternoon with the inevitable Miss Werner. I remember that she looked both cool and smart in quite a simple affair of brown holland,[52] which toned well with her complexion, and was cleverly relieved with touches of

scarlet. I quite admired her that afternoon, for her eyes were
really very good, and so were her teeth, yet I had never admired
her more directly in my own despite. For I passed them again
and again in order to get a word with Raffles, to tell him I knew
there was danger in the wind; but he would not so much as
catch my eye. So at last I gave it up. And I saw him next in the
captain's cabin.

They had summoned him first; he had gone in smiling; and
smiling I found him when they summoned me. The state-room
was spacious, as befitted that of a commander. Mackenzie sat
on the settee, his beard in front of him on the polished table;
but a revolver lay in front of the captain; and, when I had
entered, the chief officer, who had summoned me, shut the door
and put his back to it. Von Heumann completed the party, his
fingers busy with his moustache.

Raffles greeted me.

'This is a great joke!' he cried. 'You remember the pearl you
were so keen about, Bunny, the emperor's pearl, the pearl money
wouldn't buy? It seems it was entrusted to our little friend here,
to take out to Canoodle Dum,[53] and the poor little chap's gone
and lost it; *ergo*, as we're Britishers, they think we've got it!'

'But I know ye have,' put in Mackenzie, nodding to his beard.

'You will recognize that loyal and patriotic voice,' said
Raffles. 'Mon, 'tis our auld acquaintance Mackenzie, o' Scoteland Yarrd an' Scoteland itsel'!'

'Dat is enough,' cried the captain. 'Have you submid to be
searge, or do I vorce you?'

'What you will,' said Raffles, 'but it will do you no harm to
give us fair play first. You accuse us of breaking into Captain
von Heumann's state-room during the small hours of this morning, and abstracting from it this confounded pearl. Well, I can
prove that I was in my own room all night long, and I have no
doubt my friend can prove the same.'

'Most certainly I can,' said I indignantly. 'The ship's boys can
bear witness to that.'

Mackenzie laughed, and shook his head at his reflection in
the polished mahogany.

'That was vera clever,' said he, 'and like enough it would ha'

served ye had I not stepped aboard. But I've just had a look at
they ventilators, and I think I know how ye worrked it. Anyway,
captain, it makes no matter. I'll just be clappin' the darbies on
these young sparks,[54] an' then –'

'By what right?' roared Raffles, in a ringing voice, and I never
saw his face in such a blaze. 'Search us if you like; search every
scrap and stitch we possess; but you dare to lay a finger on us
without a warrant!'

'I wouldna' dare,' said Mackenzie gravely, as he fumbled in his
breast pocket, and Raffles dived his hand into his own. 'Haud his
wrist!' shouted the Scotchman; and the huge Colt[55] that had been
with us many a night, but had never been fired in my hearing,
clattered on the table and was raked in by the captain.

'All right,' said Raffles savagely to the mate. 'You can let
go now. I won't try it again. Now, Mackenzie, let's see your
warrant!'

'Ye'll no mishandle it?'

'What good would that do me? Let me see it,' said Raffles,
peremptorily, and the detective obeyed. Raffles raised his eyebrows as he perused the document; his mouth hardened, but
suddenly relaxed; and it was with a smile and a shrug that he
returned the paper.

'Wull that do for ye?' inquired Mackenzie.

'It may. I congratulate you, Mackenzie; it's a strong hand, at
any rate. Two burglaries and the Melrose necklace, Bunny!'
And he turned to me with a rueful smile.

'An' all easy to prove,' said the Scotchman, pocketing the
warrant. 'I've one o' these for you,' he added, nodding to me,
'only not such a long one.'

'To thingk,' said the captain reproachfully, 'that my shib
should be made a den of thiefs! It shall be a very disagreeable
madder. I have been obliged to pud you both in irons until we
ged to Nables.'

'Surely not!' exclaimed Raffles. 'Mackenzie, intercede with
him; don't give your countrymen away before all hands! Captain, we can't escape; surely you could hush it up for the night?
Look here, here's everything I have in my pockets; you empty
yours too, Bunny, and they shall strip us stark if they suspect

we've weapons up our sleeves. All I ask is that we are allowed to get out of this without gyves upon our wrists!'

'Webbons you may not have,' said the captain; 'but wad about der bearl dat you were sdealing?'

'You shall have it!' cried Raffles. 'You shall have it this minute if you guarantee no public indignity on board!'

'That I'll see to,' said Mackenzie, 'as long as you behave yourselves. There now, where is't?'

'On the table under your nose.'

My eyes fell with the rest, but no pearl was there; only the contents of our pockets – our watches, pocket-books, pencils, penknives, cigarette cases – lay on the shiny table along with the revolvers already mentioned.

'Ye're humbuggin' us,' said Mackenzie. 'What's the use?'

'I'm doing nothing of the sort,' laughed Raffles. 'I'm testing you. Where's the harm?'

'It's here, joke apart?'

'On that table, by all my gods.'

Mackenzie opened the cigarette cases and shook each particular cigarette. Thereupon Raffles prayed to be allowed to smoke one, and, when his prayer was heard, observed that the pearl had been on the table much longer than the cigarettes. Mackenzie promptly caught up the Colt and opened the chamber in the butt.

'Not there, not there,' said Raffles; 'but you're getting hot. Try the cartridges.'

Mackenzie emptied them into his palm, and shook each one at his ear without result.

'Oh, give them to me!'

And, in an instant, Raffles had found the right one, had bitten out the bullet,[56] and placed the emperor's pearl with a flourish in the centre of the table.

'After that you will perhaps show me such little consideration as is in your power. Captain, I have been a bit of a villain, as you see, and as such I am ready and willing to lie in irons all night if you deem it requisite for the safety of the ship. All I ask is that you do me one favour first.'

'That shall debend on wad der vafour has been.'

'Captain, I've done a worse thing aboard your ship than any of you know. I have become engaged to be married, and I want to say goodbye!'

I suppose we were all equally amazed; but the only one to express his amazement was von Heumann, whose deep-chested German oath was almost his first contribution to the proceedings. He was not slow to follow it, however, with a vigorous protest against the proposed farewell; but he was overruled, and the masterful prisoner had his way. He was to have five minutes with the girl, while the captain and Mackenzie stood within range (but not earshot), with their revolvers behind their backs. As we were moving from the cabin, in a body, he stopped and gripped my hand.

'So I've let you in at last, Bunny – at last and after all! If you knew how sorry I am . . . But you won't get much – I don't see why you should get anything at all. Can you forgive me? This may be for years, and it may be for ever, you know! You were a good pal always when it came to the scratch; some day or other you mayn't be so sorry to remember you were a good pal at the last!'

There was a meaning in his eye that I understood; and my teeth were set, and my nerves strung ready, as I wrung that strong and cunning hand for the last time in my life.

How that last scene stays with me, and will stay to my death! How I see every detail, every shadow on the sunlit deck! We were among the islands that dot the course from Genoa to Naples; that was Elba[57] falling back on our starboard quarter, that purple patch with the hot sun setting over it. The captain's cabin opened to starboard, and the starboard promenade deck, sheeted with sunshine and scored with shadow, was deserted but for the group of which I was one, and for the pale, slim, brown figure further aft with Raffles. Engaged? I could not believe it, cannot to this day. Yet there they stood together, and we did not hear a word; there they stood out against the sunset, and the long, dazzling highway of sunlit sea that sparkled from Elba to the *Uhlan*'s plates; and their shadows reached almost to our feet.

Suddenly – an instant – and the thing was done – a thing I have never known whether to admire or to detest. He caught her – he kissed her before us all – then flung her from him so that she almost fell. It was that action which foretold the next. The mate sprang after him, and I sprang after the mate.

Raffles was on the rail, but only just.

'Hold him, Bunny!' he cried. 'Hold him tight!'

And, as I obeyed that last behest with all my might, without a thought of what I was doing, save that he bade me do it, I saw his hands shoot up and his head bob down, and his lithe, spare body cut the sunset as cleanly and precisely as though he had plunged at his leisure[58] from a diver's board!

Of what followed on deck I can tell you nothing, for I was not there. Nor can my final punishment, my long imprisonment, my everlasting disgrace, concern or profit you, beyond the interest and advantage to be gleaned from the knowledge that I at least had my deserts. But one thing I must set down, believe it who will – one more thing only and I am done.

It was into a second-class cabin, on the starboard side, that I was promptly thrust in irons, and the door locked upon me as though I were another Raffles. Meanwhile a boat was lowered, and the sea scoured to no purpose, as is doubtless on record elsewhere. But either the setting sun, flashing over the waves, must have blinded all eyes, or else mine were victims of a strange illusion.

For the boat was back, the screw throbbing, and the prisoner peering through his porthole across the sunlit waters that he believed had closed for ever over his comrade's head. Suddenly the sun sank behind the Island of Elba, the lane of dancing sunlight was instantaneously quenched and swallowed in the trackless waste, and in the middle distance, already miles astern, either my sight deceived me or a black speck bobbed amid the grey. The bugle had blown for dinner: it may well be that all save myself had ceased to strain an eye. And now I lost what I had found, now it rose, now sank, and now I gave it up utterly. Yet anon it would rise again, a mere mote dancing in the dim grey distance, drifting towards a purple island, beneath a fading western sky, streaked with dead gold and cerise. And night fell before I knew whether it was a human head or not.

Notes

THE IDES OF MARCH

The Ides of March is the 15th of March in the ancient Roman calendar (where the Ides of each month fall eight days after the Nones), and the day on which Julius Caesar was murdered after he had ignored a warning from a soothsayer. The phrase 'Beware the Ides of March', from Shakespeare's *Julius Caesar*, serves as a warning of impending and certain danger.

1. *the Albany*: Or Albany, a building off Piccadilly, dating from 1770–74, named after its former owner, Frederick, Duke of Albany. It was converted into bachelor chambers in 1802 by Henry Holland, with the addition of buildings at the back on either side of a covered way or 'rope walk'. The rooms occupied by Raffles were on the first floor of the 'Mansion House', on the left side of the main entrance, although the description is based on the rooms known to Hornung, No. E4, which were occupied by George Cecil Ives (1867–1950) between 1895 and 1897.

2. *baccarat-counters*: Used to place bets in the game baccarat, a fashionable, though illegal, card game, which was introduced to Britain from the Continent. It became familiar to the public because of the 'Royal Baccarat Scandal' of 1890 when Sir William Gordon-Cumming was accused of cheating during a game of baccarat at a house-party at Tranby Croft, near Hull, and this happened while the Prince of Wales was in the room.

3. *I fagged for you at school*: A fag at a British public school was a junior boy who did menial jobs for a senior one.

4. *a Sullivan*: A cigarette made by Sullivan, Powell & Co., Ltd, of 4 George Street, Hanover Square, who specialized in handmade 'oriental cigarettes' containing the finest Egyptian tobacco.

5. *cuss*: American colloquial term, from 'cursed' ('cussed'); used affectionately as a diminutive form of 'customer'.

6. *the mag*: Based on the Uppingham School Magazine in which Hornung's earliest literary work had appeared in 1882–3.

7. *Mount Street*: A road running from Berkeley Square to Park Lane, in Mayfair. The building where Bunny lived had a lift and a uniformed concierge (see 'No Sinecure', *The Black Mask*, 1901), and could only have been Cliveden Chambers, at 104 Mount Street. Hornung may have had in mind 104F, which belonged to Wilfrid Scawen Blunt (1840–1922).

8. *a bill of sale*: A grant by deed by which ownership, but not possession, of personal goods and chattels is transferred from one person to another; it entitles the holder to sell the goods if repayments are not made on the money advanced.

9. *captain of the eleven*: Captain of the First Eleven at Cricket. Hornung had in mind J. A. Turner (1863–1924), who was captain of cricket in 1882 during his first year at Uppingham. He later described Raffles as also having been 'the fastest man in the fifteen, athletic champion, and an ornament of the Upper Sixth' (cf. *Mr Justice Raffles*), which was also true of Turner.

10. *pluck*: Fortitude, courage, spirit and inner strength; the quality which Hornung rated above all others, his favourite motto being: 'Money lost – little lost. Honour lost – much lost. Pluck lost – all lost' (quoted in *Young Blood*, 1898, IV, 39: 'It's only pluck that's everything. We must never lose that, mother, we must never lose that!').

11. *Bunny*: The narrator's nickname. His real name is given as Harry Manders in the play of 1903. It was the name of a boy who had been in the same house as Hornung at Uppingham (Tuck's, afterwards Constable's). He appears in the Uppingham School Roll, 1853–1947, thus: 'Came in May 1877: Manders, Harry. (C) Sept. 1861. Son of F. Manders, Ardmore, Donnybrook, Co. Dublin. Left Dec. 1878.'

12. *A. J. Raffles*: The initials appear here for the first time (though they had been given in the subtitle used for the serial publication). They are those of Hornung's housemaster at Uppingham, A. J. (Alfred Johnson) Tuck, and, in reverse, those of the 1882 Uppingham cricket captain, J. A. (John Alfred) Turner (see note 9). The 'A' is for 'Arthur', which was also Conan Doyle's first name and that of the author's son, Arthur Oscar Hornung (first given as 'Arturo' in 'The Fate of Faustina', and as 'Arthur' in 'An Old Flame', *The Black Mask*, 1901).

13. *backing and filling*: A nautical expression, the action of the wind on the side of a sail, 'tacking against the wind'; used figuratively to mean 'irresolute', 'constantly changing one's position'.

14. *the very secrets of my heart*: A phrase from Shakespeare, 'by and by thy bosom shall partake the secrets of my heart' (*Julius Caesar*, II, i).

15. *Love and Death ... The Blessed Damozel*: The first is a painting by George Frederic Watts (1817–1904), inspired by the early death of

the 8th Marquess of Lothian. 'Love stands upon the threshold of the House of Life, barring the entry against the fatal advance of Death,' the artist explained: 'The bright wings of the god are already crushed against the lintel of the door and the petals are falling from the roses that Love has set around the porch.' It was one of the most popular pictures of the day: 'Most people are quite familiar with this beautiful painting. Death, black-veiled and cyprus crowned, forcing his way in, notwithstanding the efforts of Love who, with glorious golden curls and shimmering wings, piteously tries to bar him out' (*Tit-Bits*, 25 September 1897). It exists in two versions. The first, painted in 1877, was given by the artist to the Whitworth Art Gallery at the University of Manchester; the second, of 1896 (in the Watts Gallery, Guildford, on loan from Tate Britain), was part of a trilogy with *Love and Life* (1896) and *Love Triumphant* (1898). The reproduction which Raffles had was by Frederick Hollyer (1837–1933) who is mentioned by name in *Mr Justice Raffles*.

The Blessed Damozel is a painting by Dante Gabriel Rossetti (1828–82), now in the Fogg Museum of Art in Boston, illustrating his poem of the same name:

> The blessed Damozel leaned out
> > From the gold bar of Heaven;
> Her eyes were deeper than the depth
> > Of waters stilled at even;
> She had three lilies in her hand,
> > And stars in her hair were seven.
> > > (*Poems*, 1870)

The first version was completed in 1877; a later version, painted in 1879, which was on display at the New Gallery in Regent Street at the time the story was written, is now in the Lady Lever Art Gallery, Port Sunlight.

16. *of the first water*: The colour or lustre of a diamond is described as its 'water', and those 'of the first water' are the finest. The term is used of any person who is outstanding in a particular field.

17. *on the side of the angels*: From the phrase used by Benjamin Disraeli (1804–81) in a speech at the Oxford Diocesan Conference on 25 November 1864 when discussing the theory of evolution ('Is man an ape or an Angel? I, my lord, am on the side of the angels'); it came to mean 'on the side of the righteous'.

18. *he was in the habit of parading the town . . . I pulled the rope up after him*: The incident was based on the author's memories of an

incident at Uppingham School. In *Fathers of Men* (1912) the hero, Jan Rutter, behaves in a similar fashion.

19. *a drag*: A restraining influence; a brake, a weight or mechanism to slow movement (as in 'drag-anchor' or 'drag-chain').

20. *by hook or crook*: In one way or another; said to derive from a shepherd's crook and bill-hook, but with criminal connotations ('by fair means or foul'): a 'hook' or 'hooker' was slang for a pickpocket; 'by crook' suggests the use of dishonest means. Raffles says of his agreement with Daniel Levy: 'My side was to get you by hook or crook a certain letter which you say you never wrote. As a matter of fact it was only to be got by crook – ' (*Mr Justice Raffles*, 1909).

21. *raise the wind*: Procure money by borrowing or other means; a nautical metaphor: to propel the ship you must raise the wind.

22. *here in Bond Street*: Bond Street was named after Sir Thomas Bond, a friend of Charles II; it runs north from Piccadilly to Oxford Street and has two parts: Old Bond Street to the south, which was laid out in 1686, and New Bond Street to the north. The Albany is not 'in Bond Street', but in the vicinity of Bond Street, as it has entrances on to Piccadilly to the south and Burlington Gardens to the north.

23. *a covert coat*: (French, *couvert*); a short overcoat or dust-coat, made of a woven twill fabric, originally designed to be worn while shooting.

24. *tearing a leaflet from a Shakesperian calendar*: An older spelling (also 'Shaksperian'), now commonly 'Shakespearean'. This refers to a calendar with quotations from Shakespeare's works appropriate to each day of the year, such as *The Shakespeare Diary and Almanack* (published by W. Kent & Co.), the *Shakespeare Daily Calendar* (issued by Bemrose & Sons), and *The Shakespeare Calendar* (published by F. W. Savory). The 'leaflet' is the small leaf, which in this instance was for '14 March'.

25. *the Ides of March, remember*: Not a direct quotation from *Julius Caesar*, but an allusion to the warning given by the soothsayer.

26. *keep their weather eye open*: Originally a nautical expression, from the watch on the weather-side of a ship from which the greatest danger comes.

27. *some windows across the road*: On the west side of Old Bond Street. The east side had a jewel broker, a watchsmith, a goldsmith, and a silversmith, but there were no such shops on the west side. Hornung had in mind the gallery of Thomas Agnew and Sons, at 39b, from which Gainsborough's painting of *The Duchess of Devonshire* was stolen in 1876.

28. *the devil of a night-bird*: Or night-hawk, underworld slang, a person who goes about by night for criminal reasons.

29. *we'll take a rise out of him*: Have a laugh at his expense; from fish, which get caught when they rise to the bait.

30. *sinking the commander in the leader*: Leading with the willing compliance of the led, rather than by the exercise of authority. This was the quality which most endeared the headmaster of Uppingham to the boys: 'We looked up at him, when he was in a mood of sternness or enthusiasm, and thought, What a soldier you would have made! How you would have ordered a charge, and led it! . . . But next and far more, we loved him as a leader. He had a cause, and he took us into it' (J. H. Skrine, *A Memory of Edward Thring*, Macmillan, 1890, pp. 67–8).

31. *chaff*: A collective term for the worthless husks of corn or other grain separated by threshing or winnowing; thus 'a jest', 'an invention'.

32. *Danby*: A fictitious jeweller, though the name has local associations; the 1st Earl of Danby (1631–72) owned part of the leasehold of Bond Street; the artist Francis Danby resided there; and the Danby brothers and Nathaniel Danby had commercial premises in Great Marlborough Street.

33. *dark lantern*: A small portable oil lamp, or torch, with a metal shutter that could be turned to close off the light, known as a 'bull's eye lantern' when it had a thick glass lens to spread the beam. 'Burglars' lanterns vary in size – they are known as "darkeys" in the profession – the better class of lantern now in use being of the police pattern' ('Crimes and Criminals', *Strand Magazine*, March 1894).

34. *rock-oil*: Petrol, oil used as a lubricant. The bottle of rock-oil found its way to the Black Museum at Scotland Yard and the use to which it was put is explained by the curator: 'That's his centre-bit, and this is the bottle of rock-oil he's supposed to have kept dipping it in to prevent making a noise' ('The Raffles Relics', *A Thief in the Night*).

35. *his razors*: Cut-throat razors become blunt after use, so it was customary for those who could afford to do so to have a case holding seven or eight razors, which would last a week and could be sharpened at one time.

36. *a skeleton key was selected from the bunch*: Skeleton keys, or 'twirls', are ground down to avoid the wards in warded locks; the term is also used of lock picks or 'pick-locks', which are made of stout wire bent at the ends. 'Of skeleton keys there is a very admirable selection at New Scotland Yard. They are made both of iron and steel – mostly of scrap-iron as it is tougher and has no grain in it. Burglars and

housebreakers usually make their own skeleton keys – some of which are very rough. The key is bought in the block, and the wards are cut out as needed' ('Burglars and Burgling', *Strand Magazine*, March 1894).

37. *jointed jemmy*: A steel crow bar in two sections which could be screwed together or fastened by a sliding collar.

38. *Chubb's safe*: The famous firm of Chubb & Sons, founded by Charles Chubb in 1818, makers of patent locks (such as the 'detector lock', which jammed when an attempt was made to pick it); according to an article in the *Strand Magazine* Chubb safes were 'practically speaking impregnable' ('Thieves v. Locks and Safes', November 1894).

39. *our finger-marks on the dusty banisters*: The unique nature of these marks was not yet recognized by the police; the Fingerprint Bureau at Scotland Yard was founded by Edward Henry on 1 July 1901, and the first conviction based on them was that of Harry Jackson in June 1902.

40. *I'm as cold as Keats's owl*: An allusion to the owl mentioned in the opening lines of 'The Eve of Saint Agnes' (1820), by John Keats (1795–1821): 'St Agnes' Eve – Ah, bitter chill it was!/The owl, for all his feathers, was a-cold.'

41. *aigrettes*: (French, egret), sprays of gems resembling the tuft or plumes on the bird's tail.

42. *the Thimbleby diamonds*: The name is found in a variety of spellings. 'Thimbleby' is the spelling used for villages in Lincolnshire and Yorkshire, and is found in *Punch* on 9 October 1897 in a humorous exchange between Mrs Thimbleby and Mrs Grimbleby. However in 'The Criminologists' Club' (in *A Thief in the Night*, 1905), Raffles is said to have taken 'the Thimblely [*sic*] diamonds and returned them to Lord Thimblely [*sic*]'. This confirms that it was the name of an aristocratic English family, and suggests that of Sir John Thimbelby [*sic*] whose wife is shown in a portrait by Van Dyck in the National Gallery.

43. *a poor lot of paste*: Paste, or strass, is a hard vitreous composition of the purest, most transparent and most highly refractive glass. Imitation gems made from it can be distinguished from the real thing by their inferior hardness (as glass will not cut glass), by chemical tests, or by the warmer sensation which they communicate to the tongue.

44. *the Dormer house-boat at Henley*: Henley-on-Thames is thirty-five miles west of London and is famous for the rowing regatta held annually since 1839. Houseboats were moored along the river front, including one owned by the American millionaire Cornelius Vanderbilt; the name recalls that of the 12th Baron Dormer (1830–1900).

45. *the Colonies*: Australia, which consisted of six colonies until the formation of the 'Commonwealth of Australia' on 1 January 1901.

46. *Gilbert's lines*: Lines by William Schwenck Gilbert (1836–1911) from 'The Policeman's Lot' in *The Pirates of Penzance* (1879):

> When a felon's not engaged in his employment
> > Or maturing his felonious little plans,
> His capacity for innocent enjoyment
> > Is just as great as any honest man's.
>
> . . .
>
> When the enterprising burglar's not a-burgling,
> > When the cut-throat isn't occupied in crime,
> He loves to hear the little brook a-gurgling,
> > And listen to the merry village chime.

47. *Nothing matters another rap*: A 'rap' is a base halfpenny worth half a farthing; and therefore something that is worthless.

A COSTUME PIECE

A 'costume piece' is a theatrical term for a costume drama.

1. *Reuben Rosenthall*: The character was based on Barney Barnato (Barnett Isaacs Barnato, 1852–97), the South African diamond magnate and speculator known as the 'Kaffir King', who had died in June 1897. 'Reuben Rosenthal' was used by Agatha Christie for a character in *The Labours of Hercules* (1947).

2. *the halfpenny evening papers*: London had six halfpenny evening papers: the *Echo* (1868–1905), *Evening Argus* (1880–97), *Evening News* (1881–1980), *Evening Standard* (from 1827), *Star* (1888–1960) and *Sun* (1893–1906). There were three other evening papers which cost a penny: the *Pall Mall Gazette*, the *St James's Gazette* and the *Globe*.

3. *St John's Wood*: An area of London, north of Regent's Park (named after a wood owned by the Knights of St John), familiar to Hornung and Raffles as the site of Lord's cricket ground.

4. *Kaffirs*: *Kafirs* or infidels; an Arabic name for Africans who were not Muslims, and used by Europeans for the Bantu races who worked in the diamond fields.

5. *a prize-fighter*: A pugilist who takes part in a match for prize money or a trophy. Barnato took up boxing in his youth, consorted with prize-fighters, and promoted matches when he was in South Africa.

6. *magisterial proceedings*: A case brought by the police before a metropolitan magistrate at one of fourteen police courts attached to police stations. Barney Barnato caused a stir in 1895 when he presented

himself at the Marlborough Street police court to stand bail for a friend
from Hatton Garden, who had been charged under the Bankruptcy
Act.

7. *Old Bohemian Club*: 'Bohemian' was used to describe the irregular
and penurious lifestyle of writers and artists. The 'Old Bohemian' was
the name used by Dr Gustave Ludwig Moritz Strauss (1807–87), a
founding member of the Savage Club and author of *Reminiscences of
an Old Bohemian* (1882) and *Stories of an Old Bohemian* (1883). The
club is based on the Savage and on the Vagabonds' Club (of which
Hornung was a member), though the inspiration for the banquet was
one held in honour of Barney Barnato at the Criterion restaurant in
May 1895.

8. *the Old Country*: Great Britain, the mother country.

9. *our bloated princes*: The sons and grandsons of Queen Victoria,
specifically her eldest son, the Prince of Wales (later Edward VII).

10. *before you could say Jack Robinson*: Immediately, instantly; the
eighteenth-century phrase is said to derive from a man of that name
who would call upon his neighbours, but would be gone before his
name could be announced.

11. *write his name in bullets on the opposite wall*: Sherlock Holmes
engaged in a similar activity in his rooms at 221b Baker Street. 'Holmes
in one of his queer humours would sit in an arm-chair with his hair-
trigger and a hundred Boxer cartridges, and proceed to adorn the
opposite wall with a patriotic V.R. done in bullet-pocks' (A. Conan
Doyle, 'The Musgrave Ritual', *The Memoirs of Sherlock Holmes*,
George Newnes, 1894).

12. *Does the painter paint for bread alone*: An echo of the biblical
saying, 'man does not live by bread alone' (Luke, 4:4).

13. *Tom of Bow and Dick of Whitechapel*: Tom and Dick (later 'Tom,
Dick and Harry') was a term for the common run of men, used here to
mean people who were representative of Bow and Whitechapel (two
working-class areas of East London where crime was rife).

14. *Art for art's sake*: A concept formulated by Benjamin Constant
(1767–1834) in his *Journal Intime* (11 February 1804): 'L'art pour
l'art est sans but; tout but denature l'art' ('Art for art's sake and without
purpose; purpose perverts art'); it was adopted by Théophile Gautier
and formed the basis of the Aesthetic Movement in England.

15. *I would rob St Paul's Cathedral*: In *Cassell's Magazine* this was: 'I
would rob a millionaire', which is less disconcerting. St Paul's is one
of London's most prominent buildings and the masterpiece of Sir
Christopher Wren. It celebrated its bicentenary on 2 December 1897.

16. *The Bank of England*: The central bank, founded in 1601 and

housed in Threadneedle Street. The building, the western side of which was designed by Sir John Soane in 1788, was considered the most secure place in England. 'The vaults usually contain about 20 million pounds in gold and silver, while there are over 25 millions of pounds sterling of the Bank's notes in circulation' (Karl Baedeker, *London and Its Environs*, Leipzig, 1894, p. 105).

17. *Billy Purvis*: The character was suggested by the pugilists who surrounded Barney Barnato, such as Bat Mullins, but the name is taken from the real Billy Purvis (1784–1853), the 'extraordinary, witty and comical showman' who was a celebrity in his day and is credited with having coined the word 'Geordie' to describe people from Newcastle.

18. *A man's reach must exceed his grasp, dear boy, or what the dickens is a heaven for*: 'Ah but a man's reach should exceed his grasp, or what's a Heaven for?' (Robert Browning, 'Andrea del Sarto', 1855, 97–8).

19. *the thickest thieves in all London*: From the phrase 'as thick as thieves', 'on very intimate terms', from the confidential and secret manner by which thieves confer.

20. *the angle formed by two broad thoroughfares*: The angle of Grove End Road and Circus Road, enclosing the area where the largest houses in St John's Wood were to be found.

21. *the four-mile radius*: London was the largest city in the world. The four-mile radius covered an area of 117 square miles and contained over four million people.

22. *a cutty pipe*: Scottish, 'short'; a short clay pipe.

23. *a battered billycock*: A hard or soft round-crowned felt hat, or bowler hat, said to have been named after William (Billy) Coke, for whom it was first designed in 1850. Sherlock Holmes made a series of deductions from 'a battered billycock' in 'The Adventure of the Blue Carbuncle' (A. Conan Doyle, *The Adventures of Sherlock Holmes*, George Newnes, 1892).

24. *Finchley Road*: A road which runs north from St John's Wood to Finchley, via Swiss Cottage, Frognal, and Golders Green. Bunny is referring to the southern end where it joins Wellington Road.

25. *an Atlas omnibus*: The 'Atlas' was a two-horse bus operated by the London General Omnibus Company and was coloured light green; it ran every eight minutes from the Eyre Arms in St John's Wood, via Wellington Road, Park Road, Baker Street, Oxford Street, Regent Street, Charing Cross, Westminster Bridge, Westminster Bridge Road, to the London Road Office, then to Walworth and the Old Kent Road. It was the bus on which Hornung travelled when going to Lord's cricket ground.

26. *another omnibus to Sloane Street*: The chocolate-coloured Chelsea bus, which ran from Hoxton and the City, through Piccadilly to Sloane Square and beyond.

27. *the King's Road*: The main artery of Chelsea (formerly the king's private road to Hampton Court) served by a local one-horse bus running from Sloane Square to Fullham. The area had a flourishing artistic community, which included James Abbott McNeill Whistler, Philip Wilson Steer and Frank Brangwyn.

28. *his silk hat*: His top hat of brushed silk. The top hat, which identified the class of the wearer, celebrated its centenary in 1897.

29. *shag*: A coarse, strong and cheap pipe tobacco. 'Shag tobacco has obtained its distinctive name from its being so finely cut that the filaments appear like so much "shag" – the old name for short and matted wool or hair. It is manufactured of the strongest and very worst kind of leaf, and is chiefly consumed by the poorer classes' (Joseph Fune, *A Paper of Tobacco*, 1839).

30. *pied-à-terre*: The studio used by Raffles was on the north side of the King's Road, a district with a thriving artistic colony (whose members met at the Chelsea Arts Club).

31. *my private pavilion*: As in cricket or sports pavilion, a place where players change before a game.

32. *Shoreditch*: A working-class suburb in the East End of London, notorious for its high level of crime and deprivation. It was said of Barney Barnato that wherever he went he 'carried a bit of Shoreditch about with him'.

33. *toggery*: Clothing, garments, costumes; slang, 'togs' ('togas').

34. *a rig*: A costume or outfit (from the rigging of a ship). This includes the black mask to cover the eyes and the 'gag' to tie around the mouth.

35. *it's the sitting with their pads on that upsets their applecart*: Pads are worn by cricketers to protect the lower legs and are put on in advance so that the cricketer is ready to take the place of an outgoing batsman. 'To upset the applecart' is to throw everything into disarray, to upset carefully laid plans (from the general disorder when a carefully piled cart of apples is overturned). Cecil Rhodes complained that Dr Jameson had 'upset his applecart' after the fiasco of the Jameson Raid into the Transvaal at the end of 1895.

36. *Illicit Diamond Buyer*: A South African term. It was the title of a series of stories by George Griffith (George Chetwynd Griffith Jones, 1859–1906), which were serialized in *Pearson's Magazine* between July and December 1897 and published as *Knaves of Diamonds*, 1899. Griffith explained the significance of the initials in a footnote to the first story:

Never since men first began to risk health and life and honour for the sake of swift-won wealth have three characters of any alphabet been brought together which in their combination connoted, as the logicians say, so much as these do, for in their internal meaning they include all the extremes and means of human fortune which may be imagined to lie between a life of luxury, and often of distinction, in which wealth makes wealth, till millions pile on millions; and fifteen years' penal servitude on the Breakwater at Capetown, which is the Portland of South Africa, with its semi-starvation and heartbreaking monotonous toil under the pitiless sub-tropical sun . . . The true import of these mystic and momentous letters may be explained better here than elsewhere. They have, in fact, two meanings – Illicit Diamond Buying, the crime specified in the various Diamond Acts, and the Illicit Diamond Buyer, one who buys 'gonivahs', or stones which he knows to have been stolen or otherwise illicitly come by.

It was widely believed that Barnato had engaged in illicit diamond buying while amassing his wealth in the mid-1870s.

37. *the breakwater at Capetown*: The breakwater in Table Bay was started in 1860 and built by convicts who were incarcerated in the neighbouring Breakwater Prison where the conditions were harsh.

38. *A brush with the heathen*: A fight with the heathen; the phrase was used by writers of the period to describe 'small wars' and minor skirmishes, as in 'A Brush with the Natives' in G. A. Henty's *Young Colonists*, or 'Brush with Afridis' (*Daily Chronicle*, 15 November 1897).

39. *Ladies with an i*: Cockneys, or 'common' women, from the way they pronounced the word. *Punch* used the spelling in a humorous filler on 4 December 1897: ' 'Arry of Cockaigne, having heard the word "Bacchylides" recently mentioned, wishes to know if it means "lidies as smoke cigarettes".'

40. *raising Cain*: Making an angry fuss or noisy disturbance, raising the devil. Cain was roused to such violent anger that he murdered his brother (Genesis 4:5) and his name became synonymous with the devil. Rudyard Kipling associates it with drunkenness in 'The Ballad of the "Bolivar" ': 'Seven men from all the world back to the docks again/ Rolling down the Ratcliffe Road drunk and raising Cain' (*Barrack-Room Ballads*, 1892).

41. *on the knees of the gods*: In the lap of the gods; a person's fate lies on the knees of the gods while they decide the outcome. The phrase is used by Homer in the *Odyssey* and the *Iliad*, and is also the title of the last story in *The Black Mask* (1901), where Raffles meets his death.

42. *a head of hair like a bath sponge*: The simile was used of the Afro-Caribbean hairstyle of Miss Joy Howard, who was also known

as the 'moss-haired girl'; she was appearing as one of the 'Human Curiosities' in Barnum and Bailey's circus, which had opened at Olympia on 26 December 1897. In *Collier's Weekly* it appeared as 'a tremendous head of hair'.

43. *The Gardenia*: A fictitious gambling den or night-club, named after the flower, and perhaps suggested by the Cocoa Tree (a gambling club in St James's) or other smaller clubs in Soho such as the International Club (which was raided by the police on 9 January 1898). Gardenias were the most fashionable flowers for the buttonholes of clubmen.

44. *the psychological moment*: German, *das Momentum*; the moment when the mind is readiest to receive suggestions from another, though commonly used to mean 'the opportune moment'.

45. *Kimberley*: A city at the centre of the diamond fields in the Northern Cape Province of South Africa, founded in 1871 and named after the then Colonial Secretary, the 1st Earl of Kimberley (1826–1902).

46. *buggins*: Little fool. Buggins was a character in a farce by Charles Selby called *Hotel Charges* (Adelphi theatre, 13 October 1853), and 'Buggins' turn' came to mean that 'even the most foolish and least qualified person should have a chance'. It is used as a school nickname in Hornung's novel, *Fathers of Men* (1912).

47. *Set a thief to ketch a thief*: The truth of this maxim was illustrated by the success of the French *sûreté*, which was run by a reformed thief, Vidocq. Raffles refers to it again in 'The Return Match', and 'To Catch a Thief' is used as the title of the fifth story in *The Black Mask* (1901).

48. *I'll drill you*: Colloquial term for 'shoot' (drill a hole).

49. '*Whort price thet brikewater*': This was perhaps the inspiration for Bill Walker's taunt in George Bernard Shaw's *Major Barbara* (1905): 'Wot prawce Selvytion nah?'

50. *a rattle in his thick neck*: A mixed metaphor, the death rattle and the menacing sound made by a rattlesnake.

51. *Jala*: An Arabic name meaning 'Clarity' and also African for 'Special One', but perhaps suggested by 'Djala' from Max Pemberton's 'The Vengeance of Djala' published in *Cassell's Magazine* in April 1898.

52. *pier-glass*: A full-length, free-standing mirror on a stand (from long mirrors designed to fill the 'pier' or narrow strip of wall between windows).

53. *a Babel*: 'A confused turbulent medley of sounds' (*OED*), uproar; from the confusion of tongues associated with the Tower of Babel (Genesis 11:9).

54. *Marylebone*: The police court at Marylebone police station, which served the St John's Wood district.

55. *The helmet is one of a collection I made up at Oxford*: Knocking off policemen's helmets was tolerated during the celebration which followed the Oxford and Cambridge boat race. Raffles implies that he was a student at Oxford University; he also later claims to have been 'up at Cambridge' in 'The Field of Philippi' (*A Thief in the Night*, 1905).

56. *hansom*: A cab (cabriolet) with two large wheels, an enclosed seat for two passengers and a high driving seat behind, patented in 1834 and named after the inventor, Joseph Aloysius Hansom (1802–82). It was redesigned in the early 1870s by Forder & Company of Wolverhampton, who transformed it into a fast and reliable conveyance. By 1897 there were over 7,500 hansom cabs in London.

57. *I sent him off to Scotland Yard with ten bob*: Scotland Yard is the headquarters of the Metropolitan Police Force and is named after its first location in Whitehall (which was the site of the Palace of the Kings of Scotland). It moved to New Scotland Yard on the Embankment, near the Palace of Westminster, in 1890 (and to its present premises in Victoria Street in 1967). 'Ten bob', or ten shillings in the pre-decimal currency, was equivalent to 50p (though then worth thirty or forty times as much).

GENTLEMEN AND PLAYERS

The Gentlemen and Players (or Gentlemen *v.* Players) matches were a highlight of the cricket season at Lord's from 1806 until 1962. An MCC resolution of 1878 stated: 'That no gentleman ought to make a profit by his services in the cricket field, and that for the future no cricketer who takes more than his expenses in any match shall be qualified to play for the Gentlemen against the Players.'

1. *Lord's*: Lord's cricket ground, the headquarters of the Marylebone Cricket Club and centre of English cricket, named after the founder, Thomas Lord (1755–1832), who opened the ground in 1787; it moved to its present site on St John's Wood Road in 1814. Hornung was a regular visitor and first went there in 1878.

2. *Mr Peace . . . playing the fiddle and taming animals*: Charlie Peace (Charles Frederick Peace, 1832–79), one of England's most notorious criminals, described by Raffles in a later story as 'the greatest of the pre-Rafflesites'. 'Peace was truly magnificent in all he undertook – in his own peculiar profession he positively arose to greatness. In the midst of his burglaries he kept up a fine house in Peckham, with two housekeepers and a servant . . . He lived the life of an independent gentleman. He was passionately fond of music, and on the night of the attempted robbery at Blackheath he had an at-home concert, and whilst one housekeeper played the piano and another sang, Charles joined in with the violin' ('Crimes and Criminals', II, *Strand Magazine*, March 1894).

3. *Jack the Ripper was a really eminent public man*: The identity of Jack the Ripper, whose name was first used on the supposed confessional letters at the time of the Whitechapel murders in 1888, remains a mystery. In 1894 Sir Melville Macnaghten, the head of the Criminal Investigation Department at Scotland Yard, named three suspects: Montague John Druitt, a barrister, who drowned in the Thames; Michael Ostrog, a conman and sneak thief; and Kosminski, a Polish Jew. Suspicion has since fallen on various eminent men, including Queen Victoria's son Prince Albert Victor and her physician, Sir William Gull.

4. *sovereigns, which he put on the stumps instead of bails*: Gold sovereigns, worth £1, placed on the three stumps in place of the bails. This is said to have been done by the great all-round cricketer Sir Francis Stanley Jackson (1870–1947), whose father had given him a sovereign for every wicket he took and every run he scored when he made his debut at Lord's, playing for Harrow against Eton in 1887.

5. *on the second Monday in July*: This suggests 1896, when the Gentlemen's first innings against the Players was played on Monday, 13 July, though the story is set some years earlier.

6. *a young fellow of the exquisite type*: Foppish, sensitive, exhibiting feminine qualities; Oscar Wilde described Lord Arthur Savile as someone who 'had lived the delicate and luxurious life of a young man of birth and fortune, and a life exquisite in its freedom from sordid care' (*Lord Arthur Savile's Crime*, 1891).

7. *the Ladies' Enclosure*: The area set aside for ladies, who attended the Gentlemen and Players and Eton and Harrow matches as part of the London season. 'When a gate-money match is on hand,' *Punch* complained, the paying public saw only 'the backs of ladies' hats, of heads of both sexes, of carriages, and of special stands' ('St John's Wood House of Lords', *Punch*, 27 November 1897).

8. *Crowley ... Last year's Harrow Eleven*: The name recalls A. S. Crawley, who impressed the cricket world when he played for Harrow against Eton, in the premier match between two great public schools in July 1895.

9. *Amersteth*: The Earl of Amersteth is an invented title which combines Amersham and Bickersteth.

10. *a cricket week*: One held on a private ground and paid for by the owner, or organized by a local club.

11. *Zingari blazer*: One with black, red and gold stripes, showing that Raffles was a member of I Zingari or 'IZ', the oldest of the wandering cricket clubs. It was founded in 1845 and takes its name from the Italian word for 'gypsies'.

12. *flog a stream*: To cast a fishing-line repeatedly over a stream.

13. *the Free Foresters*: A wandering cricket club, named after the Forest of Arden where it was founded in 1856. The Dorsetshire Gentlemen or 'Gentlemen of Dorset' was a team of skilled amateurs from the county.

14. *the bell rang*: To signify the resumption of play. Two warning bells were rung before the start of play, at the end of the lunch interval and to mark the start of a new innings.

15. *pitch and break*: The 'pitch' is the trajectory of the ball and the 'break' is the deviation from the straight, caused by the bowler's spin or cut.

16. *leg-stump*: The 'leg side' is the side of the batsman's legs (which varies according to whether he is left-or right-handed, as the bat is held in front of the wicket.

17. *dropping head-ball*: One which curves downwards on to the wicket.

18. *three for forty-one, out of the four that fell*: Three wickets for a total of forty-one runs; this appeared as 'three for thirty-eight' in *Cassell's Magazine*.

19. *swagger house-party*: Fashionable, showy, with an ostentatious display of wealth.

20. *Monday, the tenth of August*: This would make the year either 1889 or 1896, when the tenth of August fell on a Monday.

21. *Milchester Abbey, Dorset*: An invented place; the name is suggested by Silchester, or as a variant of Melchester, Thomas Hardy's name for Salisbury. Agatha Christie used Milchester as the name of a village in *A Murder is Announced* (1950) and *4.50 from Paddington* (1957).

22. *Warbeck Junction*: An invented place (a railway junction).

23. *The Dowager Marchioness of Melrose*: Melrose, in Galashiels, is the site of a famous abbey. Lady Melrose is described in the play of 1903 as the sister of the Earl of Amersteth, and in 'The Last Word' (in *A Thief in the Night*, 1905) as the aunt of Miss Carruthers, the woman with whom Bunny is in love.

24. *a great and lengthy pool*: A long game of pool; each player has a ball of a different colour with which to pocket the other balls in a fixed order.

25. *instantaneous photography*: A term loosely applied to cameras with exposures under one second (first made possible by the gelatin

plate). The Kodak hand camera, patented by George Eastman in 1888, made instantaneous photography widely accessible by using a roll of treated film in place of glass plates.

26. *Inspector Mackenzie of Scotland Yard*: The Inspector is based on Melville Leslie McNaghten (1858–1921), the Chief Constable of the Criminal Investigation Department at Scotland Yard. In the play *Raffles, The Amateur Cracksman* (1903) his role is taken by an American detective called Curtis Bedford. His assumed name, Clephane, perhaps suggested by Elizabeth Cecilia Clephane (1830–69), the author of the hymn 'Beneath the Cross of Jesus' (1868), was later used in the novel *No Hero* (1903).

27. *our mutual fence*: A 'fence' is a purchaser or receiver of stolen goods – his name is given in 'Wilful Murder' as Angus Baird. The phrase recalls a novel by Charles Dickens, *Our Mutual Friend* (1865).

28. *boodle*: American slang; illicit spoils, booty, plunder, proceeds of a burglary (Dutch, 'boedel', effects).

29. *at single wicket*: A form of cricket, popular in the early and mid nineteenth century, played with one batsman and between as few as two people.

30. *the professors*: The professional criminals; those for whom crime is a profession (as distinct from 'amateurs').

31. *mirabile dictu*: Latin: marvellous to relate, strange to say, incredible though it may seem. The phrase is used by Virgil in the *Aeneid*.

32. *Viscount Crowley's majority*: The title is an honorary one given to the eldest son of an earl; a boy reached his majority and 'came of age' on his twenty-first birthday.

33. *a trumpery match*: Showy, but worthless; trumped up, contrived.

34. *l'écrin*: Jewel-case.

35. *Est-elle bien*: This had appeared as 'Va-t-elle bien?' in *Cassell's Magazine*.

36. *Paddington*: The London terminus of the Great Western Railway, which served the West Country; it was designed by Isambard Kingdom Brunel and opened in 1854.

37. *a hansom with noiseless tyres*: One with rubber tyres, a feature of the cabs built by Forder and Company, Ltd., of Wolverhampton.

38. *working the oracle with my sheet*: Contriving a successful robbery, using his sheet as a rope. 'To work the oracle' means to secure the desired answer by tampering with priests, and is used figuratively to mean 'secure the desired result'.

LE PREMIER PAS

'Le premier pas', or 'the first step', is from the French saying: 'Le premier pas engage au second', 'the first step leads to the second', and from the famous remark by Madame du Deffand, the celebrated French wit and friend of Horace Walpole, referring to Cardinal de Polignac's account of St Denis's miraculous walk of two miles after his decapitation: 'Il n'y a que le premier pas qui coute' ('it is only the first step that costs anything').

1. *That night*: The evening of the return from Milchester was Sunday, 16 August.

2. *days that were no more*: An allusion to Tennyson's poem 'Tears, Idle Tears': 'Tears, idle tears, I know not what they mean,/Tears from the depth of some divine despair/Rise in the heart, and gather to the eyes/In looking on the happy Autumn-fields,/And thinking of the days that are no more.' Engelhardt recites this poem in *The Boss of Taroomba* (1894) and is touched by 'the sheer beauty of the idea and its words'.

3. *an Orient label*: A luggage label for the Orient Line (Orient Steam Navigation Company), which operated a fleet of ten Royal Mail steamers between England and Australia. The company was formed in 1878 and later merged with the Pacific Steam Navigation Company to form P.&O. Hornung had sailed on the Orient Line to Australia in 1884.

4. *the Melbourne Cup*: A horse race traditionally held on the first Tuesday in November at the Flemington Racecourse, near Melbourne. It was first competed for in 1861 and by the 1880s attracted crowds of over 100,000 people.

5. *they're extra fly*: Shrewd, knowing; they drive a hard bargain.

6. *a second cousin of my father's*: The son of a cousin. This is the only reference Raffles makes to his parents.

7. *cut over on the hand*: A cricketing term; a 'cut' is a stroke played with a horizontal bat to a short ball outside the off stump. Raffles had misjudged the cut and the ball had hit his hand.

8. *the National Bank*: There were two national banks: the Bank of Australasia (established in 1835) and the Union Bank of Australia (established in 1838), but the town was served by the Commercial Bank (whose premises, dating from 1887, still survive).

9. *the township of Yea*: A town in the foothills of the Great Dividing range, set in the valley formed by the Yea and Gowlborn rivers; Raffles gives the distance from Melbourne as 'fifty miles', but it is closer to

seventy miles (105 kilometres). It was established in 1855 and named after Colonel Lacy Yea (a Crimean war hero).

10. *his initials are W. F.*: The initials are those of the author's friend W. F. (Willingham Franklin) Rawnsley, who had been a boy and master at Uppingham.

11. *Can't I go by train*: The railway line reached Yea in 1883 and Whittlesea in 1889; before then the closest junction was at Kilmore (which the railway reached in 1872).

12. *Whittlesea ... Plenty Ranges*: A post town on the Plenty River, twenty-eight miles (thirty-six kilometres) north-east of Melbourne; it was settled in 1837 and laid out as a town in 1853. The Plenty Ranges are the hills north of Melbourne, which feed into the Plenty River and take their name from it.

13. *the water supply of this city ... the pure Yan Yean*: Water from the Yan Yean river was stored in a large reservoir, holding nearly six and half million gallons of water, built by the Colonial Government in 1857; the water was carried to Melbourne on an aqueduct, seven miles in length.

14. *a bovine beast*: A slow, dull animal, 'like an ox'. It is likened to an ambulance because the horse was so slow and steady that it would have been suitable for carrying the wounded.

15. *dipped into a gully and ran through a creek*: Geographical features associated with Australia (and used in the title of an anthology of Australian stories, *By Creek and Gully* (London: T. Fisher Unwin, 1899), edited by Lala Fisher, which included Hornung's story 'The Diamond of Larrikin Creek').

16. *a whole forest of gums had been ring-barked*: The 'gum tree' or Australian eucalyptus is the most common tree in Australia with over 800 species; rings were cut in the bark as a way of killing the trees when clearing the primeval forests.

17. *a beard like W. G. Grace*: A long full black beard, which was the most distinctive feature of the great English cricketer Dr William Gilbert Grace (1848–1915), who dominated the game at the end of the nineteenth century.

18. *a second Kelly gang*: The original gang consisted of Ned Kelly (1855–80), the notorious outlaw, two friends, Steve Hart and Joe Byrne, and his younger brother, Daniel Kelly. They took to the bush in 1878 after wounding a police constable and killing three policemen shortly afterwards. They were outlawed by the State of Victoria, which put a price of £500 on their heads (raised to £2000 after another killing). Their career included the holding up of the towns of Eurora and Jerilderie and culminated in the battle of Glenrowan on 28 June

1880 when Dan Kelly, Hart and Byrne were shot. Ned Kelly was captured, severely wounded, and hanged in Melbourne on 11 November 1880.

19. *caught a Tartar in you*: Met somebody who was more than their match (a Tartar is an intractable or savage person).

20. *tu quoque*: (Latin: you, also) The retort usually implies that the behaviour or circumstances of the person addressed is no better than that of the speaker, and that both are guilty of the same misdeeds, but here there is a comic confusion as each wrongly believes the other to be the fearless hero of the recent bank raid.

21. *take the cake*: Be unrivalled, carry off the prize (said to derive from the 'cake walk', when pairs of competitors walked around a cake and those judged to have deported themselves most gracefully 'took the cake').

22. *your wind bagged at footer*: To be winded or have the wind knocked out of you at football; a word play on 'wind bag' (a long-winded or bombastic speaker with little to say).

23. *Ewbank*: A surname suggested by the Sussex cricketer Christopher Cooper Ewbank (1845–1933).

24. *a funk of robbers*: Afraid of robbers; 'funk' is tobacco smoke or the strong stench of tobacco, used figuratively to describe a state of fear or trepidation.

25. *a five-barred forehead*: Heavily lined with wrinkles, similar to the five bars of a farm gate.

26. *a red moustache, and a very humorous face (not unlike Tom Emmett's)*: Tom Emmett (1841–1904) was a jovial Yorkshire cricketer, who was known as the 'smile on the face of English cricket'. Hornung had seen the 'red good-humoured face, with the crafty hook-nose and the ginger moustache' for the first time when he visited Lords at the age of twelve.

27. *a treble-seamed, hand-sewn head*: A metaphor from a 'treble seam' cricket ball.

28. *sleep like a timber-yard*: A variation of the phrase 'to sleep like a log'.

29. *the old woman of Banbury Cross*: Raffles did not wish the coins to jangle and 'make music'; he is alluding to the old lady in the nursery rhyme (found in *Gammer Gurton's Garland*, 1784):

> Ride a cock-horse to Banbury Cross,
> To see an old lady get up on her horse,
> Rings on her fingers and bells on her toes,
> And so she makes music wherever she goes.

30. *new chum*: Australian slang for a 'newcomer' (usually from England), as opposed to an 'old chum', a long-established and experienced settler.

31. *cock shots*: Objects set up as a target, and the shots fired at them.

32. *bushrangers; of course, there are no such things nowadays*: The bushranging era started in 1861 and ended with the extermination of the Kelly Gang in 1880. The heyday was during the 1860s when chivalrous and romantic bushrangers, such as Frank Gardiner (known as 'Darkie, the Prince of Highwaymen and King of the Road'), Ben Hall and Fred Ward ('Thunderbolt') held sway.

33. *Coburg*: A residential suburb, five miles (eight kilometres) north of Melbourne. It was first known as Pentridge, but was renamed in 1869 in honour of Prince Alfred, the Duke of Saxe-Coburg, and in order to dissociate itself from Pentridge prison.

34. *Every rod, pole or perch*: The words all refer to a measure or length of 5½ yards.

35. *bushed*: An Australian term, 'lost in the bush'. A man lost in the bush invariably walks in circles, and this was the subject of an earlier story by Hornung called 'Bushed' (which appeared in the *London Society* holiday number for 1889).

WILFUL MURDER

'Wilful murder' is intentional or deliberate murder for which compulsion, ignorance or accident cannot be pleaded as an excuse. A contemporary example was the wilful murder of the actor William Terriss, who was stabbed to death at the stage door of the Adelphi Theatre on 16 December 1897 by a disaffected actor, Richard Arthur Prince.

1. *the Ardagh emeralds*: Ardagh is a village in County Longford, Ireland, known for the Celtic 'Ardagh Chalice', which was discovered there in 1868, and because Oliver Goldsmith stayed at Ardagh Hall when writing *She Stoops to Conquer*.

2. *the original sinews and the final spoils of war*: 'The sinews of war' is the money essential for its prosecution: '*nervos belli pecuniam*' ('money provides the sinews for war') (Cicero, *Philippics* V, ii, 5).

3. *I had played Sister Ann*: By leaning out of the window and surveying the road; in the tale of Blue-Beard (Charles Perrault, 'La Barbe Bleue', *Histoires ou contes du temps passé avec des moralitez*, 1697), Ann climbed to the top of the tallest tower in the castle to watch for her brothers, who would save her sister Fatima, Blue-Beard's seventh wife, from execution. Sister Ann was a prominent character in the Drury

Lane pantomime of *Blue Beard*, and was played by leading male comedians such as Dan Leno.

4. *tattoo*: The beat of a drum; a distinctive knock.

5. *A stern chase and a long one*: In naval warfare a 'stern chase' is the pursuit of a ship, from the remark by the eighteenth-century American naval officer and privateer John Paul Jones (1747–92), 'a stern chase is a long one'.

6. *Baird*: Hornung may have taken the name from Mrs Thomas Baird, a friend of his mother-in-law, whom he met in Genoa on 30 November 1897, or from the actress, Dorothea Baird, Sir Henry Irving's daughter-in-law, who was best known for her performance as Trilby in the play based on George du Maurier's novel (at the Theatre Royal, Haymarket, from 30 October 1895).

7. *twang that you could cut with a paper-knife*: A (Cockney) accent so thick that it could be cut with a knife.

8. *Blackfriars . . . High Street, Kensington . . . Sloane Square*: Stations on the 'inner circle' of the underground Metropolitan Railway Line (now the Circle Line of the London underground). The first two stations were familiar to Hornung as he had worked in an office near Blackfriars and lived near High Street Kensington, while Sloane Square lies between them.

9. *like a lamplighter*: A man who carried a narrow ladder to reach the street lamps. By the end of the nineteenth century the ladder had been replaced by a pole with a flame at the top, which with one movement turned on the gas and lit the mantle.

10. *Clapham Junction . . . Twickenham . . . Richmond . . . Charing Cross*: The route was familiar to Hornung from the time he had lived in Twickenham. Raffles took the Metropolitan District Line train from Richmond to Charing Cross underground station (now called Embankment).

11. *make assurance doubly sure*: 'But yet I'll make assurance double sure' (Shakespeare, *Macbeth*, IV, i).

12. *a young blood*: A dandy, a man of fashion; it was used by Hornung in 1898 as the title of a novel (*Young Blood*, Cassell, 1898).

13. *Jack Rutter*: The name may have been suggested by the popular rhyme of 'Jimmy the Mowdy' ('Old Jack Rutter / Sent two stone of butter'). It was also the surname of Edward Rutter, the Middlesex left-hand bowler, who was for many years the honorary secretary of the Free Foresters. Hornung used it again in his novel *Fathers of Men* (Smith, Elder, 1912), where Jan Rutter is the hero.

14. *skinned him*: To fleece, to make a person pay an extortionate price.

15. *fill the bill*: Make the headlines, fill the billhead. The expression is used of posters for the music hall, where individual acts fill the bill, and are therefore suitable for it.

16. *snuff out with a flourish of extra-specials*: Be hanged with a flurry of reports in the late editions of the evening newspapers. The evening papers went through five editions, the last being designated Extra Special or Second Extra Special.

17. *you wouldn't rust with a vile repose*: Raffles is alluding to Byron's description of the prisoner of Chillon (François de Bonnivard, 1493–1570), a Genevan prelate who spent four years in the dungeon of the Chateau de Chillon: 'My limbs are bow'd, though not with toil,/But rusted with a vile repose,/For they have been a dungeon's spoil' (Lord George Gordon Byron, 1788–1824, 'The Prisoner of Chillon', I, 5–7).

18. *saddle-bag chair*: A chair upholstered with carpeting of the type used for the saddle-bags of camels.

19. *Willesden*: An area to the north-west of London, in the process of being developed at the end of the nineteenth century, but still largely rural.

20. *'I'm coming too'*: This exchange inspired the one between Sherlock Holmes and Dr Watson in 'The Adventure of Charles Augustus Milverton', where Watson asks 'When do we start?' and Holmes replies 'You are not coming' (A. Conan Doyle, *The Return of Sherlock Holmes*, 1905).

21. *We walked across St James's Park . . . the bridge*: Raffles and Bunny crossed the park on their way to Victoria station. St James's Park is the oldest of the royal parks, dating from Tudor times; it stretches north from Horse Guards Road to Buckingham Palace, between the Mall and Birdcage Walk, and has running through it a long narrow lake. The cast iron suspension bridge dated from 1857 and crossed the centre of the lake (it was replaced by a concrete bridge in 1957).

22. *We had to get out at Willesden Junction*: The train they used was the West London extension line from Victoria to Willesden Junction, via Battersea, Chelsea, West Brompton and Kensington (Addison Road). They were too late to make a connection to Kensal Rise Station on the North London Railway.

23. *champagne corks on the spikes*: A pleasing conceit. Scalpels and sharp knives were customarily kept secure in corks; but for champagne corks to have worked in this way, the spikes on the gate would have had to be sharpened to a fine point.

24. *a little pyramid of slates*: The roof of a tower.

25. *bell-wires and springs*: Trip wires which activate bells and man-traps which snap shut when trodden on.

26. *the diamond, the pot of treacle, and the sheet of brown paper*: This is known as the 'tar paper' method, using paper (or cloth) soaked in tar, honey or treacle, which is laid over the glass to muffle the sound of the hammer and to hold the broken fragments. It can be used either (as here) on a small area with a glass cutter or to remove the whole pane of glass. The description given by Hornung influenced many later writers and a number of petty criminals (including one in 1901, whose attempt at burglary was thwarted when the treated paper failed to hold the broken glass, which roused the householder: he was then caught when his identity was revealed by the shopkeeper who had supplied the treacle).

27. *break into the studies at school*: Every boy at Uppingham had his own study, and Hornung is referring here to the studies in the quadrangle of Tuck's House, which could be forced in the way described.

28. *like a cobble in a squall*: Like a boat in a storm; a 'cobble' or 'coble' is a small fishing boat found in Scotland and the North-East of England.

29. *went for him bald-headed*: Went for him without constraint, without regard for the circumstances, in an impetuous and whole-hearted fashion; from the Dutch 'balddadig', 'audaciously'.

30. *swing in a row at Newgate*: Be hanged. Raffles uses the term as a general name for prison. Newgate was the oldest and most famous of London's jails, dating from the time of Henry I. The last building on the site (dating from 1770) closed in 1880 and was demolished in 1902 to make way for the Central Criminal Court. Hornung set several scenes in Newgate in *The Rogue's March* (1896), based on the *Newgate Calendar* (the biographical record of notorious criminals begun in 1773).

31. *drunk with wine*: A biblical phrase: 'Be not drunk with wine, wherein is excess' (Ephesians 5:18).

32. *Maida Vale*: An area a mile and a half east of Kensal Rise. The route took them down Maida Vale (the road named after the district), along the Edgware Road to Marble Arch, then along Park Lane as far as the turning to Mount Street.

33. *a steerage passenger from Liverpool to New York*: Steerage passengers paid the lowest fares and were housed in cramped conditions. The ships from Liverpool to New York carried many thousands of emigrants and offered ideal anonymity to a fugitive from justice.

34. *diggings*: Rooms, lodgings (often of a temporary nature); commonly abbreviated as 'digs'.

NINE POINTS OF THE LAW

'Possession is nine points of the law': in a case of disputed ownership, the person who possesses the object has an advantage over the one from whom it was taken. *Nine Points of the Law* was also the title of a play by Tom Taylor, written in 1859.

1. *the last column of the Daily Telegraph*: The Personal, Lost & Found or 'agony' column of the newspaper, which was printed at the top right-hand side of the back page. The newspaper was first issued in 1855.

2. *a telegraphic address*: An abbreviated address of two words, consisting of a name or cognomen and the town or place of delivery, which was registered with the Post Office.

3. *five bob*: Five shillings in the pre-decimal currency. Inland telegrams cost sixpence for the first twelve words, and a halfpenny for each additional word (including the address to which it was to be sent), whereas the inland letter rate was only a penny.

4. *I signed myself Glasspool*: Perhaps taking the alias from Alfred John Glasspool, the author of *The Band of Hope Companion* (1891). In *Cassell's Magazine* Raffles used the name 'Suamarez' (recalling the British admiral James Suamarez, 1757–1836).

5. *Hickey, 38, Conduit Street; that's my tailor*: The number is given as '28' in *Cassell's Magazine*. Conduit Street; runs from Regent Street to New Bond Street and was known for its tailors and dressmakers. No. 28 had three occupants in 1897: a jeweller, an American dentist and a private resident. Hornung may have changed the number to '38' because it was vacant at the time; it had been the premises of a diamond merchant and a jeweller and was afterwards let to a firm of 'high-class lapidaries and experts in gems' with the upper floor used by the Palestine Exploration Fund. There were no tailors in London called Hickey, but this was the name of a hatter in the King's Road.

6. *Addenbrooke*: The name recalls Dr John Addenbrooke, the benefactor of the free hospital in Cambridge (opened in 1766).

7. *instanter*: Latin: instantly, immediately, at once; originally a legal term.

8. *struck off the rolls*: Removed from the official list of solicitors and prohibited from practising; the penalty for gross professional misconduct.

9. *'over the way to the court'*: The Police (or Magistrates') Court at Bow Street police station (first established in 1740). The building, designed by Sir John Taylor, dates from 1879–80 and contains three court rooms.

10. *on our beam-ends*: Penniless; a wooden ship turned on its side is 'on its beam ends' and is in danger of going under (as in the novel which Hornung wrote immediately before Raffles, *Dead Men Tell No Tales* (Methuen, 1899), which involved a shipwreck).

11. *Sir Bernard Debenham . . . Broom Hall, Esher*: Though given the name of the owner of a famous furriers and general stores (Debenham, of Debenham and Freebody), the character is based on Colonel Payne Bingham, who owned one of the Velasquez paintings of the Infanta Maria Teresa (see note 13). There was a Broom Hill in Esher, the seat of Captain Edward Seymour, and many 'Broom Halls' in other parts of the country, but Hornung was most familiar with Littleworth, the house in Esher belonging to the Martineaus, who were his friends from Uppingham. He was a frequent visitor to the town, which is in Surrey, fourteen miles south-west of London.

12. *fons et origo*: Latin: source and origin; the sole cause.

13. *Velasquez*: The Spanish court artist Diego Rodriguez de Silva y Velasquez (1599–1660), 'the head of the Spanish school of painting and one of the greatest painters the world has ever known' (*Encyclopaedia Britannica*).

14. *a portrait of the Infanta Maria Teresa*: The Infanta Maria Teresa (1638–83) was the daughter of Philip IV of Spain and Isabella de Bourbon, and became the wife of Louis XIV of France in 1666. Velasquez painted the Infanta several times as a child and as an adolescent. The most famous is a full-length portrait in the Kunsthistoriches Museum, Vienna, and there are smaller versions in the Louvre (since 1869) and the Victoria and Albert Museum (since 1878). There were three smaller portraits in private hands, which had all recently been offered for sale. The first, from the Lyne Stephens Collection, listed as 'A Young Lady called an Infanta (thought to be Maria Teresa)', was sold in May 1895 to Pierpoint Morgan (who left it to the Metropolitan Museum in New York, where it is now ascribed to Mazo). A second was offered at the Viscount Clifden sale in May 1895 and went to the Johnson Collection (now in the Philadelphia Museum of Art); a third came from the Ledieu Collection in Paris and was sold at the end of the 1890s to Colonel Payne Bingham (then to the Duveen Brothers, and finally to John S. Bache, who left it to the Metropolitan Museum in New York).

15. *another portrait of one of the Popes in Rome*: The seated portrait of Pope Innocent X (Giambattisti Pamphilii, 1574–1655) in the Galleria Doria Pamphilii, Rome, painted in late 1649 or early 1650 and the inspiration for the 'Screaming Pope' (1954) by the British artist Francis

Bacon (1909–92). Hornung was in Rome at the time he was writing the story.

16. *National Gallery*: The British national collection of paintings in Trafalgar Square, London, founded in 1824. The Spanish gallery (Room XV) had seven works by Velasquez, including two portraits of Philip IV. The painting that is now best known, 'The Rokeby Venus' (*Venus and Cupid*), did not enter the collection until 1905–6.

17. *the Hon. John Montagu Craggs, M.L.C.*: The initials stand for 'Member of the Legislative Council' (of the Queensland Parliament). There were between thirty and forty MLCs appointed by the Governor; they received no pay, but had tenure for life and the right to be known as 'The Honourable'. The surname may have been suggested by 'The Marvellous Craggs' in the *Windsor Magazine* (March 1898).

18. *the Métropole*: The Hotel Métropole, on the west side of Northumberland Avenue, one of London's grand hotels, with 600 rooms, owned by the Gordon Hotels Company; it was later converted into government offices.

19. *there's the rub*: There's the downside; from Hamlet's soliloquy: 'To sleep: perchance to dream: ay, there's the rub; for in that sleep of death what dreams may come when we have shuffled off this mortal coil, must give us pause' (Shakespeare, *Hamlet*, III, i).

20. *God wot*: The past tense of 'wit', but used here to mean 'God knows (that I am earnest)'. Thomas Edward Brown (1830–97) used the phrase in the line of poetry for which he is now best remembered: 'A Garden is a lovesome thing, God wot!' ('My Garden').

21. *the Café Royal*: A famous café at 68 Regent Street, the haunt of artists, which opened in 1865 and was extended in 1870. It had a wine cellar and billiard room in the basement; a café, luncheon bar and grill on the ground floor, and private rooms on the floors above. The old premises were demolished when Regent Street was widened in the early 1920s. The current building dates from 1924–5.

22. *an A.B.C. time-table*: The *ABC Rail Guide* listed train services from London; it was first issued in 1853 as an alternative to *Bradshaw's Monthly Rail Guide*. The times of the trains from Waterloo station to Esher were taken from a copy of the guide.

23. *end in fizzle*: American slang: end up as a ludicrous failure, come to nothing.

24. *let him gang his own gait*: Scottish, gang his ain gait, go at his own speed, do what best pleases him, decide on his own course of action.

25. *such a bear at lunch*: Behaving in a gruff or rude fashion.

26. *(there's 'copy' there!)*: 'Good copy', material that would make an

interesting article for a newspaper or other publication; in *Cassell's Magazine* the words in parentheses were 'such a rum old boy'.

27. *lied like Ananias*: Ananias was struck dead for lying ('Peter said, Ananias, why hath Satan filled thine heart to lie to the Holy Ghost . . . thou hast not lied unto men, but unto God. And Ananias hearing these words fell down, and gave up the ghost', Acts 5:5).

28. *I had the wax in the palm of my hand*: A soft wax (usually carried in a tin) into which the key was pressed, providing a mould which could be cast by a locksmith.

29. *Revolvers would be out of place in the Métropole*: In *Cassell's Magazine*, Raffles says: 'You had better take your revolver. I shall certainly take mine.' The change was made for the reason given here.

30. *a life-preserver*: A bludgeon, a cosh; a short stick loaded with lead. 'They (life preservers) are of all sorts and sizes. One swings on a piece of thick cord heavily loaded; another is made of rhinoceros hide. A pretty little invention in these specialities doubles up and fits the waistcoat pocket, the more popular examples being made out of a piece of cord twisted round a short cane with a lead shot at both ends' ('Crimes and Criminals', II, *Strand Magazine*, March 1894). The life-preserver is mentioned twice in *A Thief in the Night* (1905): it was used by Bunny in 'A Bad Night' and was one of 'The Raffles Relics' in the Black Museum at Scotland Yard.

31. *'smile and smile and be a villain'*: Said of Claudius, who had married Hamlet's mother after he had murdered her husband: 'one may smile, and smile, and be a villain' (Shakespeare, *Hamlet*, I, v).

32. *near relatives . . . I knew of none*: *Cassell's Magazine* was more categorical: 'Now, Raffles had none.' Bunny did know of the second cousin who is mentioned in 'Le Premier Pas', but he had yet to hear of the sister to whom Raffles refers in 'The Return Match'. Bunny's statement that he was a bosom pal of Raffles in town, but had never been 'to his place in the country' recalls the distinction made by Oscar Wilde in *The Importance of Being Earnest* (1895) between town and country, though the implication is not that Raffles owned a country house, but that his parents did so.

33. *a full-skin billet*: A well-paid post or job; 'skin' is thieves' slang for a purse; a 'billet' is the Australian term for employment (and lodging).

34. *Rank bad form of his mother or his aunt, and I hope she will kick the bucket*: This appeared in *Cassell's Magazine* as: 'Rank bad form of his mother or his aunt to go and kick the bucket today.'

35. *the Silly Cynic*: The Cynics were a sect of philosophers in Ancient Greece, founded by Antisthenes, a pupil of Socrates, the most famous

being Diogenes. The basis of their philosophy was a disbelief in the sincerity or goodness of human motives. According to Oscar Wilde, 'A cynic is a person who knows the price of everything and the value of nothing' (*Lady Windermere's Fan*, 1891, Act 1).

36. *a 'real, genuine, twin-screw, double-funnelled, copper-bottomed Old Master'*: 'Copper-bottomed', as on a ship, meaning watertight, absolutely genuine. Twin-screw ships, such as the SS *Königin Luise*, on which Hornung sailed to Italy, were the finest afloat.

37. *two hundred and thirty years*: Velasquez died in 1660, so if this were accurate the date of the story would be prior to 1890. The painting would more correctly have been described as 'over two hundred and forty years old'.

38. *Worth fifty thousand pounds*: The record for a painting sold at auction in 1897 stood at 14,050 guineas, and did not reach or exceed £50,000 until 1919. However, paintings by Velasquez had changed hands at high prices. Pierpoint Morgan paid a record price of £4,500 for his painting of Maria Teresa in May 1895; the National Gallery in London paid £6,300 for the portrait of Philip IV; and 45,000 guineas was paid in 1905 on its behalf for 'The Rokeby Venus'. There was a precedent as Parliament had paid £70,000 to the trustees of Blenheim Palace for Raphael's *Ansidei Madonna* in 1885.

39. *my gentleman's own key*: The key belonging to Craggs; this was originally 'my master key' in *Cassell's Magazine* (which had raised the question of how it had been come by).

40. *chloroform*: An anaesthetic used by criminals as a chemical alternative to the cosh; a colourless, sweet-smelling liquid which produces insensibility when inhaled.

41. *stertorous breaths*: Latin: *stertere*, to snore; snoring with irregular hoarse breaths.

42. *Inverness cape*: A sleeveless cloak with a removable cape, named after a town in Scotland (now often associated with Sherlock Holmes).

43. *one of the later Savoy operas . . . Mikado*: Operas by Gilbert and Sullivan named after the Savoy theatre in London: *H.M.S. Pinafore* (1878), *Patience* (1881) and *The Mikado* (1885). Their 'later Savoy operas' were *Utopia Limited* (1893) and *The Grand Duke* (1896); the phrase could also apply to the Savoy operas written by other people, such as *The Nautch Girl* (1891), *The Vicar of Bray* (1892), or J. M. Barrie's and A. Conan Doyle's *Jane Annie* (1893).

44. *Surbiton*: The station immediately preceding Esher on the line from Waterloo.

45. *ipse egomet*: Latin; alternatively *egomet memet*, myself, I alone ('*-met*' is an enclitic particle, which is used for emphasis).

THE RETURN MATCH

The 'return match' is a sporting term referring to the convention that teams play two games, one 'at home' on their own ground, and the other 'away' on the ground of their opponents. In this case the 'return match' is literally played 'at home'.

1. *to crack another crib*: Thieves' slang; a 'crib' is a house or dwelling; 'to crack a crib' is to commit a burglary or break into a house, and this is the origin of the word 'cracksman'.

2. *the card*: The printed score card on which the names of the players are listed and on which the spectators can enter the scores as they are made.

3. *Crawshay*: The character was based on William Morgan, who escaped from Dartmoor on 2 January 1898, though the name is perhaps from Richard Crawshay (1741–99), one of the great early iron-masters.

4. *Dartmoor*: The high-security convict prison at Princetown, in the centre of Dartmoor. It was first established in 1809 to hold French prisoners of war and was rebuilt in 1850.

5. *Pall Mall*: The *Pall Mall Gazette* (1865–1923), a London evening paper. This carried a similar report about the escape of William Morgan on 3 January 1898, under the heading 'Exciting Escape from Dartmoor':

A correspondent telegraphs:– Last evening, between seven and nine o'clock, a daring escape was made from Dartmoor by William Morgan, a convict undergoing a sentence of ten years' penal servitude. At nine o'clock this morning the convict was still at large. Morgan smashed the window of his cell, and, making a rope of his blanket, lowered himself into the yard. Once in the yard he climbed over the wall by the aid of a scaffold pole.

   Morgan was found to be missing at nine o'clock, and an alarm was at once given. Warders have been scouring the moor all night, but unsuccessfully.

6. *the six-foot way*: The strip of ground between the two sets of railway lines.

7. *not to go and get lagged*: Not to get sent to prison; not to be apprehended or arrested. 'Getting lagged' originally referred to being transported as a convict; also used as a noun, 'lag' (or 'old lag').

8. *Liverpool Street*: Liverpool Street station, the London railway terminus of the Great Eastern Railway and of the East London Line, serving East Anglia and the North.

9. *I have the best of sisters married to a country parson in the eastern*

counties: This was also true of Hornung, two of whose sisters had married country parsons. Hetty (Harriet Susan Hornung, 1857–97) had married Anthony Anstruther Wilkinson, Rector of Icklingham, Suffolk (1889–1900); and Ida (1859–1951) was the wife of the Revd Walter St John Field, the Vicar of Fordcombe, Kent.

10. *broadcloth*: Fine plain-woven, double-width, dressed black cloth. The word is used of the clothes made from it, but also reflects the status of the person wearing them.

11. *the cool canary*: Impertinent or audacious young wag.

12. *after my own kidney*: After my own heart; Falstaff speaks of 'a man of my kidney' in *The Merry Wives of Windsor* (III, v), when describing the disastrous effect which the dirty clothes and heat of a laundry basket had upon him.

13. *get over me*: Usually, get one over on me; get round me; you cannot deceive me.

14. *Clean heels*: Getting clean away; 'showing his heels' without being caught.

15. *'copped'*: (Slang) arrested by a policeman or 'cop'.

16. *We had the bulge*: (American slang) had the advantage of, got the better of.

17. *on the rocks for a sleep*: (Nautical) feeling wrecked for want of sleep.

18. *cuckoos*: Fools.

19. *They see the pegs, and they mean to hit 'em*: 'Pegs' is an alternative word for the cricket stumps that make up a wicket.

20. *he gets his tongue between his teeth*: He speaks to good purpose.

21. *Rightum*: Right ho, right you are.

22. *a gone coon*: (American slang, from 'racoon') a goner, a gone goose, a person in serious difficulty for whom there is no hope.

23. *driving-coat*: A long coat, extending to the shoes, with a high collar and cape, ideally suited for use as a disguise.

24. *another entrance ... on one's way to Piccadilly*: Harry Furniss took issue with Hornung on this point: 'Albany is secure, it is guarded back and front and no one can enter without he or she is known to the sturdy janitors or can give some reasonable excuse for calling' (*Paradise in Piccadilly. The Story of Albany*, The Bodley Head, 1925, p. 172).

25. *a gen'leman comes arfter rooms ... an' shows 'im the empties*: Harry Furniss also found fault with this statement: 'To obtain chambers it is necessary to write to the Secretary and await one's opportunity. To send a stray caller to the "orfice" and that "one of the clurks, 'e goes round with 'im an' shows 'im the empties", as if Albany was a

common lodging-house, shows ignorance on the author's part' (see note 24).

26. *his extry-speshul Star*: 'His extra-special', his late edition of the *Star* (1888–1960), a London evening paper.

27. *the tec*: The detective.

28. *the air of a chief commissioner*: The Chief Commissioner is the head of the Metropolitan Police Force (a post held by Sir Edward Bradford from 1890–1903); the City Police has a Commissioner and other police forces have a Chief Constable.

29. *the leads*: The roof, specifically the gutters and gulleys, which were made of lead.

30. *These bedroom windows looked into a narrow side-street*: Harry Furniss said: 'There is no narrow side-street with traffic adjoining Albany and no low window from which one could drop on to the roof of a passing cab "under the noses of the police"' (see note 24). There is, however, a passage which runs between the Albany and the Royal Academy.

31. *a congeries of little kitchens and cubicles*: A 'congeries' is a mass or heap, thus 'numerous little kitchens and rooms'. The first-floor chambers in the Albany had kitchens and servants' rooms on the floor above; the ground-floor rooms, on the floor below (though it is unlikely that Hornung ever saw them). There were also large kitchens which served the main dining-room.

32. *a crown a head*: Five shillings per person, from the crown coin (equivalent to 25 pence in decimal currency).

33. *telescope sticks*: Stout bamboo walking sticks containing a series of smaller canes, which could be screwed together to form a long pole, similar to a fishing rod; a hook at the top end with a strong silk rope could then be attached to a pipe or other projection on the building, enabling the burglar to scale the building. The telescope stick used by Raffles is fully described in 'The Criminologists' Club' (*A Thief in the Night*, 1905).

34. *the Rubicon of my life*: The decisive turning point from which there is no going back – from Julius Caesar's crossing of the Rubicon in 49 BC at the head of a legion. By crossing the river he went beyond the limits of Cisalpine Gaul and became an invader, thereby precipitating the war with the Senate which led to the overthrow of the Roman Republic.

35. *P 34*: The divisional letter and number, worn on the collar (the 'collar number'), which identifies the policeman and his division.

36. *stuck pig in buttons*: From staring like a stuck pig, gaping and

staring in astonishment or dismay; describing the appearance of a pig that is being killed. 'In buttons' refers to a uniform (and specifically to the tunic worn by the policeman, which had eight buttons on the front), and is a play on the saying 'You can dress a pig in buttons and bows, but it is still a pig.' Pig-sticking had been the favourite sport of the Chief Commissioner Sir Edward Bradford when he served in India, and even after he lost an arm, he continued to take part by holding the reins between his teeth.

37. *he'll do by us as we've done by him*: This is the Golden Rule: 'Do as you would be done by', 'Do unto others as you would have them do unto you' ('all things whatsoever ye would that men should do to you, do ye even so to them: for this is the law and the prophets' – Matthew 7:12; 'as ye would that men should do to you, do ye also to them likewise', Luke 6:31).

THE GIFT OF THE EMPEROR

'The gift of the Emperor' was used by the Roman emperors on their public works, with the abbreviation 'D. I.', 'Dedit Imperator'. The formation of the Austrian Reichstag in 1848 and the granting of the Meiji Constitution of 1889 were also described as 'the gift of the Emperor'.

1. *King of the Cannibal Islands*: The Cannibal Islands was a name given to various Polynesian islands (including Tahiti, Tonga, Samoa and the Marquesas) on which cannibalism was once practised, but specifically to Fiji under King Cakobau, which was ceded to Britain in 1875. The King of the Cannibal Islands was a bogey figure in pantomime, and the title of a popular song written in 1830, by A. W. Humphreys:

> Hokey Pokey, whisky, thrum
> How do you like your potatoes done?
> Boiled in whisky, boiled in rum,
> Says the King of the Cannibal Islands.

2. *made faces at Queen Victoria*: Used metaphorically, snubbed the British advances and repudiated the hand of friendship.

3. *a European monarch*: The German Emperor, Kaiser Wilhelm II (Friedrich Wilhelm Victor Albrecht, 1859–1941), the eldest son of Frederick III and grandson of Queen Victoria on his mother's side. He reigned as the ninth King of Prussia and third German Emperor from 1888 until forced to abdicate at the end of the First World War in 1918.

4. *set the cables tingling with his compliments*: Led to unfavourable comment and caused an uproar in the press; the submarine or land cables ('wires') were used to transmit news. The Kaiser had angered the British in 1896 when he sent a congratulatory telegram to President Kruger after the Jameson Raid, and again in 1898 when he visited Abdul Hamid in Constantinople.

5. *a pearl of price unparalleled*: This recalls the one given to Queen Victoria in 1897 by the people of Queensland in honour of her Diamond Jubilee. The Bible compares the Kingdom of Heaven to a 'pearl of great price' (Matthew 13:4–6).

6. *a Polynesian setting*: Polynesia comprises all the small islands of the Pacific Ocean, east of Australia (also known as the Oceanic or the South Sea Islands). Those with pearl fisheries included the Tuamatu Islands (Tahiti), the Society Island, the Marquesas, the Fiji Islands, Penhryn (Tongareva), and New Caledonia (where pearls were discovered for the first time in 1897).

7. *a godsend to the Press a few weeks later*: During the period known as the 'silly season', which followed the end of the London season and coincided with the Parliamentary recess when there was no social or political news of any consequence.

8. *the Daily Chronicle devoting half its literary page*: The *Daily Chronicle and Clerkenwell News* (1872–1930) was the most widely read newspaper of the day and was noted for its literary reviews and for the 'Writers and Readers' column, which appeared on Wednesdays and Fridays. Max Pemberton, Hornung's editor at *Cassell's Magazine*, believed that his success as a writer was due to a good review in the *Daily Chronicle*, which he described as 'the one paper at that time which really influenced the booksellers' (*Sixty Years Ago and After*, Hutchinson, 1936, p. 116).

9. *the new Pall Mall*: The latest issue of the *Pall Mall Gazette*. There were three '*Pall Malls*': the *Pall Mall Gazette* (see note 5 for 'The Return Match'); the weekly *Pall Mall Budget* (1888–94); and the monthly *Pall Mall Magazine*, which was started in 1893; but only the *Gazette* matches the description given here.

10. *blow to flinders*: 'Flinders' is from a Norwegian word meaning 'fragments' or 'splinters'. The pun implies that Flinders is also the capital of the Cannibal Islands, and this sounds very convincing because the name was found in that part of the world. Captain Matthew Flinders (1774–1814), the explorer and navigator, had given his name to Flinders Land and Flinders River in Southern Australia, and to Flinders Island (Furneaux Islands).

11. *Thames Ditton*: A parish on the river Thames opposite Hampton

Court Palace, fourteen miles south-west of London. It was familiar to Hornung from the time he lived in Teddington (which is further up the river).

12. *To personal paragraphs ... I would not stoop*: Contributions to gossip columns were paid for at a rate of a penny a line.

13. *the old red wall of Hampton Court*: The wall built by Henry VIII on the south side of Hampton Court Palace along the river Thames. The palace has towers, turrets, a Water Gallery, an elaborate summer house, and a water-gate.

14. *qua verses*: Latin; in their capacity as verses (the ablative singular form of *qui*, 'who').

15. *fifty thousand pounds*: No pearl approached this value (let alone twice that sum); the Hope Pearl, the largest known, which was owned by Garrard, the Crown jewellers, was valued at £9,000.

16. *'apostasy'*: Abandonment of religous faith, vows, or principles, but here used in a contrary sense.

17. *a winter at St Moritz ... Cannes or Cairo*: Three of the most fashionable winter resorts for British travellers. St Moritz, in the Upper Engadine in the Swiss Grisons, was a centre for skating and tobogganing. Cannes, in the south of France, was a resort made fashionable by Lord Brougham in the 1830s and visited by Queen Victoria in 1887; and Cairo, which had been under British control since 1882, had luxurious hotels and was the starting point for the Nile cruises operated by Thomas Cook.

18. *North German Lloyd special*: The train from London to Southampton docks, reserved for passengers travelling on the North German Lloyd or Norddeutscher Lloyd line. The company was founded in 1856, and had monthly departures for the Far East, calling at Genoa, Naples, Egypt, Aden, Colombo, Singapore, Hong Kong, Shanghai and the Japanese ports. Raffles was not the first to commit a crime on board a Norddeutscher Lloyd steamer; nearly £2,500 belonging to the Chartered Bank of India, Australia and China had been stolen from the mail room during a voyage from Yokohama to London (cf. *Pall Mall Gazette*, 17 November 1897).

19. *Uhlan*: A special type of cavalryman or lancer in various European armies, but specifically in the Prussian army. The ship is based on the SS *Königin Luise*, a 10,000-ton, twin-screw, steel ship of the Barbarossa class, built in 1896 – the one on which Hornung sailed to Naples in November 1897.

20. *we were bound for Capri*: The island of Capri, on the south side of the Bay of Naples, where the Emperor Tiberius is buried. It is also

famous for its Blue Grotto. Oscar Wilde and Lord Alfred Douglas visited the island in 1897 to lay flowers on the tomb of Tiberius and to lunch with the Swedish physician Axel Munthe (1857–1949).

21. *the Island of the Lotos-eaters*: A fabulous land visited by Odysseus (Homer, *Odyssey*, IX), where those who ate the lotus-fruit forgot their homes and desired to remain for ever. It is the subject of 'The Lotos-Eaters' (1832), a poem by Alfred, Lord Tennyson (1809–92):

> Most weary seem'd the sea, weary the oar,
> Weary the wandering fields of barren foam.
> Then some one said, 'We will return no more';

22. '*and for a while forget*': From 'Let us be Drunk', by William Ernest Henley (1849–1903):

> Let us be drunk, and for a while forget,
> Forget, and, ceasing even from regret,
> Live without reason and despite of rhyme,
> As in a dream preposterous and sublime,
> Where place and hour and means for once are met.

23. '*faery lands forlorn*': From the 'Ode to a Nightingale' (1820), by John Keats (1795–1821):

> Thou wast not born for death, immortal Bird!
>   No hungry generations tread thee down;
> The voice I hear this passing night was heard
>   In ancient days by emperor and clown: . . .
>   The same that oft-times hath
> Charmed magic casements, opening on the foam
>   Of perilous seas, in faery lands forlorn.

24. *Bremen*: A former Hanseatic League town in north Germany, the home port of the Norddeutscher Lloyd fleet.

25. *a-hunting I must go*: From 'A-Hunting We Will Go', a song by Henry Fielding (1707–54):

> The hounds all join in glorious cry,
> The huntsman winds his horn:
> And a-hunting we will go.

26. *long chairs*: Deck chairs, long-armed, reclining chairs.

27. *drill coat*: A coat made of a coarse twilled linen or cotton fabric.

28. *by light of nature*: A philosophical term for the understanding of God by natural revelation. 'The knowledge of man is as the waters, some descending from above, and some springing from beneath; the one informed by the light of nature, the other inspired by divine revelation. The light of nature consisteth in the actions of the mind and the reports of the senses' (Francis Bacon, *The Advancement of Learning*, 1605, Bk. II).

29. *with perpendicular moustaches*: The ends turned up, in the style favoured by the German Kaiser.

30. *Herr Capitain Wilhelm von Heumann*: The name no doubt suggested by Wilhelm von Schuckman, who was the captain of SS *Königin Luise*.

31. *against nature*: Unnatural; the phrase was used as the title for the translation of *A Rebours* (1884) by Joris Karl Huysmans, which described the morbid tastes of the decadent aristocrat des Esseintes.

32. *a board of chequers*: An allusion to the famous lines by Edward Fitzgerald (1809–93) found in his translation of *Omar Khayyam* (1859, I.xlix):

> 'Tis all a Chequer-board of Nights and Days
> Where Destiny with Men for Pieces plays;
> Hither and thither moves, and mates, and slays,
> And one by one back in the closet lays.

33. *old Virgil*: Publius Vergilius Maro (70–19 BC), the Roman poet, author of the *Aeneid*. His fame survived into the Middle Ages when he gained the sobriquet 'old': 'Old poets foster'd under friendlier skies,/ Old Virgil who would write ten lines, they say,/ At dawn, and lavish all the golden day/ To make them wealthier in his readers' eyes' (Tennyson, 'Poets and Their Bibliographies').

34. *to climb out of Avernus*: A reference to the famous lines in the sixth book of the *Aeneid*, describing the descent of Aeneas into the underworld through the cave of Avernus:

> *Facilis descensus Averno;*
> *Noctes atque dies patet atri janua Ditis;*
> *Sed revocare gradum, superasque evadere ad auras,*
> *Hoc opus, hic labor est.*

> Smooth the descent, and easy is the way:
> (The Gates of Hell stand open night and day);
> But to return, and view the cheerful skies,
> In this the task and mighty labour lies.
>
> (trans. Dryden)

The lines were imprinted on Hornung's memory for reasons which he gave when describing a visit to the Blue Mountains in New South Wales: 'I remembered with many a pang – and many a pant – a certain passage of my old enemy, Virgil, who describes a descent, that, like ours, was *easy* – extremely easy – *sed revocare gradum*! (N.B. I once had it to write out)' ('A Visit to the Blue Mountains, New South Wales', Uppingham School Magazine, February 1885, pp. 4–8).

35. *the Solent*: A channel, between two and five miles in width, which separates the north-west shore of the Isle of Wight from the mainland, and through which ships pass from Southampton to the sea.

36. *chit*: A small or slender young woman.

37. *his experience of women*: This recalls Dr Watson, whose experience of women was said to have extended 'over many countries and three separate continents' (A. Conan Doyle, *The Sign of Four*, 1890).

38. *a murderous scar . . . a present from Heidelberg*: A duelling scar, a highly prized honour among the German student fraternities, in particular those of the University of Heidelberg. Members, dressed in a light shirt and trousers, with their eyes protected by goggles, would stand face to face, and without moving their feet would slash at each other with a sabre or '*Schlager*' until the wound had been inflicted. The 'badge of honour' is here compared to a cheap souvenir, such as 'A Present from Margate'.

39. *bowling him out as he was 'getting set'*: A batsman 'gets set' by centring the bat on the wicket at the opening of his innings.

40. *diddle*: Cheat, swindle.

41. *Few travellers tempt the Red Sea*: Few travellers brave the dangers of the Red Sea; the Arabian Gulf or Red Sea, which was joined to the Mediterranean when the Suez canal opened in 1869, was notorious for its extreme heat in summer.

42. *'Achilles sulking in his bunk'*: Achilles, the hero on the Greek side during the Trojan War, was described by Homer in the *Iliad* as having sulked in his tent after a quarrel with Agamemnon over a servant girl, Briseis. The death of his friend Patroclus roused him to fury and led him to triumph over the Trojans.

43. *sentry-go*: On duty, pacing up and down as a sentry.

44. *pi*: School and university slang for 'pious', virtuous, sanctimonious. Raffles had already referred to Bunny as a 'pious rabbit'.

45. *Samson was the unlucky hero, and one Delilah the heroine*: The story of Samson and Delilah is found in the Old Testament, Judges 16.

46. *wealthy squatter*: In the Australian sense: 'one occupying a tract of pastoral land as a tenant of the crown; a grazier or sheep farmer, especially on a large scale' (*OED*).

47. *draw stumps*: Raffles would 'end his career of crime'; the cricket stumps are drawn (pulled from the ground) at the end of a match.

48. *a filbert*: Or filbert nut, a cultivated hazelnut, named after St Philbert, on whose feast day (22 August) the nuts are deemed to be ripe enough to eat.

49. *a filibustering age*: Filibusters (from the Dutch *vrijbuiter*, via French *flibustiers*) was the name given to freebooters and buccaneers who plundered the coast of America in the sixteenth and seventeenth centuries, and to others who engaged in unauthorized warfare against foreign states. The Jameson Raid at the end of 1895 (an attempt by Dr L. S. Jameson to overthrow the Transvaal Government of Paul Kruger) and the raids on the coast of Cuba by American ships during the Cuban war between America and Spain in 1897 suggested that filibustering was again in vogue.

50. *German cap*: Also known as a Teutonic cap, a soft cap with a high front and narrow peak, typically worn by students. Edward Thring, the headmaster of Uppingham School, had decreed that boys should wear German caps in place of mortar boards.

51. *the lighthouse*: 'La Lanterna', the principal building and emblem of Genoa, dating from the 1540s; it gained an emotional significance at the end of the nineteenth century by being the last building which emigrants saw when leaving Italy.

52. *brown holland*: An unbleached linen fabric.

53. *Canoodle Dum*: From 'The King of Canoodle Dum' (*The Bab Ballads*, 1876), by William Schwenck Gilbert (1836–1911):

> The story of Frederick Gowler,
> A mariner of the sea,
> Who quitted his ship, the Howler,
> A-sailing in Caribbee.
> For many a day he wandered,
> Till he met in a state of rum
> Calamity Pop Von Peppermint Drop,
> The King of Canoodle-Dum.
>
> . . .

> Alliance with Kings of Europe
>   Is an honour Canoodlers seek,
> Her monarchs don't stop with Peppermint Drop
>   Every day in the week.

54. *clappin' the darbies on these young sparks*: Handcuffing; the phrase is thought to derive from a rigid form of usurer's bond, called 'father Darby's bonds'; 'clapping' means applying them quickly.

55. *Colt*: An American revolver patented in 1835 and named after its inventor, Colonel Sam Colt.

56. *bitten out the bullet*: This is used literally, but is also a play on words as 'to bite the bullet' means 'to face trouble with fortitude'.

57. *Elba*: The island where Raffles would land after his disappearance: 'Deadly, my dear Bunny, is not the word for that glorified snag, or for the molluscs its inhabitants ... Napoleon couldn't stand it, you remember, but he held on longer than I did. I put in a few weeks in their infernal mines, simply to pick up a smattering of Italian; then got across to the mainland in a little wooden timber-tramp; and ungratefully glad I was to leave Elba blazing in just such a sunset as the one you won't forget.' ('The Fate of Faustina', *The Black Mask*, 1901)

58. *as though he had plunged at his leisure*: The disappearance of Raffles may have been suggested by the death of Barney Barnato, who drowned on 14 June 1897 when he threw himself (or was thrown) over the rail of the Union Mail steamer *Scot*, but it also recalls the death of Shelley, who drowned off the coast of Italy on 8 July 1822.